The
Highs and Lows
of Being Mia

# MEG CABOT

# The Highs and Lows of Being Mia

## The Princess Diaries, Volumes III & IV

AVON BOOKS
*An Imprint of* HarperCollins*Publishers*

ACKNOWLEDGMENTS for *The Princess Diaries,*
*Volume III: Princess in Love*:
Many thanks to Beth Ader, Jennifer Brown,
Barbara Cabot, Sarah Davies, Laura Langlie, Abby McAden,
and David Walton.

DEDICATION for *The Princess Diaries, Volume III:*
*Princess in Love*:
For Benjamin, with love

ACKNOWLEDGMENTS for *The Princess Diaries,*
*Volume IV: Princess in Waiting*:
Many thanks to Beth Ader, Alexandra Alexo, Jennifer Brown,
Kim Goad Floyd, Darcy Jacobs, Laura Langlie, Amanda
Maciel, Abby McAden, and Benjamin Egnatz.

Belated thanks to the Beckham family, especially Julie,
for so generously allowing me to borrow Molly's
sock-swallowing habit!

DEDICATION for *The Princess Diaries, Volume IV:*
*Princess in Waiting*:
For Walter Schretzman, and the many others who scatter
largesse so selflessly throughout New York City. Don't think
we haven't noticed. With thanks.

Originally published as *The Princess Diaries, Volume III: Princess in Love* and
*The Princess Diaries, Volume IV: Princess in Waiting.*

Library of Congress Cataloging-in-Publication Data

Cabot, Meg.
    The highs and lows of being Mia / Meg Cabot.— 1st Avon ed.
        p.    cm. — (The princess diaries ; v. 3 & 4)
    Summary: Presents the third and fourth volumes in the Princess Diaries series, in
which Mia copes with final exams at school in New York and is introduced to her
Genovian subjects.
    ISBN 0-06-059001-7 (pbk.)
    1. Princesses—Juvenile fiction. [1. Princesses—Fiction. 2. Identity—Fiction. 3.
Schools—Fiction. 4. Love—Fiction. 5. Dating (Social customs)—Fiction. 6. New York
(N.Y.)—Fiction. 7. Diaries—Fiction. 8. Humorous stories.] I. Cabot, Meg. Princess in
waiting. 2004. II. Title. III. Series.
PZ7.C11165Hi 2004
[Fic]--dc22                                                                        2004009033

First Avon edition, 2004

# The Princess Diaries
## Volume III

*"One of Sara's 'pretends' is that she is
a princess,"* said Jessie. *"She plays it
all the time—even in school. She
wants Ermengarde to be one, too, but
Ermengarde says she is too fat."*

*"She is too fat,"* said Lavinia.
*"And Sara is too thin."*

*"Sara says it has nothing to do
with what you look like, or what you
have. It has only to do with what you
think of, and what you do,"* Jessie
explained.

A LITTLE PRINCESS
*Frances Hodgson Burnett*

Assignment (Due December 8): Here at Albert Einstein High School, we have a very diverse student population. Over one hundred and seventy different nations, religions, and ethnic groups are represented by our student body. In the space below, describe the manner in which your family celebrates the uniquely American holiday, Thanksgiving. Please utilize appropriate margins.

## MY THANKSGIVING
### by Mia Thermopolis

6:45 a.m.–Roused by the sound of my mother vomiting. She is well into her third month of pregnancy now. According to her obstetrician, all the throwing up should stop in the next trimester. I can't wait. I have been marking the days off on my 'N Sync calendar. (I don't really like 'N Sync. At least, not that much. My best friend, Lilly, bought me the calendar as a joke. Except that one guy really is pretty cute.)

7:45 a.m.–Mr. Gianini, my new stepfather, knocks on my door. Only now I am supposed to call him Frank. This is very difficult to remember due to the fact that at school, where he is my first-period Algebra teacher, I am supposed to call him Mr. Gianini. So I just don't call him anything (to his face).

It's time to get up, Mr. Gianini says. We are having Thanksgiving at his parents' house on Long Island. We have to leave now if we are going to beat the traffic.

8:45 a.m.–There is no traffic this early on Thanksgiving Day. We arrive at Mr. G's parents' house in Sagaponic three hours early.

Mrs. Gianini (Mr. Gianini's mother, not my mother. My mother is still Helen Thermopolis because she is a fairly well-known modern painter under that name, and also because she does not believe in the cult of the patriarchy) is still in curlers. She looks very surprised. This might not only be because we arrived so early, but also because no sooner had my mother entered the house than she was forced to run for the bathroom with her hand pressed over her mouth, on account of the smell of the roasting turkey. I am hoping this means that my future half-brother or -sister is a vegetarian, since the smell of meat cooking used to make my mother hungry, not nauseated.

My mother had already informed me in the car on the way over from Manhattan that Mr. Gianini's parents are very old-fashioned and are used to enjoying a conventional Thanksgiving meal. She does not think they will appreciate hearing my traditional Thanksgiving speech about how the Pilgrims are guilty of committing mass genocide by giving their new Native American friends blankets filled with the smallpox virus, and that it is reprehensible that we as a country annually celebrate this rape and destruction of an entire culture.

Instead, my mother said, I should discuss more neutral topics, such as the weather.

I asked if it was all right if I discussed the astonishingly high rate of attendance at the Reykjavik opera house in Iceland (over 98 percent of the country's population has seen *Tosca* at least once).

My mother sighed and said, "If you must," which I take to be a sign that she is beginning to tire of hearing about Iceland.

Well, I am sorry, but I find Iceland extremely fascinating, and I will not rest until I have visited the ice hotel.

9:45 a.m.–11:45 a.m.–I watch the Macy's Thanksgiving Day parade with Mr. Gianini Senior in what he calls the rec room.

They don't have rec rooms in Manhattan.

Just lobbies.

Remembering my mother's warning, I refrain from repeating another one of my traditional holiday rants, that the Macy's Thanksgiving Day parade is a gross example of American capitalism run amok.

At one point during the broadcast, I catch sight of Lilly standing in the crowd outside of Office Max on Broadway and Thirty-Seventh, her videocamera clutched to her slightly squished-in face (so much like a pug) as a float carrying Miss America and William Shatner of *Star Trek* fame passes by. So I know Lilly is going to take care of denouncing Macy's on the next episode of her public access television show, *Lilly Tells It Like It Is* (every Friday night at nine, Manhattan cable channel 67).

12:00 p.m. – Mr. Gianini Junior's sister arrives with her husband, their two kids, and the pumpkin pies. The kids, who are my age, are twins, a boy, Nathan, and a girl, Claire. I know right away Claire and I are not going to get along, because when we are introduced she looks me up and down the way the cheerleaders do in the hallway at school and goes, in a very snotty voice, "*You're* the one who's supposed to be a princess?"

And while I am perfectly aware that at five foot nine inches tall, with no visible breasts, feet the size of snowshoes, and hair that sits in a tuft on my head like the cotton on the end of a Q-tip, I am the biggest freak in the freshman class of Albert Einstein High School for Boys (made coeducational circa 1975), I do not appreciate being reminded of it by girls who do not even bother finding out that beneath this mutant facade beats the heart of a person who is only striving, just like everybody else in this world, to find self-actualization.

Not that I even care what Mr. Gianini's niece Claire thinks of me. I mean, she is wearing a pony-skin miniskirt. And it is not even imitation pony skin. She must know that a horse had to die just so she could have that skirt, but she obviously doesn't care.

Now Claire has pulled out her cell phone and gone out onto the deck, where the reception is best (even though it is thirty degrees outside, she apparently doesn't mind. She has that pony skin to keep her warm, after all). She keeps looking in at me through the sliding glass doors and laughing as she talks on her phone.

Nathan—who is dressed in baggy jeans and has a pager, in addition to a lot of gold jewelry—asks his grandfather if he can change the channel. So instead of traditional Thanksgiving viewing options, such as football or the Lifetime Channel's made-for-TV movie marathon, we are now forced to watch MTV2. Nathan knows all the songs and sings along with them. Most of them have dirty words that have been bleeped out, but Nathan sings them anyway.

1:00 p.m.—The food is served. We begin eating.

1:15 p.m.—We finish eating.

1:20 p.m.—I help Mrs. Gianini clean up. She says not to be ridiculous, and that I should go "have a nice gossip" with Claire.

It is frightening, if you think about it, how clueless old people can be sometimes.

Instead of going to have a nice gossip with Claire, I stay where I am and tell Mrs. Gianini how much I am enjoying having her son live with us. Mr. G is very good about helping around the house, and has even taken over my old job of cleaning the toilets. Not to mention the thirty-six-inch TV, pinball machine, and foozball table he brought with him when he moved in.

Mrs. Gianini is immensely gratified to hear this, you can just tell. Old people like to hear nice stuff about their kids, even if their kid, like Mr. Gianini, is thirty-nine and a half years old.

3:00 p.m.—We have to leave if we are going to beat the traffic home. I say good-bye. Claire does not say good-bye back to me, but Nathan does. He advises me to keep it real. Mrs. Gianini gives us a lot of leftover turkey. I thank her, even though I don't eat turkey, being a vegetarian.

6:30 p.m.—We finally make it back into the city, after spending three and a half hours in bumper-to-bumper traffic along the Long Island Expressway. Though there is nothing very express about it, if you ask me.

I barely have time to change into my baby-blue floor-length Armani sheath dress and matching ballet flats before the limo honks downstairs, and Lars, my bodyguard, arrives to escort me to my second Thanksgiving dinner.

7:30 p.m.—Arrive at the Plaza Hotel. I am greeted by the concierge, who announces me to the masses assembled in the Palm Court:

"Presenting Her Royal Highness Princess Amelia Mignonette Grimaldi Thermopolis Renaldo."

God forbid he should just say Mia.

My father, the prince of Genovia, and his mother, the dowager princess, have rented the Palm Court for the evening in order to throw a Thanksgiving banquet for all of their friends. Despite my strenuous objections, Dad and Grandmère refuse to leave New York City until I have learned everything there is to know about being a princess . . . or until my formal introduction to the Genovian people the day before Christmas, whichever comes first. I have assured them that it isn't as if I am going to show up at the castle and start hurling olives at the ladies-in-waiting and scratching myself under the arms. I mean, I am fourteen years old: I do have some idea how to act, for crying out loud.

But Grandmère, at least, does not seem to believe this, and so she is still subjecting me to daily princess lessons. Lilly recently contacted the United Nations to see whether these lessons constitute a human rights violation. She believes it is unlawful to force a minor to sit for hours practicing tipping her soup bowl away from her—"Always, always, *away* from you, Amelia!"—in order to scrape up a few drops of lobster bisque. The UN has so far been unsympathetic to my plight.

It was Grandmère's idea to have what she calls an "old-fashioned" Thanksgiving dinner, featuring mussels in a white wine sauce, squab stuffed with foie gras, lobster tails, and Iranian caviar, which you could never get before because of the embargo. She has invited two hundred of her closest friends, plus the emperor of Japan and his wife, since they were in town anyway for a world trade summit.

That's why I have to wear ballet flats. Grandmère says it's rude to be taller than an emperor.

8:00 p.m.–11:00 p.m.—I make polite conversation with the empress while we eat. Like me, she was just a normal person until one day she married the emperor and became royal. I, of course, was born royal. I just didn't know it until September, when my dad found out he couldn't have any more kids, due to his chemotherapy for testicular cancer having rendered him sterile. Then he had to admit he was actually a prince and all, and that though I am "illegitimate," since my dad and my mom were never married, I am still the sole heir to the Genovian throne.

And even though Genovia is a very small country (population 50,000) crammed into a hillside along the Mediterranean Sea between Italy and France, it is still this very big deal to be princess of it.

Not a big enough deal for anyone to raise my allowance higher than ten dollars a week, apparently. But a big enough deal that I have to have a bodyguard follow me around everywhere I go, just in case some Euro-trash terrorist in a ponytail and black leather pants takes it into his head to kidnap me.

The empress knows all about this—what a bummer it is, I mean, being just a normal person one day, and then having your face on the cover of *People* magazine the next. She even gave me some advice: She told me I should always make sure my kimono is securely fastened before I raise my arm to wave to the populace.

I thanked her, even though I don't actually own a kimono.

11:30 p.m.—I am so tired on account of having gotten up so early to go to Long Island, I have yawned in the empress's face twice. I have tried to hide these yawns the way Grandmère taught me to, by clenching my jaw and refusing to open my mouth. But this only makes my eyes water, and the rest of my face stretch out like I am hurtling through a black hole. Grandmère gives me the evil eye over her salad with pears and walnuts, but it is no use. Even her malevolent stare cannot shake me from my state of extreme drowsiness.

Finally, my father notices, and grants me a royal reprieve from dessert. Lars drives me back to the apartment. Grandmère is clearly upset because I am leaving before the cheese course. But it is either that, or pass out in the *fromage bleu*. I know that in the end, Grandmère will have retribution, undoubtedly in the form of forcing me to learn the names of every member of the Swedish royal family, or something equally as heinous.

Grandmère always gets her way.

12:00 a.m.—After a long and exhausting day of giving thanks to the founders of our nation—those genocidal hypocrites known as the Pilgrims—I finally go to bed.

And that concludes Mia Thermopolis's Thanksgiving.

Over.

That is what my life is. O-V-E-R.

I know I have said that before, but this time I really mean it.

And why? Why THIS TIME? Surprisingly, it's not because:

Three months ago, I found out that I'm the heir to the throne of a small European nation, and that at the end of this month, I am going to have to go to said small European nation and be formally introduced for the first time to the people over whom I will one day reign, and who will undoubtedly hate me, because given that my favorite shoes are my combat boots and my favorite TV show is *Baywatch*, I am so not the royal-princess type.

Or because:

My mother, who is expecting to give birth to my Algebra teacher's child in approximately seven months, recently eloped with said Algebra teacher.

Or even because:

At school they've been loading us down with so much homework—and after school, Grandmère's been torturing me so endlessly with all the princess stuff I've got to learn by Christmas—that I haven't even been able to keep up with this journal, let alone anything else.

Oh, no. It's not because of any of that. Why is my life over?

Because I have a boyfriend.

At fourteen years of age, I suppose it's about time. I mean, all my friends have boyfriends. All of them, even Lilly, who blames the male gender for most, if not all, of society's ills.

And okay, Lilly's boyfriend is Boris Pelkowski, who may, at the age of fifteen, be one of the nation's leading violin virtuosos, but that doesn't mean he doesn't tuck his sweater into his pants, or that he doesn't have food in his braces more often than not. Not what I would call ideal boyfriend material, but Lilly seems to like him, which is all that matters.

I guess.

I have to admit, when Lilly—possibly the pickiest person on this planet (and I should know, having been best friends with her since kindergarten)—got a boyfriend, and I still didn't have one, I pretty much started to think there was something wrong with me. Besides my gigantism and what Lilly's parents, the Drs. Moscovitz, who are psychiatrists, call my inability to verbalize my inner rage.

And then, one day, out of the blue, I got one. A boyfriend, I mean.

Well, okay, not out of the blue. Kenny started sending me all these anonymous love letters. I didn't know it was him. I kind of thought (okay, hoped) someone else was sending them. But in the end, it turned out to be Kenny. And by then I was in too deep, really, to get out. So *voila*! I had a boyfriend.

Problem solved, right?

Not. So not.

And it isn't that I don't like Kenny. I do. I really do. We have a lot in common. For instance, we both appreciate the preciousness of not just human, but *all* life forms, and refuse to dissect fetal pigs and frogs in Bio. Instead, we are writing term papers on the life cycles of various grubs and mealworms.

And we both like science fiction. Kenny knows a lot more about it than I do, but he has been very impressed so far by the extent of my familiarity with the works of Robert A. Heinlein and Isaac Asimov, both of whom we were forced to read in school (though he doesn't seem to remember this).

I haven't told Kenny that I actually find most science

fiction boring, since there seem to be very few girls in it.

There are a lot of girl characters in Japanese anime, which Kenny also really likes, and which he has decided to devote his life to promoting (when he is not busy finding a cure for cancer). I have noticed that most of the girls in Japanese anime seem to have misplaced their bras.

Plus I really think it might be detrimental to a fighter pilot to have a lot of long hair floating around in the cockpit while she is gunning down the forces of evil.

But like I said, I haven't mentioned any of this to Kenny. And mostly, we get along great. We have a fun time together. And in some ways, it's very nice to have a boyfriend. Like, I don't have to worry now about not being asked to the Albert Einstein High School Nondenominational Winter Dance (so called because its former title, the Albert Einstein High School Christmas Dance, offended many of our non– Christmas-celebrating students).

And why is it that I do not have to worry about not being asked to the biggest dance of the school year, with the exception of the prom?

Because I'm going with Kenny.

Well, okay, he hasn't exactly asked me yet, but he will. Because he is my boyfriend.

Isn't that great? Sometimes I think I must be the luckiest girl in the whole world. I mean, really. Think about it: I may not be pretty, but I am not grossly disfigured; I live in New York City, the coolest place on the planet; I'm a princess; I have a boyfriend. What more could a girl ask for?

Oh, God.

WHO AM I KIDDING?????

This boyfriend of mine? Here's the scoop:

I DON'T EVEN LIKE HIM.

Well, okay, it's not that I don't like him. But this boyfriend thing, I just don't know. Kenny's a nice enough guy and all—don't get me wrong. I mean, he is funny and not boring to be with, certainly. And he's pretty cute, you know, in a tall, skinny sort of way.

It's just that when I see Kenny walking down the hall, my heart so totally doesn't start beating faster, the way girls' hearts start beating faster in those teen romances my friend Tina Hakim Baba is always reading.

And when Kenny takes my hand, at the movies or whatever, it's not like my hand gets all tingly in his, the way girls' hands do in those books.

And when he kisses me? Those fireworks people always talk about? Forget about it. No fireworks. Nil. Nada.

It's funny, because before I got a boyfriend, I used to spend a lot of time trying to figure out how to get one, and once I got him, how I'd get him to kiss me.

But now that I actually have a boyfriend, mostly all I do is try to figure out how to get out of kissing him.

One way that I have found that works quite effectively is the head turn. If I notice his lips coming toward me, I just turn my head at the last minute, so all he gets is my cheek, and maybe some hair.

I guess the worst thing is, when Kenny gazes deeply into my eyes—which he does a lot—and asks me what I am thinking about, I am usually thinking about this one certain person.

And that person isn't Kenny. It isn't Kenny at all. It is Lilly's older brother, Michael Moscovitz, whom I have loved for, oh, I don't know, MY ENTIRE LIFE.

Wait, though. It gets worse.

Because now it's like everybody considers me and Kenny this big Item. You know? Now we're Kenny-and-Mia. Now, instead of Lilly and me hanging out together Saturday nights, it's Lilly-and-Boris and Kenny-and-Mia. Sometimes my friend Tina Hakim Baba and her boyfriend, Dave

Farouq El-Abar, and my other friend Shameeka Taylor and her boyfriend, Daryl Gardner, join us, making it Lilly-and-Boris and Kenny-and-Mia and Tina-and-Dave and Shameeka-and-Daryl.

So if Kenny and I break up, who am I going to hang around with on Saturday nights? I mean, seriously. Lilly-and-Boris and Tina-and-Dave and Shameeka-and-Daryl won't want just plain Mia along. I'll be just like this seventh wheel.

Not to mention, if Kenny and I break up, who will I go to the Nondenominational Winter Dance with? I mean, if he ever gets around to asking me.

Oh, God, I have to go now. Lilly-and-Boris and Tina-and-Dave and Kenny-and-Mia are supposed to go ice-skating at Rockefeller Center.

All I can say is, be careful what you wish for. It just might come true.

I thought my life was over because I have a boyfriend now and I don't really like him in that way, and I have to break up with him without hurting his feelings, which is, I guess, probably impossible.

Yeah, well, I didn't know *how* over my life could actually be.

Not until tonight, anyway.

Tonight, Lilly-and-Boris and Tina-and-Dave and Mia-and-Kenny were joined by a new couple, Michael-and-Judith.

That's right: Lilly's brother Michael showed up at the ice-skating rink, and he brought with him the president of the Computer Club—of which he is treasurer—Judith Gershner.

Judith Gershner, like Lilly's brother Michael, is a senior at Albert Einstein High School.

Judith Gershner, like Michael, is on the honor roll.

Judith Gershner, like Michael, will probably get into every college she applies to, because Judith Gershner, like Michael, is brilliant.

In fact, Judith Gershner, like Michael, won a prize last year at the Albert Einstein High School Annual Biomedical Technology Fair for her science project, in which she actually cloned a fruit fly.

*She cloned a fruit fly.* At home. In her *bedroom.*

Judith Gershner knows how to clone fruit flies in her bedroom. And me? I can't even multiply fractions.

Hmmm. Gee, I don't know. If you were Michael Moscovitz—you know, a straight-A student who got into Columbia, early decision—who would you rather go out with? A girl who can clone fruit flies in her bedroom, or a girl who is getting a D in Freshman Algebra, in spite of the fact that *her mother is married to her Algebra teacher?*

Not that there's even a chance of Michael ever asking me out. I mean, I have to admit, there were a couple of times when I thought he might. But that was clearly just wishful thinking on my part. I mean, why would a guy like Michael, who does really well in school and will probably excel at whatever career he ultimately chooses, ever ask out a girl like me, who would have flunked out of the ninth grade by now if it hadn't been for all those extra tutoring sessions with Mr. Gianini, and, ironically, Michael himself?

But Michael and Judith Gershner, on the other hand, are perfect for each other. Judith even looks like him, a little. I mean, they both have the same curly black hair and pale skin from being inside all the time, looking up stuff about genomes on the Internet.

But if Michael and Judith Gershner are so suited for each other, how come when I first saw them walking toward us while we were lacing up our rental skates, I got this very bad feeling inside?

I mean, I have absolutely no right to be jealous of the fact that Michael Moscovitz asked Judith Gershner to go skating with him. Absolutely no right at all.

Except that when I first saw them together, I was shocked. I mean, Michael hardly ever leaves his room, on account of always being at his computer, maintaining his webzine, *Crackhead*. The last place I'd ever expected to see him is the ice-skating rink at Rockefeller Center during the height of the Christmas-tree–lighting hysteria. Michael generally avoids places he considers tourist traps, like pretty much everywhere north of Bleecker Street.

But there he was, and there was Judith Gershner, in her overalls and Rockports and ski parka, chatting away with him about something—probably something really smart, like DNA.

I nudged Lilly in the side—she was lacing up her skates—and said, in this voice that I hoped didn't show what I was feeling inside, "Look, there's your brother."

And Lilly wasn't even surprised to see him! She looked over and saw him and went, "Oh, yeah. He said he might show up."

Show up with a *date*? Did he mention *that*? And would it have been too much for you, Lilly, to have mentioned this to me beforehand, so I could have had time for a little mental preparation?

Only Lilly doesn't know how I feel about her brother, so I guess it never occurred to her to break it to me gently.

Here's the subtle way in which I handled the situation. It was really smooth (NOT).

As Michael and Judith were looking around for a place to put on their skates:

Me:       (Casually, to Lilly) I didn't know your brother and Judith Gershner were going out.

Lilly:    (Disgusted for some reason) Please. They're not. She was just over at our place, working with Michael on some project for the stupid Computer Club. They heard we were all going skating, and Judith said she wanted to come, too.

Me:       Well, that sounds like they're going out to me.

Lilly:    Whatever. Boris, must you constantly *breathe* on me?

Me:       (To Michael and Judith as they walk up to us) Oh, hi, you guys. Michael, I didn't know you knew how to ice-skate.

Michael:  (shrugging) I used to be on a hockey team.

Lilly:    (snorting) Yeah, Pee Wee Hockey. That was

15

before he decided that team sports were a
waste of time because the success of the team
was dictated by the performance of all the
players as a whole, as opposed to sports
determined by individual performance such as
tennis and golf.

Michael:   Lilly, don't you ever shut up?

Judith:    I love ice-skating! Although I'm not very
           good at it.

And she certainly isn't. Judith is such a bad skater, she
had to hold on to both of Michael's hands while he skated
backwards in front of her, just to keep from falling flat on
her face. I don't know which astonished me more: that
Michael can skate backwards, or that he didn't seem to
mind having to tow Judith all around the rink. I mean, I
may not be able to clone a fruit fly, but at least I can remain
upright unaided in a pair of ice skates.

Kenny, however, seemed to really think Michael and
Judith's method of skating was way preferable to skating the
old-fashioned way—you know, solo—so he kept coming up
and trying to get me to let him tow me around the way
Michael was towing Judith.

And even though I was all, "Duh, Kenny, I know how to
skate," he said that that wasn't the point. Finally, after he'd
bugged me for like half an hour, I gave in, and let him hold
both my hands as he skated in front of me, backwards.

Only the thing is, Kenny isn't very good at skating backwards. I can skate forward, but I'm not good enough at it
that if someone is wobbling around in front of me, I can
keep from crashing into him if he falls down.

Which was exactly what happened. Kenny fell down,
and I couldn't stop, so I crashed into him, and my chin hit
his knee and I bit my tongue and all this blood filled up my

mouth, and I didn't want to swallow it so I spat it out. Only unfortunately it went all over Kenny's jeans and onto the ice, which clearly impressed all of the tourists standing along the railings around the rink, taking pictures of their loved ones in front of the enormous Rockefeller Center Christmas tree, since they all turned around and started taking pictures of the girl spitting up blood on the ice below, a truly New York moment.

And then Lars came *shoosh*ing over—he is a champion ice-skater, thanks to his Nordic upbringing; quite a contrast to his bodyguard training in the heart of the Gobi desert—picked me up, looked at my tongue, gave me his handkerchief and told me to keep pressure on the wound, and then said, "That's enough skating for one night."

And that was it. Now I've got this bloody gouge in the tip of my tongue, and it hurts to talk, and I was totally humiliated in front of millions of tourists who'd come to look at the stupid tree at stupid Rockefeller Center, not to mention in front of my friends and, worst of all, Judith Gershner, who it turns out also got accepted early decision at Columbia (great, the same school Michael's going to in the fall), where she will be pre-med, and who advised me that I should go to the hospital, as it seemed likely to her that I might need stitches. In my *tongue*. I'm lucky, she said, I didn't bite the tip of it off.

Lucky!

Oh, yeah, I'll tell you how lucky I am: I'm so lucky that while I lie here in bed writing this, with no one but my twenty-five-pound cat, Fat Louie, to keep me company (and Fat Louie only likes me because I feed him), the boy I've been in love with since like forever is up at midtown right now with a girl who knows how to clone fruit flies and can tell if wounds need stitches or not.

One good thing about this tongue, though: if Kenny was

thinking about moving on to Frenching, we totally can't until I heal. And that could, according to Dr. Fung—whom my mom called as soon as Lars brought me home—take anywhere from three to ten days.

*Yes!*

## TEN THINGS I HATE ABOUT THE HOLIDAY SEASON IN NEW YORK CITY

1. Tourists who come in from out of town in their giant sport-utility vehicles and try to run you over at the crosswalks, thinking they are driving like aggressive New Yorkers. Actually, they are driving like morons. Plus there is enough pollution in this city. Why can't they just take public transit, like normal people?
2. Stupid Rockefeller Center tree. They asked me to be the person who throws the switch to light it this year, as I am considered "New York's own Royal" in the press, but when I told them how cutting down trees contributes to the destruction of the ozone layer, they rescinded their invitation and had the mayor do it instead.
3. Stupid Christmas carols blaring from outside all the stores.
4. Stupid ice-skating with stupid boys who think they can skate backwards when they can't.
5. Pressure to buy stupid "meaningful" gifts for everyone you know.
6. Final exams.
7. Stupid lousy New York weather. No snow, just cold, wet rain, every single day. Whatever happened to a white Christmas? I'll tell you: Global warming. You know why? Because everybody keeps driving SUVs and cutting down trees!
8. Stupid manipulative Christmas specials on TV.
9. Stupid manipulative Christmas commercials on TV.

10. Mistletoe. This stuff should be banned. In the hands of adolescent boys, it becomes a societally approved excuse to demand kisses. This is sexual harassment, if you ask me.

Plus all the wrong boys have it.

*Sunday, December 7*

Just got back from dinner at Grandmère's. All of my efforts to get out of having to go—even my pointing out that I am currently suffering from a perforated tongue— were in vain.

And this one was even worse than usual. That's because Grandmère wanted to go over my itinerary for my trip to Genovia, which, by the way, looks like this:

*Sunday, December 21*
3 p.m.
Arrive in Genovia

3:30 p.m.–5 p.m.
Meet and greet palace staff

5 p.m.–7 p.m.
Tour of palace

7 p.m.–8 p.m.
Change for dinner

8 p.m.–11 p.m.
Dinner with Genovian dignitaries

*Monday, December 22*
8 a.m.–9:30 a.m.
Breakfast with Genovian public officials

10 a.m.–11:30 a.m.
Tour of Genovian public schools

12 p.m.–1 p.m.
Meet with Genovian schoolchildren

1:30 p.m.–3 p.m.
Lunch with members of Genovian Teachers
Association

3:30 p.m.–4:30 p.m.
Tour of Port of Genovia and Genovian naval cruiser
(the *Prince Phillipe*)

5 p.m.–6 p.m.
Tour of Genovian General Hospital

6 p.m.–7 p.m.
Visit with hospital patients

7 p.m.–8 p.m.
Change for dinner

8 p.m.–11 p.m.
Dinner with the dowager princess, prince, and
Genovian military advisors

*Tuesday, December 23*
8 a.m.–9 a.m.
Breakfast with members of Genovian Olive Growers
Association

10 a.m.–11 a.m.
Christmas Tree Lighting ceremony, Genovia Palace
Courtyard

11:30 a.m.–1 p.m.
Meet with Genovian Historical Society

1 p.m.–3 p.m.
Lunch with Genovian Board of Tourism

3:30 p.m.–5:30 p.m.
Tour of Genovian National Art Museum

6 p.m.–7 p.m.
Visit Genovian War Veterans Memorial,
place flowers on grave of Unknown Soldier

7:30 p.m.–8:30 p.m.
Change for dinner

8:30 p.m.–11:30 p.m.
Dinner with Royal Family of Monaco

And so on.

It all culminates in my appearance on my dad's annual nationally televised Christmas Eve address to the people of Genovia, during which he will introduce me to the populace. I am then supposed to make a speech about how thrilled I am to be Dad's heir, and how I promise to try to do as good a job as he has at leading Genovia into the twenty-first century.

Nervous? Me? About going on TV and promising fifty thousand people that I won't let their country down?

Nah. Not me.

I just want to throw up every time I think about it, that's all.

Whatever. Not that I thought my trip to Genovia was going to be like going to Disneyland, but still. You'd think they'd have scheduled in *some* fun time. I'm not even asking for Mr. Toad's Wild Ride. Just, like, some swimming or horseback riding.

But apparently, there is no time for fun in Genovia.

As if going over my itinerary wasn't bad enough, I also had to meet my cousin Sebastiano. Sebastiano Grimaldi is my dead grandfather's sister's daughter's kid. Which I guess actually makes him my cousin a couple times removed. But not removed enough that, if it weren't for me, he wouldn't be inheriting the throne to Genovia.

Seriously. If my dad had died without ever having had a kid, Sebastiano would be the next prince of Genovia.

Maybe that's why my dad, every time he looks at Sebastiano, heaves this big shudder.

Or maybe it's just because my dad feels about Sebastiano the way I feel about my cousin Hank: I like him in theory, but in actual practice, he kind of bugs me.

Sebastiano doesn't bug Grandmère, though. You can tell that Grandmère just loves him. Which is really weird, because I always supposed Grandmère was incapable of loving anyone. Well, with the exception of Rommel, her miniature poodle.

But you can tell she totally adores Sebastiano. When she introduced him to me, and he bowed with this big flourish and kissed the air above my hand, Grandmère was practically beaming beneath her pink silk turban. Really.

I have never seen Grandmère beam before. Glare, plenty of times. But never beam.

Which might be why my dad started chewing the ice in his whiskey and soda in a very irritated manner. Grandmère's smile disappeared right away when she heard all that crunching.

"If you want to chew ice, Phillipe," Grandmère said, coldly, "you can go and have your dinner at McDonald's with the rest of the proletariat."

My dad stopped chewing his ice.

It turns out Grandmère brought Sebastiano over from Genovia so that he could design my dress for my nationally televised introduction to my countrymen. Sebastiano is a very up-and-coming fashion designer—at least according to Grandmère. She says it is important that Genovia supports its artists and craftspeople, or they will all flee to New York, or even worse, Los Angeles.

Which is too bad for Sebastiano, since he looks like the type who might really enjoy living in LA. He is thirtyish, with long, dark hair tied back in a ponytail, and is all tall and flamboyant-looking. Like for instance, tonight, instead of a tie, Sebastiano was wearing a white silk ascot. And he had on a blue velvet jacket with leather pants.

I am fully prepared to forgive Sebastiano for the leather pants if he designs me a dress that is nice enough. A dress that, should he happen to see me in it, will make Michael Moscovitz forget all about Judith Gershner and her fruit flies, and fill his head with nothing but thoughts of me, Mia Thermopolis.

Only of course the chances of Michael ever actually seeing me in this dress are very slim, as my introduction to the Genovian people is only going to be on Genovian television, not CNN or anything.

Still, Sebastiano seemed ready to rise to the challenge. After dinner, he even took out a pen and began sketching— right on the white tablecloth!—a design he thought might accentuate what he called my narrow waist and long legs.

Only, unlike my dad, who was born and raised in Genovia but speaks fluent English, Sebastiano doesn't have a real keen grasp of the language. He kept forgetting the second syllables of words. So *narrow* became "nar." Just like *coffee* became "coff," and when he described something as magical, it came out as "madge." Even the butter wasn't safe. When Sebastiano asked me to please pass him the "butt," I had to practically stuff my napkin in my mouth to keep from laughing out loud.

All my efforts to stifle myself didn't do any good, though, since Grandmère caught me and, raising one of her drawn-on eyebrows, went, "Amelia, kindly do not make light of other people's speech habits. Your own are not even remotely perfect."

Which is certainly true, considering the fact that, with my swollen tongue, I can't really say any word that starts with *s*.

Not only did Grandmère not mind Sebastiano saying the word *butt* at the dinner table, she didn't mind his drawing on the tablecloth, either. She looked down at his sketch and said, "Brilliant. Simply brilliant. As usual."

Sebastiano looked very pleased. "Do you real think so?" he asked.

Only I didn't think his sketch was so brilliant. It just looked like an ordinary dress to me. Certainly nothing to make anyone forget the fact that I'm about as likely to clone a fruit fly as I am to use animal-tested hair products.

"Um," I said. "Can't you make it a little more . . . I don't know . . . sexy?"

Grandmère and Sebastiano exchanged looks. "Sexy?" Grandmère echoed, with an evil laugh. "How? By making it lower cut? But you haven't got anything there to show!"

Now, seriously. I would expect to hear this kind of thing from the cheerleaders at school, who have made demeaning other people—especially me—a sort of new Olympic sport. But what kind of person says things like this to her only grandchild? I had meant, of course, a side slit, or maybe some fringe. I wasn't asking for anything Jennifer Lopez-ish.

But trust Grandmère to turn it into something like that.

Why do I have to be cursed with a grandmother who shaves off her eyebrows and seems to enjoy making light of my inadequacies? Why can't I have a normal grandmother, who bakes me cookies and can't stop bragging to her friends in her bridge club about how wonderful I am?

It was while Grandmère and Sebastiano were cackling to themselves over this great witticism at my expense that my dad abruptly got up and left the table, saying he had to make a call. I suppose it's every man for himself where Grandmère is concerned, but you would think my own father would stick up for me once in a while.

I don't know, maybe I was feeling odd about the giant hole in my tongue (which doesn't even have a nice hypoallergenic stud in it so I can pretend to have done it on purpose to be controversial). I sat there listening to Grandmère and Sebastiano chatter away about how pathetic it was that I would never be able to wear anything strapless, unless some miracle of nature occurred one night that inflated me from a 32A to a 34C, and I couldn't help thinking that probably, given my luck, it will turn out that Sebastiano isn't in town just to design me a dress for my royal introduction, but to kill me so that he can assume the throne of Genovia himself.

Or, as Sebastiano would say, "ass" the throne.

Seriously. That kind of stuff happens on *Baywatch* all the time. You wouldn't believe the number of royal family members Mitch has had to save from assassination.

Like supposing I put on the dress that Sebastiano has designed for me to wear when I'm introduced to the people of Genovia, and it ends up squeezing me to death, just like that corset Snow White puts on in the original version of the story by the Brothers Grimm. You know, the part they left out of the Disney movie because it was too gruesome.

Anyway, what if the dress squeezes me to death, and then I'm lying in my coffin, looking all pale and queenly, and

Michael comes to my funeral and ends up gazing down at me and doesn't realize until right then that he has always loved me?

Then he'll *have* to break up with Judith Gershner.

Hey. It could happen.

Okay, well, probably not, but thinking about that was better than listening to Grandmère and Sebastiano talk about me as if I weren't even there. Seriously. I was roused from my pleasant little fantasy about Michael pining for me for the rest of his life by Sebastiano saying suddenly, "She has bute bone struck," which, when I realized I was the *she* he was referring to, I took to be a compliment about my bone structure.

Only a second later it wasn't such a compliment when he went, "I put makeup on her that make her look like a mod."

Implying I don't look like a model without makeup (although of course I don't).

Grandmère certainly wasn't about to come to my defense, however. She was feeding bits of her leftover veal marsala to Rommel, who was sitting on her lap, shivering as usual, since all of his fur has fallen out due to canine allergies.

"I wouldn't count on her father letting you," she said to Sebastiano. "Phillipe is hopelessly old-fashioned."

Which is so the pot calling the kettle black! I mean, Grandmère still thinks that cats go around trying to suck the breath out of their owners while they are sleeping. Seriously. She is always trying to convince me to give Fat Louie away.

So while Grandmère was going on about how old-fashioned her son is, I got up and joined him on the balcony.

He was checking his messages on his cell phone. He's supposed to play racquetball tomorrow with the prime minister of France, who is in town for the same summit as the emperor of Japan.

"Mia," he said, when he saw me. "What are you doing out here? It's freezing. Go back inside."

"I will, in a minute," I said. I stood there next to him and looked out over the city. It really is kind of awe-inspiring, the view of Manhattan from the penthouse of the Plaza Hotel. I mean, you look at all those lights in all those windows, and you think, for each light there's probably at least one person, but maybe even more, maybe even like ten people, and that's, well, pretty mind-boggling.

I've lived in Manhattan my whole life. But it still impresses me.

Anyway, while I was standing there looking at all the lights, I suddenly realized that one of them probably belonged to Judith Gershner. Judith was probably sitting in her room right this moment cloning something new. A pigeon, or whatever. I got yet another flashback of her and Michael looking down at me after I'd split open my tongue. Hmmm, let me see: girl who can clone things, or girl who bit her own tongue? I don't know, who would *you* choose?

My dad must have noticed something was wrong, since he went, "Look, I know Sebastiano is a bit much, but just put up with him for the next couple of weeks. For my sake."

"I wasn't thinking about Sebastiano," I said sadly.

My dad made this grunting noise, but he made no move to go back inside, even though it was about forty degrees out there, and my dad, well, he's completely bald. I could see that the tips of his ears were getting red with cold, but still he didn't budge. He didn't even have a coat on, just another one of his charcoal-gray Armani suits.

I figured this was invitation enough to go on. You see, ordinarily my dad is not who I would go to first if I had a problem. Not that we're not close. It's just that, you know, he's a guy.

On the other hand, he's had a lot of experience in the

romance department, so I figured he might just be able to offer some insight into this particular dilemma.

"Dad," I said. "What do you do if you like someone, but they don't, you know, know it?"

My dad went, "If Kenny doesn't know you like him by now, then I'm afraid he's never going to get the message. Haven't you been out with him every weekend since Halloween?"

This is the problem with having a bodyguard who is on your father's payroll: All of your personal business totally gets discussed behind your back.

"I'm not talking about Kenny, Dad," I said. "It's someone else. Only like I said, he doesn't know I like him."

"What's wrong with Kenny?" my dad wanted to know. "I like Kenny."

Of course my dad likes Kenny. Because the chances of me and Kenny ever getting past first base are like, nil. What father doesn't want his teenage daughter to date a guy like that?

But if my dad has any serious hope of keeping the Genovian throne in the hands of the Renaldos, and not allowing it to slip into Sebastiano's control, he had better get over the whole Kenny thing, because I'm pretty sure that Kenny and I will not be doing any procreating. In this lifetime, anyway.

"Dad," I said. "Forget Kenny, okay? Kenny and I are just friends. I'm talking about someone else."

My dad was looking over the side of the balcony railing like he wanted to spit. Not that he ever would. I don't think. "Do I know him? This someone else, I mean?"

I hesitated. I've never really admitted to anyone out loud that I have a crush on Michael. Really. Not to anybody. I mean, who could I tell? Lilly would just make fun of me, or worse, tell Michael. And Mom, well, she's got her own problems.

"It's Lilly's brother," I said in a rush, to get it over with. My dad looked alarmed. "Isn't he in college?"

"Not yet," I said. "He's going in the fall." When he still looked alarmed, I said, "Don't worry, Dad. I don't stand a chance. Michael is very smart. He'd never like someone like me."

Then my dad got all offended. It was like he couldn't figure out which to be, worried about my liking a senior, or angry that that senior didn't like me back.

"What do you mean, he'd never like someone like you?" my father demanded. "What's wrong with you?"

"Duh, Dad," I said. "I practically flunked Algebra, remember? Michael is going to an Ivy League school in the fall, for crying out loud. What would he want with a girl like me?"

Now my dad was *really* annoyed: "You may take after your mother as far as your aptitude with numbers is concerned, but you take after me in every other respect."

This was surprising to hear. I stuck out my chin and tried to believe it. "Yeah," I said.

"And you and I, Mia, are not unintelligent," my dad went on. "If you want this Michael fellow, you must let him know it."

"You think I should just go up to him and be like, 'Hey, I like you'?"

My dad shook his head in disgust. "No, no, no," he said. "Of course you must be more subtle than that. Tell him by *showing* how you feel."

"Oh," I said. I may take after my father in every respect except my math aptitude, but I had no idea what he was talking about.

"We'd better get back in," my father said. "Or your grandmother will suspect us of plotting against her."

So what else is new? Grandmère is always suspecting

somebody of plotting something against her. She thinks the launderers at the Plaza are plotting against her. She blames the soap they use on their linens for making all of Rommel's fur fall out.

Reminded of plots, I asked my dad, "Do you think Sebastiano's plotting to kill me so he can ascend the throne himself?"

My dad made a strangled noise, but he managed not to burst out laughing. I guess that wouldn't have seemed very princely.

"No, Mia," he said. "I do not."

But my dad, he really doesn't have much of an imagination. I have decided to stay on alert about Sebastiano, just in case.

My mom just poked her head into my room to say that Kenny is on the phone for me.

I suppose he wants to ask me to the Nondenominational Winter Dance. Really, it is about time.

Okay. I am in shock. Kenny so did NOT ask me to the Nondenominational Winter Dance. Instead, this is how our conversation went:

Me:      Hello?
Kenny:   Hi, Mia. It's Kenny.
Me:      Oh, hi, Kenny. What's the matter?

Kenny sounded funny, which is why I asked.

Kenny:   Well, I just wanted to see if you were okay. I
         mean, if your tongue was okay.
Me:      It's a little better, I guess.
Kenny:   Because I was really worried. You know. I
         really, really didn't mean to—
Me:      Kenny, I know. It was just an accident.

This is when I started realizing I'd asked my dad the wrong question. I should have asked him what's the best way to break up with somebody, not what's the best way to let someone know you like them.

Anyway, to get back to what Kenny said:

Kenny:   Well, I just wanted to call and wish you a
         good night. And say that I hope you feel bet-
         ter. And also to let you know . . . well, Mia,
         that I love you.
Me:      . . . .

I didn't say anything right away, because I was completely FREAKED OUT!!!! It wasn't exactly as if it happened out of the blue, because we are sort of going out, after all.

But still, what kind of guy calls a girl on the phone and says I love you??? Except for weird psycho stalkers? And Kenny's not a weird psycho stalker. He's just Kenny. So what's he doing calling me on the phone and telling me he loves me????

And then, brilliant me, here's what I do. Because he was still on the phone, waiting for an answer, and all. So I go:

Me:        Um, okay.

*Um, okay.*

A boy says he loves me, and this is how I respond: "Um, okay." Oh, yeah, good thing my future career lies in the diplomatic corps.

So then, poor Kenny, he's like waiting for some response other than "Um, okay," as anybody would.

But I am perfectly incapable of giving him one. Instead, I just go:

Me:        Well, see you tomorrow.

AND I HUNG UP!!!!!

Oh, my God, I am the meanest, most ungrateful girl in the world. After Sebastiano kills me, I am going to burn in hell.

Seriously.

## TO DO BEFORE LEAVING FOR GENOVIA

1. Detailed list for Mom and Mr. G: How to care for Fat Louie while I am away
2. Stock up on cat food, litter
3. Christmas/Hannukah presents! For:
   Mom—electric breast pump? Check on this.
   Mr. G—new drumsticks
   Dad—book on vegetarianism. He should eat better if he wants to keep his cancer in remission.
   Lilly—what she always wants, blank videotapes for her show
   Lars–See if Prada makes a shoulder holster that would fit his Glock
   Kenny—gloves? Something NON-romantic
   Fat Louie—catnip ball
   Grandmère–What do you get for the woman who has everything, including an eighty-nine-carat sapphire pendant given to her by the Sultan of Brunei? Soap on a rope?
4. Break up with Kenny. . . . Only how can I? He LOVES me.

But not enough to ask me to the Nondenominational Winter Dance, I've noticed.

Lilly doesn't believe me about Kenny calling and saying he loves me. I told her in the car on the way to school this morning (thank God Michael had a dentist appointment and wasn't there. I would sooner die than discuss my love life in front of him. It's bad enough having to discuss it in front of my bodyguard. If I had to discuss it in front of this person I've been worshiping for half my life, I think I'd probably go completely borderline personality disorder).

Anyway, so Lilly went, "I categorically refuse to believe Kenny would do something like that."

"Lilly," I said. I had to keep my voice down so the driver wouldn't hear. "I am dead serious. He told me he loves me. *I love you.* That is what he said. It was completely random and weird."

"He probably didn't say that. He probably said something else, and you misunderstood him."

"Oh, what? I *glove* you?"

"Well, of course not," Lilly said. "That doesn't even make any sense."

"Well, then what? What could Kenny have said that sounded like *I love you*, but wasn't *I love you*?"

Lilly got mad then. She went, "You know, you have been acting weird about Kenny for the past month. Since the two of you started going out, practically. I don't know what's wrong with you. All I ever heard before was 'Why don't I have a boyfriend? How come everybody I know has a boyfriend but me? When am I going to get a boyfriend?' And now you've got one and you aren't the least bit appreciative of him."

Even though what she was saying was true, I acted offended, because I have been trying really hard not to let the fact that I am not in love with Kenny show.

"That is so false," I said. "I completely appreciate Kenny."

"Oh, yeah? I think the truth of the matter is, you, Mia, simply aren't ready to have a boyfriend."

Boy did I see red after *that* remark.

"*Me?* Not ready to have a boyfriend? Are you kidding? I've been waiting my whole life to have a boyfriend!"

"Well, if that's true"—Lilly was looking very superior—"why won't you let him kiss you on the lips?"

"Where did you hear *that*?" I demanded.

"Kenny told Boris, of course, who told me."

"Oh, great," I said, trying to remain calm. "So now our boyfriends are talking about us behind our backs. And you're condoning this?"

"Of course not," Lilly said. "But I do find it intriguing, from a psychological point of view."

This is the problem with being best friends with someone whose parents are psychiatrists. Everything you do is interesting to them from a psychological point of view.

"Where I let anybody kiss me," I exploded, "is *my* business! Not yours, and not Boris's, either."

"Well," Lilly said. "I'm just saying, if Kenny did say what you say he said—you know, the L word—then maybe he said it because he can't express the depth of his feelings any other way. You know. Other than *verbally*. Since you won't *let* him, physically."

So I suppose that technically I should be thankful that Kenny chose merely to *say* the words I love you, rather than enacting them physically, which, God knows, might have actually involved his tongue.

Oh, God, I don't even want to think about it anymore.

They just passed out the final exam schedules. Here is mine:

## FINAL EXAM SCHEDULE

### December 15
Reading Day

### December 16
Periods One and Two

For me, that means the Algebra and English finals will be on the same day. But that's okay. I'm doing pretty good in English. Well, except for that sentence diagramming thing. As if I'll ever need to do *that* in my future role as princess of the smallest nation in Europe.

Unfortunately, Algebra, I am told, I will probably need to know. DAMN!

### December 17
Periods Three and Four

World Civ: Easy. I mean, Grandmère has told me enough stories about post–World War II Europe for me to pass any test. I probably know more about it than the teacher. And PE? How can you give a final in PE? We already had the Presidential Fitness Test (I did okay on everything but the V-sit reach).

## December 18
### Periods Five, Six, and Seven

Gifted and Talented? No exam there. They don't give finals in classes that are basically study hall. That will be a snap. I have French sixth period. I do okay in oral, not so great in written. Fortunately Tina's in the same class. Maybe we can study together.

But I have Bio seventh period. That won't be so easy. The only reason I'm not flunking Bio is because of Kenny. He slips me most of the answers.

And if I break up with him, that will be the end of that.

## December 19
### Nondenominational Winter Carnival and Dance

The Winter Carnival should be fun. All the different school clubs and groups are going to have booths, with traditional winter fare, like hot cider. This will be followed in the evening by the dance I am supposed to go to with Kenny. If he ever asks me to it, I mean.

Unless, of course, I do the right thing and break up with him.

In which case, I won't be able to go at all, because you can't go without a date.

I wish Sebastiano would just hurry up and off me already.

WHY???? WHY can't I ever remember my Algebra notebook?????

FIRST—Evaluate exponents
SECOND—Multiply and divide in order, left to right
THIRD—Perform addition and subtraction in order, left to right
EXAMPLE: $2 \times 3 - 15 \div 5 = 6 - 3 = 3$

Oh, God. Lana Weinberger just tossed me a note.

What now? This can't be good. Lana's had it out for me forever. Don't ask me why. I mean, I could kind of understand her resenting me for when Josh Richter asked me to the Cultural Diversity Dance instead of her. But he only asked me because of the princess thing—and they got back together right after. Besides, Lana hated me long before that.

So I open the note. Here's what it says:

> *I heard what happened to you at the skating rink this weekend. Guess the BF is going to have to wait a little longer if he wants to see any tongue action, huh?*

Oh, my God. Does *everyone* in the entire school know that Kenny and I have not yet French kissed?

It is all Kenny's fault, of course.

What next? The cover of the *Post*?

I'm telling you, if our parents knew what actually goes on every day in the typical American high school, they would totally opt for homeschooling.

It's clear what I have to do.

I've always known it, of course, and if it hadn't been for, you know, the dance, I would have done it long before now.

But it is clear now that I cannot afford to wait until after the dance. I should have done it last night when he called, but you can't really do something like that over the phone. Well, I mean, a girl like Lana Weinberger probably could, but not me.

No, I don't think I can put it off another day: I have got to break up with Kenny. I simply cannot continue living this lie.

Fortunately, I do have the support of at least one person in this plan: Tina Hakim Baba.

I didn't want to tell her. I didn't plan on telling anybody. But it all sort of slipped out today in the girls' room between second and third periods while Tina was putting on her eye makeup. Her dad won't let her wear makeup, you see, so Tina has to wait until she gets to school to put it on. She has a deal with her bodyguard, Wahim. Tina won't tell her parents how much Wahim flirts with Mademoiselle Klein, our French teacher, if Wahim doesn't tell Mr. and Mrs. Hakim Baba about Tina's Maybelline addiction.

Anyway, all of a sudden I just couldn't take it anymore, and I ended up telling Tina what Kenny said last night on the phone—

And a lot more than that actually.

But first the part about Kenny's phone call:

Unlike Lilly, *Tina* believed me.

But Tina also had the totally wrong reaction. She thought it was great.

"Oh, my God, Mia, you are so lucky," she kept saying. "I wish Dave would tell me he loves me! I mean, I know he is fully committed to our relationship, but his idea of romance is paying to have my fries super-sized at Mickey D's."

This was so not the kind of support I was looking for.

"But, Tina," I said. I felt Tina, with her extensive reading of romances, would understand. "The thing is, I don't love him."

Tina widened her mascaraed eyes at me. "You don't?"

"No," I said, miserably. "I mean, I really like him, as a friend. But I'm not in love, or anything. Not with him."

"Oh, God," Tina said, reaching out and grabbing my wrist. "There's someone else, isn't there?"

We only had a few minutes before the bell rang. We both had to get to class.

And yet, for some reason, I chose this moment to make my big confession. I don't know why. Maybe since I'd already spilled it to my dad, it didn't seem too hard to tell someone else, especially Tina. Also, I can't stop thinking about what my dad said. You know, about showing the guy I like how I feel. Tina, I felt, was the only person I knew who would know how to help me do that.

So I went, "Yes."

Tina nearly spilled her cosmetics bag, she was so excited.

"I knew it!" she yelled. "I knew there was a reason you wouldn't let him kiss you!"

My jaw dropped. "*You* know about that, too?"

"Well." Tina shrugged. "Kenny told Dave, who told me."

Jeez! What's that Oprah is always complaining about, about how men aren't in touch with their emotions, and don't share enough? It sounds to me like Kenny's been doing enough sharing recently to make up for several centuries' worth of masculine reticence.

"So who is he?" Tina asked, all eager as she packed up her eyelash curler and lipliner. "The guy you like?"

I went, "It doesn't matter. Besides, the whole thing is completely futile. He sort of has a girlfriend. I think."

Tina whipped her head around to look at me, making her thick, black braid smack her in her own face, which is chubby, but in a good way.

"It's Michael, isn't it?" she demanded, grabbing my arm again. She was holding on so tight it hurt.

My instinct, of course, was to deny it. In fact, I even opened my mouth, all set to have the word *No* come out of it.

But then I was like, Why? Why should I deny it to Tina? Tina wouldn't tell anyone. And Tina might be able to help me.

So instead of saying No, I took a deep breath, and said, "If you tell anyone, I'll kill you, understand? KILL YOU."

Tina did a strange thing then. She let go of my arm and started jumping up and down in a circle.

"I knew it, I knew it, I knew it," she said, as she jumped. Then she stopped jumping and grabbed my arm again. "Oh, Mia, I always thought you two would make the cutest couple. I mean, I like Kenny and all, but he's, you know." She wrinkled up her nose. "Not Michael."

If I had thought it felt strange last night telling my dad the truth about my feelings for Michael, that was nothing—NOTHING—compared to how it felt to be telling someone my own age. The fact that Tina hadn't burst out laughing or gone, "Yeah, right," in a sarcastic way meant more to me than I ever would have expected.

And the fact that she seemed to understand—even applaud—my feelings for Michael made me want to fling my arms around her and give her a great big hug.

Only there was no time for that, since the bell was about to ring.

Instead, I gushed, "Really? You really don't think it's stupid?"

"Duh," Tina said. "Michael is *hot. And* he's a senior." Then she looked troubled. "But what about Kenny? And Judith?"

"I know," I said, my shoulders slumping in a manner that would have caused Grandmère to rap me on the back of the head, if she'd seen them. "Tina, I don't know what to do."

Tina's dark eyebrows furrowed with concentration.

"I think I read a book where this happened once," she said. "*Listen to My Heart*, it was called, I think. If I could just remember how they resolved everything—"

But before she could remember, the bell rang. We were both totally late to class.

But if you ask me, it was worth it. Because now, at least, I don't have to worry alone. I have somebody else worrying with me.

Lunch was a disaster.

Considering that everybody in the entire school seems to know, in the minutest detail, exactly what I've been doing—or not doing—with my tongue lately, I guess I shouldn't have been surprised. But it was even worse than I could have imagined.

That's because I ran into Michael at the salad bar. I was creating my usual chickpea-and-pinto-bean pyramid when I saw him headed for the burger grill (despite my best efforts, both Moscovitzes remain stubbornly carnivorous).

Seriously, all I did was say "Fine" when he asked how I was doing. You know, on account of how last time he saw me, I was bleeding out of the mouth (what a nice picture that must have been. I am so glad that I have been able to maintain an appearance of dignity and beauty at all times in front of the man I love).

Anyway, then I asked him, just to be polite, you know, how his dentist appointment went. What happened next was not my fault.

Which was that Michael started telling me about how he'd had to have this cavity filled, and that his lips were still numb from the novocaine. Seeing as how I have experienced a certain amount of sensation-deadening, what with my gouged tongue, I could relate to this, so I just sort of, you know, *looked* at Michael's lips while he was talking, which I have never really done before. I mean, I have looked at other parts of Michael's body (particularly when he comes into the kitchen in the morning with no shirt on, like he does every time I have a sleepover at Lilly's). But I've never really looked at his lips. You know. Up close.

Michael actually has very nice lips. Not thin lips, like mine. I don't know if you should say this about a boy's lips, but Michael's lips look like if you kissed them, they'd be very soft.

It was while I was noticing this about Michael's lips that the very bad thing happened: I was looking at them, you know, and wondering if they'd be soft to kiss, and as I looked, I sort of actually pictured us kissing, you know, in my head. And right then I got this very warm feeling—the one they talk about in all of Tina's romance novels—and RIGHT THEN was when Kenny went by on his way to get his usual lunch: Coke and an ice-cream sandwich.

I know Kenny can't read my mind—if he could, he totally would have broken up with me by now—but maybe he caught some hint as to what I was thinking, and that's why he didn't say *Hi* back, when Michael and I said "Hi" to him.

Well, that and the whole part where I said, "Um, okay," after he said he loved me.

Kenny must have known something was up, if my face was anywhere near as red-hot as it felt. Maybe *that*'s why he didn't say *Hi* back. Because I was looking so guilty. I'd certainly *felt* guilty. I mean, there I was, looking at another guy's lips and wondering what it would be like to kiss them, and my boyfriend goes walking by.

I am so going to bad-girl hell when I die.

You know what I wish? I wish everyone *could* read my mind. Because then Kenny would never have asked me out. He'd have known I don't think of him that way. And Lilly wouldn't make fun of me for not letting Kenny kiss me. She would know the reason I don't is that I'm in love with someone else.

The bad part is, she'd know who that someone else is.

And that someone probably won't even speak to me again, because it's totally uncool for a senior to go out with a freshman. Especially one who can't go anywhere without a bodyguard.

Besides, I'm almost positive he's going out with Judith Gershner, because after he came back from the grill, he went and sat down next to her.

So that settles that.

I wish I were leaving for Genovia tomorrow instead of in two weeks.

In spite of that disastrous incident at lunch, I had a pretty good time in Gifted and Talented. In fact, it was almost like old times again. I mean, before we all started going out with each other and everyone became so obsessed with the inner workings of my mouth, and all that.

Mrs. Hill spent the whole class period in the teachers' lounge across the hall, yelling at American Express on the phone, leaving us free to do what we usually do during her class . . . whatever we wanted. For instance, those of us who, like Lilly's boyfriend Boris, wanted to work on our individual projects (Boris's is learning to play some new sonata on his violin), which is what Gifted and Talented class is supposedly for, did so.

Those of us, however, like Lilly and me, who did not want to work on our individual projects (mine is studying for Algebra; Lilly's is working on her cable access TV show) did not.

This was especially satisfying, because Lilly had completely forgotten about the whole kissing thing between Kenny and me. The reason for this is that now she's mad at Mrs. Spears, her honors English teacher, who shot down her term paper proposal.

It really was unfair of Mrs. Spears to turn it down, because it was actually very well thought out, and quite creative. I made a copy of it:

# How to Survive High School
## *by Lilly Moscovitz*

Having spent the past two months locked in that institution of secondary education commonly referred to as high school, I feel that I am a qualified authority on the subject. From pep rallies to morning announcements, I have observed high-school life and all of its complexities. Sometime in the next four years, I will be granted my freedom from this festering hellhole, and then I will publish my carefully compiled *High School Survival Guide*.

Little did my peers and teachers know that as they went about their daily routines, I was recording their activities for study by future generations. With my handy guide, every ninth grader's sojourn in high school can be a little more fruitful. Students of the future will learn that the way to settle their differences with their peers is not through violence, but through the sale of a really scathing screenplay—featuring characters based on those very individuals who tormented them all those years—to a major Hollywood movie studio. That, not a Molotov cocktail, is the path to true glory.

Here, for your reading pleasure, are a few examples of the topics I will explore in *How to Survive High School*, by Lilly Moscovitz:

1. High-School Romance, or How I Cannot Open My Locker Because Two Oversexed Adolescents are Leaning Up Against It, Making Out
2. Cafeteria Food: Can Corndogs Legally Be Listed as a Meat Product?
3. How to Communicate with the Subhumans Who Populate the Hallways
4. Guidance Counselors: Who Do They Think They're Kidding?
5. Get Ahead by Forging: The Art of the Hall Pass

Does that sound good, or what? Now look what Mrs. Spears had to say about it:

> *Lilly—Sorry as I am to hear that your experience thus far at AEHS has not been a positive one, I am afraid I am going to have to make it worse by asking you to find another topic for your term paper. A for creativity, as usual, however.*
>
> *—Mrs. Spears*

Can you believe that? Talk about unfair! Lilly's been censored! By rights, her proposal ought to have brought the school's administration to its knees. Lilly says she is appalled by the fact that, considering how much our tuition costs, this is the kind of support we can expect from our teachers. Then I reminded her that that isn't true of Mr. Gianini, who really goes beyond the call of duty by staying after school every day to conduct help sessions for people like me, who aren't doing so well in Algebra.

Lilly says Mr. Gianini probably only started pulling that staying-after-school thing so that he could ingratiate himself with my mother, and now he can't stop, because then she'll realize it was all just a setup and divorce him.

I don't believe that, however. I think Mr. G would have stayed after school to help me whether he was dating my mom or not. He's that kind of guy.

Anyway, the upshot of it all is that now Lilly has launched another one of her famous campaigns. This is actually a good thing, as it will keep her mind off me and where I am putting (or not putting) my lips. Here's how it started:

Lilly:     The real problem with this school isn't the teachers. It's the apathy of the student body.

|          | For instance, let's say we wanted to stage a walkout. |
|----------|------------------------------------------------------|
| Me:      | A walkout? |
| Lilly:   | You know. We all get up and walk out of the school at the same time. |
| Me:      | Just because Mrs. Spears turned down your term paper proposal? |
| Lilly:   | No, Mia. Because she's trying to usurp our individuality by forcing us to bend to corporate feudalism. Again. |
| Me:      | Oh. And how is she doing that? |
| Lilly:   | By censoring us when we are at our most fertile, creatively speaking. |
| Boris:   | (leaning out of the supply closet, where Lilly made him go when he started practicing his latest sonata) Fertile? Did someone say *fertile*? |
| Lilly:   | Get back in the closet, Boris. Michael, can you send a mass e-mail tonight to the entire student body, declaring a walkout tomorrow at eleven? |
| Michael: | (working on the booth he and Judith Gershner and the rest of the Computer Club are going to have up at the Winter Carnival) I can, but I won't. |
| Lilly:   | WHY NOT? |
| Michael: | Because it was your turn to empty the dishwasher last night, but you weren't home, so I had to do it. |
| Lilly:   | But I TOLD Mom I had to go down to the studio to edit the last few finishing touches on this week's show! |

Lilly's TV program, *Lilly Tells It Like It Is*, is now one of the highest-ranked shows on Manhattan cable. Of course, it's public access, so it's not like she's making any money off it, but a bunch of the major networks picked up this interview she did of me one night when I was half asleep and played it. I thought it was stupid, but I guess a lot of other people thought it was good, because now Lilly gets tons of viewer mail, whereas before the only mail she got was from her stalker, Norman.

Michael:   Look, if you're having time-management issues, don't take it out on me. Just don't expect me to meekly do your bidding, especially when you already owe me one.

Me:   Lilly, no offense, but I don't think this week's a good time for a walkout, anyway. I mean, after all, it's almost finals.

Lilly:   SO???

Me:   So some of us really need to stay in class. I can't afford to miss any review sessions. My grades are bad enough as it is.

Michael:   Really? I thought you were doing better in Algebra.

Me:   If you call a D plus better.

Michael:   Aw, come on. You have to be making better than a D plus. Your mom is married to your Algebra teacher!

Me:   So? That doesn't mean anything. You know Mr. G doesn't play favorites.

Michael:   I would think he'd cut his own stepdaughter a little slack, is all.

Lilly:   WOULD YOU TWO PLEASE PAY ATTEN-TION TO THE SITUATION AT HAND,

## WHICH IS THE FACT THAT THIS SCHOOL IS IN VITAL NEED OF SERIOUS REFORM?

Fortunately at that moment the bell rang, so no walkout tomorrow as far as I know. Which is a good thing, because I really need the extra study time.

You know, it's funny about Mrs. Spears not liking Lilly's term paper proposal, because she was very enthusiastic about my proposal, *A Case Against Christmas Trees: Why We Must Curtail the Pagan Ritual of Chopping Down Pine Trees Every December if We Are Going to Repair the Ozone Layer.*

And my IQ isn't anywhere near as high as Lilly's.

Kenny just passed me the following note:

> *Mia—I hope what I said to you last night didn't make you feel uncomfortable. I just wanted you to know how I feel.*
> *Sincerely,*
> *Kenny*

Oh, God. *Now* what am I supposed to do? He's sitting here next to me, waiting for an answer. In fact, that's what he thinks I'm writing right now. An answer.

What do I say?

Maybe this is my perfect opportunity to break up with him. *I'm sorry, Kenny, but I don't feel the same way—let's just be friends.* Is that what I should say?

It's just that I don't want to hurt his feelings, you know? And he is my Bio partner. I mean, whatever happens, I am going to have to sit next to him for the next two weeks. And I would much rather have a Bio partner who likes me than one who hates me.

And what about the dance? I mean, if I break up with him, who am I going to go to the Nondenominational Winter Dance with? I know it is horrible to think things like this, but this is the first dance in the history of my life to which I already have a date.

Well, I mean, if he'd ever get around to asking me.

And how about that final, huh? Our Bio final, I mean. No way am I going to be able to pass without Kenny's notes. NO WAY.

But what else can I do? I mean, considering what happened today at the salad bar.

This is it. Good-bye, date for the Nondenominational Winter Dance. Hello, Friday-night television.

*Dear Kenny,*
*It isn't that I don't think of you as a very dear friend. It's just that—*

*Monday, December 8, 3 p.m.,*
*Mr. Gianini's Algebra review*

Okay, so the bell rang before I had time to finish my note.

That doesn't mean I'm not going to tell Kenny exactly how I feel. I totally am. Tonight, as a matter of fact. I don't care if it's cruel to do something like that over the phone. I just can't take it anymore.

HOMEWORK

Algebra: review questions at the end of Chapters 1–3
English: term paper
World Civ: review questions at the end of Chapters 1–4
G&T: none
French: review questions at the end of Chapters 1–3
Biology: review questions at the end of Chapters 1–5

All right. So I didn't break up with him.

I totally meant to.

And it wasn't even because I didn't have the heart to do it over the phone, either.

It was something *Grandmère*, of all people, said.

Not that I feel right about it. Not breaking up with him, I mean. It's just that after Algebra review, I had to go to the showroom where Sebastiano is flogging his latest creations, so that he could have his flunkies take my measurements for my dress. Grandmère was going on about how from now on, I should really only wear clothes by Genovian designers, to show my patriotism, or whatever. Which is going to be hard, because, uh, there's only one Genovian clothing designer that I know of, and that's Sebastiano. And let's just say he doesn't make very much out of denim.

But whatever. I so had more important things to worry about than my spring wardrobe.

Which I guess Grandmère must have caught on to, because midway through Sebastiano's description of the beading he was going to have sewn onto my gown's bodice, Grandmère shouted, "Amelia, what is the matter with you?"

I must have jumped about a foot in the air. "What?"

"Sebastiano asked if you prefer a sweetheart or square-cut neckline."

I stared at her blankly. "Neckline for what?"

Grandmère gave me the evil eye. She does this quite frequently. That's why my father, even though he has the neighboring hotel suite, never stops by during my princess lessons.

"Sebastiano," my grandmother said. "You will please leave the princess and me for a moment."

And Sebastiano—who was wearing a new pair of leather pants, these in a tangerine color (the new gray, he told me;

and white, you might be surprised to know, is the new black)—bowed and left the room, followed by the slinky ladies who'd been taking my measurements.

"Now," Grandmère said imperiously. "Something is clearly troubling you, Amelia. What is it?"

"It's nothing," I said, turning all red. I knew I was turning all red because: a) I could feel it, and b) I could see my reflection in the three full-length mirrors in front of me.

"It is not nothing." Grandmère took in a healthy drag from her Gitanes, even though I have asked her repeatedly not to smoke in my presence, as breathing secondhand smoke can cause just as much lung damage as actually smoking. "What is it? Trouble at home? Your mother and the math teacher fighting already, I suppose. Well, I never expected *that* marriage to last. Your mother is much too flighty."

I have to admit, I kind of snapped when she said that. Grandmère is always putting my mother down, even though Mom has raised me pretty much single-handedly and I certainly haven't gotten pregnant or shot anyone yet.

"For your information," I said, "my mom and Mr. Gianini are blissfully happy together. I wasn't thinking about them at all."

"What is it, then?" Grandmère asked in a bored voice.

"Nothing," I practically yelled. "I just—well, I was thinking about the fact that I have to break up with my boyfriend tonight, that's all. Not that it's any of your business."

Instead of taking offense at my tone, which any self-respecting grandparent would have found insolent, Grandmère only took a sip of her drink and suddenly looked way interested.

"Oh?" she said, in a totally different tone of voice—the same tone of voice she uses when someone mentions a stock tip she thinks might be useful for her portfolio. "What boyfriend is this?"

God, what did I ever do to be cursed with such a grand-mother? Seriously. Lilly and Michael's grandma remembers the names of all their friends, makes them rugelach all the time, and always worries that they're not getting enough to eat, even though their parents, the Drs. Moscovitz, are wholly reliable at bringing home groceries, or at least order-ing out.

Me? I get the grandma with the hairless poodle and the nine-carat diamond rings whose greatest joy in life is to tor-ture me.

And why is that, anyway? I mean, why does Grandmère love to torture me so much? I've never done anything to her. Nothing except be her only grandchild, anyway. And it isn't exactly like I go around advertising how I feel about her. You know, I've never actually *told* her I think she's a mean old lady who contributes to the destruction of the environ-ment by wearing fur coats and smoking filterless French cigarettes.

"Grandmère," I said, trying to remain calm. "I have only one boyfriend. His name is Kenny." I've only told you about fifty thousand times, I added, in my head.

"I thought this Kenny person was your Biology partner," Grandmère said, after taking a sip of her Sidecar, her favorite drink.

"He is," I said, a little surprised that she'd managed to remember something like that. "He's also my boyfriend. Only last night he went completely schizo on me, and told me he loves me."

Grandmère patted Rommel, who was sitting in her lap looking miserable (his habitual expression), on the head.

"And what is so wrong," Grandmère wanted to know, "about a boy who says he loves you?"

"Nothing," I said. "Only I'm not in love with him, see? So it wouldn't be fair of me to, you know, lead him on."

Grandmère raised her painted-on eyebrows. "I don't see why not."

How had I ever gotten into this conversation? "Because, Grandmère. People just don't go around *doing* things like that. Not nowadays."

"Is that so? Well, my observations of people are to the contrary. Except, of course, if one happens to be in love with someone else. Then shedding an unwanted suitor might be considered wise, so that one can make oneself available to the man one truly desires." She eyed me. "Is there someone like that in your life, Amelia? Someone—ahem—special?"

"No." I lied, automatically.

Grandmère snorted. "You're lying."

"No, I'm not." I lied again.

"Indeed you are. I oughtn't tell you this, but I suppose as it is a bad habit for a future monarch, you ought to be made aware of it, so that in the future, you can try to prevent it: When you lie, Amelia, your nostrils flare."

I threw my hands up to my nose. "They do not!"

"Indeed," Grandmère said, clearly enjoying herself immensely. "If you do not believe me, look in the mirror."

I turned around to face the nearby full-length mirrors. Taking my hands from my face, I examined my nose. My nostrils weren't flaring. She was crazy.

"I'll ask you again, Amelia," Grandmère said, in a lazy voice, from her chair. "Are you in love with anyone right now?"

"No." I lied, automatically. . . .

And my nostrils flared right out!

Oh, my God! All these years I've been lying, and it turns out whenever I do, my nostrils totally give me away! All anyone has to do is look at my nose when I talk, and they'll know for sure whether or not I'm telling the truth.

How could no one have pointed this out to me before?

And Grandmère—Grandmère, of all people—was the one who figured it out! Not my mother, with whom I've lived for fourteen years. Not my best friend, whose IQ is higher than Einstein's.

No. Grandmère.

If this got out, my life was over.

"Fine," I cried dramatically, spinning away from the mirror to face her. "All right, yes. Yes, I am in love with somebody else. Are you happy now?"

Grandmère raised her painted-on eyebrows.

"No need to shout, Amelia," she said, with what I might have taken for amusement in anyone other than her. "Who might this special someone be?"

"Oh, no," I said, holding out both my hands. If it wouldn't have been totally rude, I'd have made a little cross out of my index fingers and held it up toward her—that's how much she scares me. And if you think about it, with her tattooed eyeliner, she does look a little like Nosferatu. "You are not getting that information out of me."

Grandmère stamped out her cigarette in the crystal ashtray Sebastiano had provided, and went, "Very well. I take it, then, that the gentleman in question does not return your ardor?"

There was no point in lying to her. Not now. Not with my nostrils.

My shoulders sagged. "No. He likes this other girl. This really smart girl who knows how to clone fruit flies."

Grandmère snorted. "A useful talent. Well, never mind that now. I don't suppose, Amelia, that you are acquainted with the expression, dirty dishwater is better than none?"

I guess she must have been able to tell from my perplexed expression that this was one I hadn't heard before, since she went on, "Do not throw away this Kenny until you have managed to secure someone better."

I stared at her, horrified. Really, my grandmother has

said—and done—some pretty cold things in her time, but this one took the cake.

"Secure someone better?" I couldn't believe she actually meant what I thought she meant. "You mean I shouldn't break up with Kenny until I've got someone else?"

Grandmère lit another cigarette. "But of course."

"But Grandmère." I swear to God, sometimes I can't figure out if she's human or some kind of alien life force sent down from some other planet to spy on us. "You can't do that. You can't just string a guy along like that, knowing that you don't feel the same way about him that he feels about you."

Grandmère exhaled a long plume of blue smoke. "Why not?"

"Because it's completely unethical!" I shook my head. "No. I'm breaking up with Kenny. Right away. Tonight, as a matter of fact."

Grandmère stroked Rommel under the chin. He looked more miserable than ever, as if instead of stroking him, she was peeling the skin away from his body. He really is the most heinous excuse for a dog I have ever seen.

"That," Grandmère said, "is your prerogative, of course. But allow me to point out to you that if you break off your relationship with this young man, your Biology grade will suffer."

I was shocked. But mostly because this was something I had already thought of myself. I was amazed Grandmère and I had actually shared something.

Which was really the only reason I exclaimed, "Grandmère!"

"Well," Grandmère said, flicking ash from her cigarette into the ashtray. "Isn't it true? You are only making what, a C, in this class? And that is only because that young man allows you to copy his answers to the homework."

"Grandmère!" I squealed again. Because, of course, she was right.

She looked at the ceiling. "Let me see," she said. "With your D in Algebra, if you get anything less than a C in Biology, your grade-point average will take quite a little dip this semester."

"Grandmère." I couldn't believe this. She knew all about my grades! And she was right. She was so right. But still. "I am not going to postpone breaking up with Kenny until after the final. That would be just plain wrong."

"Suit yourself," Grandmère said with a sigh. "But it certainly will be awkward having to sit beside him for the next—how long is it until the end of the semester?—Oh, yes, two weeks. Especially considering the fact that after you break things off with him, he probably won't even speak to you anymore."

God, so true. And not something I hadn't thought of myself. If Kenny got mad enough over me breaking up with him to not want to speak to me anymore, seventh period was going to be plenty unpleasant.

"And what about this dance?" Grandmère rattled the ice in her Sidecar. "This Christmas dance?"

"It's not a Christmas dance," I said. "It's a nondenominational—"

Grandmère waved a hand. This spiky charm bracelet she was wearing tinkled.

"Whatever," she said. "If you stop seeing this young man, who will you go to the dance with?"

"I won't go with anybody," I said, firmly, even though, of course, my heart was breaking at the thought. "I'll just stay home."

"While everyone else has a good time? Really, Amelia, you aren't being at all sensible. What about this other young man?"

"What other young man?"

"The one you claim to be so in love with. Won't he be at this dance with the housefly girl?"

"Fruit fly," I corrected her. "And I don't know. Maybe."

The thought that Michael might ask Judith Gershner to the Nondenominational Winter Dance had never occurred to me. But as soon as Grandmère mentioned it, I felt that same sickening sensation I'd felt at the ice-skating rink when I'd first seen them together: kind of like the time when Lilly and I were crossing Bleecker Street and this Chinese food delivery man crashed into us on his bicycle, and I had the wind completely knocked out of me.

Only this time, it wasn't just my chest that hurt, but my tongue. It had been feeling a lot better, but now it started to throb again.

"It seems to me," Grandmère said, "that one way to get this young man's attention might be to show up at this dance on the arm of this other young man, looking perfectly divine in an original creation by Genovian fashion designer Sebastiano Grimaldi."

I just stared at her. Because she was right. She was so right. Except . . .

"Grandmère," I said. "The guy I like? Yeah, he likes girls who can clone *insects*. Okay? I highly doubt he is going to be impressed by a *dress*."

I didn't mention that I had, of course, just the night before, been hoping that very thing. But almost as if she could read my mind, Grandmère just went, "Hmmm," in this knowing way.

"Suit yourself," she continued. "Still, it seems a bit cruel to me, your breaking things off with this young man at this time of year."

"Why?" I asked, confused. Had Grandmère inadvertently stumbled across some TV channel playing *It's a Wonderful*

*Life*, or something? She had never shown one speck of holiday spirit before now. "Because it's *Christmas*?"

"No," Grandmère said, looking very disgusted with me, I guess over the suggestion that she might ever be moved by the anniversary of the birth of anyone's savior. "Because of your exams. If you truly wish to be kind, I think you might at least wait until after the final exams are over before breaking the poor little fellow's heart."

I had been all ready to argue with whatever excuse for me not breaking up with Kenny Grandmère came up with next—but this one, I had not expected. I stood there with my mouth hanging open. I know it was hanging open, because I could see it reflected in the three full-length mirrors.

"I cannot imagine," Grandmère went on, "why you do not simply allow him to believe that you return his ardor until your exams are over. Why compound the poor boy's stress? But you must, of course, do what you think is best. I suppose this—er—Kenny is the sort of boy who bounces back easily from rejection. He'll probably do quite well on his exams, in spite of his broken heart."

Oh, God! If she had stabbed a fork in my stomach and twisted my intestines around the tines like spaghetti, she couldn't have made me feel worse. . . .

And, I have to admit, a little relieved. Because of course I can't break up with Kenny now. Never mind my Bio grade and the dance: You can't break up with someone right before finals. It's, like, the meanest thing you can do.

Well, aside from the kind of stuff Lana and her friends pull. You know, girls' locker-room stuff, like going up to someone who is changing and asking her why she wears a bra when she obviously doesn't need one, or making fun of her just because she doesn't happen to like being kissed by her boyfriend. That kind of thing.

So here I am. I *want* to break up with Kenny, but I can't.

I *want* to tell Michael how I feel about him, but I can't do that either.

I can't even quit biting my fingernails. I am going to gross out an entire European nation with my bloody cuticles.

I am a pathetic mess. No wonder in the car this morning—after I accidentally closed the door on Lars's foot—Lilly said that I should really look into getting some therapy, because if there's anybody who needs to find inner harmony between her conscious and her subconscious, it's me.

### TO DO BEFORE LEAVING FOR GENOVIA

1. Get cat food, litter for Fat Louie
2. Stop biting fingernails
3. Achieve self-actualization
4. Find inner harmony between conscious and subconscious
5. Break up with Kenny—but not until after finals/Nondenominational Winter Dance

*What was THAT just now in the hallway? Did Kenny*
*Showalter just say what I think he said to you?*

Yes. Oh, my God, Shameeka, what am I going to do?
I'm shaking so hard I can barely write.

*What do you mean, what are you going to do? The boy is*
*warm for your form, Mia. Go for it.*

People can't just be allowed to go around saying
things like that. Especially so loud. Everyone must
have heard him. Do you think everyone heard him?

*Everybody heard him, all right. You should have seen*
*Lilly's face. I thought she was going to suffer one of those*
*synaptic breakdowns she's always talking about.*

You think EVERYBODY heard him? I mean, like the
people coming out of the Chemistry lab? Do you
think they heard?

*How could they not? He yelled it pretty loud.*

Were they laughing? The people coming out of
Chemistry? They weren't laughing, were they?

*Most of them were laughing.*

Oh, God! Why was I ever born????

*Except Michael. He wasn't laughing.*

He WASN'T? REALLY? Are you pulling my leg?

*No. Why would I do that? And what do you care what*
*Michael Moscovitz thinks, anyway?*

I don't. I don't care. What makes you think I care?

*Um, for one thing because you won't shut up about it.*

People shouldn't go around laughing at other people's
misfortunes. That's all.

*I don't see what the big misfortune is. So the guy loves*
*you? A lot of girls would really like it if their boyfriend*
*yelled that at them between first and second period.*

Yeah, well, NOT ME!!!!

Use <u>transitive verbs</u> to create brief, vigorous sentences.

<u>Transitive</u>: He soon regretted his words.
<u>Intransitive</u>: It was not long before he was very sorry that he had said what he said.

Gifted and Talented was so not fun today. Not that Bio is any better, on account of the fact that I am stuck here next to Kenny, who seems to have calmed down a little since this morning.

Still, I really think that people who are not actually enrolled in certain classes have no business showing up in them.

For instance, just because Judith Gershner has study hall for fifth period is no reason that she should be allowed to hang around the Gifted and Talented classroom for fifty minutes during that period. She should never have been let out of study hall in the first place. I don't think she even had a pass.

Not that I would turn her in, or anything. But this kind of flagrant rule-breaking really shouldn't be encouraged. If Lilly is going to go through with this walkout thing, which she is still trying to garner support for, she should really add to her list of complaints the fact that the teachers in this school play favorites. I mean, just because a girl knows how to clone things doesn't mean she should be allowed to roam the school freely any time she wants.

But there she was when I walked in, and there's no doubt about it: Judith Gershner has a total crush on Michael. I don't really know how he feels about her, but she was wearing tan-colored panty hose instead of the black cotton tights she normally wears, so you *know* something is up. No girl wears tan panty hose without a good reason.

And okay, so maybe they are working on their booth for the Winter Carnival, but that is no reason for Judith to drape her arm across the back of Michael's chair like that. Plus he used to help me with my Algebra homework during G and T, but now he can't, because Judith is monopolizing all his time. I would think he might resent the intrusion.

Plus Judith really has no business butting into my private conversations. She hardly even knows me.

But did that stop her from letting me know, when she overheard Lilly's formal apology for not having believed me about Kenny's weird phone call—any doubts about the veracity of which he managed to scatter today with his display of unbridled passion in the third-floor hallway—that she feels sorry for him? Oh, no.

"Poor kid," Judith said. "I heard what he said to you in the hallway. I was in the chem lab. What was it again? 'I don't care if you don't feel the same way, Mia, I will always love you,' or something like that?"

I didn't say anything. That's because I was busy picturing how Judith would look with a pencil sticking out of the middle of her forehead.

"It's really sweet," Judith said. "If you think about it. I mean, the guy's clearly got it bad for you."

This is the problem, see. Everyone thinks what Kenny did was so cute and everything. Nobody seems to understand that it wasn't cute. It wasn't cute at all. It was completely humiliating. I don't think I've ever been so embarrassed in my whole life.

And believe me, I've lived through more than my fair share of embarrassing incidents, especially since this whole princess thing started.

But I'm apparently the only person in this entire school who thinks what Kenny did was the least bit wrong.

"He's obviously very in touch with his emotions." Even Lilly was taking Kenny's side in the whole thing. "Unlike *some* people."

I have to say, this makes me so mad when I think about it, because the truth is, ever since I started writing things down in journals, I have gotten very in touch with my emotions.

I usually know almost exactly how I feel.

The problem is, I just can't tell anyone.

I don't know who was the most surprised when Michael suddenly came to my defense against his sister—Lilly, Judith Gershner, or me.

"Just because Mia doesn't go around shouting about how she feels in the third-floor hallway," Michael said, "doesn't mean she isn't in touch with her emotions."

How does he do that? How is it that he is able to magically put into words exactly what I feel, but seem to have so much trouble saying? This, you see, is why I love him. I mean, how could I not?

"Yeah," I said triumphantly.

"Well, you could have said something back to him." Lilly always gets disgruntled when Michael comes to my rescue—especially when he does it while she is attacking me about the lack of honesty in my emotional life. "Instead of just leaving him hanging there."

"And what," I demanded—injudiciously, I now realize—"should I have said to him?"

"How about," Lilly said, "that you love him back?"

WHY? That's all I want to know. WHY was I cursed with a best friend who doesn't understand that there are some things you just don't say in front of EVERYONE IN THE ENTIRE GIFTED AND TALENTED CLASSROOM, INCLUDING HER BROTHER????

The problem is, Lilly has never been embarrassed about anything in her life. She simply does not know the meaning of the word *embarrassment*.

"Look," I said, feeling my cheeks begin to burn. I couldn't lie, of course. How could I lie, considering what I now knew about my nostrils? And okay, Lilly hadn't figured it out yet, but it was only a matter of time. I mean, if *Grandmère* knew . . . "I really and truly value Kenny's companionship,"

I said, carefully. "But love. I mean, *love*. That is a very big thing. I'm not, I mean, I don't . . ."

I dribbled off pathetically, acutely aware that everyone in the room, most especially Michael, was listening.

"I see," Lilly said, narrowing her eyes. "Fear of commitment."

"I do not fear commitment," I insisted. "I just—"

But Lilly's dark eyes were already shining in eager anticipation. She was getting ready to psychoanalyze me, one of her favorite hobbies, unfortunately.

"Let's examine the situation, shall we?" she said. "I mean, here you've got this guy going around the hallways, screaming about how much he loves you, and you just stare at him like a rat caught in the path of the D train. What do you suppose that means?"

"Have you ever considered," I demanded, "that maybe the reason I didn't tell him I love him back is because I—"

I almost said it. Really. I did. I almost said that I don't love Kenny.

But I couldn't. Because if I'd said that, somehow it would have gotten back to Kenny, and that would be even worse than my breaking up with him. I couldn't do it.

So all I said instead was, "Lilly, you know perfectly well I do not fear commitment. I mean, there are lots of boys I—"

"Oh, yeah?" Lilly seemed to be enjoying herself way more than usual. It was almost as if she was playing to an audience. Which, of course, she was. The audience of her brother and his girlfriend. "Name one."

"One what?"

"Name a boy that you could see yourself committing to for all eternity."

"What do you want, a list?" I asked her.

"A list would be nice," Lilly said.

So I drew up the following list:

GUYS MIA THERMOPOLIS COULD
SEE HERSELF COMMITTING TO FOR
ALL ETERNITY

1. Wolverine of the *X-Men*
2. That *Gladiator* guy
3. Will Smith
4. Tarzan from the Disney cartoon
5. The Beast from *Beauty and the Beast*
6. That hot soldier guy from *Mulan*
7. The guy Brendan Fraser played in *The Mummy*
8. Angel
9. Tom on *Daria*
10. Justin Baxendale

But this list turned out to be no good, because Lilly totally took it and analyzed it, and it works out that half the guys on it are actually cartoon characters; one is a vampire; and one is a mutant who can make spikes shoot out of his knuckles.

In fact, except for Will Smith and Justin Baxendale—the good-looking senior who just transferred from Trinity and who a lot of girls at Albert Einstein High School are already in love with—all the guys I listed are fictional creations. Apparently, the fact that I could list no guy I had a hope of actually getting together with—or who even lives in the third dimension—is indicative of something.

Not, of course, indicative of the fact that the guy I like was actually in the room at the time, sitting next to his new girlfriend, and so I couldn't list him.

Oh, no. Nobody thought of *that*.

No, the lack of actual attainable men on my list was apparently indicative of my unrealistic expectations where men are concerned, and further proof of my inability to commit.

Lilly says if I don't lower my expectations somewhat, I am destined for an unsatisfactory love life.

As if the way things have been going, I've ever expected anything else.

Kenny just tossed me this note:

*Mia—I'm sorry about what happened today in the hallway. I understand now that I embarrassed you. Sometimes I forget that even though you are a princess, you are still quite introverted. I promise never to do anything like that again. Can I make it up to you by taking you to lunch at Big Wong on Thursday?*
*—Kenny*

I said yes, of course. Not just because I really like Big Wong's steamed vegetable dumplings, or even because I don't want people thinking I fear commitment. I didn't even say yes because I suspect that, over dumplings and hot tea, Kenny is finally going to ask me to the Nondenominational Winter Dance.

I said yes because in spite of it all, I really do like Kenny, and I don't want to hurt his feelings.

And I'd feel the same way even if I weren't a princess, and always had to do the right thing.


HOMEWORK

Algebra: review questions at the end of Chapters 4–7
English: term paper

World Civ: review questions at the end of Chapters 5–9
G&T: none
French: review questions at the end of Chapters 4–6
Biology: review questions at the end of Chapters 6–8

The following conversation took place between Mr. Gianini and me today after Algebra review:

Mr. G:     Mia, is everything all right?
Me:        (Surprised) Yes. Why wouldn't it be?
Mr. G:     Well, it's just that I thought you'd pretty much grasped the FOIL method, but on today's pop quiz, you got all five problems wrong.
Me:        I guess I've sort of had a lot on my mind.
Mr. G:     Your trip to Genovia?
Me:        Yeah, that, and . . . other things.
Mr. G:     Well, if you want to talk about the, um, other things, you know I'm always here for you. And your mother. I know we might seem preoccupied with the baby coming and everything, but you're always number one on our list of priorities. You know that, don't you?
Me:        (Mortified) Yes. But there's nothing wrong. Really.

Thank God he doesn't know about my nostrils.

And really, what else *could* I have said? "Mr. G, my boyfriend is a nut case but I can't break up with him on account of finals, and I'm in love with my best friend's brother?"

I highly doubt he'd be able to offer any meaningful advice on any of the above.

I don't believe this. I'm home before *Baywatch Hawaii* starts for the first time in, like, months. Something must be wrong with Grandmère. Although she seemed pretty normal at our lesson today. I mean, for her. Except that she stopped me in the middle of my reciting the Genovian pledge of allegiance (which I have to memorize, of course, for when I am visiting schools in Genovia. I don't want to look like an idiot in front of a bunch of five-year-olds for not knowing it) to ask me what I'd decided to do about Kenny.

It's kind of funny about her taking an interest in my personal life, since she certainly never has before. Well, not very much, anyway.

And she kept on saying stuff about how ingenious it had been of Kenny, sending me those anonymous love letters last October, the ones I thought (well, okay, *hoped*, not really thought) Michael was writing.

I was all, "What was so ingenious about *that*?" to which Grandmère just replied, "Well, you're his girlfriend now, aren't you?"

Which I never really thought about, but I guess she's right.

Anyway, my mom was so surprised to see me home so early, she actually let me be in charge of choosing the takeout (pizza margherita for me. I let her get rigatoni bolognese, even though the sausage in the sauce is probably steeped in nitrates that could harm a developing fetus. Still, it was sort of a special occasion, what with me actually being home for dinner for a change. Even Mr. Gianini got a little wild and had something with porcini mushrooms in it).

I am psyched to be home early, because you wouldn't believe all the studying I have to do, plus I should probably start my term paper, then there's figuring out what I'm going to get people for Christmas and Hannukah, not to mention going over the thank-you speech I have to make to the people of Genovia in my nationally televised (in Genovia, anyway) introduction to the people I will one day rule.

I had really better buckle down and get to work!

Okay, so I was taking a study break, and I just realized something. You can learn *a lot* from watching *Baywatch*. Seriously.

I have compiled this list:

## THINGS I HAVE LEARNED FROM WATCHING BAYWATCH

1. If you are paralyzed from the waist down, you just need to see a kid being attacked by a murderer, and you will be able to get up and save him.
2. If you have bulimia, it is probably because two men love you at the same time. Just tell the two of them you only want to be friends, and your bulimia will go away.
3. It is always easy to get a parking place near the beach.
4. Male lifeguards always put a shirt on when they leave the beach. Female lifeguards don't need to bother.
5. If you meet a beautiful but troubled girl, she is probably either a diamond smuggler or suffering from split personality disorder: Do not accept her invitation to dinner.
6. Dick van Patten, though a senior citizen, can be surprisingly hard to quell in a fistfight.
7. If people are mysteriously dying in the water, it is probably because a giant electric eel has escaped from a nearby aquarium.

8. A girl who is thinking about abandoning her baby should just leave it on the beach. Chances are, a nice lifeguard will take it home, adopt it, and raise it as his own.
9. It is very easy to outswim a shark.
10. Wild seals make adorable and easily trained pets.

I just got an e-mail from Lilly. I'm not the only one who got it, either. Somehow she figured out how to do a mass e-mail to every kid in school.

Well, I shouldn't be surprised, I guess. She *is* a genius. Still, she has clearly developed atrophy of the brain from too much studying, because look what she wrote:

## ATTENTION ALL STUDENTS AT
## ALBERT EINSTEIN HIGH SCHOOL

Stressed from too many exams, term papers, and final projects? Don't just passively accept the oppressive workload handed down to us by the tyrannical administration! A silent walkout has been scheduled for tomorrow. At 10 A.M. exactly, join your fellow students in showing our teachers how we feel about inflexible exam schedules, repressive censorship, and having only one reading day on which to prepare for our finals. Leave your pencils, leave your books, and gather on East 75th Street between Madison and Park (use doors by main administration offices, if possible) for a rally against Principal Gupta and the trustees. Let your voice be heard!

I am so sure. I can't walk out tomorrow at 10 A.M. That's right in the middle of Algebra. Mr. Gianini's feelings will be so hurt if we all just get up and leave.

But if I say I'm not going to take part in it, Lilly will be furious.

But if I do take part in it, my dad will kill me. Not to mention my mom. I mean, we could all get suspended, or something. Or hit by a delivery truck. There are a lot of them on 75th at that time of day.

Why? Why must I be saddled with a best friend who is so clearly a sociopath?

*Tuesday, December 9, 8:45 p.m.*

I just got the following Instant Message from Michael:

CRACKING: Did you just get that whacked-out mass e-mail from my sister?

I replied at once.

FTLOUIE: Yes.

CRACKING: You're not going along with her stupid walkout, are you?

FTLOUIE: Oh, right. She won't be too mad if I don't, or anything.

CRACKING: You don't have to do everything she says, you know, Mia. I mean, you've stood up to her before. Why not now?

Um, because I have enough to worry about right now—for instance, finals; my impending trip to Genovia; and, oh, yeah, the fact that I love you—without adding a fight with my best friend to the list.

But I didn't say that, of course.

FTLOUIE: I find that the path of least resistance is often the safest one when dealing with your sister.

CRACKING: Well, I'm not doing it. Walking out, I mean.

FTLOUIE: It's different for you. You're her brother. She has to remain on speaking terms with you. You live together.

CRACKING: Not for much longer. Thank God.

Oh, right. He's going away to college soon.

Well, not too far away. But about a hundred blocks or so.

FTLOUIE: That's right. You got accepted to Columbia. Early decision, too. I never did congratulate you. So congratulations.

CRACKING: Thanks.

FtLouie: You must be happy that you'll know at least one other person there. Judith Gershner, I mean.

CracKing: Yeah, I guess so. Listen, you're still going to be in town for the Winter Carnival, right? I mean, you're not leaving for Genovia before the 19th are you?

All I could think was, *Why is he asking me this? I mean, he can't be going to ask me to the dance. He must know I'm going with Kenny. I mean, if Kenny ever gets around to asking me, that is. Besides, it isn't as if Michael is available. Isn't he going with Judith? Well? ISN'T HE?*

FtLouie: I'm leaving for Genovia on the 20th.

CracKing: Oh, good. Because you should really stop by the Computer Club's booth at the Carnival, and check out this program I've been working on. I think you'll like it.

I should have known. Michael isn't going to ask me to any dance. Not in this lifetime, anyway. I should have known it was just his stupid computer program he wanted me to see. Who even cares? I suppose dumb army guys will pop out at me, and I'll have to shoot them, or whatever. Judith's idea, I'm sure.

I wanted to write to him, *Don't you have the slightest idea what I'm going through? That the only person with whom I can see myself committing to for all eternity is YOU? Don't you KNOW that by now????*

But instead I wrote:

FtLouie: Can't wait. Well, I have to go. Bye.

Sometimes I completely hate myself.

You're never going to believe this. Something *Grandmère* said is keeping me awake.

Seriously. I was dead asleep—well, as asleep as you can be with a twenty-five-pound cat purring on your abdomen—when all of a sudden, I woke up with this totally random phrase going around in my head:

"Well, you're his girlfriend now, aren't you?"

That's what Grandmère said when I asked her what was so ingenious about Kenny's having sent me those anonymous love letters.

And do you know what?

SHE'S RIGHT.

It seems totally bizarre to admit that Grandmère might be right about something, but I think it's true. Kenny's anonymous love letters *did* work. I mean, I *am* his girlfriend now.

So what's to keep me from writing some anonymous love letters to the boy *I* like? I mean, really? Besides the fact that I already have a boyfriend, and the guy I like already has a girlfriend?

I think this is a plan that might have some merit. It needs more work, of course, but hey, desperate measures call for desperate times. Or something like that. Too sleepy to figure it out.

Okay, I was up all night thinking about it, and I'm pretty sure I've got it figured out. Even as I sit here, my plan is being put into action, thanks to Tina Hakim Baba and a stop at Ho's Deli before school started.

Actually, Ho's didn't really have what I wanted. I wanted a card that was blank inside, with a picture on the front that was sophisticated but not too sexy. But the only blank cards they had at Ho's (that weren't plastered with pictures of kittens) were ones with photos of fruit being dipped into chocolate sauce.

I tried to choose a non-phallic fruit, but even the strawberry I got is kind of sexier than I would have liked. I don't know what's sexy about fruit with chocolate sauce dripping off it, but Tina was like, "Whoa," when she saw it.

Still, she gamely agreed to print my poem on the inside of the card, so Michael won't recognize my handwriting. She even liked my poem, which I came up with at five this morning:

> *Roses are Red*
> *Violets are Blue*
> *You may not know it*
> *But someone loves you.*

Not my best work, I will admit, but it was really hard to come up with something better after only three hours of sleep.

I hesitated somewhat over the use of the L word. I thought maybe I should substitute *like* for *love*. I don't want him to think there's a creepy stalker after him, and all.

But Tina said *love* was absolutely right. Because, as she put it, "It's the truth, isn't it?"

And since it's anonymous, I guess it doesn't matter that I am laying open my soul.

Anyway, Tina goes by Michael's locker right before we have PE, so she's going to slip it to him then.

I can't believe that this is the low I have stooped to. But like Dad once told me, Faint heart never won fair lady.

Lars just pointed out that I'm not exactly risking anything, seeing as how I didn't sign the card and even went to the extreme of having someone else write out the poem for me (Lars knows all about this, on account of I had to explain to him why we had to go into Ho's at eight fifteen in the morning). He helped pick the card, but I would be happy if that was the extent of his contribution to this particular project. Because he's a man, I cannot imagine his input is at all valuable.

Besides, he's been married like four times, so I highly doubt he knows anything about romance.

Also, he should know by now we're not allowed to talk during Homeroom.

I just saw Lilly in the hallway. She whispered, "Don't forget! Ten o'clock! Don't let me down!"

Well, the truth is, I did forget. The walkout! The stupid walkout!

And poor Mr. Gianini, standing up there going over Chapter Five, not suspecting a thing. It's not his fault Mrs. Spears didn't like Lilly's term paper topic. Lilly can't just arbitrarily punish all the teachers in school for something one teacher did.

It's already nine thirty-five. What am I going to do?

Lana just leaned back and hissed, "You gonna walk out with your fat friend?"

I take real objection to this. Only in a culture as screwed up as ours, where girls like Christina Aguilera are held up as models of beauty when clearly they are in fact suffering from some sort of malnutrition (scurvy?), would Lilly ever be considered fat. Because Lilly isn't fat. She is just round, like a puppy.

I hate it here.

*Wednesday, December 10, Algebra, 9:50 a.m.*

Ten minutes until the walkout. I can't take this. I'm getting out.

Okay. I'm standing in the hallway next to the fire alarm by the second-floor drinking fountain. I got a hall pass from Mr. G. I told him I had to go to the bathroom.

Lars is with me, of course. I wish he'd stop laughing. He does not seem to realize the seriousness of the situation. Plus Justin Baxendale just walked by with a hall pass of his own, and he gave us this really weird look.

And yeah, I probably do look a little strange, hanging out in the hallway with my bodyguard, who is currently experiencing a fit of the giggles, but still—I do not need to be looked at weirdly by Justin Baxendale.

His eyelashes are really long and dark and they make his eyes look sort of smoky. . . .

OH, MY GOD! I CAN'T BELIEVE I AM WRITING ABOUT JUSTIN BAXENDALE'S EYELASHES AT A TIME LIKE THIS!

I mean, I am in a real bind here:

If I do not walk out with Lilly, I'll lose my best friend.

But if I do walk out with everyone, I will be totally dissing my stepfather.

So I really only have one choice.

Lars just offered to do it for me. But I can't let him. I can't let him take the fall for me if we get caught. I am the princess. I have to do it myself.

I just told him to get ready to run. This is one time being so tall comes in handy. I have a pretty long stride.

Well, here goes.

I don't get why she's so mad. I mean, yeah, if everyone evacuates the building due to a fire alarm going off, it's not the same thing as everyone leaving in protest against the repressive teaching techniques of some of the teachers.

But we're still all standing in the middle of the street in the rain, and nobody has coats on because they wouldn't let us stop at our lockers for fear we'd all be consumed in a fiery conflagration, so we're probably going to get hypothermia from the cold and die.

That's what she wanted, right?

But no. She can't even be happy about that.

"Somebody ratted us out!" she keeps yelling. "Somebody told! Why else would they schedule a fire drill for exactly the same time as my walkout? I'm telling you, these bureaucrats will stop at nothing to keep us from speaking out against them. Nothing! They'll even make us stand out in freezing drizzle, hoping to weaken our immune systems so we'll no longer have the strength to fight them. Well, I for one refuse to catch cold! I refuse to succumb to their petty abuses!"

I suggested to Lilly that she write her term paper on the suffragettes, because they, like us, had to put up with numerous indignities in their battle for equal rights.

Lilly, however, told me not to be facile.

God, being best friends with a genius is hard.

I can't tell if Michael got the note or not!!!!

Worse, stupid Judith Gershner is here AGAIN. Why can't she stay in her own class? Why is she always hanging around ours? We were all getting along perfectly well until *she* came along.

My life is pathetic.

I thought about going across the hall to the teachers' lounge and asking Mrs. Hill a question about something—like why she had the custodians remove the door to the supply closet so we can't lock Boris in there anymore—so she'd maybe look over and NOTICE that there's a girl in our classroom who is *not* supposed to be there.

But I couldn't bring myself to do it, because of Michael. I mean, Michael obviously *wants* Judith here, or else he'd tell her to go away.

RIGHT?????

Anyway, with Michael so busy and all with Miss Gershner, I guess I am on my own with the whole Algebra review thing.

That's all right. I'm completely fine with that. I can study on my own just fine. Watch:

A, B, C = disjoint partition of universal set
Collection of non-empty subsets of U that are pairwise disjoint and whose union is equal to the set of U

I get that. I totally get what that means. Who needs Michael's help? Not me. I am totally cool with the collection of non-empty subsets.

TOTALLY COOL WITH IT.

Oh, Michael
You have made my heart
a disjoint partition.

Why can't you see
that we were meant to be
a universal set?

Instead, you have turned my soul
into a collection
of non-empty subsets.

I cannot believe
that our love was meant to be
pairwise disjoint.

But rather
a union—
equal to the set of
U and me.

You know what else I just realized? That if this thing works—you know, if I do manage to get Michael away from Judith Gershner, and I break up with Kenny, and I end up, you know, in a potentially romantic situation with Lilly's brother—I will not know what to do.

Seriously.

Take kissing, for instance. I have only ever kissed one person before, and that's Kenny. I cannot believe that what Kenny and I did really encompassed the whole of the kissing experience, because it certainly wasn't as fun as people always make it look on TV.

This is a very disturbing thought, and has led me to an equally disturbing conclusion: I know very little about kissing.

In fact, it seems to me that if I am going to be doing any kissing with anybody, I should get some advice beforehand. From a kissing expert, I mean.

Which is why I am consulting Tina Hakim Baba. She may not be allowed to wear makeup to school, but she has been kissing Dave Farouq El-Abar—who goes to Trinity—for close to three months now, *and* liking it, so I consider her an expert on the subject.

I am enclosing the results of this highly scientific document for future reference.

Tina—

I need to know about kissing. Can you please answer each of the following questions IN DETAIL????
And DO NOT show this to anyone!!!! DO NOT lose this paper!!!!      —Mia

1. Can a boy tell if the person he is with is inexperienced? How does an inexperienced kisser kiss (so I can avoid that)?

> *The guy may sense a feeling of nervousness coming from you, or that you are uneasy, but everyone is nervous when they are kissing someone new. It's natural! But kissing is easy to catch on to—believe me! An inexperienced kisser might break away too soon because he or she is scared or whatever. But that is normal. It's SUPPOSED to be weird. That's what makes it fun.*

2. Is there such a thing as a great kisser? If so, what are the qualifications? (So I know what to practice.)

> *Yes, there is such a thing as a great kisser. A great kisser is always affectionate and gentle and patient and not demanding.*

3. How much pressure do you exert on his lips? I mean, do you push, or like in a handshake, are you just supposed to be firm? Or are you just supposed to stand there and let him do all the work?

> *If you want a gentle kiss (a caring one) don't apply too much pressure (this is also true if he is wearing braces—you don't want to cause any lacerations). If*

you give a guy a "harsh" kiss (too much pressure), he might think you are desperate or that you want to go further than you probably do.

Of course you aren't supposed to just stand there and let him do all the work: Kiss him back! But always kiss him the way YOU want to be kissed. That is how guys learn. If we didn't show them how to do everything, we'd never get anywhere!

4. How do you know when it's time to stop?

Stop when he stops, or when you feel like you've had enough, or don't want to go any further. Just gently (so you don't freak him out) move your head back, or if the moment is right, you can change the kiss into a hug, then step back.

5. If you are in love with him, is it still gross?

Of course not! Kissing is never gross!

Well, okay, I guess I could see that maybe with Kenny, it might be. It is always better with someone you actually like.

Of course, even with someone you really like, sometimes kissing can be gross. Once Dave licked me on the chin, and I was all, Get away. But I think that was by accident (the licking).

6. If he is in love with you, does he even care if you are bad? (Define bad kisser. See above.)

If the guy likes/loves you, he won't care if you are a good kisser or not. In fact, even if you are a bad kisser, he will probably think you are a good one. And vice *versa. He should like you for what you are—not how you kiss.*

*DEFINITION OF BAD KISSER: A bad kisser is someone who gets your face all wet, slobbers on you, sticks his tongue in when you're not ready, has bad breath, OR sometimes there can be kissers whose tongues are all dry and prickly like a cactus but I have never experienced one of those, just heard about them.*

7. When do you know if it's time to open your mouth (thus turning it into a French)?

*You will probably feel his tongue touch your lips. If you want to pursue the idea, open your lips a little. If not, keep them closed.*

*Coming au demain—Chapter II: How to French!!!!*

HOMEWORK

Algebra: review questions at the end of Chapters 8–10
English: English Journal: Books I Have Read
World Civ: review questions at the end of Chapters 10–12
G&T: none
French: review questions at the end of Chapters 7–9
Biology: review questions at the end of Chapters 9–12

I am so tired I can hardly write. Grandmère made me try on every single dress in Sebastiano's showroom. You wouldn't believe the number of dresses I've had on today. Short ones, long ones, straight-skirted ones, poufy-skirted ones, white ones, pink ones, blue ones, and even a lime-green one (which Sebastiano declared brought out the 'col' in my cheeks).

The purpose of all this dress-trying-on business was to choose one to wear on Christmas Eve, during my first official televised speech to the Genovian people. I have to look regal, but not too regal. Beautiful, but not too beautiful. Sophisticated, but not too sophisticated.

I tell you, it was a nightmare of hollow-cheeked women in white (the new black) buttoning and zipping and snapping me in and out of dresses. Now I know how all those supermodels must feel. No wonder they do so many drugs.

Actually, it *was* kind of hard to choose my dress for my first big televised event, because surprisingly, Sebastiano turned out to be a pretty good designer. There were several dresses I actually wouldn't be embarrassed to be caught dead in.

Oops. Slip of the tongue. I wonder, though, if Sebastiano really does want to kill me. He seems to like being a fashion designer, which he couldn't do if he were prince of Genovia: He'd be too busy turning bills into law and stuff like that.

Still, you can tell he'd totally enjoy wearing a crown. Not that, as ruler of Genovia, he'd ever get to do this. I've never seen my dad in a crown. Just suits. And shorts when he plays racquetball with other world leaders.

Ew, I wonder if I will have to learn to play racquetball. But if Sebastiano became prince of Genovia, he would totally wear a crown all the time. He told me nothing brings out the sparkles in someone's eyes like pear-shaped diamonds. He prefers Tiffany's. Or as he calls it, Tiff's.

Since we were getting so chummy and all, I told Sebastiano about the Nondenominational Winter Dance, and how I have nothing to wear to it. Sebastiano seemed disappointed when he learned I would not be wearing a tiara to my school dance, but he got over it and started asking me all these questions about the event. Like "Who do you go with?" and "What he look like?" and stuff like that.

I don't know what it was, but I found myself actually telling Sebastiano all about my love life. It was so weird. I totally didn't want to, but it all just started spilling out. Thank God Grandmère wasn't there. . . . she'd gone off in search of more cigarettes, and to have her Sidecar refreshed.

I told Sebastiano all about Kenny and how he loves me but I don't love him, and how I actually like someone else, but he doesn't know I'm alive.

Sebastiano is actually quite a good listener. I don't know how much, if anything, he understood of what I said, but he didn't take his eyes off my reflection as I talked, and when I was done, he looked me up and down in the mirror, and just said one thing: "This boy you like. How you know he no like you back?"

"Because," I said. "He likes this other girl."

Sebastiano made an impatient motion with this hands. The gesture was made more dramatic by the fact that he was wearing sleeves with these big frilly lace cuffs.

"No, no, no, no, no," he said. "He help you with your Al home. He like you, or he no do that. Why he do that, if he no like you?"

I took "He help you with your Al home" to mean "He helps you with your Algebra homework." I thought for a minute about why Michael had always been so willing to do that. Help me with my Algebra, I mean. I guess just because I am his sister's best friend, and he isn't the type of person who can sit around and watch his sister's best friend flunk out of high school without, you know, at least trying to do something about it.

While I was thinking about that, I couldn't help remembering how Michael's knees, beneath our desks, sometimes brush against mine as he's telling me about integers. Or how sometimes he leans so close to correct something I've written wrong that I can smell the nice, clean scent of his soap. Or how sometimes, like when I do my Lana Weinberger imitation or whatever, he throws back his head and laughs.

Michael's lips look extra nice when he is smiling.

"Tell Sebastiano," Sebastiano urged me. "Tell Sebastiano why this boy help you, if he no like you."

I sighed. "Because I'm his little sister's best friend," I said sadly. Really, could there *be* anything more humiliating? I mean, clearly Michael has never been impressed with my keen intellect or ravishing good looks, given my low grade-point average and of course my gigantism.

Sebastiano tugged on my sleeve and went, "You no worry. I make dress for dance, this boy, he no think of you as little sister's best friend."

Yeah. Sure. Whatever. Why must all my relatives be so weird?

Anyway, we picked out what I'm going to wear on Genovian national TV during my introduction. It's this white taffeta job with a huge poufy skirt and this light blue sash (the royal colors are blue and white). But Sebastiano had one of his assistants take photos of me in all the dresses, so I can see how I looked in them and then decide. I thought this was fairly professional for a guy who calls breakfast "breck."

But all that isn't what I want to write about. I'm so tired,

I hardly know what I'm doing. What I want to write about is what happened today after Algebra review.

Which was that Mr. Gianini, after everyone but me had left, went, "Mia, I heard a rumor that there was supposed to have been some kind of student walkout today. Had you heard that?"

Me:                (freezing in my seat) Um, no.

Mr. Gianini:    Oh. So you wouldn't know then if somebody—maybe in protest of the protest—threw the second-floor fire alarm? The one by the drinking fountain?

Me:                (wishing Lars would stop coughing suggestively) Um, no.

Mr. Gianini:    That's what I thought. Because you know the penalty for pulling one of the fire alarms—when there is, in fact, no sign of a fire—is expulsion.

Me:                Oh, yes. I know that.

Mr. Gianini:    I thought you might have seen who did it, since I believe I gave you a hall pass shortly before the alarm went off.

Me:                Oh, no. I didn't see anybody.

Except Justin Baxendale, and his smoky eyelashes. But I didn't say that.

Mr. Gianini:    I didn't think so. Oh, well. If you ever hear who did it, maybe you could tell her from me never to do it again.

Me:                Um. Okay.

Mr. Gianini:    And tell her thanks from me, too. The last thing we need right now, with tensions running so high over finals, is a student

walkout. (Mr. Gianini picked up his
briefcase and jacket.) See you at home.

Then he winked at me. WINKED at me, like he knew I
was the one who'd done it. But he couldn't know. I mean,
he doesn't know about my nostrils (which were fully flaring the whole time; I could *feel* them!) Right? RIGHT????

Lilly is going to drive me crazy.

Seriously. Like it's not enough I have finals and my introduction to Genovia and my love life and everything to worry about. I have to listen to Lilly complain about how the administration of Albert Einstein High is out to get her. The whole way to school this morning she just droned on and on about how it's all a plot to silence her because she once complained about the Coke machine outside the gym. Apparently the Coke machine is indicative of the administration's efforts to turn us all into mindless soda-drinking, Gap-wearing clones, in Lilly's opinion.

If you ask me, this isn't really about Coke, or the attempts by the school's administration to turn us into mindless pod-people. It's really just because Lilly's still mad she can't use a chapter of the book she's writing on the high-school experience as her term paper.

I reminded Lilly if she doesn't submit a new topic, she's going to get an F as her nine-week grade. Factored in with her A for the last nine weeks, that's only like a C, which will significantly lower her grade-point average, and put her chances of getting into Berkeley, which is her first-choice school, at risk. She may be forced to fall back on her safety school, Brown, which I know would be quite a blow.

She didn't even listen to me. She says she's having an organizational meeting of this new group (of which she is president) Students Against the Corporatization of Albert Einstein High School (SACAEHS) on Saturday, and I have to come, because I am the group's secretary. Don't ask me how *that* happened. Lilly says I write everything down anyway, so it shouldn't be any trouble for me.

I wish Michael had been there to protect me from his sister, but like he has every day this week, he took the subway to school early so he could work on his project for the Winter Carnival.

I wouldn't doubt Judith Gershner has been showing up to school on the early side, too, this week.

Speaking of whom, I picked up another greeting card, this one from the Plaza gift shop on the way to Sebastiano's showroom last night. It's a lot better than that stupid one with the strawberry. This one has a picture of a lady holding a finger to her lips. Inside, it says, *Shhhh . . .*

Under that, I am having Tina write:

> *Roses are red*
> *But cherries are redder*
> *Maybe she can clone fruit flies*
> *But I like you better.*

What I meant was that I like him more than Judith Gershner does, but I'm not really sure that comes through in the poem. Tina says it does, but Tina thinks I should have used love instead of like, so who knows if her opinion is of any value? This is a poem clearly calling for a like and not a love.

I should know. I write enough of them.

Poems, I mean.

This semester, we have read several novels, including *To Kill a Mockingbird, Huckleberry Finn,* and *The Scarlet Letter.* In your English journal, please record your feelings about the books we have read, and books in general. What have been your most meaningful experiences as a reader? Your favorite books? Your least favorite?

Please utilize <u>transitive</u> verbs.

## Books I Have Read, and What They Meant to Me
### *by Mia Thermopolis*

Books that were good:

1. *Jaws*—I bet you didn't know that in the book version of this, Richard Dreyfuss and Roy Scheider's wife have sex. But they do.
2. *The Catcher in the Rye*—This is totally good. It has lots of bad words.
3. *To Kill a Mockingbird*—This is an excellent book. They should do a movie version of this with Mel Gibson as Atticus, and he should blow Mr. Ewell away with a flame thrower at the end.
4. *A Wrinkle in Time*—Only we never find out the most important thing: whether or not Meg has breasts. I'm thinking she probably did, considering the fact that she already had the glasses and braces. I mean, all of that, and flat-chested, too? God wouldn't be so cruel.
5. *Emanuelle*—In the eighth grade, my best friend and I found this book on top of a trash can on East Third Street. We took turns reading it out loud. It was very, very good. At least the parts I remember. My mom caught us reading it and took it away before we'd gotten a chance to finish it.

## Books that sucked*

1. *The Scarlet Letter*—You know what would have been cool? If there had been a rift in the space-time continuum, and one of those Euro-trash terrorists Bruce Willis is always chasing in the *Die Hard* movies dropped a nuclear bomb on the town where Arthur Dimmesdale and all those losers lived, and blew it sky high. That's about the only thing I can think of that would have made this book even remotely interesting.

2. *Our Town*—Okay, this is a play and not a book, but they still made us read it, and all I have to say about it is that basically, you find out when you die that nobody cared about you and we're all alone forever, the end. Okay! Thanks for that! I feel much better now!

3. *The Mill on the Floss*—I don't want to give anything away here, but midway through the book, just when things were going good and there were all these hot romances (not as hot as in *Emanuelle*, though, so don't get your hopes up) someone very crucial to the plot DIES, which if you ask me is just a cop-out so the author could make her deadline on time.

4. *Anne of Green Gables*—All that blah-blah-blah about imagination. I tried to imagine some car chases or explosions that would actually make this book good, but I must be like all of Anne's drippy unimaginative friends, because I couldn't.

5. *Little House on the Prairie*—Little yawn on the big snore. I have all ninety-seven thousand of these books, because people kept on giving them to me when I was little, and all I have to say is if Half Pint had lived in Manhattan, she'd have gotten her you-know-what kicked from here to Avenue D.

* Mrs. Spears, I believe the word *sucked* is transitive in this instance.

No PE today!

Instead there is an assembly.

And it's not because there's a sporting event they want us all to show our support for. No! This was no pep rally. There wasn't a cheerleader in sight. Well, okay, there were cheerleaders in sight, but they weren't in uniform or anything. They were sitting in the bleachers with the rest of us. Well, not really with the rest of us, since they were in the best seats, the ones in the middle, all jostling to see who could sit next to Justin Baxendale, who has apparently ousted Josh Richter as hottest guy in school, but whatever.

No. Instead, it appears that there has been a major disciplinary infraction at Albert Einstein High School. An act of random vandalism that has shaken the administration's faith in us. Which was why they called an assembly, so that they could better convey their feelings of—as Lilly just whispered in my ear—disillusionment and betrayal.

And what was this act that has Principal Gupta and the trustees so up in arms?

Why, someone pulled a fire alarm yesterday, that's what.

Oops.

I have to say, I have never done anything really bad before—well, I dropped an eggplant out a sixteenth-floor window a couple of months ago, but no one got hurt or anything—but there really is something sort of thrilling about it. I mean, I would never want to do anything *too* bad, like anything where someone might get hurt.

But I have to say, it is immensely gratifying to have all these people coming up to the microphone and decrying my behavior.

I probably wouldn't feel so good about it if I'd gotten caught, though.

I am being urged to come forward and turn myself in even as I write this. Apparently, the guilt for my action is going to hound me well past my teen years, possibly even into my twenties and beyond.

Okay, can I just tell you how much I'm NOT going to think about high school when I am in my twenties? I am going to be way too busy working with Greenpeace to save the whales to worry about some stupid fire alarm I pulled in the ninth grade.

The administration is offering a reward for information leading to the identity of the perpetrator of this heinous crime. A reward! You know what the reward is? A free movie pass to the Sony Imax theater. That's all I'm worth! A movie pass!

The only person who could possibly turn me in isn't even paying attention to the assembly. I can see Justin Baxendale has got a Gameboy out, and is playing it with the sound off, while Lana and her fellow cheer cronies look over his broad shoulders, probably panting so hard they're fogging up the screen.

I guess Justin hasn't put two and two together yet. You know, about seeing me in the hallway just before that fire alarm went off. With any luck, he never will.

Mr. Gianini, though. That's another story. I see him over there, talking to Mrs. Hill. He has obviously not told anyone that he suspects me.

Maybe he doesn't suspect me. Maybe he thinks Lilly did it, and I know about it. That could be. I can tell Lilly really wishes she'd done it, because she keeps on muttering under her breath about how, when she finds out who did it, she's going to kill that person, etc.

She's just jealous, of course. That's because now it seems like some kind of political statement, instead of what it actually was: a way to prevent a political statement.

Principal Gupta is looking at us very sternly. She says that it is always natural to want to burn off a little steam right before finals, but that she hopes we will choose positive channels for this, such as the penny drive the Community Outreach Club is holding in order to benefit the victims of Tropical Storm Fred, which flooded several suburban New Jersey neighborhoods last November.

Ha! As if contributing to a stupid penny drive can ever give anybody the same kind of thrill as committing a completely random act of civil disobedience.

## LILLY MOSCOVITZ'S LIST OF THE
## TOP TEN BEST MOVIES OF ALL TIME
### (with commentary by Mia Thermopolis)

*Say Anything*: Kick-boxing iconoclast Lloyd Dobler, as played by John When-Is-He-Going-to-Run-for-President-So-We-Can-Have-Someone-Cute-in-the-Oval-Office Cusack, goes after the class brain (Ione Skye), who soon learns what we all know: Lloyd is every girl's dream date. He understands us. He longs to protect us from broken glass in the parking lot of the local 7-Eleven. Need we say more? (*This movie also contains classic song, "Joe Lies."*)

*Reckless*: Rebel from wrong side of tracks (Aidan Quinn) goes after straight-arrow cheerleader (Daryl Hannah). A classic example of teens struggling to break the yoke of parental expectation. (*Plus you get to see Aidan Quinn's you-know-what!*)

*Desperately Seeking Susan*: Bored suburban housewife finds man of her dreams in East Village. An Eighties manifesto about female empowerment. Also starring Madonna and that lady who played Roseanne's sister Jackie. (*Also starring Aidan Quinn as the East Village hottie, only you don't really get to see his you-know-what in this one. But you do get to see his butt!*)

*Ladyhawke*: Star-crossed lovers are caught in an evil spell that only Matthew Broderick can help them break. Rutger Hauer makes a powerful Navarre, a knight who lives only to exact vengeance upon the man who wronged his fair Isabeau, played by Michelle Pfeiffer. An elegant and moving love story. (*But what is with Matthew Broderick's hair?*)

*Dirty Dancing*: Spoiled teenage Baby learns a lot more than the cha-cha from long-haired summer resort dance instructor Johnny.

A classic tale of coming-of-age in the Catskills, with important messages about the class system in America. (*Only you don't get to see anyone's butt.*)

*Flashdance*: A welder by day and an exotic dancer by night, Jennifer Beals's Alex is a feminist in a thong, the Elizabeth Cady Stanton of the lap dance, who longs to audition for the Pittsburgh ballet. (*But first she sleeps with her totally hot boss Michael Nouri and throws a big rock through his window!*)

*The Cutting Edge*: Former hockey stud D.B. Sweeney is paired with figure skater and prissy rich girl Moira Kelly in an unlikely quest for Olympic gold. Interesting for its strategic build-up of sexual tension through ice dancing. (*Toe-pick. Toooooooe-pick.*)

*Some Kind of Wonderful:* Victory of tomboy Mary Stuart Masterson over prissy Lea Thompson for the heart of Eric Stolz. As usual, keen insight by John Hughes into the teen psyche/social structure. (*Last movie in which Eric Stolz was actually cute.*)

*Reality Bites*: Who will indie filmmaker Winona Ryder choose, smart aleck slacker Ethan Hawke, or clean-cut go-getter Ben Stiller? (*Isn't it obvious?*)

*Footloose*: Out-of-towner flaunts small town's anti-dancing laws. Starring Kevin Bacon, who saves Lori Singer from her abusive hick boyfriend. Most notable for scene at the PTA meeting in which Kevin Bacon's character reveals he has actually done homework, as illustrated by his quoting from several Biblical passages which support dancing. (*In the movies* Wild Thing *and* Hollow Man *you get to see Kevin Bacon's you-know-what.*)

Today was my lunch with Kenny at Big Wong.

I really don't have anything to say about it, except that he didn't ask me to the Nondenominational Winter Dance. Not only that, but it appears that Kenny's passion for me has ebbed significantly since it hit its zenith on Tuesday.

I of course was beginning to suspect this, since he's stopped calling me after school, and I haven't had one Instant Message from him since before the great Ice-Skating Debacle. He says it's because he's so busy studying for finals and all, but I suspect something else:

He knows. He knows about Michael.

I mean, come on. How can he not?

Well, okay, maybe he doesn't know about Michael *specifically*, but Kenny must know *generally* that he is not the one who lights my fire.

If I had a fire, that is.

No, Kenny is just being nice.

Which I appreciate, and all, but I just wish he'd come out and say it. All of this kindness, this solicitousness, it's just making me feel worse. I mean, how could I? Really? How could I have ever agreed to be Kenny's girlfriend, knowing full well I liked someone else? By rights, Kenny should go to *Majesty* magazine and spill all. "Royal Betrayal," they could call it. I totally would understand it, if he did.

But he won't. Because he's too nice.

Instead, he ordered steamed vegetable dumplings for me, and pork buns for him (one encouraging sign that Kenny might not love me as much as he used to insist: he's eating meat again) and talked about Bio and what had happened at assembly (I didn't tell him it was me who pulled the alarm, and he didn't ask me, so there was no need to shield my nostrils). He mentioned again how sorry he was about my tongue, and asked how I was doing in Algebra, and offered to come over and tutor me if I wanted (Kenny tested out of freshman Algebra), even though of course I live with an Algebra teacher. Still, you could tell he meant to be nice.

Which just makes me feel worse. Because of what I'm going to have to do after finals and all.

But he didn't ask me to the dance.

I don't know if this means we aren't going, or if it means he considers the fact we are going a given.

I swear, I do not understand boys at all.

As if lunch wasn't bad enough, G and T isn't too great, either. No, Judith Gershner isn't here . . . but neither is Michael. The guy is AWOL. Nobody knows where he is. Lilly had to tell Mrs. Hill, when she took attendance, that her brother was in the bathroom.

I wonder where he really is. Lilly says that since he started writing this new program that the Computer Club will be unveiling at the Winter Carnival, she's hardly seen him.

Which is no real change, since Michael hardly comes out of his room anyway, but still. You'd think he'd come home once in a while to study.

But I guess, seeing as how he already got into his first-choice college, his grades don't really matter anymore.

Besides, like Lilly, Michael is a genius. What does he need to study for?

Unlike the rest of us.

I wish they'd put the door back on the supply closet. It is extremely hard to concentrate with Boris scraping away on his violin in there. Lilly says this is just another tactic by the trustees to weaken our resistance, so we will remain the mindless drones they are trying to make us, but I think it's just on account of that time we all forgot to let him out, and he was stuck in there until the night custodian heard his anguished pleas to be released.

Which is Lilly's fault, if you think about it. I mean, she's his girlfriend. She should really take better care of him.

HOMEWORK

Algebra: practice test
English: term paper
World Civ: practice test
G&T: none
French: *l'examen pratique*
Biology: practice test

*Thursday, December 11, 9 p.m.*

Grandmère is seriously out of control. Tonight she started quizzing me on the names and responsibilities of all of my dad's cabinet ministers. Not only do I have to know exactly what they do, but also their marital status and the names and ages of their kids, if any. These are the kids I am supposedly going to have to hang out with while celebrating Christmas at the palace. I am figuring they will probably hate me as much, if not more, than Mr. Gianini's niece and nephew hated me at Thanksgiving.

All of my holidays from now on are apparently going to be spent in the company of kids who hate me.

You know, I would just like to say that it is totally not my fault I am a princess. They have no right to hate me so much. I have done everything I could to maintain a normal life in spite of my royal status. I have totally turned down opportunities to be on the covers of *CosmoGirl*, *Teen People*, *Seventeen*, *YM*, and *Girl's Life*. I have refused invitations to go on *TRL* and introduce the number-one video in the country, and when the mayor asked if I wanted to be the one to press the button that drops the ball in Times Square on New Year's Eve, I said no (aside from the fact I am going to be in Genovia for New Year's, I oppose the mayor's mosquito spraying campaign, as runoff from the pesticides used to kill the mosquitos that may be carrying the West Nile virus has infected the local horseshoe crab population. A compound in the blood of horseshoe crabs, which nest all along the eastern seaboard, is used to test the purity of every drug and vaccine administered in the U.S. The crabs are routinely gathered, drained of a third of their blood, then re-released into the sea . . . a sea which is now killing them as well as many other arthropods, such as lobsters, thanks to the amount of pesticide in it).

Anyway, I am just saying, all the kids who hate me should just chill, because I have never once sought the spotlight I have been thrust into. I've never even called my own press conference.

But I digress.

So Sebastiano was there, drinking aperitifs and listening as I rattled off name after name (Grandmère has made flashcards out of the pictures of the cabinet ministers—kind of like those bubble gum cards you can get of the Backstreet Boys, only the cabinet ministers don't wear as much leather). I was kind of thinking maybe I was wrong about Sebastiano's commitment to fashion, and that maybe Sebastiano was there to try and pick up some pointers for after he's thrust me into the path of an oncoming limo or whatever.

But when Grandmère paused to take a phone call from her old friend General Pinochet, Sebastiano started asking me all these questions about clothes, in particular what clothes my friends and I like to wear. What were my feelings, he wanted to know, on velvet stretch pants? Spandex tube tops? Sequins?

I told him all of that sounded, you know, okay for Halloween or Jersey City, but that generally in my day-to-day life I prefer cotton. He looked saddened by this, so I told him that I really felt orange was going to be the next pink, and that perked him right up, and he wrote a bunch of stuff down in this notebook he carries around. Kind of like I do, now that I think about it.

When Grandmère got off the phone, I informed her— quite diplomatically, I might add—that, considering how much progress we'd made in the past three months, I felt more than prepared for my impending introduction to the people of Genovia, and that I did not feel it would be necessary to have lessons next week, as I have FIVE finals to prepare for.

But Grandmère got totally huffy about it! She was all, "Where did you get the idea that your academic education is more important than your royal training? Your father, I suppose. With him, it's always education, education, education. He doesn't realize that education is nowhere near as important as deportment."

"Grandmère," I said. "I need an education if I'm going to run Genovia properly." Especially if I'm going to convert the palace into a giant animal shelter—something I'm not going to be able to do until Grandmère is dead, so I see no point in mentioning it to her now . . . or ever, for that matter.

Grandmère said some swear words in French, which wasn't very dowager-princessy of her, if you ask me. Thankfully right then my dad walked in, looking for his Genovian Air Force medal, since he had a state dinner to go to over at the embassy. I told him about my finals and how I really needed time off from princess stuff to study, and he was all, "Yes, of course."

When Grandmère protested, he just went, "For God's sake, if she hasn't got it by now, she never will."

Grandmère pressed her lips together and didn't say anything more after that. Sebastiano used the opportunity to ask me about my feelings on rayon. I told him I didn't have any.

For once, I was telling the truth.

HERE'S WHAT I HAVE TO DO:

1. Stop thinking about Michael, especially when I should be studying.
2. Stop telling Grandmère anything about my personal life.
3. Start acting more:
   A. Mature
   B. Responsible
   C. Regal
4. Stop biting my fingernails.
5. Write down everything Mom and Mr. G need to know about how to take care of Fat Louie while I'm gone.
6. CHRISTMAS/HANNUKAH PRESENTS!
7. Stop watching *Baywatch* when I should be studying.
8. Stop playing Pod Racer when I should be studying.
9. Stop listening to music when I should be studying.
10. Break up with Kenny.

Well, I guess it's official now:

I, Mia Thermopolis, am a juvenile delinquent.

Seriously. That fire alarm I pulled was only the beginning, it appears.

I really don't know what's come over me lately. It's like the closer I get to actually going to Genovia and performing my first official duties as its princess, the less like a princess I act.

I wonder if I'll be expelled.

If I am, it is totally unfair. Lana started it. I was sitting there in Algebra, listening to Mr. G go on about the Cartesian plane, when suddenly Lana turns around in her seat and slaps a copy of *USA Today* down in front of me. There is a headline screaming:

# TODAY'S POLL

*Most Popular Young Royal*

Fifty-seven percent of readers say that **Prince William of England** is their favorite young royal, with Will's little brother **Harry** coming in at 28 percent. America's own royal, **Princess Mia Renaldo of Genovia**, comes in third, with 13 percent of the votes, and Prince Andrew and Sarah Ferguson's daughters, **Beatrice** and **Eugenie**, round out the votes with 1 percent each.

The reasons given for Princess Mia's third-place finish? "Not outgoing" is the most common answer. Ironically, Princess Mia is perceived as being as shy as Princess Diana—the mother of William and Harry—when she first stepped into the harsh glare of the media spotlight.

Princess Mia, who only recently learned she was heir to the throne of Genovia, a small principality located on the Côte d'Azur, is expected to make her first official trip to that country next week. A representative for the princess describes her as looking forward to her visit with "eager anticipation." The princess will continue her education in America, and will reside in Genovia only during the summer months.

I read the stupid article and then passed the paper back to Lana.

"So?" I whispered to her.

"So," Lana whispered. "I wonder how popular you'd be—especially with the people of Genovia—if they found out their future ruler goes around pulling fire alarms when there isn't any fire."

She was only guessing, of course. She couldn't have seen me. Unless . . .

Unless maybe Justin Baxendale did figure it out! You know, seeing me in the hallway like that, just before the alarm went off—and he mentioned it to Lana. . . .

No. Not possible. I am so far out of the sphere of Justin Baxendale's consciousness as to be nonexistent to him. He didn't tell Lana anything. Lana, like Mr. G, obviously thinks it's a little coincidental that on that fateful Wednesday, the fire alarm went off about two minutes after I'd disappeared from class with the pass to the bathroom.

But even so. Even though she could only have been guessing, it seemed to me like she knew, like she was going to make sure I never heard the end of it.

I really don't know what came over me. I don't know if it was

A. The stress of finals
B. My impending trip to Genovia
C. This thing with Kenny
D. The fact that I'm in love with this guy who is going out with a human fruit fly
E. The fact that my mother is going to give birth to my Algebra teacher's baby
F. The fact that Lana has been persecuting me practically my whole life and pretty much getting away with it, or
G. All of the above.

Whatever the reason, I snapped. Just snapped. Suddenly, I found myself reaching for Lana's cell phone, which was lying on her desktop beside her calculator.

And then the next thing I knew, I had put the tiny little pink thing on the floor, and crushed it into a lot of pieces beneath the heel of my size-ten combat boot.

I guess I can't really blame Mr. G for sending me to the principal's office.

Still, you would expect a little sympathy from your own stepfather.

Uh-oh. Here comes Principal Gupta.

Well, that's it then. I'm suspended.

Suspended. I can't believe it. ME! Mia Thermopolis! What is happening to me? I used to be such a good kid!

And okay, it's just for one day, but still. It's going on my permanent record! What are the Genovian cabinet ministers going to say?

I am turning into Courtney Love.

And yeah, it's not like I'm not going to get into college because I was suspended for one day in the first semester of my freshman year, but how totally embarrassing! Principal Gupta treated me like I was some kind of *criminal* or something.

And you know what they say: Treat a person like a criminal, and pretty soon, she'll end up like one. At least I think that's what they say. The way things are going, I wouldn't be surprised if pretty soon I start wearing ripped-up fishnet stockings and dyeing my hair black. Maybe I'll even start smoking and get my ears double pierced or something. And then they'll make a TV movie about me, and call it *Royal Scandal*. It will show me going up to Prince William and saying, "Who's the most popular young royal now, huh, punk?" and then headbutting him or something.

Except I practically fainted the first time I got my ears pierced, and smoking is really bad for you, and I always thought it must hurt to headbutt someone.

I guess I don't have the makings of a juvenile delinquent after all.

My dad doesn't think so, either. He's all ready to set the royal Genovian lawyers on Principal Gupta. The only problem, of course, is that I won't tell him—or anybody else, for that matter—what Lana said to make me assault her cell phone. It's kind of hard to prove the attack was provoked if the attacker won't say what the provocation was. My dad pleaded with me for a while when he came to pick me up from school, after having received The Call from Principal Gupta. But when I wouldn't tell him what he wanted, and Lars just looked carefully blank, my dad just went, "Fine," and his mouth got all scrunchy like it does when Grandmère has one too many Sidecars and starts calling him Papa Cueball.

But how can I tell him what Lana said? If I do that, then everyone will know I'm guilty of not just one crime, but two!

Anyway, now I'm home, watching the Lifetime channel with my mother. She hasn't been doing much painting at her studio since she got pregnant. This is on account of her being exhausted. It's quite hard to paint lying down, she's discovered. So instead she has been doing a lot of sketching from bed, mostly line drawings of Fat Louie, who seems to enjoy having someone home all day with him. He sits for hours on her bed, watching the pigeons on the fire escape outside her window.

But since I'm home today, Mom did some drawings of me. I think she is making my mouth too big, but I'm not saying anything, as Mr. Gianini and I have discovered it's better not to upset my mother in her current hormonal state. Even the slightest criticism—like asking her why she left the phone bill in the vegetable crisper—can lead to an hour-long crying jag.

While she sketched me, I watched a very excellent movie called *Mother, May I Sleep With Danger?* starring Tori Spelling, of *Beverly Hills 90210* fame, as a girl who has an abusive boyfriend. I really don't get why any girl would stay with a guy who hits her, but my mom says it's all about self-esteem and your relationship with your father. Except that my mom doesn't have that great a relationship with Papaw, and if any guy ever tried to slug her, you can bet she'd put him in the hospital, so go figure.

As my mom drew, she tried to get me to spill my guts to her, you know, about what Lana said that made me go on a cell-phone-stomping rampage. You could tell she was trying really hard to be all TV mom about it.

I guess it must have worked, because all of a sudden I found myself telling her all of it, every last thing: the stuff about Kenny and about my not liking to kiss him and about him telling everybody, and about how I plan to break up with him as soon as finals are over.

And along the way, I mentioned Michael and Judith Gershner and Tina and the greeting cards and the Winter Carnival and Lilly and her protest group and how I'm secretary of it, and just about everything else, except the part about pulling the fire alarm.

After a while my mom stopped drawing and just looked at me.

Finally, when I was done, she said, "You know what I think you need?"

And I said, "What?"

And she said, "A vacation."

So then we had a sort of vacation, right there on her bed. I mean, she wouldn't let me go study. Instead, she made me order a pizza, and together we watched the satisfying but completely unbelievable end of *Mother, May I Sleep with Danger?*, which was followed, much to our joy, by the dishiest made-for-TV movie ever, *Midwest Obsession*, in which Courtney Thorne-Smith plays the local Dairy Princess, who goes around in a pink Cadillac wearing cow earrings and kills people like Tracey Gold (deep in the throes of her post–*Growing Pains* anorexia) for messing with her boyfriend. And the best part was, it was all *based on a true story*.

For a while, there on my mom's bed, it was almost like old times. You know, before my mom met Mr. Gianini and I found out I was a princess.

Except, of course, not really, because she's pregnant, and I'm suspended.

But why quibble?

Oh, my God, I just checked my e-mail. I am being inundated with supportive messages from my friends!

They all want to congratulate me on my decisive handling of Lana Weinberger. They sympathize with my suspension and encourage me to stay firm in my refusal to back down from my stand against the administration (what stand against the administration? All I did was destroy a cell phone. It has nothing to do with the administration). Lilly went so far as to compare me with Mary, Queen of Scots, who was imprisoned and then beheaded by Elizabeth I.

I wonder if Lilly would still think that if she knew that the reason I smashed Lana's cell phone was because she was threatening to spill the beans about my having pulled the fire alarm that ruined Lilly's walkout.

Lilly says it's all a matter of principle, that I was banished from the school for refusing to back down from my beliefs. But actually, I was banished from school for destroying someone else's private property—and I only did it to cover up for another crime that I committed.

No one knows that but me, though. Well, me and Lana. And even she doesn't know for sure why I did it. I mean, it could have been just one of those random acts of violence that are going around.

Everyone else, however, is seeing it as this great political act. Tomorrow, at the first meeting of the Students Against the Corporatization of Albert Einstein High School, my case is going to be held up as an example of one of the many unjust decisions of the Gupta Administration.

I think tomorrow I might develop a case of weekend strep throat.

Anyway, I wrote back to everyone, telling them how much I appreciate their support, and not to make a bigger deal out of this than it actually is. I mean, I'm not proud of what I did. I would much rather have NOT done it, and stayed in school.

One bright note: Michael is definitely getting the cards I've been sending him. Tina walked by his locker today after PE and saw him take the latest one out and put it in his backpack! Unfortunately, according to Tina, he did not wear an expression of dazed passion as he slipped the card into his bag, nor did he gaze at it tenderly. He did not even put it away very carefully: Tina regretted to inform me that he slipped his iMac laptop into his backpack next, undoubtedly squashing the card.

But he wouldn't, Tina hastened to assure me, have done that if he'd known it was from you, Mia! Maybe if you'd signed it . . .

But if I signed it, he'd know I like him! More than that, he'd know I love him, since I do believe the L word was mentioned in at least one card. And what if he doesn't feel the same way about me? How embarrassing! Way worse than being suspended.

Oh, no! As I was writing this, I got Instant Messaged by, of all people, Michael himself! I freaked out so bad, I shrieked and scared Fat Louie, who was sleeping on my lap as I wrote. He sank all of his claws into me, and now I have little puncture marks all over my thighs.

Michael wrote:

CRACKING: Hey, Thermopolis, what's this I hear about you getting suspended?

I wrote back:

FTLOUIE: Just for one day.
CRACKING: What'd you do?

128

FtLOUIE: Crushed a cheerleader's cellular phone.

CracKING: Your parents must be so proud.

FtLOUIE: If so, they've done a pretty good job of disguising it so far.

CracKING: So are you grounded?

FtLOUIE: Surprisingly, no. The attack on the cell phone was provoked.

CracKING: So you'll still be going to the Carnival next week?

FtLOUIE: As secretary to the Students Against the Corporatization of Albert Einstein High School, I believe my attendance is required. Your sister is planning for us to have a booth.

CracKING: That Lilly. She's always looking out for the good of mankind.

FtLOUIE: That's one way of putting it.


We probably would have talked longer, but right then my mom yelled at me to get offline, since she's waiting to hear from Mr. Gianini, who, surprisingly, still wasn't home from school, even though it was past dinnertime. So I logged off.

This is the second time Michael's asked if I'm going to the Winter Carnival. What's up with that?

Now we know why Mr. G was so late getting home:

He stopped along the way to buy a Christmas tree.

Not just any Christmas tree, either, but a twelve-footer that must be at least six feet wide at the base.

I didn't say anything negative, of course, because my mom was so happy and excited about it, and immediately lugged out all of her Dead Celebrity Christmas ornaments (my mom doesn't use pretty glass balls or tinsel on her Christmas tree, like normal people. Instead, she paints pieces of tin with the likenesses of celebrities who have died that year, and hangs those on the tree. Which is why we probably have the only tree in North America with ornaments commemorating Richard and Pat Nixon, Elvis, Audrey Hepburn, Kurt Cobain, Jim Henson, John Belushi, Rock Hudson, Alec Guiness, Divine, John Lennon, and many, many more).

And Mr. Gianini kept looking over at me, to see if I was happy, too. He got the tree, he said, because he knew what a bad day I'd had, and he didn't want it to be a total loss.

Mr. G, of course, has no idea what my English term paper topic is.

What was I supposed to say? I mean, he'd already gone out and bought it, and you know a tree that size had to have cost a lot of money. And he'd meant to do a nice thing. He really had.

Still, I wish the people around here would consult me about things before just going out and doing them. Like the whole pregnancy thing, and now this tree. If Mr. G had asked me, I would have been like, Let's go to the Big Kmart on Astor Place and get a nice fake tree so we don't contribute to the destruction of the polar bear's natural habitat, okay?

Only he didn't ask me.

And the truth is, even if he had, my mom would never have gone for it. Her favorite part of Christmas is lying on the floor with her head under the tree, gazing up through the branches and inhaling the sweet tangy smell of pine sap. She says it's the only memory of her Indiana childhood she actually likes.

It's hard to think about the polar bears when your mom says something like that.

*Saturday, December 13, 2 p.m.,*
*Lilly's apartment*

Well, the first meeting of the Students Against the Corporatization of Albert Einstein High School is a complete bust.

That's because nobody showed up but me and Boris Pelkowski. I am a little miffed that Kenny didn't come. You would think that if he really loves me as much as he says he does, he would take any opportunity whatsoever to be near me, even a boring meeting of the Students Against the Corporatization of Albert Einstein High School.

But I guess even Kenny's love is not that great. As should be obvious to me by now, considering the fact that there are exactly six days until the Nondenominational Winter Dance, and Kenny STILL HASN'T ASKED ME IF I WANT TO GO WITH HIM.

Not that I'm worried, or anything. I mean, a girl who set off a fire alarm AND smashed Lana Weinberger's cell phone, worried about not having a date to a stupid dance?

All right. I'm worried.

But not worried enough to pull a Sadie Hawkins and ask *him* to the dance.

Lilly is pretty much inconsolable over the fact that no one but Boris and me showed up for her meeting. I tried to tell her that everybody is too busy studying for finals to worry about privatization at the moment, but she doesn't seem to care. Right now she is sitting on the couch, with Boris speaking to her in a soothing voice. Boris is pretty gross and all—with his sweaters that he always tucks into his pants, and that weird retainer his orthodontist makes him wear—but you can tell he genuinely loves Lilly. I mean, look at the tender way he is gazing at her as she sobs about how she is going to call her congressmember.

It makes my heart hurt, looking at Boris looking at Lilly.

I guess I must be jealous. I want a boy to look at *me* like that. And I don't mean Kenny, either. I mean a boy who I actually like back, as more than just a friend.

I can't take it anymore. I am going into the kitchen to see what Maya, the Moscovitzes' housekeeper, is doing. Even helping to wash things has to be better than this.

Maya wasn't in the kitchen. She was here, in Michael's room, putting away his school uniform, which she just finished ironing. Maya is going around picking up Michael's things and telling me about her son Manuel. Thanks to the help of the Drs. Moscovitz, Manuel was recently released from the prison in the Dominican Republic where he'd been wrongfully held for suspicion of having committed crimes against the state. Now Manuel is starting his own political party, and Maya is just as proud as can be, except she is worried he might end up back in prison if he doesn't tone down the anti-government stuff a little.

Manuel and Lilly have a lot in common, I guess.

Maya's stories about Manuel are always interesting, but it is much more interesting to be in Michael's room. I have been in it before, of course, but never while he was gone (he is at school, even though it is Saturday, working in the computer lab on his project for the Carnival; apparently the school's modem is faster than his. Also, I suppose, though I hate to admit it, he and Judith Gershner can freely practice their downloading there, without fear of parental interruption).

So I am lying on Michael's bed while Maya putters around, folding shirts and muttering about sugar, one of her native land's main exports and apparently a source of some consternation to her son's political platform, while Michael's dog, Pavlov, sits next to me, panting on my face. I can't help thinking, *This is what it's like to be Michael*: *This is what Michael sees when he looks up at his ceiling at night* (he has put glow-in-the-dark stars up there, in the form of the spiral galaxy Andromeda) and *This is how Michael's sheets smell* (springtime fresh, thanks to the detergent Maya uses) and *This is what the view of Michael's desk looks like from his bed.*

Except that looking over at his desk, I just noticed something. It's one of my cards! The one with the strawberry on it!

It isn't exactly on display, or anything. It's just sitting on his desk. But hey, that's a far cry from being crumpled at the bottom of his backpack. It shows that the cards mean something to him, that he hasn't buried them under all the other junk on his desk—the DOS manuals and anti-Microsoft literature—or worse, thrown them away.

This is somewhat heartening.

Uh-oh. I just heard the front door open. Michael??? Or the Drs. Moscovitz???? I better get out of here. Michael doesn't have all those Enter At Your Own Risk signs on the door for nothing.

How, you might ask, did I go from the Moscovitzes' apartment to my grandmother's suite at the Plaza in the space of a mere half hour?

Well, I'll tell you.

Disaster has struck, in the form of Sebastiano.

I always suspected, of course, that Sebastiano was not the sweet-tempered innocent he pretended to be. But now it looks like the only murder Sebastiano needs to worry about is his own. Because if my dad ever gets his hands on him, Sebastiano is one dead fashion designer.

Looking at it objectively, I think I can safely say I'd prefer to have been murdered. I mean, I'd be dead and all, which would be sad—especially since I still haven't written down those instructions for caring for Fat Louie while I'm gone—but at least I wouldn't have to show up for school on Monday.

But now, not only do I have to show up for school on Monday, but I have to show up for school on Monday knowing that every single one of my fellow classmates is going to have seen the supplement that arrived in the Sunday *Times*: the supplement featuring about twenty photos of ME standing in front of a triple mirror in dresses by Sebastiano, with the words "Fashion Fit for a Princess" emblazoned all over the place.

Oh, yes. I'm not kidding. Fashion Fit for a Princess.

I can't really blame him, I guess. Sebastiano, I mean. I suppose the opportunity was too much for him to resist. He is, after all, a businessman, and having a princess model your clothes . . . well, you can't buy exposure like that.

Because you know all the other papers are going to pick up on the story. You know, Princess of Genovia Makes Modeling Debut. That kind of thing.

So with just one little photo spread, Sebastiano is going to get virtual worldwide coverage of his new clothing line.

A clothing line that it looks like I have endorsed.

Grandmère doesn't understand why my dad and I are so upset. Well, I think she gets why my dad is upset. You know the whole "My daughter is being used" thing. She just doesn't get why *I'm* so unhappy. "You look perfectly beautiful," she keeps saying.

Yeah. Like that helps.

Grandmère thinks I am overreacting. But hello, have I ever aspired to tread in Claudia Schiffer's footsteps? I don't think so. Fashion is so not what I'm about. What about the environment? What about the rights of animals? What about the HORSESHOE CRABS??????

People are not going to believe I didn't pose for those photos. People are going to think I am a sellout. People are going to think I am a stuck-up model snob.

I would so rather that they think I am a juvenile delinquent, I can't tell you.

Little did I know when I heard the front door to the Moscovitzes' apartment opening, and I hustled out of Michael's room, that I was about to be greeted by the disastrous news. It was only Lilly's parents, after all, coming home from the gym, where they'd met with their personal trainers. Afterward, they'd stopped to have a latte and read the Sunday *Times*, large sections of which arrive, for reasons no one understands, on Saturday, if you have a subscription.

What a surprise they had had, when they'd opened up the paper and saw the Princess of Genovia hawking this hot new fashion designer's spring collection.

What a surprise I had, when the Drs. Moscovitz congratulated me on my new modeling career, and I was all, "What are you talking about?"

So, while Lilly and Boris looked on with curiosity, Dr. Moscovitz opened her paper and showed me:

And there it was, in all of its four-color-layout glory.

I'm not going to lie and say I looked bad. I looked okay. What they had done was, they had taken all the photos Sebastiano's assistant had snapped of me trying to decide which dress to wear to my introduction to the people of Genovia and laid them all out on this purple background. I'm not smiling in the pictures, or anything. I'm just looking at myself in the mirror, clearly going, in my head, *Ew, could I look more like a walking toothpick?*

But of course, if you didn't know me, and didn't know WHY I was trying on all these dresses, I'd seem like some freak who cares WAY too much about how she looks in a party dress.

Which is exactly the kind of person I've always wanted to be portrayed as.

NOT!!!!!!!

I have to admit, I am a little hurt. I'd thought, when he'd asked me all those questions about Michael, Sebastiano and I had kind of made a connection. But I guess not. Not if he could do something like this.

My dad has already called the *Times* and demanded that they remove the supplement from all the papers that haven't been delivered yet. He has called the concierge of the Plaza and insisted on Sebastiano being listed as persona non grata, which means the cousin to the prince of Genovia won't be allowed to set foot on hotel property.

I thought this was a little harsh, but not as harsh as what my dad *wanted* to do, which was call the NYPD and press charges against Sebastiano for using the likeness of a minor without the consent of her parents. Thank God Grandmère talked him out of that. She said there'd be enough publicity about this without the added humiliation of a royal arrest.

My dad is still so mad he can't sit still. He is pacing back and forth across the suite. Rommel is watching him very nervously from Grandmère's lap, his head moving back and forth, back and forth, his eyes following my dad as if he were watching the US Open or something.

I bet if Sebastiano *were* here, my dad would smash up a lot more than just his cell phone.

Well.

All I can say is, Grandmère's really done it this time.

I'm serious. I don't think my dad is ever going to speak to her again.

And I know *I* never will.

And okay, she's an old lady and she didn't know that what she was doing was wrong, and I should really be more understanding.

But for her to do *this*—for her not to even take into consideration my feelings—I frankly don't think I will ever be able to forgive her.

What happened was, Sebastiano called right before I was getting ready to leave the hotel. He was completely perplexed about why my dad is so mad at him. He tried to come upstairs to see us, he said, but Plaza security stopped him.

When my dad, who'd answered the phone, told Sebastiano that the reason Plaza security stopped him was because he'd been PNG'd, and then explained why, Sebastiano was even more upset. He kept going, "But I had your permish! I had your permish, Phillipe!"

"My permission to use my daughter's image to promote your tawdry rags?" My father was disgusted. "You most certainly did not!"

But Sebastiano kept insisting he had.

And little by little, it came out that he *had* had permission, in a way. Only not from me. And not my dad, either. Guess who, it appears, gave it to him?

Grandmère went, all indignantly, "I only did it, Phillipe, because Amelia, as you know, suffers from a terrible self-image, and needed a boost."

But my dad was so enraged, he wouldn't even listen to

her. He just thundered, "And so to repair her self-image, you went behind her back and gave permission for her photo to be used in an advertisement for *women's clothing?*"

Grandmère didn't have much to say after that. She just stood there, going "Uhn . . . uhn . . . uhn . . . " like someone in a horror movie who'd been pinned to a wall with a machete but wasn't quite dead yet (I always close my eyes during parts like this, so I know exactly what it sounds like).

It became clear that even if Grandmère had had a reasonable excuse for her behavior, my father wasn't going to listen to it—or let me listen to it, either. He stalked over to me, grabbed my arm, and marched me right out of the suite.

I thought we were going to have a bonding moment, like fathers and daughters always do on TV, where he'd tell me that Grandmère was a very sick woman and that he was going to send her somewhere where she could take a nice, long rest, but instead all he said was, "Go home."

Then he handed me over to Lars—after slamming the door to Grandmère's suite VERY loudly behind him, before storming off in the direction of his own suite.

Jeez.

It just goes to show, even a royal family can be dysfunctional.

Couldn't you just see us on *Ricki Lake?*

| Ricki: | Clarisse, tell us: Why did you allow Sebastiano to put your granddaughter's photos in that *Times* advertising supplement? |
| Grandmère: | That's Your Royal Highness to you, Ms. Lake. I did it to boost her self-esteem. |

I just know that when I get to school on Monday, every-body is going to be all, "Oh, look, here comes Mia, that big FAKE, with her vegetarianism and her animal-rights activism and her looks-aren't-important-it's-what's-on-the-inside-that-matters-ism. But I guess it's all right to pose for *fashion photo shoots*, isn't it, Mia?"

As if it wasn't enough to be suspended. Now I am going to be sneered at by my peers, too.

I'm home now, trying to pretend none of it ever hap-pened. This is difficult, of course, because when I walked back into the loft, I saw that my mom had already pulled the supplement out of our paper and drawn little devil horns coming out of my head in every picture, then stuck the whole thing onto the refrigerator.

While I appreciate this bit of whimsy, it does not make the fact that I will have to show my face—now plastered all over advertising supplements throughout the tristate area—in school on Monday any easier.

Surprisingly, there is one good thing that's come out of all of this: I know for sure I look best in the white taffeta number with the blue sash. My dad says over his dead body am I going to wear it, or any other Sebastiano creation, again. But there isn't another designer in Genovia who could do as good a job, let alone finish the dress in time. So it looks like the dress by Sebastiano, which got delivered to the loft this morning, is it.

Which is one thing off my mind, anyway.

I guess.

I've already gotten seventeen e-mails, six phone calls, and one visitor (Lilly) about the fashion thing. Lilly says it's not as bad as I think, and that most people throw the supplements away without even looking at them.

If that's true, I said, why are all these people calling and e-mailing me?

She tried to make out like it was all members of the Students Against the Corporatization of Albert Einstein High School, calling to show their solidarity with my suspension, but I think we both know better:

It's all people who want to know what I was thinking, selling out like that.

How am I ever going to explain that I had nothing to do with it, that I didn't even *know* about it? Nobody is going to believe that. I mean, the proof is right there: I'm *wearing* the proof. There's photographic evidence of it.

My reputation is going down the drain, even as I sit here. Tomorrow morning, millions of subscribers to *The New York Times* are going to open their papers and be like, "Oh, look, Princess Mia. Sold out already. Wonder how much she got paid? You wouldn't think she'd need the money, what with being royal, and all."

Finally I had to ask Lilly to please go home, because I'd developed a bad headache. She tried to cure it with some shiatsu, which her parents frequently employ on their patients, but it didn't work. All that ended up happening was that I think she burst a blood vessel or something between my thumb and index finger, since it really hurts.

Now I am determined to start studying, even though it's Saturday night, and everyone else my age is out having fun.

But haven't you heard? Princesses never get to have any fun.

## HERE IS WHAT I HAVE TO DO

Algebra: review Chapters 1–10
English: term paper, 10 pages, double spaced; utilize
    appropriate margins; also, review Chapters 1–7
World Civ: review Chapters 1–12
G&T: none
French: *revue Chapitres Un–Neuf*
Biology: review Chapters 1–12
Write out instructions on how to care for Fat Louie
Christmas/Hannukah shopping:
    Mom–Bon Jovi maternity T
    Dad—Book on anger management
    Mr. G—Swiss Army knife
    Lilly—blank videotapes
    Tina Hakim Baba—copy of *Emanuelle*
    Kenny—combination TV/VCR (I don't think this
    is too extravagant. And no, it's not guilt, either.
    He really wants one.)
Grandmère—NOTHING!!!!!!
Paint fingernails (maybe presence of foul-tasting
    polish will prevent biting them off)
Break up with Kenny
Organize sock drawer

I am going to start with the sock drawer, because that is
clearly the most important. You can't really concentrate on
anything if your socks aren't right.

Then I will move on to Algebra because that is my worst
subject, and also my first test. I am going to pass it if it's the
last thing I do. NOTHING is going to distract me. Not this
thing with Grandmère, not the fact that four of those seventeen e-mails are from Michael, not the fact that two are
from Kenny, not the fact that I am leaving for Europe at the

end of next week, not the fact that my mother and Mr. Gianini are in the next room watching *Die Hard*, my favorite Christmas movie, NOTHING.

I WILL PASS ALGEBRA THIS SEMESTER, and NOTHING IS GOING TO DISTRACT ME FROM STUDYING FOR THE FINAL!!!!!!!!!!!!

I just had to go out and see the part where Bruce Willis throws the explosives down the elevator shaft, but now I am back at work.

I was really curious about what Michael could possibly want, so I read his e-mails—just his. One was about the supplement (Lilly had told him, and he wanted to know if I was thinking of abdicating, ha ha) and the other three were jokes that I guess were supposed to make me feel better. They weren't very funny, but I laughed anyway.

I bet Judith Gershner doesn't laugh at Michael's jokes. She's too busy cloning things.

## HOW TO CARE FOR FAT LOUIE
## WHILE I AM AWAY

A.M.:

In the morning, please fill Fat Louie's bowl with DRY FOOD. Even if there is already food in the bowl, he likes to have some fresh served on top so he can feel like he is having breakfast like the rest of us.

In my bathroom is a BLUE PLASTIC CUP sitting by the bathtub. Please fill that every morning with water from the bathroom sink. You must use water from the bathroom sink, because water from the kitchen sink isn't cold enough. And you have to put it in the BLUE CUP because that is the cup Fat Louie is used to drinking out of while I am brushing my teeth.

He has a bowl in the hallway outside my room. Rinse that out and fill it with water from the WATER FILTER PITCHER in the refrigerator. It must be water from the WATER FILTER PITCHER because even though New York tap is said to be contaminant-free, it is good for Louie to get at least some water that is definitely pure. Cats need to drink a lot of water to flush out their systems and prevent kidney and urinary tract infections, so always leave lots of water out, and not just by his food bowls, but other places as well.

Do not confuse the bowl in the hall with the BOWL BY THE CHRISTMAS TREE. That bowl is there to discourage Louie from drinking out of the tree holder. Too much tree resin could make him constipated.

In the morning, Fat Louie likes to sit on the windowsill in my room and look at the pigeons on the fire escape. NEVER OPEN THIS WINDOW, but be sure the curtains are open so he can see out.

Also, sometimes he likes to look out the windows by the TV. If he cries while he is doing this, it means you should pet him.

P.M.:

At dinnertime, give Fat Louie CANNED FOOD. Fat Louie only likes three flavors: CHICKEN AND TUNA FEAST (FLAKED), SHRIMP AND FISH FEAST (FLAKED), and OCEAN FISH FEAST (FLAKED). He won't eat anything with BEEF or PORK. He must have the contents of the can on a new, CLEAN saucer, or he won't eat. Also, he won't eat if the contents don't retain their CANLIKE SHAPE on the plate, so don't chop up his food.

After eating his canned food, Fat Louie likes to stretch out on the carpet in front of the front door. This is a good time to give him his exercise. When he stretches out, just put your hand under his front legs and straighten them (he likes this) until he bends like a comma. Then dig your thumbs between his shoulder blades and give him a kitty massage. He will purr if you do it right. If you do it wrong you will know, because he will bite you.

Fat Louie gets bored very easily, and when he gets bored, he walks around crying, so here are some games he likes to play:

149

Take some pieces of CAT TREAT and line them up on top of the stereo for Fat Louie to knock off and chase.

Put Fat Louie in my COMPUTER CHAIR and then hide behind the bookshelf and throw one end of a shoelace over the back of the chair so he can't see where it is coming from.

Make a FORT out of pillows on my bed and put Fat Louie inside of it and then stick your hand into any openings between the pillows (I recommend wearing an oven mitt during this game).

Put some catnip in an OLD SOCK and throw it to Fat Louie. Then leave him alone for four to five hours, because catnip makes him a little free with his claws.

## THE LITTER BOX

Mr. Gianini, this one is for you. Mom must not clean out the litter box or touch anything that may have come in contact with it, or she might develop toxoplasmosis, and the baby might get sick. Always wash your hands in warm, soapy water after changing Fat Louie's litter box, even if you don't think you got anything on your hands.

Fat Louie's box needs to be scooped out EVERY DAY. Always use clumping litter, and then just scoop out the clumps into a Grand Union bag and dispose. Nothing could be simpler. He tends to do number 2 about two hours after his evening meal. You will be able to tell from the odor wafting from his box in my bathroom.

## MOST IMPORTANT OF ALL

Remember not to disturb Fat Louie's SPECIAL AREA BEHIND THE TOILET in my bathroom. That is where he keeps his collection of shiny objects. If he takes something of yours and you find it there, be sure not to take it out while he is looking, or for weeks he will try to bite you every time he sees you. I talked to the vet about it, but she said short of hiring an animal behaviorist at $70/hr there is nothing that can be done. We just have to put up with it.

ABOVE ALL, BE SURE TO PICK FAT LOUIE UP SEVERAL TIMES A DAY AND HUG AND SQUEEZE HIM!!!!! (HE LIKES THIS.)

I can't believe it's midnight already, and I am still only on Chapter One of *An Introduction to Algebra*!

This book is incomprehensible. I sincerely hope whoever wrote it did not make very much money off of it.

I should just go and ask Mr. G what's going to be on the final.

No, that would be cheating.

Wouldn't it?

Only forty-eight hours until the Algebra final, and I am still on Chapter One.

Lilly just came over again. She wants to study for World Civ together. I told her I can't worry about World Civ when I am only on Chapter One in my Algebra review, but she said we could alternate: She would quiz me on Algebra for an hour, then I could quiz her on World Civ for an hour. I said okay, even though it really isn't fair: She is getting an A in Algebra, so her quizzing me isn't really helping her any, while my quizzing her in World Civ helps me study for it, too.

But that's what friends are for, I guess.

Tina just called. Her little brother and sisters are driving her crazy. She wanted to know if she could come down and study here. I said sure.

What else could I say? Besides, she promised to stop at H&H for bagels and vegetable cream cheese. And she said she thought the photos of me in the supplement were beautiful and that I shouldn't care if people call me a sellout, because I look so hot.

Michael told Boris where Lilly is, so now Boris is here, too.

Lilly's right. Boris really does breathe too loudly. It's very distracting.

And I wish he wouldn't put his feet on my bed. The least he could do is take his shoes off first. But when I suggested it, Lilly said that would be a bad idea.

Ew. I don't know why Lilly puts up with a boyfriend who is not only a mouth breather but also has stinky feet.

Boris may be a musical genius, but he has a lot to learn about hygiene, if you ask me.

*Sunday, December 14, 12:30 p.m., the loft*

Now Kenny's here. I don't know how I am supposed to get any studying done with all of these people around. Plus, Mr. Gianini has decided that now would be a good time to practice his drums.

Sunday, December 14, 8 p.m., the loft

I told Lilly, and she agreed, that once Boris and Kenny showed up, the whole studying thing kind of went down the drain. Plus, Mr. G's drumming didn't help. So we decided it would be best to take a study break and go to Chinatown for dim sum.

We had a good time at Great Shanghai eating vegetable dumplings and dried sauteed string beans with garlic sauce. I ended up sitting by Boris, and he really made me laugh, engineering it so that whenever the waiters brought something new, the only empty spot on the table was in front of him, so they had to put it there, and then Boris and I got first dibs on it.

Which made me realize that in spite of the sweaters and the mouth-breathing, Boris really is a funny and nice person. Lilly is so lucky. I mean, that the boy she loves actually loves her back. If only I could love Kenny the way Lilly loves Boris!

But I don't seem to have any control over who I fall in love with. Believe me, if I did, I would NOT love Michael. I mean, for one thing, he is my best friend's older brother, and if Lilly ever found out I liked him, she would NOT understand. Also, of course, he is a senior and is graduating soon.

And oh, yeah, he already has a girlfriend.

But what am I supposed to do? I can't *make* myself fall in love with Kenny any more than I can *make* him stop liking me, you know, in that special way.

Although he still hasn't asked me to the dance. Or mentioned it, anyway. Lilly says I should just call him and be like, "So are we going, or not?" After all, she keeps pointing out, I had the guts to smash up Lana's cell phone. Why don't I have the guts to call my own boyfriend and ask him whether or not he is taking me to the school dance?

But I smashed up Lana's cell phone in the heat of passion. I cannot summon up anything like passion where Kenny is concerned. There is a part of me that doesn't want to go to the dance with him at all, and that part of me is relieved that he hasn't mentioned anything about it.

Okay, it is a very small part of me, but it's still *there*.

So actually, even though I was having fun sitting by Boris at the restaurant and all, it was also a little depressing, on account of the whole Kenny thing.

And then things got even more depressing. That's because some little Chinese-American girls came up to me as I was opening my fortune cookie and wanted to know if they could have my autograph. Then they handed me pens and the advertising supplement that had appeared in that day's *Times* for me to sign.

I seriously thought about killing myself, only I couldn't think how I'd do it, except for maybe stabbing myself through the heart with a chopstick.

Instead I just signed the stupid thing for them and tried to smile. But inside, of course, I was FREAKING OUT, especially when I saw how happy the little girls were to have met me. And why? No, not because of my tireless work on behalf of the polar bears or the whales or starving kids. Which I haven't actually done yet, but I fully intend to do.

No, because I'd been in a magazine in a bunch of pretty dresses, and I'm tall and skinny like a model.

Which is no accomplishment at all!

After that, my headache came back, and I said I had to go home.

Nobody protested very much, I think because everybody realized all of a sudden how much time we'd wasted, and how much studying we all had left to do. So we left, and now I am home again, and my mom says that while I was gone, Sebastiano called four times, AND he had another dress delivered.

Not just any dress, either. It is a dress Sebastiano designed just for me, to wear to the Nondenominational Winter Dance. It's not sexy. It isn't sexy at all. It's dark green velvet with long sleeves and a wide, square neckline.

But when I put it on and looked at my reflection in the mirror in my room, something funny happened:

I looked good. *Really* good.

There was a note attached to the dress that said,

> *Please forgive me.*
> *I promise this dress will not make him think of*
> *you as his little sister's best friend.*
> *S.*

Which is very sweet. Sad, but sweet. Sebastiano can't know, of course, that the Michael situation is completely hopeless, and that no *dress* is going to make any difference, no matter how nice I look in it.

But hey, at least Sebastiano *apologized*. That's a lot more, I've noticed, than Grandmère has done.

Of course I forgive Sebastiano. I mean, none of it is his fault, really.

And I guess someday I'll probably forgive Grandmère, since she's too old to know any better.

But the person I will never, ever forgive is myself, for getting into this situation in the first place. I totally should have known better. I should have told Sebastiano, No photos, please. Only I was so carried away, looking at myself in all those beautiful dresses, that I forgot that being a princess is more than just wearing pretty dresses: It's being an example to a lot of people . . . people you don't even know and may not ever even meet.

Which is why if I don't pass this Algebra test, I am dead.

Here are the number of students at Albert Einstein High School who (so far) have felt compelled to make comments to me about my smashing Lana Weinberger's cell phone last Friday: 37

Here are the number of students at Albert Einstein High School who (so far) have felt compelled to mention my suspension last Friday: 59

Here are the number of students at Albert Einstein High School who (so far) have felt compelled to make comments to me about my appearance in an advertising supplement to *The New York Times* over the weekend: 74

Total number of comments made to me so far today by students at Albert Einstein High School:  170

Oddly, after wading through all of this, when I got to my locker, I found something that seemed extremely out of place: a single yellow rose, sticking out of the door.

What can this mean? Can there be someone in this school who does not despise me?

Apparently so. But when I looked around, wondering who my one supporter could be, I saw only Justin Baxendale, being stalked (as usual) by a horde of worshipful girls.

I suppose my anonymous rose-leaver must be Kenny, trying to cheer me up. He will not admit it, but who else could it be?

It is Reading Day today, which means we are supposed to spend the whole day—except for lunch—sitting in Homeroom, studying for our finals, which begin tomorrow. This is fine by me, since at least this way, there's no chance I'll run into Lana. Her homeroom is on a whole other floor.

The only problem is that Kenny's in this class. We have to sit alphabetically, so he's way up at the front of this row, but he keeps passing notes back to me. Notes that say things like, *Keep on smilin'!* and *Hang in there, Sunshine!*

He won't fess up to the rose thing, though.

By the way, want to know the total number of comments made to me so far today by Michael Moscovitz? 1

And it wasn't even really a comment. He told me in the hallway that my combat boot had come untied.

And it had.

My life is so over.

Four days until the Nondenominational Winter Dance, and still no date.

Distance formula: $d - 10xrt$

$r = 10$

$t = 2$

$d = 10 + (10)(2)$

$\quad = 10 + 20 = 30$

Variables are placeholders for numbers (letters)
Distributive law

$5x + 5y - 5$

$5 (x + y - 1)$

$2a - 2b + 2c$

$2 (-1) - 2(-2) + 2 (5)$

$-2 + 4 + 10 = 12$

Four times a number is added to three. The result is five times the number.

Find the number.

$x = $ *the number*

$\quad 4x + 3 \quad = 5x$

$\underline{-4x \qquad\quad -4x}$

$\qquad\quad 3 = x$

*Regardes les oiseaux stupides.*

Cartesian coordinate system divides the plane into four parts called quadrants

Quadrant 1 (positive, positive)

Quadrant 2 (negative, positive)

Quadrant 3 (negative, negative)

Quadrant 4 (positive, negative)

Slope: slope of a line is line denoted *m*

Find slope
negative slopes
positive slopes
zero slope
Vertical line has no slope
Horizontal line has 0 slope
Collinear—points that lie on the same line
Parallel lines have the same slope

$4x + 2y = 6$
$2y = -4x + 6$
$y = -2x + 3$

Active voice indicates that the subject of the verb is acting

Passive voice indicates that the subject of the verb is being acted upon

Algebra and English finals completed.
Only three more, plus term paper, to go.

76 comments today, 53 of them negative:
"Sellout" = 29 times
I-Must-Think-I'm-All-That = 14 times
Here Comes Miss Thang = 6 times

Lilly says, "Who cares what people are saying? You know the truth, right? And that's all that matters."
That's easy for Lilly to say. Lilly's not the one who people are saying all those mean things about. *I* am.

Somebody left another yellow rose in my locker. What is up with that? I asked Kenny again if it was him, but he denied it. Strangely, he seemed to get very red in the face about it. But this might have been because Justin Baxendale, who was walking by at the time, stepped on Kenny's foot. Kenny has very large feet, larger even than mine.

Three more days until the Nondenominational Winter Dance, and nada on the date front.

World Civ exam *finis*.
Two more, plus term paper, to go.

62 comments, 34 negative:
Don't give up your day job = 12 times
Sellout = 5 times
"If I was flat-chested like you, Mia, I could be a model, too" = 6 times

One rose, yellow, still no indication who left it. Perhaps someone is mistaking my locker for Lana's. She is, after all, always hanging out in that area, waiting for Josh Richter, whose locker is next door to mine, so that the two of them can suck face. It's possible that someone thinks he is leaving roses for her.

God knows no one at Albert Einstein High School would want to leave flowers for me. Unless I were dead, maybe, and they could fling them onto my grave and say, "Good riddance, Miss Thang."

Two more days until the dance. Still nothing.

*Thursday, December 18, 1 a.m.*

It just occurred to me:

Maybe Kenny is lying about the roses. Maybe they really *are* from him. Maybe he's leaving them as kind of teasers, leading up to asking me to the dance tomorrow night.

Which is kind of insulting, really. I mean, him waiting this long to finally ask. For all he knows, I could have said yes to somebody else by now.

As if somebody else might have asked.
HA!

THAT'S IT!!!!!
I'M DONE!!!!!!
DONE WITH FINALS!!!!!!!!!!!!!
And guess what?

I'm pretty sure I passed all of them. Even Algebra. The grades aren't posted until tomorrow, during the Winter Carnival, but I bugged Mr. G so much he finally said, "Mia, you did fine. Now leave me alone, all right?"

Got that????? He said I did FINE!!!!!!!!!! You know what *fine* means, don't you?

IT MEANS I PASSED!!!!!!!!!!!!!!!!!

Thank God all of that's over. Now I can concentrate on what's important:

My social life.

I am serious. It is in a state of total disrepair. Everyone at school—with the exception of my friends—thinks I am this total sellout. They're like, "You talk the talk, Mia, but you don't walk the walk."

Well, I'm going to show them. Right after the World Civ exam yesterday, it hit me like a ton of bricks. I knew *exactly* what to do. It's what Grandmère would do.

Well, okay, maybe not *quite* what Grandmère would do, but it will solve the whole problem. Granted, Sebastiano isn't going to like it very much. But then, he should have asked ME, not Grandmère, if it was all right to run those photos in an ad for his clothes. Right?

I have to say, this is the most princessy thing I've done so far. I am very, very nervous. Seriously. You wouldn't believe how much my palms are sweating.

But I cannot continue to lie back and meekly take this abuse. Something must be done about it, and I think I know what.

The best part is, I am doing it all by myself, with no help from anyone.

Well, all right, the concierge at the Plaza helped by getting me a room, and Lars helped by making all the calls on his cell phone.

And Lilly helped me write down what I was going to say, and Tina did my makeup and hair just now.

But other than that, it was all me.

Okay, we're here.

Here goes nothing.

I have now watched myself on all four major networks, plus New York 1, CNN, Headline News, MSNBC, and Fox News Channel. Apparently, they are also going to show it on *Entertainment Tonight*, *Access Hollywood*, and *E! Entertainment News*.

And I have to say, for a girl who supposedly has issues with her self-image, I think I did a fine job. I didn't mess up, not even once. If I maybe spoke a little too fast, well, you could still *understand* me. Unless, you know, you're a non–English-speaker or something.

I looked good, too. I probably should have worn something other than my school uniform, but you know, royal blue comes off pretty good on TV.

The phone has been ringing off the hook ever since the press conference was first aired. The first time it rang, my mom picked it up, and it was Sebastiano, screaming incomprehensibly about how I've ruined him.

Only he can't say ruined. It just came out "rued."

I felt really bad. I mean, I didn't mean to ruin him. Especially after he was so nice about designing me that dress for the dance.

But what was I supposed to do? I tried to make him look on the bright side:

"Sebastiano," I said, when I got on the phone, "I haven't ruined you. Really. It's just the proceeds from the sales of the dresses I'm wearing in the ad that will go to Greenpeace."

But Sebastiano completely failed to look at the big picture. He kept screaming, "Rued! I'm rued!"

I pointed out that, far from ruining him, his donating all the proceeds from sales of the dresses I modeled to Greenpeace was going to be perceived in the industry as a brilliant stroke of marketing genius, and that I wouldn't be surprised

171

if those dresses flew off the racks, since girls like me, who are really the people his fashions are geared for, care a great deal about the environment.

I must have picked up a thing or two during my princess lessons with Grandmère, since in the end, I totally won him over. By the time I hung up, I think Sebastiano almost believed the whole thing had been his idea in the first place.

The next time the phone rang, it was my dad. I may have to scratch the plan to get him a book on anger management, because he was laughing his head off. He wanted to know if it had been my mom's idea, and when I said, "No, it was all me," he went, "You really *have* got the princess thing down, you know."

So, in a weird way, I feel like I passed that final, too.

Except of course that I'm still not speaking to Grandmère. Not a single one of the calls I've gotten tonight—from Lilly and Tina and Mamaw and Papaw back in Indiana, who saw the broadcast on a local affiliate—have been from her.

Really, I think she should be the one to apologize, because what she did was totally underhanded.

Almost as underhanded, my mom pointed out to me over dinner from Number One Noodle Son, as what *I* did.

Which is sort of shocking. I mean, I never thought about it before, but it's true: What I did tonight—it was as sneaky as anything Grandmère's ever done.

But I guess that shouldn't be very surprising. We *are* related, after all.

Then again, so were Luke Skywalker and Darth Vader.

Must go. *Baywatch* is on. This is the first time in a while I've been home to watch it.

Tina just called. She didn't want to talk about the press conference. She wanted to know what I got from my Secret Snowflake. I was all, "Secret Snowflake? What are you talking about?"

"You know," Tina said. "Your Secret Snowflake. You remember, Mia. We signed up for it like a month ago. You put your name in the jar, and then someone draws it, and they have to be your Secret Snowflake for the last week of school before Winter Break. They're supposed to surprise you with little gifts and stuff. You know, as a stress breaker. Since it's finals week, and all."

I dimly remembered, one day before Thanksgiving Break, Tina dragging me over to a folding table where some nerdy-looking kids from the student government were sitting on one side of the cafeteria with a big jar filled with little pieces of paper. Tina had made me write my name on a slip of paper, then pick someone else's name out of the jar.

"Oh, my God!" I cried. With all the stress of finals and everything, I had forgotten all about it!

Worse, I had forgotten that I had drawn Tina's name. No real coincidence, since she'd stuffed her slip of paper into the jar right before I picked. Still, what kind of heinous friend am I, that I would forget something like this?

Then I realized something else. The yellow roses. They hadn't been put in my locker by mistake! And they really weren't from Kenny, either! They had to be from my Secret Snowflake.

Which was kind of upsetting in a way. I mean, it's really starting to look as if Kenny has no intention whatsoever of asking me to tomorrow night's dance.

"I can't believe you forgot about it," Tina said, sounding amused. "You *have* been getting stuff for your Secret

Snowflake, haven't you, Mia?"

I felt a rush of guilt. I had totally blown it. Poor Tina!

"Uh, sure," I said, wondering where I was going to find a present for her by tomorrow morning, the last day of the Secret Snowflake thing. "Sure, I have."

Tina sighed. "I guess nobody picked me," she said. "Because I haven't gotten anything."

"Oh, don't worry," I said, hoping the guilt washing over me wasn't noticeable in my voice. "You will. Your Secret Snowflake is probably waiting, you know, until the last day because she's—or he's—gotten you something really good."

"Do you think so?" Tina asked, wistfully.

"Oh, yes," I gushed.

Reassured, Tina got businesslike.

"Now," she said, "that finals are over . . ."

"Um, yes?"

". . . when are you going to tell Michael that you're the one who sent him those cards?"

Shocked, I went, "How about never?"

To which Tina replied, tartly, "Mia, if you don't tell him, then what was the point of sending those cards?"

"To let him know that there are other girls out there who might like him, besides Judith Gershner."

Tina said, severely, "Mia, that's not enough. You've got to tell him it was you. How are you ever going to get him if he doesn't know how you feel?" Tina Hakim Baba, surprisingly, has a lot in common with my dad. "Remember Kenny? That's how Kenny got you. He sent the anonymous notes, but then he finally fessed up."

"Yeah," I said, sarcastically. "And look how great *that* turned out."

"It'll be different with you and Michael," Tina insisted. "Because you two are destined for each other. I can just *feel* it. You've got to tell him, and it's got to be tomorrow, because the next day, you are leaving for Genovia."

Oh, God. In my self-congratulations over having successfully maneuvered my first press conference, I'd forgotten about that, too. I am leaving for Genovia the day after tomorrow! With Grandmère! To whom I am not even speaking anymore!

I told Tina that I'd confess to Michael tomorrow. She hung up all happy.

But it was a good thing she hadn't been able to see my nostrils, because they were flaring like crazy, on account of the fact that I was totally lying to her.

Because there is no way I am ever telling Michael Moscovitz how I feel about him. No matter what my dad says. I *can't*.

Not to his face.

Not ever.

They are holding us hostage here in Homeroom until they've passed out our final semester grades. Then we are free to spend the rest of the day at the Winter Carnival in the gym, and then, later this evening, the dance.

Really. We don't have any more classes after this. We are just supposed to have fun.

As if. I am so never having fun again.

That is because—you know, aside from my many other problems, including the fact that I don't love my boyfriend, who also apparently does not love me anymore, at least not enough to ask me to the school dance, but I do love my best friend's brother, who is not even remotely aware of my feelings—that I think I know who my Secret Snowflake is.

Really, there is no other explanation. Why else would Justin Baxendale—who, even though he's so new, is still totally popular, not to mention way good-looking—be hanging around my locker so much? I mean, seriously. This is the third time I've spotted him lurking around there this week. Why else would he be hanging around there, except to leave those roses?

Unless he's planning on blackmailing me about the whole fire-alarm thing.

But Justin Baxendale doesn't exactly strike me as the black-mailer type. I mean, he looks to me like somebody who'd have something better to do than blackmail a princess.

Which leaves only one other explanation for why he could possibly be spending so much time around my locker: He is my Secret Snowflake.

And how totally embarrassing is it going to be when I go out there when the bell rings, and Justin comes up to me to confess—because that's the rule, it turns out: You have to reveal your identity to your Secret Snowflake today—and I have to look up into his smoky eyes with those long lashes and give a big fake smile and go, "Oh, gee, thanks, Justin. I had no idea it was you!"

Whatever. This is actually the least of my problems, right? I mean, considering that I am the only girl in this entire school who does not have a date to the dance tonight. And that tomorrow I have to leave for a country I am princess of, with my lunatic grandmother who isn't speaking to my father, and who, I know from past experience, is not above smoking in the airplane lavatory if the urge strikes her.

Really. Grandmère is a flight attendant's worst nightmare.

But that's not even half of it. I mean, what about my mom and Mr. Gianini? Sure, they're acting like they don't mind my spending the holidays in another country, and yes, we're going to have our own private little Christmas among ourselves before I leave, but really, I bet they mind. I bet they mind a lot.

And what about my grade in Algebra? Oh, Mr. Gianini says it's fine, but what is fine, exactly? A D? A D is not fine. Not considering the number of hours I've put into raising my grade from an F, it isn't. A D is *not* acceptable.

And what—oh God, *what*—am I going to do about Kenny?

At least I got Tina's present out of the way. I went online last night and signed her up for a teen romance book-of-the-month club. I printed out the certificate, saying she is an official member, and will give it to her when the bell rings.

When the bell rings, which is also when I have to go out there and face Justin Baxendale.

It wouldn't be so bad if it weren't for those eyes of his. Why does he have to be so good-looking? And why did a good-looking person have to pick me as his Secret Snowflake? Beautiful people, like Lana and Justin, can't help but be repulsed by ordinary-looking people, like me.

He probably didn't even pull my name from that jar at all. Probably, he picked Lana's name and has been putting those roses in my locker, thinking it's Lana's, seeing as how God knows she never hangs out in front of her own locker.

What's even worse is, Tina told me yellow roses mean love *everlasting*.

Which of course was why I figured maybe it was Kenny after all.

Oh, great. They are passing around the printouts with our grades on them. I am not looking. I don't even care. I DO NOT CARE ABOUT MY GRADES.

Thank God for the bell. I'm just going to slip out of here—not looking at my grades, totally not looking at my grades—and go about my business like nothing out of the ordinary is going on.

Except of course when I get to my locker, Justin is there, looking for someone. Lana is there, too, waiting for Josh.

You know, I really don't need this. Justin revealing that he is my Secret Snowflake right in front of Lana, I mean. God only knows what she's going to say, the girl who has been suggesting I wear Band-Aids instead of a bra every day since the two of us hit puberty. Plus, it isn't like she's been super happy with me since the whole cell-phone thing. I'll bet she'll have something extra mean all prepared for the occasion. . . .

"Dude," Justin says.

Dude? I'm not a dude. Who is Justin talking to?

I turn around. Josh is standing there, behind Lana.

"Dude, I've been looking for you all week," Justin says, to Josh. "Do you have those Trig notes for me, or not? I've got to make up the final in one hour."

Josh says something, but I don't hear him. I don't hear him because there's a roaring sound in my ears. There's a roaring sound in my ears because standing behind Justin is Michael. *Michael Moscovitz.*

And in his hand is *a yellow rose.*

Oh, God.

I am in so much trouble.

Again.

And it isn't even my fault this time. I mean, I couldn't help myself. It just *happened*, you know? And it doesn't mean anything. It was just, you know, one of those things.

And besides, it's not what Kenny thinks. Not even. I mean, if you think about it, it is a complete and total let-down. For me, anyway.

Because of course the first thing Michael says, when he sees me standing there gaping at him while he is holding that flower, is, "Here. This just fell out of your locker."

I took it from him in a complete daze. I swear to God my heart was beating so hard, I thought I was going to pass out.

Because I thought they'd been from him. The roses, I mean. For a minute there, I really did think Michael Moscovitz had been leaving me roses.

But of course this time, there's a note attached to the rose. It says:

*Good luck on your trip to Genovia! See you when you get back!*
*Your Secret Snowflake,*
*Boris Pelkowski*

Boris Pelkowski. Boris Pelkowski is the one who's been leaving those roses. Boris Pelkowski is my Secret Snowflake.

Of course Boris wouldn't know that a yellow rose represents love everlasting. Boris doesn't even know not to tuck his sweater into his pants. How would he know the secret language of flowers?

I don't know which was actually stronger, my feeling of

relief that it wasn't Justin Baxendale leaving those roses after all . . .

. . . or my feeling of disappointment that it wasn't Michael.

Then Michael went, "Well? What's the verdict?"

To which I responded by staring at him blankly. I still hadn't quite gotten over it. You know, those brief few seconds when I'd thought—I'd actually thought, fool that I am—that he loved me.

"What did you get in Algebra?" he asked, slowly, as if I were dense.

Which, of course, I am. So dense that I never realized how much in love with Michael Moscovitz I was until Judith Gershner came along and swept him right out from under my nose.

Anyway, so I opened the computer printout containing my grades, and would you believe that I had raised my F in Algebra all the way up to a B minus?

Which just goes to show that if you spend nearly every waking moment in your life studying something, the likelihood is that you are going to retain at least a little of it.

Enough to get a B minus on the final, anyway.

I'm trying really hard not to gloat, but it's difficult. I mean, I'm so happy.

Well, except for the whole not-having-a-date-to-the-dance thing.

Still, it's hard to be unhappy. There is absolutely no way I got this grade because the teacher happens to be my step-father. In Algebra, either you get the right answer, or you don't. There's nothing subjective about it, like in English. There's no interpretation of the facts. Either you're right, or you're not.

And I was right. Eighty percent of the time.

Of course it helped that I knew the answer to the final's

extra-credit question: What instrument did Ringo, in the Beatles, play?

But that was only worth two points.

Anyway, here's the part where I got into trouble. Even though, of course, it isn't my fault.

I was so happy about my B minus, I completely forgot for a minute how much I am in love with Michael. I even forgot, for a change, to be shy around him. Instead, I did something really unlike me.

I threw my arms around him.

Seriously. Threw my arms right around his neck and went, "Wheeeeeee!!!!!"

I couldn't help it. I was so happy. Okay, the whole rose thing had been a little bit of a bummer, but the B minus made up for it. Well, almost.

It was just an innocent hug. That's *all* it was. Michael had, after all, tutored me almost the whole semester. He had some stake in that B minus, too.

But I guess Kenny, who Tina now tells me came around the corner right as I was doing it—hugging Michael, I mean—doesn't see it that way. According to Tina, Kenny thinks there's something going on between Michael and me.

To which, of course, I can only say, I WISH!

But I can't say that. I have to go find Kenny now, and let him know, you know, it was just a friendly hug.

Tina's all, "Why? Why don't you tell him the truth—that you don't feel the same way about him that he feels about you? This is your big chance!"

But you can't break up with someone during the Winter Carnival. I mean, really. How mean.

Why must my life be so fraught with trauma?

Well, I still haven't found Kenny, but I really have to hand it to the administrators: Grasping they might be, but they sure do know how to throw a party. Even Lilly is impressed.

Of course, signs of corporatization are everywhere: There are McDonald's orange drink dispensers on every floor, and it looks as if there was a run on Entenmann's, there are so many cake-and-cookie-laden tables scattered around.

Still, you can tell they are really trying to show us a good time. All of the clubs are offering activities and booths. There's ballroom dancing in the gym, courtesy of the Dance Club; fencing lessons in the auditorium, thanks to the Drama Club; even cheerleading lessons in the first-floor hallway, brought to us by—you guessed it—the junior varsity cheerleaders.

I couldn't find Kenny anywhere, but I ran into Lilly at the Students for Amnesty International booth (Students Against the Corporatization of Albert Einstein High School did not submit their application for a booth in time to get one, so Lilly is stuck running the Amnesty International booth instead). And guess what? Guess who got an F in something?

That's right.

Lilly. I couldn't believe it.

"Mrs. Spears gave you an F in English? *YOU* got an F?"

She didn't seem too bothered by it, though.

"I had to take a stand, Mia," she said. "And sometimes, when you believe in something, you have to make sacrifices."

"Sure," I said. "But an *F*? Your parents are going to kill you."

"No, they won't," Lilly said. "They'll just try to psycho-analyze me."

Which is true.

Oh, God. Here comes Tina.

I hope she doesn't remember—

She does.

We're going over to the Computer Club's booth right now.

I don't want to go to the Computer Club's booth. I already looked over there, and I know what's going on. Michael and Judith and the rest of the computer nerds are sitting there behind all these color monitors. When somebody comes up, they get to sit down in front of one of the monitors, and play a computer game the club designed where you walk through the school and all of the teachers are in funny costumes. Like Principal Gupta is wearing a leather dominatrix's outfit, and holding a whip, and Mr. Gianini is in footie pajamas with a teddy bear that looks exactly like him.

They used a different program when the club applied to be part of the Carnival, of course, so none of the teachers or administrators know what everyone is sitting there look-ing at. You would think they'd wonder why all of the kids are laughing so hard.

Whatever. I don't want to do it. I don't want to go any-where near it.

But Tina says I have to.

"Now's the perfect time to tell him," she says. "I mean, Kenny's nowhere to be seen."

Oh, God. This is what comes from telling your friends anything.

Well, I'm in the girls' room again. And I think I can state with certainty that this time, I'm never coming out.

No, I think I'll just stay in here until everyone has gone home. Only then will it be safe. Thank God I am leaving the country tomorrow. Maybe by the time I get back, everyone involved in this little incident will have forgotten about it.

But I doubt it. Not with my luck, anyway.

Why do these kinds of things always happen to me? I mean, seriously? What did I ever do to turn the gods against me? Why don't these kinds of things ever happen to Lana Weinberger? Why me? Why always *me*?

All right, so here's what happened.

I had no intention whatsoever of actually telling Michael anything. I mean, let me get that out right away. I was only going along with Tina because, well, it would have looked weird if I had completely avoided the Computer Club's booth. Plus Michael had asked me so many times to make sure I stopped by. So there was no way I could avoid it.

But I never intended to say a word about You-Know-What. I mean, Tina was just going to have to learn to live with the disappointment. You don't love somebody for, like, as long as I have loved Michael and then just go up to him at a school fair and be like, "Oh, by the way, yeah, I love you."

Okay? You don't *do* that.

But whatever. So I went up to the stupid booth with Tina. Everyone was all giggly and excited, because their program was so popular that there was this really long line to see it. But Michael saw us, and went, "Come on up!"

Like we were supposed to cut in front of all these other people. I mean, we did it, of course, but everyone behind us grumbled, and who can blame them? They'd been waiting a long time.

But I guess because of the thing the night before—you know, when I explained on national television that the only reason I'd done that clothing ad was because the designer was donating all the proceeds to Greenpeace—I have been noticeably more popular (positive comments so far: 243. Negative: 1. From Lana, of course). So the grumbling wasn't as bad as it could have been.

Anyway, Michael was all, "Here, Mia, sit at this one." And he pulled out a chair in front of this one computer monitor.

So I sat down and waited for the stupid thing to come on, and all around me other kids were laughing at what they were seeing on their screens. I just sat there thinking, for some reason, *Faint heart never won fair lady.*

Which was stupid, because, number one, I was NOT going to tell him I like him and number two, Michael is darkhaired, *not* fair. And he isn't a lady either, obviously.

Then I heard Judith go, "Wait, what are you doing?"

And then I heard Michael say, "No, that's okay. I have a special one for her."

Then the screen in front of my eyes flickered. I sighed. *Okay*, I thought. *Here goes the stupid teacher thing. Be sure to laugh so they think you like it.*

So I was sitting there, and I was actually kind of depressed, because I really didn't have anything to look forward to, if you think about it. I mean, everybody else was all excited, because later on they were going to the dance, but no one had asked me to the dance—not even my supposed boyfriend—so I didn't even have that to look forward to. And everyone else I knew was going skiing or to the Bahamas or wherever for Winter Break, but what did I get to do? Oh, hang out with a bunch of members of the Genovian Olive Growers

Society. I'm sure they are all really nice people, but come on.

And before I even leave for my boring trip to Genovia, I have to break up with Kenny, something I totally don't want to do, because I really do like him, and I don't want to hurt his feelings, but I guess I sort of have to.

Although I have to say, the fact that he still hasn't so much as mentioned the dance is making the idea of breaking up with him seem a lot less heinous.

*Then tomorrow,* I thought, *I'll leave for Europe on a plane with Dad and Grandmère, who still aren't speaking to each other* (and since I'm not speaking to Grandmère either, it should be a really fun flight), *and when I come back, knowing my luck, Michael and Judith will be engaged.*

That's what I was sitting there thinking in the split second the screen in front of me flickered. That, and, *You know, I'm not really in the mood to see any of my teachers in funny outfits.*

Only when the flickering stopped, that's not what I saw. What I saw instead was this castle.

Seriously. It was a castle, like out of the Knights of the Round Table, or *Beauty and the Beast*, or whatever. The picture zoomed in until we were over the castle walls and inside this courtyard, where there was a garden. And in the garden, all these big, fat, red roses were blooming. Some of the roses had lost their petals, and you could see them lying on the courtyard floor. It was really, really pretty, and I was like, *Hey, this is cooler than I thought it would be.*

And I sort of forgot I was sitting there in front of a computer monitor at the Winter Carnival, with like two dozen people all around me. I began to feel like I was actually *in* that garden.

Then this banner waved across the screen, in front of the roses, like it was blowing in the wind. The banner had some words written on it in gold leaf. When it stopped flapping, I could read what the words said:

> *Roses are red*
> *Violets are blue*
> *You may not know it*
> *But I love you, too*

I screamed and jumped up out of my chair, tipping it over behind me.

Everyone started laughing. I guess they thought I'd seen Principal Gupta in her leather catsuit.

Only Michael knew I hadn't.

And Michael wasn't laughing.

Only I couldn't look at Michael. I couldn't look anywhere, really, except at my own feet. Because I couldn't believe what had just happened. I mean, I couldn't process it. What did it *mean*? Did it mean Michael knew I was the one who'd been sending him those notes, and that he felt the same way?

Or did it mean he knew I was the one who'd been sending him those notes, and he was trying to get back at me, as a kind of joke?

I didn't know. All I knew was that if I didn't get out of there, I was going to start crying . . .

. . . and in front of everyone in the entire school.

I grabbed Tina by the arm and yanked her, *hard*, after me. I guess I was figuring I could tell her what I'd seen, and maybe *she'd* be able to figure out what it meant, since I sure couldn't.

Tina shrieked—I must have grabbed her harder than I thought—and I heard Michael call, "Mia!"

But I just kept going, lugging Tina behind me, and pushing through the crowd for the door, thinking only one thing:

Must get to the girls' room. Must get to the girls' room before I start bawling my head off.

Somebody, with about as much force as I'd grabbed Tina, grabbed me. I thought it was Michael. I knew if I so much as looked at him, I'd burst into big baby sobs. I said, "Get *off*," and jerked my arm away.

It was Kenny's voice that said, "But Mia, I *have* to talk to you!"

"Not *now*, Kenny," Tina said.

But Kenny was totally inflexible. He went, "Yes, *now*," and you could tell from his face he meant it.

Tina rolled her eyes and backed off. I stood there, my back to the Computer Club's booth, and prayed, *Please, please don't come over here, Michael. Please stay where you are. Please, please,* please *don't come over here.*

"Mia," Kenny said. He looked more uncomfortable than I'd ever seen him, and I've seen Kenny look plenty uncomfortable. He's an awkward kind of guy. "I just want to . . . I mean, I just want you to know. Well. That I know."

I stared at him. I had no idea what he was talking about. Seriously. I'd forgotten all about that hug he'd seen in the hallway. The one I'd given Michael. All I could think was, *Please don't come over here, Michael. Please don't come over here, Michael. . . .*

"Look, Kenny," I said. I don't even know how I got my tongue to work, I swear. I felt like a robot somebody had switched into the Off position. "This really isn't a good time. Maybe we could talk later—"

"Mia," Kenny said. He had a funny look on his face. "I *know*. I saw him."

I blinked.

And then I remembered. Michael, and the B-minus hug.

"Oh, Kenny," I said. "Really. That was just . . . I mean, there's nothing—"

"You don't have to worry," Kenny said. And then I realized why his face looked so funny. It was because he was wearing an expression on it that I had never seen before. At least, not on Kenny. The expression was resignation. "I won't tell Lilly."

Lilly! Oh, God! The last person in the world I wanted to know how I felt about Michael!

Maybe it wasn't too late. Maybe there was still a chance I could . . .

But no. No, I couldn't lie to him. For once in my life, I could not summon up a lie.

"Kenny," I said. "I am so, so sorry."

I didn't realize until I said it that it was too late to run for the girls' room: I had already started crying. My voice broke, and when I put my hands to my face, they came away wet.

Great. I was crying, and in front of the entire student body of Albert Einstein High School.

"Kenny," I said, sniffling. "I honestly meant to tell you. And I really do like you. I just don't . . . love you."

Kenny's face was very white, but he didn't start crying—not like me. Thank God. In fact, he even managed to smile a little in that weird, resigned way as he said, shaking his head, "Wow. I can't believe it. I mean, when it first hit me, I was like *no way*. Not Mia. No way would she do that to her best friend. But . . . well, I guess it explains a lot. About, um, us."

I couldn't look him in the face any longer. I felt like a worm. Worse than a worm, because worms are very environmentally helpful. I felt like . . . like . . .

Like a fruit fly.

"I guess I've suspected for a long time that there was someone else," Kenny went on. "You never . . . well, you never exactly seemed to return my ardor when we . . . you know."

I knew. Kissed. Nice of him to bring it up though, here in the gym, in front of everyone.

"I knew you just weren't saying anything because you didn't want to hurt my feelings," Kenny said. "That's the kind of girl you are. And that's why I put off asking you to the dance," Kenny admitted. "Because I figured you'd just say no. On account of you, you know, liking someone else. I mean, I know you'd never lie to me, Mia. You're the most honest person I've ever met."

HA! Was he joking? *Me?* Honest? Obviously, he did not have the slightest clue about my nostrils.

"That's how I know how much this must be tearing you up inside. I just think you'd better tell Lilly soon," Kenny said somberly. "I started to suspect, you know, at the restaurant. And if I figured it out, other people will, too. And you wouldn't want her to hear it from somebody else."

I had reached up to try to wipe some of my tears away with my sleeve, but paused with my hand only halfway there, and stared at him. "Restaurant? What restaurant?"

"You know," Kenny said, looking uncomfortable. "That day we all went to Chinatown. You and he sat next to each other. You kept laughing. . . . You looked pretty chummy."

Chinatown? But Michael hadn't gone with us that day to Chinatown. . . .

"And you know," Kenny said, "I'm not the only one who's noticed him leaving you those roses all week, either."

I blinked. I could barely see him through my tears. "W–what?"

"You know." He looked around, then dropped his voice to a whisper. "Boris. Leaving you all those roses. I mean, come on, Mia. If you two want to carry on behind Lilly's back, that's one thing, but—"

The roaring in my ears that had been there just after I'd read Michael's poem came back. BORIS. BORIS PELKOWSKI. My boyfriend just broke up with me because he thinks I am having an affair with BORIS PELKOWSKI.

BORIS PELKOWSKI, who always has food in his braces.

BORIS PELKOWSKI, who wears his sweaters tucked inside his pants.

BORIS PELKOWSKI, my best friend's boyfriend.

Oh, God. My life is so over.

I tried to tell him. You know, the truth. That Boris isn't my secret love, but my Secret Snowflake.

But Tina darted forward, grabbed me by the arm, and went, "Sorry, Kenny, Mia has to go now." Then she dragged me into the girls' room.

"I have to tell him," I kept saying, over and over, like a crazy person, as I tried to break free of her grip. "I have to tell him. I have to tell him the truth."

"No, you do not," Tina said, pushing me past the toilet stalls. "You two are broken up. Who cares why? You're through, and that's all that matters."

I blinked at my tear-stained reflection in the mirror above the sinks. I looked awful. Never in your life have you seen anyone who looked less like a princess than I did just then. Just looking at myself made me break out into a fresh new wave of tears.

Of course Tina says she's sure Michael wasn't trying to make fun of me. Of course she says that he must have figured out that I was the one who was sending him those cards and was trying to let me know that he felt the same way about me.

Only of course I can't believe that. Because if that were true—*if that were true*—why did he let me go? Why didn't he try to stop me?

Tina has pointed out that he did try. But my shrieking when I read his poem, and then running in tears from the room, might not have seemed to him like a very encouraging sign. In fact, it might have actually looked to him like I was displeased by what I'd seen. Furthermore, Tina pointed out, even if Michael had tried to go after me, there'd been Kenny cornering me on my way out. It had certainly looked as if the two of us were Having A Moment—which we most certainly were—and didn't wish to be disturbed.

All of which could be true.

But it could also be true that Michael had just been joking. It was a very mean joke, under the circumstances, but Michael doesn't know that I adore him with every fiber of my being. Michael doesn't know that I've been in love with him all my life. Michael doesn't know that without him, I will never, ever achieve self-actualization. I mean, to Michael, I'm just his kid sister's best friend. He probably didn't mean to be cruel. He probably thought he was being funny.

It isn't his fault that my life is over, and that I am never, ever leaving this bathroom.

I'll just wait until everybody is gone, and then I'll sneak out, and no one will see me again until next semester starts, by which time, hopefully, all of this will have blown over.

Or, better yet, maybe I'll just stay in Genovia. . . .

Hey, yeah. Why not?

I don't know why people can't just leave me alone.

Seriously. I may be done with finals, but I still have a lot to do. I mean, I have to pack, don't I? Don't people know that when you are leaving for your royal introduction to the people over whom you will one day reign, you have to do a lot of packing?

But no. No, people keep on calling, and e-mailing, and coming over.

Well, I'm not talking to anybody. I think I have made that perfectly clear. I am not speaking to Lilly or Tina or my dad or Mr. Gianini or my mother and ESPECIALLY not Michael, even though at last count, he'd called four times.

I am *way* too busy to talk to anybody.

And with my headphones on, I can't even hear them pounding on the door. It's kind of nice, I have to say.

People have a right to their privacy. If I want to go into my room and lock the door and not come out or have to deal with anyone, I should have a right to. People should *not* be allowed to take the hinges off of my door and *remove* it. That is completely unfair.

But I have found a way to foil them. I am out on the fire escape. It's about thirty degrees out here, and snowing, by the way, but guess what? So far no one has followed me.

Fortunately I bought one of those pens that's also a flashlight, so I can see to write. The sun went down a while ago, and I have to admit, my butt is freezing. But it's actually sort of nice out here. All you can hear is the hiss of the snow as it lands on the metal of the fire escape, and the occasional siren or car alarm. It is restful, in a way.

And you know what I'm finding out? I need a rest. Big time.

Really. I need to like, go and lie on a beach somewhere, or something.

There's a nice beach in Genovia. Really. With white sand, palm trees, the whole bit.

Too bad while I'm there, I'm never going to have time to visit it, since I'm going to be too busy christening battleships, or whatever.

But if I *lived* in Genovia . . . you know, moved there, and lived there full time . . .

Oh, I'll miss my mom, of course. I've already considered that. She's leaned out the window about twenty times already, begging me to come inside or at least put on a coat. My mom's a nice lady. I'll really miss her.

But she can come visit me in Genovia. At least up until her eighth month. Then air travel might be a little risky.

195

But she can come after my baby brother or sister is born. That would be nice.

And Mr. G, he's okay, too. He just leaned out and asked if I wanted any of the four-alarm chili he just made. He left out the meat, he says, just for me.

That was nice of him. He can come visit me in Genovia, too.

It will be nice to live there. I can hang out with my dad all the time. He's not such a bad guy, either, once you get to know him. He wants me to come in off the fire escape, too. I guess my mom must have called him. He says he's really proud of me, on account of the press conference and my B minus in Algebra and all. He wants to take me out to dinner to celebrate. We can go to the Zen Palate, he says. A totally vegetarian restaurant. Isn't that nice of him?

Too bad he let Lars take my door down, or I might have gone with him.

Ronnie, our next door neighbor, just looked out her window and saw me. Now she wants to know what I'm doing, sitting out on the fire escape in December.

I told her I needed some privacy, and that this appears to be the only way I can get it.

Ronnie went, "Honey, don't I know how that is."

She said I was going to freeze without a coat though, and offered me her mink. I politely declined, as I cannot wear the skins of dead animals.

So she loaned me her electric blanket, which she has plugged into the outlet beneath her air conditioner. I must say, this is an improvement.

Ronnie's getting ready to go out. It's nice to watch her put on her makeup. As she does it, she keeps up a running conversation with me through her open window. She asked me if I was having trouble at school, and if that was why I'm on the fire escape, and I said I was. She asked what kind, and I told her. I told her I am being persecuted: that I am in love with my best friend's brother, but that to him it is apparently all this really big joke. Oh, and also that everyone apparently thinks I am having an affair with a mouth-breathing violinist who happens to be my best friend's boyfriend.

Ronnie shook her head and said it was good to know things haven't changed since she was in high school. She says she knows what it is like to be persecuted, because Ronnie used to be a man.

I told Ronnie that it really doesn't matter, because I'm moving to Genovia. Ronnie said she was sorry to hear that. She'll miss me, as I have really improved conditions in the apartment building's incinerator room since I insisted on installing separate recycling bins for newspapers and cans and bottles.

Then Ronnie said she has to go because she's meeting her boyfriend for cocktails at the Carlyle. She said I could keep using the electric blanket, though, so long as I remember to return it when I'm done.

God. Even my next door neighbor, who used to be a man, has a boyfriend. WHAT IS WRONG WITH ME????

Uh-oh. I hear footsteps in my room. Who's coming now?

*Friday, December 19, 7:30 p.m.*

Well. You could knock me over with a feather.

Guess who just came out onto the fire escape and sat with me for half an hour?

Grandmère.

I'm not even kidding.

I was sitting here, feeling all depressed, when all of a sudden this big furry sleeve appeared out my window, and then a foot in a high-heeled shoe, and then a big blonde head, and next thing I knew, Grandmère was sitting there, blinking at me from the depths of her full-length chinchilla.

"Amelia," she said, in her most no-nonsense tone. "What are you doing out here? It's snowing. Come back inside."

I was shocked. Shocked that Grandmère would even consider coming out onto the fire escape (it's an indelicate thing for a princess to mention, but there is actually a lot of bird poop out here), but also that she would dare to speak to me, after what she did.

But she addressed that issue right away.

"I understand that you are upset with me," she said. "And you have a right to be. But I want you to know that what I did, I did for you."

"Oh, right!" Even though I swore I was never going to speak to her again, I couldn't help myself. "Grandmère, how can you possibly say that? You completely humiliated me!"

"I didn't mean to," Grandmère said. "I meant to show you that you are just as pretty as those girls in the magazines you are always wishing you look like. It's important that you know that you are not this hideous creature that you apparently think you are."

"Grandmère," I said. "That's nice of you and all—I guess—but you shouldn't have done it that way."

"What other way could I do it?" Grandmère demanded.

198

"You will not pose for any of the magazines that have offered to send photographers. Not for *Vogue*, or *Harper's Bazaar*. Don't you understand that what Sebastiano said about your bone structure is really true? You really are quite beautiful, Amelia. If only you'd just have a little more confidence in yourself, show off once in a while. Think how quickly that boy you like would leave the housefly girl for you!"

"Fruit fly," I said. "And Grandmère, I told you, Michael likes her because she's really smart. They have a lot of stuff in common, like computers. It has nothing to do with how she looks."

"Oh, Mia," Grandmère said. "Don't be naive."

Poor Grandmère. It really wasn't fair to blame her, because she comes from such a different world. In Grandmère's world, women are valued for being great beauties—or, if they aren't great beauties, they are revered for dressing impeccably. What they do, like for a living, isn't important, because most of them don't do anything. Oh, maybe they do some charity work, or whatever, but that's it.

Grandmère doesn't understand, of course, that today being a great beauty doesn't count for much. Oh, it matters in Hollywood, of course, and on the runways in Milan. But nowadays, people understand that perfect looks are the result of DNA, something the person has nothing to do with. It's not like it's any great accomplishment, being beautiful. That's just genetics.

No, what matters today is what you do with the brain *behind* those perfect blue eyes, or brown eyes, or green, or whatever. In Grandmère's day, a girl like Judith, who could clone fruit flies, would be viewed as a piteous freak, unless she managed to clone fruit flies *and* look stunning in Dior.

And even in this remarkably enlightened age, girls like Judith still don't get as much attention as girls like Lana— which isn't fair, since cloning fruit flies is probably way more important than having totally perfect hair.

The really pathetic people are the ones like me: I can't clone fruit flies, *and* I've got bad hair.

But that's okay. I'm used to it by now.

Grandmère's the one who still needs convincing that I am an absolutely hopeless case.

"Look," I said to Grandmère. "I told you. Michael is not the type of guy who is going to be impressed because I'm in a Sunday *Times* supplement in a strapless ballgown. *That's why I like him.* If he were the kind of guy who was impressed by stuff like that, I wouldn't want anything to do with him."

Grandmère didn't look very convinced.

"Well," she said. "Perhaps you and I must agree to disagree. In any case, Amelia, I came over to apologize. I never meant to distress you. I meant only to show you what you can do, if you'd only try." She spread her gloved hands apart. "And look how well I succeeded. Why, you planned and executed an entire press conference, all on your own!"

I couldn't help smiling a little at that one. "Yes," I said. "I did."

"And," Grandmère said, "I understand that you passed Algebra."

I grinned wider. "Yes. I did."

"Now," Grandmère said, "there is only one thing left for you to do."

I nodded. "I know. I've been thinking a lot about it, and I think it might be best if I extended my stay in Genovia. Like maybe I could just live there from now on. What do you think about that?"

Grandmère's expression, I could see in the light coming from my room, was one of disbelief.

"Live in . . . live in Genovia?" For once, I'd caught her off guard. "What are you talking about?"

"You know," I said. "They have schools there. I could

just finish ninth grade there. And then maybe I could go to one of those Swiss boarding schools you're always going on about."

Grandmère just stared at me. "You'd hate it."

"No," I said. "It might be fun. No boys, right? That would be great. I mean, I'm kind of sick of boys right now."

Grandmère shook her head. "But your friends . . . your mother . . ."

"Well," I said, reasonably. "They could come visit."

Then Grandmère's face hardened. She peered at me from between the heavily mascaraed slits her eyes had become.

"Amelia Mignonette Grimaldi Renaldo," she said. "You are running away from something, aren't you?"

I shook my head innocently. "Oh, no, Grandmère," I said. "Really. I'd like to live in Genovia. It'd be neat."

"NEAT?" Grandmère stood up. Her high heels went through the slots between the metal bars of the fire escape, but she didn't notice. She pointed imperiously at my window.

"You get inside right now," she ordered, in a voice I had never heard her use before.

I have to admit, I was so startled, I did exactly what she said. I unplugged Ronnie's electric blanket and crawled right back into my room. Then I stood there while Grandmère crawled back in, too.

"You," she said, when she'd straightened out her skirt, "are a princess of the royal house of Renaldo. A princess," she said, going to my closet, and rifling through it, "does not shirk her responsibilities. Nor does she run at the first sign of adversity."

"Um, Grandmère," I said. "What happened today was hardly the first sign of adversity, okay? What happened today was the last straw. I can't take it anymore, Grandmère. I'm getting out."

Grandmère pulled from my closet the dress Sebastiano had designed for me to wear to the dance. You know, the one that was supposed to make Michael forget that I am his little sister's best friend.

"Nonsense," Grandmère said.

That was all.

Just nonsense. Then she stood there, tapping her toes, staring at me.

"Grandmère," I said. Maybe it was all that time I'd spent outside. Or maybe it was that I was pretty sure my mom and Mr. G and my dad were all in the next room, listening. How could they not be? There was no *door*, or anything, to separate my room from the living room.

"You don't understand," I said. "I can't go back there."

"All the more reason," Grandmère said, "for you to go."

"No," I said. "First of all, I don't even have a date for the dance, okay? And P.S., only losers go to dances without dates."

"You are not a loser, Amelia," Grandmère said. "You are a princess. And princesses do not run away when things become difficult. They throw their shoulders back, and they face what disaster awaits them head on. Bravely, and without complaint."

I said, "Hello, we are not talking about marauding visigoths, okay, Grandmère? We are talking about an entire high school that seems to think that I am in love with Boris Pelkowski."

"Which is precisely," Grandmère said, "why you must show them that it doesn't matter to you what they think."

"Why can't I show them that it doesn't matter by not going?"

"Because that," Grandmère said, "is the cowardly way. And you, Mia, as you have shown amply this past week, are not a coward. Now get dressed."

I don't know why I did what she said. Maybe it was because somewhere deep inside, I knew that for once, Grandmère was right.

Or maybe it was because secretly, I guess I was a little curious to see what would happen.

But I think the real reason was because, for the first time in my entire life, Grandmère didn't call me Amelia.

No. She called me Mia.

And because of my stupid sentimentalism, I am in a car right now, going back to stupid, crappy Albert Einstein High School, the dust from which I thought I'd managed to shake permanently from my feet not four hours ago.

But no. Oh, no. I'm going back, in the stupid velvet party dress Sebastiano designed for me. I'm going back, with no date. I'm going back, and I will probably be ridiculed for being the dateless biological freak that I am.

I am, however, a princess, and apparently that means I am expected to take whatever is dished out at me, no matter how cruel, unfair, or undeserved it might be.

And regardless of what happens, I can always comfort myself with the knowledge of one thing:

Tomorrow, I will be thousands of miles away from all of this.

Oh, God. We're here.

I think I'm going to be sick.

When I was about to turn six years old, all I wanted for my birthday was a cat.

I didn't care what kind of cat. I just wanted one. I wanted a cat of my very own. We had been to visit my mom's parents at their farm in Indiana, and they had a lot of cats. One of them had had kittens, little fluffy orange and white ones, which purred loudly when I held them under my chin, and liked to curl up inside the bib of my overalls and take naps. More than anything in the world, I wanted to keep one of those kittens.

I should mention that at the time, I had a thumb-sucking problem. My mother had tried everything to get me to stop sucking my thumb, including buying me a Barbie, in spite of her fundamental stand against Barbie and all that she stands for, as a sort of bribe. Nothing worked.

So when I started whining to her about wanting a kitten, my mom came up with a plan. She told me she would get me a kitten for my birthday if I quit sucking my thumb.

Which I did, immediately. I wanted a cat of my own *that badly.*

Yet, as my birthday rolled around, I had my doubts my mother would live up to her end of the bargain. For one thing, even at the age of six, I knew my mom wasn't the most responsible person. Why else was our electricity always being turned off? And about half the time I would show up at school wearing a skirt AND pants, because my mother let *me* decide what to wear. So I wasn't sure she'd remember about the kitten—or that, if she did remember, she'd know where to get one.

So as you can imagine, when the morning of my sixth birthday rolled around, I wasn't holding out much hope.

But when my mother came into my bedroom holding

this tiny ball of yellow and white fur, and plopped it into my chest, and I looked into Louie's (he didn't become Fat Louie until about twenty-something pounds later) great big blue eyes (this was before they turned green), I knew a joy such as I had never known before in my life, and never expected to feel again.

That is, until last night.

I am totally serious.

Last night was the best night of my ENTIRE life. After that whole fiasco with Sebastiano and the photos, I thought I would never ever feel anything like gratitude to Grandmère EVER again.

But she was SO RIGHT to make me go to that dance. I am SO GLAD I went back to Albert Einstein, the best, the loveliest school in the whole country, if not the whole world!!!!!!!

Okay, here's what happened:

Lars and I pulled up in front of the school. There were twinkly white lights in all the windows, that I guess were supposed to represent icicles, or whatever.

I was sure I was going to throw up and I mentioned this to Lars. He said I couldn't possibly throw up because to his certain knowledge I hadn't eaten anything since the Entenmann's cake way before lunch, and that was probably all digested by now. With that piece of encouraging information, he escorted me up the steps and into the school.

There were masses of people teeming around the coat check in the front entrance. Lars checked our coats while I stood there waiting for someone to come up and ask me what I was doing there without a date. All that happened, however, was that Lilly-and-Boris and Tina-and-Dave descended upon me and started acting all nice and said how happy they were that I'd come (Tina told me later that she'd already explained to everyone that Kenny and I had broken up, although she hadn't told them why, THANK GOD).

So, fortified, by my friends, I went into the gym, which was decorated all wintry, with cut-out paper snowflakes, one of those disco balls, and fake snow everywhere, which I must say looked a lot whiter and cleaner than the snow that was starting to pile up on the ground outside.

There were tons of people there. I saw Lana and Josh (ugh), Justin Baxendale with his usual flock of adoring fans, and Shameeka and Ling Su and a bunch of other people. Even Kenny was there, though when he saw me, he turned bright red and turned around and started talking to this girl from our Bio class. Oh well.

Everyone was there, except the one person I'd been most dreading. Or hoping to see. I didn't know which.

Then I saw Judith Gershner. She had changed out of her overalls and looked quite pretty in this red Laura Ashley–ish dress.

But she wasn't dancing with Michael. She was dancing with some boy I'd never seen before.

So I looked around for Lilly, and finally spotted her using one of the pay phones. I went up to her and was like, "Where's your brother?"

Lilly hung up the phone. "How should I know?" she demanded. "It's not my turn to baby-sit him."

Oddly comforted by her demeanor—which simply proved that no matter how much other things change, Lilly always stayed the same—I went, "Well, Judith Gershner is here, so I just figured—"

"For God's sake," Lilly said. "How many times do I have to tell you? *Michael and Judith are not going out.*"

I went, "Oh, right. Then why have they spent every waking moment together for the past two weeks?"

"Because they were working on that stupid computer program for the Carnival," she said. "Besides, Judith

Gershner already has a boyfriend." Lilly grabbed me by the shoulders and turned me around so I could see Judith on the dance floor. "He goes to Trinity."

I looked at Judith Gershner as she slow-danced with a boy who looked a lot like Kenny, only older and not as uncoordinated.

"Oh," I said.

"*Oh* is right," Lilly said. "I don't know what is wrong with you today, but I can't deal with you when you're acting like such a freak. Sit down right here—" She pulled out a chair. "And don't you dare get up. I want to know where to find you when I need to."

I didn't even ask Lilly why she might need to find me. I just sat down. I felt like I couldn't stand up anymore. I was *that* tired.

It wasn't that I was disappointed. I mean, I didn't want to see Michael. At least, part of me didn't.

Another part of me *really* wanted to see him and ask him just what he'd meant by that poem.

But I was sort of afraid of the answer.

Because it might not be the one I was hoping it would be.

After a while, Lars and Wahim came and sat down next to me. I felt like a complete tool. I mean, there I was, sitting at a dance with two bodyguards, who were deep in a discussion about the advantages versus the disadvantages of rubber bullets. Nobody was asking me to dance. Nobody would, either. I mean, I'm a huge, colossal loser. A huge, colossal loser without a date.

Who, by the way, is supposedly in love with Boris Pelkowski.

Why was I even staying? I had done what Grandmère said. I had shown up. I had proved to everyone that I wasn't a coward. Why couldn't I leave? I mean, if I wanted to?

I stood up. I said to Lars, "Come on. We've been here

long enough. I still have a lot of packing to do. Let's go."

Lars said okay, and started to get up. Then he stopped. I saw that he was looking at something behind me. I turned around.

And there was Michael.

He had obviously just gotten there. He was out of breath. His bow tie wasn't tied. And there was still snow in his hair.

"I didn't think you were coming," he said.

I knew my face had gone as red as Judith Gershner's dress. But there wasn't anything I could do about that. I said, "Well, I almost didn't."

He said, "I called you a bunch of times. Only you wouldn't come to the phone."

I said, "I know." I was wishing the floor of the gym would open up, like in *It's a Wonderful Life*, and that I'd fall into the pool underneath it and drown and not have to have this conversation.

"Mia," he said. "With that thing today. I didn't mean to make you cry."

Or the floor would open and I could just fall, and keep falling, forever and ever and ever. That would be okay, too. I stared at the floor, willing it to crack apart and swallow me up.

"It didn't." I lied. "I mean, it wasn't that. It was something Kenny said."

"Yeah," Michael said. "Well, I heard you two broke up."

Yeah. Probably by now the whole school had. Now, I knew, my face was even redder than Judith's dress.

"The thing is," Michael went on, "I knew it was you. Who was leaving those cards."

If he had reached inside my chest, pulled out my heart, flung it to the floor, and kicked it across the room, it could not possibly have hurt as much as hearing that. I could feel

208

my eyes filling up with tears all over again.

"You did?" You know, it's one thing to have your heart broken. But to have it happen at a school dance, in front of everyone . . . well, that's harsh.

"Of course I did," he said. He sounded impatient. "Lilly told me."

For the first time, I looked up into his face.

"*Lilly* told you?" I cried. "How did *she* know?"

He waved his hand. "I don't know. Your friend Tina told her, I guess. But that's not important."

I looked around the gym and saw Lilly and Tina on the far side of it, both staring in my direction. When they saw me looking at them, they turned around really fast and pretended to be deeply absorbed in conversation with their dates.

"I'm going to kill them," I murmured.

Michael reached out and grabbed both my shoulders. "Mia," he said, giving me a little shake. "It doesn't *matter*. What matters is that I meant what I wrote. And I thought you did, too."

I didn't think I could have heard him right. I went, "Of course I meant it."

He shook his head. "Then why did you freak out like that today at the Carnival?"

I stammered, "Well, because . . . because . . . I thought . . . I thought you were making fun of me."

"Never," he said.

And that's when he did it.

No fuss. No asking my permission. No hesitation whatsoever. He just leaned down and kissed me, right on the lips.

And I found out, right then, that Tina was right:

It *isn't* gross if you're in love with the guy.

In fact, it's the nicest thing in the whole world.

And do you know what the best part is?

I mean, aside from Michael being in love with me, and

having kept it a secret almost as long as I have, if not longer?

And Lilly knowing all along but not saying anything up until a few days ago because she found it an interesting social experiment to see how long it would take us to figure it out on our own (a long time, it turned out)?

And the fact that Michael's going to Columbia next year, which is only a few subway stops away, so I'll still be able to see him as much as I want?

Oh, and Lana walking by while we were kissing, and going, in this disgusted voice, "Oh, God, get a room, would you please?"

And slow dancing with him all night long, until Lilly finally came up and said, "Come on you guys, it's snowing so hard, if we don't leave now, we'll never get home"?

And kissing good night outside the stoop to my loft, with the snow falling all around us (and grumpy Lars complaining he was getting cold)?

No, the best part is that we moved right into Frenching without any trouble at all. Tina was right—it just seemed perfectly natural.

And now the royal Genovian flight attendant says we have to put away our tray tables for takeoff, so I'll have to quit writing in a minute.

Dad says if I don't stop talking about Michael, he's going to go sit up front with the pilot for the flight.

Grandmère says she can't get over the change in me. She says I seem taller. And you know, maybe I am. She thinks it's because I'm wearing another one of Sebastiano's original creations, designed just for me, just like the dress that was supposed to make Michael see me as more than just his little sister's best friend . . . except that it turned out he did anyway. But I know that's not it.

And it isn't love, either. Well, not entirely.

I'll tell you what it is: self-actualization.

Well, that and the fact that it turns out I'm really a princess, after all. I must be, because guess what?

I'm living happily ever after.

# The Princess Diaries
## Volume IV

*"If I was a princess," she murmured, "I could scatter largess to the populace. But even if I am only a pretend princess, I can invent little things to do for people. I'll pretend that to do things for people is scattering largess."*

A LITTLE PRINCESS
*Frances Hodgson Burnett*

## MY NEW YEAR'S RESOLUTIONS
## BY PRINCESS AMELIA MIGNONETTE
## GRIMALDI THERMOPOLIS RENALDO,
## AGE 14 YEARS AND 8 MONTHS

1. I will stop biting my fingernails, including the fake ones.
2. I will stop lying. Grandmère knows when I am lying anyway, thanks to my traitorous nostrils, which flare every time I tell a fib, so it's not like there is even a point in trying to be less than truthful.
3. I will never veer from prepared script while delivering televised address to the Genovian public.
4. I will stop accidentally saying *merde* in front of the ladies-in-waiting.
5. I will stop asking François, my Genovian bodyguard, to teach me French swear words.
6. I will apologize to the Genovian Olive Growers Association for that thing with the pits.
7. I will apologize to the Royal Chef for slipping Grandmère's dog that slice of foie gras (even though I have told the palace kitchen repeatedly that I do not eat liver).
8. I will stop lecturing the Royal Genovian Press Corps on the evils of smoking. If they all wish to develop lung cancer, that is their prerogative.
9. I will achieve self-actualization.

10. I will stop thinking so much about Michael
    Moscovitz.

Oh, wait. It's okay for me to think about Michael
Moscovitz, BECAUSE HE IS MY BOYFRIEND
NOW!!!!!!!!

MT + MM = TRUE LOVE 4-EVER

You know, I am supposed to be on vacation. Seriously. I mean, this is my winter break. I am supposed to be having fun, mentally recharging for the coming semester, which is not going to be easy, as I will be moving on to Algebra II, not to mention Health and Safety class. Everybody at school was all, *Oh, you are so lucky, you get to spend Christmas in a castle being waited on hand and foot.*

Well, first of all, there is nothing so great about living in a castle. Because guess what? Castles are totally old. And yeah, it's not like this one was built in 4 A.D., or whenever it was my ancestress Princess Rosagunde first became ruler of Genovia. But it was still built in, like, the 1600s, and let me tell you what they didn't have in the 1600s:

1. Cable
2. DSL
3. Toilets

Which is not to say there isn't a satellite dish now, but, hello, this is my dad's place; the only channels he has got programmed are, like, CNN, CNN Financial News, and the golf channel. Where is MTV 2, I ask you? Where is the Lifetime Movie Channel for Women?

Not that it matters because I am spending all my time being run off my feet. It isn't as if I ever even get a free moment to pick up a remote and go, "Ho hum, I wonder if there's a Tracey Gold movie on."

Oh, yeah, and the toilets? Let me just tell you that back in the 1600s, they didn't know so much about sewage. So now, four hundred years later, if you put one square too much toilet paper in the bowl and try to flush, you create a mini indoor tsunami.

So that's it. That is my life in Genovia.

Every other kid I know is spending his or her winter break in Aspen skiing, or in Miami getting tanned.

But me? What am *I* doing for my winter break?

Well, here are the highlights from the new *datebook* Grandmère gave me for Christmas (what girl wouldn't love to get a *datebook* for Christmas?) of what I have done so far:

### Sunday, December 21
Royal Daily Schedule

Arrived in Genovia. Due to large bagful of Skittles consumed on flight over, almost barfed on official Genovian welcome committee who came to airport to greet me as I disembarked from the plane.

One full day since I last saw Michael. Tried calling him at his grandparents' house in Boca Raton, where the Moscovitzes have gone for winter break, but no one answered, perhaps because of time difference, Genovia being six hours ahead of Florida.

While touring naval cruiser, the *Prince Phillipe*, tripped over anchor, accidentally knocking Admiral Pepin into the Genovian harbor. He was okay, though. They fished him out with a harpoon.

But why am I the only one in this country who thinks pollution is an important issue? If people are going to dock their yachts in the Genovian harbor, they really ought to pay attention to what they are throwing overboard. I mean, porpoises get their noses stuck in those plastic six-pack holders all the time, and then they starve to death because they can't open their mouths to eat. All people have to do is snip the loops before they throw the holders out, and everything would be fine.

Well, all right, not *everything*, since you shouldn't be throwing trash overboard in the first place.

I simply cannot stand idly by while helpless sea creatures are being abused by a bunch of Bain de Soleil addicts in search of that perfect Saint-Tropez tan.

Two days since last saw Michael. Tried calling him twice. First time, no answer. Second time, Michael's grandmother answered and said I had just missed him, as Michael had gone to the pharmacy to pick up his grandfather's prescription foot powder. This is so like him, always thinking of others before himself.

At breakfast with Genovian Olive Growers Association, mentioned unseasonable drought afflicting Mediterranean area must be the "pits." No one seemed to think this joke particularly amusing, particularly members of Olive Growers Association.

Three days since last saw Michael. No time to call due to pit controversy.

Gave televised Christmas Eve greeting to Genovian public. Strayed somewhat from prepared speech by mentioning amount of revenue generated in five boroughs of New York City by parking meters, and expressed belief that installing parking meters in Genovia would contribute greatly to national economy, while also discouraging cheapskate day-trippers from venturing across our border. Still have no idea why Grandmère was so mad about the whole thing. New York City parking meters are NOT hideously ugly blights on landscape. Most of the time, I never even notice them at all.

Four days SLSM (since last saw Michael)

SPOKE TO MICHAEL AT LAST!!!!!! Was finally able to get
through to him. Conversation somewhat stilted, however, as
my father, grandmother, and cousin René were all in room
from which I was calling, and Michael's parents, grandparents, and sister were in room in which he received call.

He asked me if I got anything good for Christmas, and
I said no, nothing but a *datebook* and a scepter. What I
wanted was a cell phone. Asked Michael if he got anything
good for Hannukah, and he said no, nothing but a color
printer. Which is still better than what I got, if you ask me.
Although scepter excellent for pushing back cuticles.

I am so relieved that Michael hasn't forgotten all about
me. I know my boyfriend is vastly superior to all the other
members of his species—guys, I mean. But everyone knows
that guys are like dogs—their short-term memory is completely nil. You tell them your favorite fictional character is
Xena, Warrior Princess, and next thing you know, they are
going on about how your favorite fictional character is Xica
of Telemundo. Boys just don't know any better, on account
of how their brains are too filled up with stuff about modems
and *Star Trek Voyager* and Limp Bizkit and all.

Michael is no exception to this rule. Oh, I know he is
co-valedictorian of his class and got a perfect score on his
SATs and was accepted early decision to one of the most
prestigious universities in the country. But you know it took
him about five million years even to admit he liked me. And
that was only after I'd sent him all these anonymous love
letters. Which turned out not to be so anonymous because
he fully knew it was me the whole time, thanks to all of my
friends, including his little sister, having such exceptionally
large mouths.

But whatever. I am just saying, five days is a long time to go without a word from your one true love. I mean, Tina Hakim Baba's boyfriend, Dave Farouq El-Abar, sometimes goes that long without calling her, and Tina always becomes convinced that Dave's met a girl who is better than she is. She even confronted him about it once, telling him that she loved him and that it hurt her when he didn't call . . . which only caused him not to call anymore, since Dave turns out to be commitment-phobic.

It would be very easy for Michael to meet a girl who is better than me. I mean, there must be millions of girls out there who have things actually going for them, aside from being a princess, and who don't have to spend their holidays cooped up in a palace with their crazy grandma and her freakish hairless toy poodle.

And even though when Tina starts insisting Dave's dumping her, and we all go, "Oh, he's not," I think I am starting to know how she feels.

Talked to Mom and Mr. Gianini. They are both doing fine, though my mom still won't let the doctor tell her what it is she's having—a boy or a girl. Mom says she doesn't want to know, since if it's a boy she won't push, due to not wanting to bring another Y-chromosomed oppressor into the world (Mr. G says that is just the hormones talking, but I'm not so sure. My mom can be pretty anti–Y-chromosome when she puts her mind to it). They put Fat Louie up to the phone so I could wish him a merry Christmas, and he growled with annoyance, so I know he is doing fine as well.

5 DSLSM

Forced to watch father and cousin René play in charity golf tournament against Tiger Woods. Tiger won (no surprise) as Dad is middle-aged and Prince René confessed to having attended grappa-tasting party the night before. Only sport more boring than golf is polo. Going to be forced to watch Dad and cousin René play *that* next month—although technically anyway, René is barely even my cousin. He's, like, eleven hundred times removed.

And even though he is a prince, he is no longer allowed by Italian law to set foot in his native land, due to the social-ists running all members of the Italian royal family out of town. Poor René's ancestral palace now belongs to a famous shoe designer, who has turned it into a resort for wealthy Americans to come for the weekend and make their own pasta and drink two-hundred-year-old balsamic vinegar.

René doesn't seem to mind, though, because here in Genovia everyone still calls him His Highness Prince René, and he is extended every privilege given a member of a royal household.

Still, just because René is four years older than me and a prince and a freshman at some French business school, doesn't mean he has the right to patronize me. I mean, I believe gambling is morally wrong, and the fact that René spends so many hours at the roulette wheel instead of uti-lizing his time in a more productive fashion irks me.

I mentioned this to him. It just seems to me that René needs to realize there is more to life than racing around in his Alfa Romeo, or swimming in the palace indoor pool wearing nothing but one of those little black Speedos, which are very stylish here in Europe (I asked my dad to please, for the love of all that is holy, stick to trunks, which, thankfully, he has).

And okay, René just laughed at me.

But at least I can rest easy knowing I have done everything I can to show one extremely self-absorbed prince the error of his profligate ways.

6 DSLSM

### Saturday, December 27
#### Royal Daily Schedule

V. depressing day, as twenty-fifth anniversary of Grandpère's death. Had to hang wreath on grave, wear black veil, etc. Veil stuck to lip gloss, could not get it off by blowing, finally had to pull it off, causing hat to be swept by wind into Genovian harbor. Prince René fished it out with the help of some friendly topless sunbathers, but hat will clearly never be the same.

7 DSLSM

### Sunday, December 28
#### Royal Daily Schedule

Prince René was caught entertaining friendly topless sunbathers in pool house. Major ballistics from my dad, who thinks at eighteen René should be aware that he has a rep for being "Prince William of the Continent," minus the crown jewels, as René's side of the family have only name and not fortune to go with it anymore, and that those girls were only using him. René says he doesn't mind being used in that fashion, and if *he* doesn't mind, why should Dad? This only made my dad madder, however. Should have warned René it isn't wise to antagonize Dad when vein in center of forehead is throbbing, but there was no time.

Tried calling Michael; got busy signal for four hours. He must have been online. Would have e-mailed him, but only computers in palace with Internet access in administrative offices, and doors were locked.

8 DSLSM

*Monday, December 29*
*Royal Daily Schedule*

Met with Genovian casino operators. Was discouraged by their insistence on maintaining valet parking for their patrons. Explained substantial increase in revenue generated by parking meters, but was rebuffed.

Asked Dad for own key to administrative offices, so that I can e-mail Michael whenever I want, but he rebuffed me, too, due to René having been caught in administrative offices last week, photocopying his nether region. Assured Dad I would never do something this asinine, not being homeless Speedo-wearing prince filled with testosterone, but argument clearly fell on deaf ears.

Nine days since I last saw Michael, and I think I am going INSANE!!!!!!!!!!!!!!!!!!

*Tuesday, December 30*
*Royal Daily Schedule*

MESSAGE FROM MICHAEL via palace phone operators. Says, *Miss you, will try to call at bonne nuit.* Asked palace operators if they are sure this is what Michael said, and they insist it was. Except this message makes no sense. *Bonne nuit* means "good night," it is not a time. Possibly there is word in Klingon that sounds like *bonne nuit*? No time to call Michael myself, however, as was ensconced all day long with Genovian Minister of Defense, learning what to do in unlikely case of military incursion by hostile enemy forces.

10 DSLSM

Posed for royal portrait. Was instructed not to move, and especially not to smile. Was very hard not to, however, as Rommel, Grandmère's toy poodle, was wandering around with one of those plastic cones around his head so he won't lick away what is left of his fur. Rommel is the only dog I know with an obsessive-compulsive disorder that is causing him to lick himself bald. The American vets all thought Rommel's hair loss was due to allergies. Then, when we got to Genovia, the Royal Vet was all, "*Alors! Eet is Oh Cee Dee!*"

I do not like to make fun of the plight of any four-legged creature, but Rommel was funny, the way he'd lost his peripheral vision and kept bumping into suits of armor and stuff.

Royal portrait painter says he despairs of me. Let me out early to attend palace New Year's party. Was big letdown, due to not having Michael there to kiss at midnight. Tried calling him, but Moscovitzes must have been out at some beach or pool party, as no one answered.

You know what they have a lot of in Florida? Beach and pool parties. You know who goes to beach and pool parties? Girls in bikinis. Like the girls from that movie *Blue Crush*. Like that one, Kate Bosworth, who had the one blue eye and the one brown eye and the tiny shorts. Yeah, that one. How is anyone supposed to compete against a surfer girl with one blue eye and one brown eye, I'd like to know?????

René tried to kiss me at midnight, but I told him to go kiss Grandmère instead. He'd had so much champagne, he actually did it. Grandmère hit him with a decorative swan carved from a pineapple.

11 DSLSM

GOT E-MAIL FROM MICHAEL!!!!!!! René stole key to administrative offices because he said he had to "look some things up" on Netscape (he was fully scoring people on Are You Hot or Not—I caught him) and I happened to be walking by on my way to the indoor palace pool, so I demanded to be let in. René had too big of a headache from all the champagne he drank last night to fight me on the matter.

So I got online and there was this e-mail from Michael!!!!!!!! It turns out he was NOT at a party with Kate Bosworth–like girls last night:

Mia (he wrote), sorry to have missed your call, I was at my grand-parents' retirement complex's New Year's bash (they played Ricky Martin and thought they were on the cutting edge). Didn't you get my message? Well, anyway, happy New Year and I really miss you and all of that.

P.S. Are they keeping you locked in a tower over there or what? Because even prisoners get phone privileges. Am I going to have to come to Genovia and climb up your hair to get you out or something?

Has there ever BEEN a more romantic note than this? He really misses me and *all of that*! And you know what *all of that* means. Love. Right? Isn't that what *all of that* means?

Made mistake of asking René. He said a man who isn't willing to put his true feelings for a woman down on paper isn't a true man at all.

I told him it wasn't paper, just e-mail, which is different. Isn't it?

Spent all day visiting patients at Genovian General Hospital. V. depressing, not because of patients, but because of the clown that the hospital hired to cheer up the sick children. HATE CLOWNS!!!! Clowns v. scary to me ever since I read that Stephen King book *It*, which was made into a TV movie starring that guy from *The Waltons*. It is awful the way writers can take a perfectly innocent thing like a clown and turn it into vessel of evil! Had to spend entire time in hospital dodging clown, just in case he was spawn of Satan.

## 12 DSLSM

And now here I am, on January 2, just sitting in on a session of the Royal Genovian Parliament, pretending to be paying attention while these really old guys in wigs go on and on about parking.

Which I realize is fully my own fault. I mean, if I had never opened my mouth about the whole parking-meter thing in the first place, none of this would be happening.

But how could they not know that if we don't charge for parking, it will just encourage more people to drive over the French and Italian borders instead of taking the train, clogging up Genovia's already very busy streets and causing yet more strain on our already deteriorating infrastructure?

And I guess I should be flattered that they are taking my suggestion so seriously. I mean, yeah, I'm the Princess of Genovia, but what do *I* know? Just because I am of royal birth and happen to be in the Gifted and Talented program at Albert Einstein High School does not mean that I am actually gifted OR talented. In fact, the opposite is true. I am clearly *not* gifted, being average in just about every category you could name, with the possible exception of foot size, in which I am somewhat over-endowed. And I have no talents to speak of. In fact, I was put into Gifted and Talented class only because I was flunking Algebra and everyone decided I needed an extra period in which to study.

So really, if you think about it, it is very kind of the members of the Genovian Parliament to listen to anything I have to say.

But I can't really feel very grateful to them considering that every moment I spend here is another moment I am forced to spend away from my one true love. I mean, it has been thirteen days and eighteen hours since I last saw Michael. That is nearly two weeks. And during that entire time, I have only spoken to him once by phone, due to the time difference between here and the U.S. and my UNFAIR, entirely UNREALISTIC schedule of duties. I mean, where in my grueling schedule am I supposed to find time to call my boyfriend? Where?

I am telling you, it is enough to make even a nearly fifteen-year-old girl weep, the way the fates are working against Michael and me. I have not even had time to shop for his birthday, which is in three days.

I have only been his girlfriend for thirteen days, and already I am letting him down.

Well, he will just have to get in line. According to Grandmère, who should know, I am letting everyone down: Michael, the Genovian people, my dad, her, you name it.

I really don't get it. I mean, they're only *parking meters*, for crying out loud.

Thirteen days, nineteen hours since I last saw Michael.

*8 a.m.–9 a.m.*
*Breakfast with Genovian Olympic Equestrian Team*

I really have nothing against horsey people, because horses are totally cool. But *what* does the palace kitchen staff have against ketchup? Seriously, ever since I gave up on the no dairy/egg thing, on account of I can't live without cheese and McDonald's has started treating the hens that lay the eggs for their Egg McMuffins humanely, I like nothing better than an egg-and-cheese omelet for breakfast. BUT HOW CAN I ENJOY IT WITHOUT KETCHUP???? When I come back to Genovia next time, I am fully bringing a bottle of Heinz with me.

*9:30 a.m.–Noon*
*Dedicate new modern wing of Royal Genovian Museum of Art*

Hello, I paint better than some of these dudes, and I am completely talentless. At least they put one of my mom's paintings in there (Portrait of the Artist's Daughter at Age Five Refusing to Eat Hot Dogs) so that's okay.

*12:30 p.m.–2 p.m.*
*Lunch with Genovian ambassador to Japan*
*Domo arigato.*

*2:30 p.m.–4:30 p.m.*
*Sit in on meeting of Genovian Parliament*

*Again????* Spent entire session thinking about Michael. When Michael smiles, sometimes one corner of his mouth goes up higher than the other. Also, he has extremely nice lips. And very nice, dark eyes. Eyes that can see to the depths of my soul. I miss him so much!!!!!! This sucks. I should call Amnesty International—IT IS CRUEL AND UNUSUAL PUNISHMENT TO KEEP ME FROM THE MAN I LOVE FOR SO LONG!!!

*5 p.m.–6 p.m.*
*Tea with Genovian Historical Society*
They actually had a lot of very interesting things to say about some of my relatives. It was too bad Prince René was in Monte Carlo buying a new polo pony. He might have learned a thing or two.

*7 p.m.–10 p.m.*
*Formal dinner with members of Genovian Trade Association*
Okay, René was lucky to miss this.

14 DSLSM

I don't think I'll be able to stand this much longer.

*Poem for M. M.*

*Across the deep blue shining sea,*
*is Michael, far away from me.*
*But he doesn't seem so far away—*
*though I haven't seen him for fourteen days—*
*because in my heart Michael stays*
*and there he'll beat forever always.*

I can see I am going to have to work harder if I am to come up with a fitting tribute to my love.

*9 a.m.–10 a.m.*
*Mass in Royal Genovian Chapel*
I thought going to church was supposed to fill you with a sense of spiritual well-being and succor. But all I feel is sleepy.

*10:30 a.m.–4 p.m.*
*Outing with Monaco's Royal Family, Royal Genovian Yacht*
Why am I the least-tan person in Genovia? And what is up with René and the Speedos? I mean, you can totally tell he thinks he's all that. And all those girls screaming his name on the dock just encourage him. I wonder if they'd still be so crazy about him if someone told them that I caught René singing an Enrique Iglesias song in front of the mirrored wall in the Reception Room, using my scepter as a pretend microphone?

*4:30 p.m.–7 p.m.*
*Princess lessons with Grandmère*
Even in Genovia, it doesn't end. As if I don't totally get why everybody is so mad about the whole speech thing. I mean, I have already sworn I will never again veer from the prepared script while addressing the Genovian populace. Why does she have to keep HARPING?

*7 p.m.–10 p.m.*
*Formal dinner with prime minister of France and his family*
René disappeared for four hours with the prime minister's twenty-year-old daughter. They said they just went to

play roulette, but if that's true, why were they smirking so much when they got back? If René doesn't watch it, he is going to have a Little Prince to look out for, sooner than he thinks.

### 15 DSLSM

Tried to call him twice today. Michael's grandmother answered the first time and said Michael had gone to the computer store to buy a new toner cartridge. Then his dad answered and said Michael and Lilly had gone with their grandparents to go see the latest James Bond at the dollar cinema. Lucky ducks!!!!!!!!!!!!!!!!!!!!!!

*8 a.m.–9 a.m.*
*Breakfast with Royal Genovian Ballet Company*
This is the first time I have ever seen René up before 10 A.M.

*9:30 a.m.–Noon*
*Attend ballet workshops, private performance of* Sleeping Beauty

I don't know if Lilly is right about ballet being totally sexist. I mean, the guys have to wear tights, too. Which is actually too much information, if you know what I mean.

*12:30 p.m.–2 p.m.*
*Lunch with Genovian minister of tourism*
Will no one acknowledge that my parking-meter idea has merit? Furthermore, all the foot traffic from the day-trippers coming off the cruise ships that dock out in the Genovian harbor is destroying some of our most historically important bridges, such as the Pont des Vierges (Bridge of the Virgins), so named after my great-great-great-great-great-great-great-grandmother Agnes, who threw herself off it rather than become a nun like her father wanted her to be (she was all right: the royal navy fished her out and she ended up eloping with the ship's captain, much to the consternation of the house of Renaldo). I don't care how much of Genovia's gross national product is dependent on cruise ship day-trippers. They are ruining EVERYTHING!

*2:30 p.m.–4:30 p.m.*
*Attend father's address to local media on importance of Genovia as a global player in today's international economy*

Whatever. Could I be more bored? Michael! Oh, Michael! Where art thou, Michael?

*5 p.m.–6 p.m.*
*Tea with Grandmère and fellow members of Genovian Ladies Aid Society*

Spilled tea on new satin shoes that had been dyed to match tea gown.

Now they match tea.

*7 p.m.–11 p.m.*
*Formal dinner with very famous former Soviet leader and his wife*

René AWOL through most of dinner. Was found after dessert cavorting in palace garden fountain with prima ballerina from Royal Genovian ballet. Dad v. upset. Tried to soothe his frazzled nerves by making small talk with his date, Miss Czech Republic, so she would feel welcome to the family, should the occasion arise.

16 DSLSM

If this goes on much longer, I will probably develop aphasia like that girl in *Firestarter*, and start thinking my dad is a hat.

*Tuesday, January 6,*
*Royal Quarters of the Dowager Princess*

HE CALLED ME!!!!!!!!!!!!!!!!

Except that I wasn't here (as usual). I was at the Royal Genovian Opera House, watching stupid *La Bohème*, which I was enjoying until all the characters I liked DIED.

He left a message with the palace operators. The message said, *Hi.*

*Hi!* Michael said HI!

I tried to call him back, of course, the minute I got to a phone, but the Moscovitzes were all at Le Crabbe Shacque enjoying the Senior Citizen early-bird discount . . . all except Dr. Moscovitz (Mrs.) who had to stay back at the condo due to one of her patient's needing emergency counseling (a shopaholic who was having a relapse due to all the post-holiday sales).

Dr. Moscovitz said she would be sure to give Michael the message that I'd called him back. The message was: *Hi.*

Well, I wanted to say something more romantic, but it is really hard to say the word *love* to your boyfriend's mother, it turns out.

Oh, my God, Grandmère is yelling at me again. She has been lecturing me all day about this stupid ball that's coming up—my farewell-for-now ball, the one they're holding the night before I leave to go back to America . . . and to my love.

The thing is, Prince William is going to be at the ball, because he's going to be in Genovia anyway for the charity polo match my dad and René are playing in, and Grandmère is all worried I am going to make the same kind of social gaffe in front of Prince Wills that I made during my televised introduction to the Genovian people.

Like I am really going to stand there and talk about

parking meters with Prince William. But whatever.

"I swear I do not know what is wrong with you," Grandmère is saying. "Your head has been in the clouds ever since we left New York. Even more so than usual." She is narrowing her eyes at me—always a very scary thing, because Grandmère had black kohl tattooed all around her lids so that she could spend her mornings shaving off her eyebrows and drawing new ones on rather than messing around with mascara and eyeliner. "You are not thinking about *that boy*, are you?"

*That boy* is what Grandmère has started calling Michael, ever since I announced that he was my reason for living. Well, except for my cat, Fat Louie, of course.

"If you are speaking of Michael Moscovitz," I just replied to her, in my most regal voice, "I most certainly am. He is never far from my thoughts, because he is my heart's breath."

Grandmère's response to this is a snort.

"Puppy love," she says. "You'll get over it soon enough."

Um, I beg your pardon, Grandmère, but I so fully will not. I have loved Michael for approximately eight years, except perhaps for a brief two-week period of time when I thought I was in love with Josh Richter. Eight years is more than half my life. A deep and abiding passion such as this cannot be dismissed as easily as that, nor can it be defined by your pedestrian grasp of human emotion.

I didn't say any of that out loud, though, on account of how Grandmère has those really sharp nails that she tends to "accidentally" poke people with.

Except that even though Michael really is my reason for living and my heart's breath, I don't think I'll be decorating my Algebra notebook with hearts and flowers and curlicue *Mrs. Michael Moscovitz*es, the way Lana Weinberger decorated hers (only with *Mrs. Josh Richter*s, of course).

Not only because doing stuff like that is completely lame and because I do not care to have my identity subjugated by taking my husband's name, but also because as consort to the regent of Genovia, Michael will of course have to take my name. Not Thermopolis. Renaldo. Michael Renaldo. That looks kind of nice, now that I think about it.

Thirteen more days until I see the lights of New York and Michael's dark brown eyes again. Please God, let me live that long.

HRH Michael Renaldo
M. Renaldo, prince consort
Michael Moscovitz Renaldo of Genovia

Seventeen days since I last saw Michael.

All I have to say about today is that if these people WANT their infrastructure to be destroyed by gas-guzzling sports utility vehicles driven by German tourists, that is entirely their prerogative. Who am I to try to stand in their way?

Oh, I'm sorry, just their PRINCESS.

18 DSLSM

*8 a.m.–9 a.m.*
*Breakfast with ambassador to Spain*
Still no ketchup!!!

*9:30 a.m.–Noon*
*Final touch-ups to royal portrait*
I am not allowed to see finished product until unveiling at Farewell Ball. Hope artist did not include large zit I have begun sprouting on chin. That could be kind of embarrassing.

*12:30 p.m.–2 p.m.*
*Lunch with Genovian minister of finance*
FINALLY! Someone who agrees with me on fiscal importance of parking meters. Minister of finance is *the man*!

Sadly, Grandmère still not convinced. And she, far more than Dad or Parliament, is the one with the most influence over public opinion.

*2:30 p.m.–4:30 p.m.*
*More coaching on what is okay versus not okay to say to Prince William when I meet him*
Example:
"I am very pleased to make your acquaintance." —Okay

"Has anyone ever told you that you look like Heath Ledger?" —Not okay

René strolled by in the middle of my coaching session on his way to the palace weight room and suggested that I ask Wills what really happened between him and Britney Spears. Grandmère says that if I do, she will leave Rommel in my care next time she goes to Baden-Baden to get a face peel. Ew! to both taking care of Rommel *and* the face peel. And to René, too, for that matter.

*7 p.m.–11 p.m.*
*Formal dinner with largest import/exporter of Genovian olive oil*
Whatever.

19 DSLSM

This just occurred to me:

When Michael said he loved me that night during the Nondenominational Winter Dance, he might have meant love in the platonic sense. Not love in the tides of flaming passion sense. You know, like, maybe he loves me like a friend.

Only you don't generally stick your tongue in your friend's mouth, do you?

Well, maybe here in Europe you might. But not in America, for God's sake.

Except Josh Richter used tongue that time he kissed me in front of the school, and he was certainly never in love with me!!!!!!!!!

This is very upsetting. Seriously. I realize it is the middle of the night and I should be at least trying to sleep since tomorrow I have to cut the ribbon at the new Royal Genovian Foundling Home.

But how can I sleep when my boyfriend could be in Florida loving me as a friend and possibly at this very minute actually falling in love with Kate Bosworth? I mean, unlike me, Kate is actually good at something (surfing). Kate belongs in Gifted and Talented, *not me.*

Why am I so stupid? Why didn't I demand that Michael specify when he said he loved me? Why didn't I go, "Love me how? Like a friend? Or like a life partner?"

I am such an idiot.

I am never going to be able to sleep now. I mean, how can I, knowing that the man I love could conceivably think of me only as a friend he likes to French kiss?

There is just one thing I can do: I have to call the only

person I know who might be able to help me. And it is okay to call her because

    1. it is only seven o'clock where she is, and

    2. she got her own cell phone for Christmas, so even though right now she is skiing in Aspen, I can still reach her, even if she is on a ski lift, or whatever.

Thank God I have my own phone in my room. Even though I *do* have to dial 9 to get a line outside of the palace.

20 DSLSM

Tina answered on the very first ring! She totally wasn't on a ski lift. She sprained her ankle on a slope yesterday. Oh, thank you, God, for causing Tina to sprain her ankle, so that she could be there for me in my hour of need.

And it is okay, because she says it only hurts when she moves.

Tina was in her room at the ski lodge, watching the Lifetime Movie Channel when I called (*Co-ed Call Girl*, in which Tori Spelling portrays a young woman struggling to pay for her college education with money earned working as an escort—based on a true story).

At first it was very difficult to get Tina to focus on the situation at hand. All she wanted to know about was what I'm going to say when I meet Prince William. I tried to explain to her that according to Grandmère, I am not allowed to say anything to Prince William beyond *It is very nice to meet you.* She is apparently fearful that I will launch into my treatise on parking meters, which she finds less than scintillating.

Besides, what does it even matter what I say to him? My heart belongs to another.

This response was extremely dissatisfying to Tina.

"The least you can do," she said, "is get his e-mail address for me. I mean, not everyone is in as an emotionally satisfying romantic relationship as you are, Mia."

Ever since she started going out with him, Tina's boyfriend, Dave, has shied away from commitment, saying that a man can't let himself get tied down before the age of sixteen. So even though Tina claims Dave is her Romeo in cargo pants, she has been keeping her eyes open for a nice boy willing to make a commitment. Although I think Prince

William is too old for her. I suggested she try for Will's little brother, Harry, who I hear is actually very cute as well, but Tina said then she'd never get to be queen, a sentiment I guess I can understand, although believe me, being royal loses a lot of its glamour once it actually happens to you.

"Okay," I said. "I'll do my best to get Prince William's e-mail address for you. But I do have other things on my mind, Tina. Like for instance that there is a distinct possibility that Michael only likes me as a friend."

"What?" Tina was shocked. "But I thought you said he used the L word the night of the Non-denominational Winter Dance!"

"He did," I said. "Only he didn't say he was in love with me. He just said he loved me."

Fortunately I didn't have to explain any further. Tina has read enough romance novels to know exactly what I was getting at.

"Guys don't say the word *love* unless they mean it, Mia," she said. "I *know*. Dave never uses it with me." There was a throb of pain in her voice.

"Yes, I know," I said, sympathetically. "But the question is, *how* did Michael mean it? I mean, Tina, I've heard him say he loves his dog. But he is not *in* love with his dog."

"I guess I can see what you mean," Tina said, though she sounded kind of doubtful. "So, what are you going to do?"

"That's why I called you!" I said. "I mean, do you think I should just ask him?"

Tina let out a cry of pain. I thought it was because she'd jiggled her sprained ankle, but really it was because she was so horrified by what I'd asked.

"Of course you can't just come out and ask him!" she cried. "You can't put him on the spot like that. You've got to be more subtle. Remember, he's Michael, which of course makes him vastly superior to most guys . . . but he's still a guy."

I hadn't thought of this. I hadn't thought of a lot of things, apparently. I couldn't believe that I had just been going along on this sea of bliss, happy just to know Michael even liked me, while the whole time, he could have been falling in love with some other, more intellectually or athletically gifted girl.

"Well," I said. "Maybe I should just be like, 'Do you like me as a friend, or do you like me as a girlfriend?'"

"Mia," Tina said. "I really do not think you should ask Michael point-blank like that. He might run away in fear, like a startled fawn. Boys have a tendency to do that, you know. They aren't like us. They don't like to talk about their feelings."

It is just so sad that to get any kind of trustworthy advice about men, I have to call someone eight thousand miles away. Thank God for Tina Hakim Baba, is all I have to say.

"So what do you think I should do?" I asked.

"Well, it's going to be hard for you to do anything," Tina said, "until you get back here. The only way to tell what a boy is feeling is to look into his eyes. You'll never get anything out of him over the phone. Boys are no good at talking on the phone."

This was certainly true, if my ex-boyfriend Kenny had been any sort of indication.

"I know," Tina said, sounding like she'd just gotten a good idea. "Why don't you ask Lilly?"

"I don't know," I said. "I'd feel kind of funny about dragging her into something that's between Michael and me—" The truth was, Lilly and I still hadn't really even talked about me liking her brother, and her brother liking me back. I had always thought she'd be kind of mad about it. But then it turned out in the end she actually kind of helped us get together, by telling Michael I was the one who'd been sending him those anonymous love letters.

"Just ask her," Tina said.

"But it's really late there," I said.

"Late? It's only, like, nine o'clock in Florida!"

"Yeah, and that's what time Lilly and Michael's grandparents go to bed. I don't want to call and wake them up. Then they'll hate me forever." *And it will make things uncomfortable at the wedding.* I didn't say this part out loud. Although probably I could have, and Tina would have understood.

"They won't care if you wake them up, Mia," Tina said. "You're calling from a different time zone. They'll understand. And be sure to call me back after you talk to her! I want to know what she says."

I have to admit that, as I dialed, my fingers were shaking. Not so much because I was afraid of waking up Mr. and Mrs. Moscovitz and having them hate me for it forever, but because there was a chance Michael might answer. What was I going to say if he did? I had no idea. The only thing I knew for sure was that I was not going to say, "Do you like me as a friend, or do you like me as a girlfriend?" Because Tina had told me not to.

Lilly answered on the first ring. Our conversation went like this:

Lilly: Whoa. It's you.

Me: Is it too late to call? I didn't wake up your grandparents, did I?

Lilly:  Well, yeah. Kinda. But they'll get over it. So. How is it?

Me:  You mean Genovia? Um, okay, I guess.

Lilly:  Oh, yes. I'm sure it's just okay, being waited on hand and foot, having your every need tended to by servants, and wearing a crown all the time.

Me:  The crown kind of hurts. Look. Just tell me the truth, Lilly. Has Michael found another girl?

Lilly:  Another girl? What are you talking about?

Me:  You know what I mean. Some Floridian girl, who can surf. Some girl named Kate, or possibly Anne Marie, with one blue eye and one brown eye. Just tell me, Lilly, I can take the truth, I swear.

Lilly:  First of all, for Michael to have met another girl, that would mean he'd have to tear himself from his laptop and leave the condo, which he has done only for meals and to buy more computer equipment the entire time we have been here. He is as pasty-skinned as ever. Secondly, he is not going to go out with some girl named Kate, because he likes *you.*

Me:  (practically crying with relief) Really, Lilly? You swear? You aren't just lying to make me feel better?

Lilly:  No, I'm not. Though I don't know how long his devotion to you is going to last, considering you didn't even remember his birthday.

I felt something clutch at my throat. Michael's birthday! I had forgotten Michael's birthday! I had written it in my new datebook and everything, but with everything that had been going on . . .

"Oh, my God, Lilly," I shrieked. "I completely forgot!"

"Yes," Lilly said. "You did. But don't worry. I'm pretty sure he didn't expect a card or anything. I mean, you're off being the Princess of Genovia. How can you be expected to remember something as important as your boyfriend's birthday?"

This seemed really unfair to me. I mean, Michael and I have only been going out for twenty-two days, and for twenty-one of them, I have been very, very busy. I mean, it is all very well for Lilly to joke, but I haven't seen her christening any battleships or crusading for the installation of public parking meters. It may never have occurred to anyone, but this princess stuff is hard work.

"Lilly," I said. "Can I talk to him, please? Michael, I mean?"

"Sure," Lilly said. Then she screamed, "Michael! Phone!"

"Lilly!" I cried, shocked. "Your grandparents!"

"Puh-*lease*," she said. "This'll get them back for slamming the front door at five every single morning when they go to pick up the *Times*."

It was a long time after that that I finally heard some footsteps, and then Michael going to Lilly, "Thanks." Then Michael picked up the phone and went, kind of curiously, since Lilly hadn't told him who it was, "Hello?"

Just hearing his voice made me forget all about how it was after three in the morning and I was miserable and hating my life. Suddenly it was like it was two in the afternoon and I was lying on one of the beaches I was working

251

so hard to protect from erosion and pollution by tourists, with the warm sun pouring down on me and someone offering me an ice-cold Orangina from a silver tray. That's how Michael's voice made me feel.

"Michael," I said. "It's me."

"Mia," he said, sounding genuinely happy to hear from me. I don't think it was my imagination, either. He really did sound pleased, and not like he was getting ready to dump me for Kate Bosworth at all. "How are you?"

"I'm okay," I said. Then, to get it out as soon as possible, I went, "Listen, Michael, I can't believe I missed your birthday. I suck. I can't believe how much I suck. I am the most horrible person who ever walked the face of the planet."

Then Michael did a miraculous thing. He laughed. Laughed! Like missing his birthday was nothing!

"Oh, that's all right," he said. "I know you're busy over there. And there's that time-zone thing, and all. So. How's it going? Has your grandmother let you off for that parking-meter thing, or is she still on your case about it?"

I practically melted right there in the middle of my big, fancy royal bed, with the phone clutched to my ear and everything. I couldn't believe he was being so nice to me, after the terrible thing I had done. It wasn't like twenty days had gone by at all. It was like we were still standing in front of my stoop, with the snow coming down and looking so white against Michael's dark hair and Lars getting mad in the vestibule because we wouldn't stop kissing and he was cold and wanted to go inside already.

I couldn't believe I had ever thought Michael might fall in love with some Floridian girl with multicolored eyes and a surfboard. I mean, I still wasn't exactly sure he was in love with me, or anything. But I was pretty sure he *liked* me.

And right there, at three in the morning, sitting by myself

in my royal bedchamber in the Palais de Genovia, that was enough.

So then I asked him about his birthday, and he told me how they'd gone to Red Lobster and Lilly'd had an allergic reaction to her shrimp cocktail and they'd had to cut the meal short to go to Promptcare because she'd swollen up like Violet in *Willy Wonka and the Chocolate Factory*, and now she has to carry a syringe filled with adrenaline around with her in case she accidentally ingests shellfish ever again, and how Michael's parents got him a new laptop for when he goes to college and how when he gets back to New York he is thinking about starting a band since he is having trouble finding sponsors for his webzine *Crackhead* on account of how he did that groundbreaking exposé on how much Windows sucks and how he only uses Linux now.

Apparently a lot of *Crackhead*'s former subscribers are frightened of the wrath of Bill Gates and his minions.

I was so happy to be listening to Michael's voice that I didn't even notice what time it was or how sleepy I was getting until he went, "Hey, isn't it, like, four in the morning there?" which by that point it was. Only I didn't care because I was so happy just to be talking to him.

"Yes," I said dreamily.

"Well, you'd better get to bed," Michael said. "Unless you get to sleep in. But I bet you have stuff to do tomorrow, right?"

"Oh," I said, still all lost in rhapsody, which is what the sound of Michael's voice sends me into. "Just a ribbon-cutting ceremony at the hospital. And then lunch with the Genovian Historical Society. And then a tour of the Genovian zoo. And then dinner with the minister of culture and his wife."

"Oh, my God," Michael said, sounding alarmed. "Do you have to do that kind of stuff every day?"

"Uh-huh," I said, wishing I was there with him, so that I could gaze into his adorably brown eyes while hearing his adorably deep voice, and thus know whether or not he loved me, since this was, according to Tina, the only way you could tell with boys.

"Mia," he said, with some urgency. "You'd better get some sleep. You have another huge day ahead of you."

"Okay," I said happily.

"I mean it, Mia," he said. He can be so authoritative sometimes, just like the Beast in *Beauty and the Beast*, my favorite movie of all time. Or the way Patrick Swayze bosses Baby around in *Dirty Dancing*. So, so exciting. "Hang up the phone and go to bed."

"You hang up first," I said.

Sadly, he got less bossy after this. Instead, he started talking in this voice I had only ever heard him use once before, and that was on the stoop in front of my mom's apartment building the night of the Nondenominational Winter Dance, when we did all that kissing.

Which was actually even more exhilarating than when he was bossing me around, to be truthful.

"No," he said. "You hang up first."

"No," I said, thrilled to pieces. "You."

"No," he said. "You."

"Both of you hang up," Lilly said, very rudely, over the extension. "I have to call Boris before his nightly Benadryl kicks in."

So we both said good-bye very hastily and hung up.

But I'm almost positive Michael would have said I love you if Lilly hadn't been on the line.

Ten days until I see him again. I can hardly WAIT!!!!!!!

*1 p.m.–3 p.m.*
*Lunch with Genovian Historical Society*

Grandmère can be so mean. Seriously. Imagine pinching me, just because she thought I had dozed off for a few seconds at lunch! I swear I am going to have a bruise now. It's a good thing I don't have any time to go to the beach, because if I did and anyone saw the mark she'd left, they'd probably call Genovian Child Protective Services, or whatever.

And I wasn't asleep, either. I was just resting my eyes.

Grandmère says it is thoughtless of "that boy" to keep me up all hours whispering sweet nothings in my ear. She says Prince René would never treat any of his girlfriends so cavalierly.

I informed her very firmly that Michael had actually *told* me to hang up, because he cares very deeply about me, and that *I* was the one who kept on talking. And that we don't whisper sweet nothings to each other, we have substantive discussions about art and literature and Bill Gates's stranglehold on the software industry.

To which Grandmère replied, *"Pfuit!"*

But you can tell she is totally jealous because she would like a boyfriend who is as smart and thoughtful as mine. But that will so never happen, because Grandmère is too mean, and besides, there is that whole thing she does with her eyebrows. Boys like girls with real eyebrows, not painted-on ones.

Nine days until I am once more in the arms of my love.

I am so excited! Tina, not being able to join her family on
the ski slopes, spent all day in an Aspen Internet café looking up all of her friends' horoscopes. Last night she faxed
over me and Michael's horoscopes! I am taping them here
in my datebook so I won't lose them. They are so accurate
it is making my spine tingle.

### Michael—Date of Birth = January 5

Capricorn is the leader of the Earth signs. Here is a sta-
bilizing force, one of the hardest-working signs of the
Zodiac. The Mountain Goat has intense powers of self-
concentration, but not in an egotistical sense. Members of
this sign find a great deal more confidence in what they do
than in who they are. Capricorn is one very high achiever!
Without balance, however, Capricorn can become too rigid,
and focus too much on achievement. Then they forget the
little joys in life. When the Goat finally relaxes and enjoys
life, his or her most delightful secrets emerge. No one has
a better sense of humor than the Capricorn. Oh, that Cap
might let us bask in that warm smile!

### Mia—Date of Birth = May 1

Ruled by loving Venus, Taurus has great emotional
depth. Friends and lovers rely on the warmth and emotional accessibility of the Bull. Taurus represents consistency,
loyalty, and patience. Fixed earth can be very rigid, too
cautious to take some of the risks necessary in life. Sometimes
the Bull ends up temporarily stuck in the mud. He or she
may not want to rise to every challenge or potential. And
stubborn? Yes! The Taurean Bull may always surface. This
sign's Yin energy can also go too far, causing Taurus to

become very, very passive. Still, you cannot ask for a better lover or more loyal friend.

### Michael + Mia

Courageous, ambitious Earth signs, Taurus and Capricorn seem to be made for each other. Both value career success and share a love of beauty and of lasting, classical foundations. Capricorn's irony charms the Bull, while the latter's expert sensuality rescues the Goat from his or her obsession with career. They enjoy talking together, and communication is excellent. They confide in each other, one promising never to offend or betray the other. This could be a perfect couple.

See? We're perfect for each other! But expert sensuality? *Me?* Um, I don't think so.

Still . . . I'm so happy! Perfect! You can't get better than perfect!

### Sunday, January 11
#### Royal Daily Schedule

*9 a.m.–10 a.m.*
*Mass in Royal Genovian Chapel*

Oh, my God, I have only been Michael's girlfriend for twenty-four days, and already I'm terrible at it. The girl-friend thing, I mean. I can't even figure out what to get him for his birthday. He is the love of my life, the reason my heart beats. You would think I would know what to get the guy.

But no. I haven't got a clue.

Tina says the only appropriate thing to get for a boy you have only been officially dating for less than four weeks is a sweater. And she says even that is pushing it, since Michael and I have not even been out on an official date yet—so technically, how can we be dating?

But a *sweater*? I mean, that is so unromantic. That is the kind of thing I would get my dad—if he wasn't so in need of anger management manuals, which is what I got for him for Christmas. I would get a sweater for my step-dad for sure.

But my *boyfriend*?

I was kind of surprised Tina would suggest something so banal, as she is basically the resident romance expert of our little group. But Tina says the rules about what to give boys are actually very strict. Her mom told them to her. Tina's mom used to be a model and international jet-setter who once dated a sultan, so I guess she would know. The rules for presents for guys, according to Mrs. Hakim Baba, go:

| Length of Time Going Out: | Appropriate Gift: |
| --- | --- |
| 1–4 months | Sweater |
| 5–8 months | Cologne |
| 9–12 months | Cigarette lighter* |
| 1 year + | Watch |

But this is better at least than Grandmère's list of what is appropriate to give boyfriends, which she presented to me yesterday, as soon as I mentioned to her my horrible faux pas of missing Michael's birthday. Her list goes:

| Length of Time Going Out: | Appropriate Gift: |
| --- | --- |
| 1–4 months | Candy |
| 5–8 months | Book |
| 9–12 months | Handkerchief |
| 1 year + | Gloves |

Handkerchiefs? Who gives handkerchiefs anymore? Handkerchiefs are completely unhygienic!

And candy? For a *guy*????

But Grandmère says the same rules apply for girls as for boys. Michael is not allowed to give me anything but candy or possibly flowers for my birthday, either!

Overall, I think I prefer Mrs. Hakim Baba's list.

Still, this whole dating/present-giving thing is so difficult! Everybody says something different. Like, last night I called my mom and asked her what I should give Michael, and she said silk boxer shorts.

But I can't give Michael UNDERWEAR!!!!!!!

I wish my mom would hurry up and have this baby already so she would stop acting so weird. She is pretty much useless to me in her current state of hormonal imbalance.

Out of desperation, I asked my dad what I should get Michael, and he said a pen, so Michael could write to me while I am in Genovia, instead of my calling him all the time and breaking the bank of Genovia.

Whatever, Dad. Like anyone writes with a pen anymore.

And hello, I am only going to be in Genovia for Christmas and summers, as per our agreement drawn up last September.

A pen. I am so sure. Am I the only person in my family with a modicum of romance in my bones?

Oops, gotta stop writing, Father Christoff is looking this way. But it is his own fault. I wouldn't write in my journal during mass if his sermons were even semi-inspiring. Or at least in English.

*12 p.m.–2 p.m.*
*Lunch with Director of Royal Genovian Opera, leading mezzo soprano*
I thought *I* was a picky eater, but it turns out mezzo-sopranos are way pickier than even princesses.

My zit is growing out of all proportion despite application of toothpaste last night before I went to bed.

*3 p.m.–5 p.m.*
*Meeting with Genovian Homeowners Association*
You would think that the Homeowners Association, at least, would be on my side on the parking meter issue. After all, it's *their* houses these tourists keep parking in front of. You'd think they'd want to bring in a little more income for sidewalk repairs. But NOOOOOOOOOOO.

I swear I don't know how my dad does this every day. I really don't.

*7 p.m.–10 p.m.*
*Formal Dinner with ambassador to Chile and his wife*
Huge controversy due to René "borrowing" Chilean ambassador's convertible Porsche—and his wife—for a jaunt into Monte Carlo after dessert. Couple eventually found playing tennis on royal court.

Sadly, it was strip tennis.

Eight days until I see him again. Oh, joy! Oh, rapture!

I just got off the phone with Michael. I *had* to call him. It wasn't like I had a choice. I had to find out what he wanted for his birthday. I know that is cheating—*asking* someone what they want—but I seriously can't think what to get him. Of course if I were the Kate Bosworth type I would so totally have gotten him the perfect gift already, like maybe a charming friendship bracelet that I wove myself out of seaweed or whatever.

But I am not Kate Bosworth. I do not even know how to weave. OH, MY GOD, I DON'T EVEN KNOW HOW TO WEAVE!!!!!!!!!!

I *have* to get him something *really* good, since I forgot. About his birthday, and all. And then of course there's the whole thing about how he is saddled with a talentless freak princess for a girlfriend, instead of a hot Kate Bosworth type who can surf and weave and is self-actualized and never gets zits and everything. I have to get him something that is so fabulous that he forgets that I am nothing but a non-surfing, fingernail-biting freshman who happened to have been born royal.

Of course Michael says he doesn't want anything, that I am the only thing he needs (if only I could believe this!!!!!!!!!!) and that he will see me in eight days, and that is the best present anyone could get him.

This seems to indicate that he might actually be in love with me, as opposed to only loving me as a friend. I will of course have to check with Tina to see what she thinks, but I would have to say that in this case, Signs Point to Yes!

But of course he is only saying that. That he doesn't want anything for his birthday, I mean. I have to get him *something*. Something really good. Only what?

Anyway, I really did have a reason to call him. I didn't do it just because I wanted to hear the sound of his voice, or anything. I mean, I am *not* that far gone.

Oh, all right, maybe I am. How can I help it? I have only been in love with Michael since, like, forever. I love the way he says my name. I love the way he laughs. I love the way he asks my opinion, like he really cares what I think (God knows nobody around here feels that way. I mean, make a suggestion—like, that it might save water to turn off the fountain in front of the palace at night, when no one is around anyway—and everybody practically acts like one of the suits of armor in the Grand Hall started talking).

Well, okay, not my dad. But I see him less here in Genovia than I do back home, practically, because he is so caught up in parliamentary meetings and racing his yacht in regattas and hanging out with Miss Czech Republic.

Anyway, I like talking to Michael. Is that so wrong? I mean, he *is* my boyfriend, after all.

If only I were worthier of him! I mean, between my not having remembered his birthday, my not being able to figure out what to get him, and my not really being that good at anything, the way he is, it's a wonder he's even interested in me at all!

So we were just saying good-bye after having had a perfectly pleasant conversation about the Genovian Olive Growers Association and Michael's band that he is trying to put together (he is so talented!), and whether it is off-putting to call a band Frontal Lobotomy, and I was just working up the guts to go, "I miss you," or "I love you," thus leaving an opening for him to say something similar back to me and therefore resolve the does-he-just-love-me-like-a-friend-or-is-he-in-love-with-me dilemma once and for all, when I heard Lilly in the background, demanding to talk to me.

Michael went, "Get away," but Lilly kept on shrieking, "I have to talk to her, I just remembered I have something really important to ask her."

Then Michael went, "Don't tell her about that," and my heart skipped a beat because I thought Lilly had all of a sudden remembered that Michael had been going out with some girl named Anne Marie behind my back after all. Before I could say another word, Lilly had wrestled the phone away from him (I heard Michael grunt, I guess in pain because she must have kicked him or something), and then she was going, "Oh, my God, I forgot to ask. Did you see it?"

"Lilly," I said, since even eight thousand miles away, I could feel Michael's pain—Lilly kicks hard. I know, because I have been the recipient of quite a few kicks of hers over the years. "I know that you are used to having me all to yourself, but you are going to have to learn to share me with your brother. Now, if this means we are going to have to set boundaries in our relationship, then I guess we will have to. But you can't just go around ripping the phone out of Michael's hand when he might have had something really important to—"

"Shut up about my sainted brother for a minute. Did . . . you . . . see . . . it?"

"See what? What are you talking about?" I thought maybe somebody had tried to jump into the polar bear cage at the Central Park Zoo again.

"Oh, just the movie," Lilly said. "Of your life. The one that was on TV the other night. Or hadn't you heard your life story has been made into a movie of the week?"

I wasn't very surprised to hear this. I had already been

warned that a TV movie about my life was in the works. But I'd been assured by the palace publicity staff that the movie wouldn't be shown until February sweeps. I guess the joke was on us.

Whatever. There are already four unauthorized biographies about me floating around out there. One of them made the best-seller list for about half a second. I read it. It wasn't that good. But maybe that's just because I already knew how it all turned out.

"So?" I said. I was kind of mad at Lilly. I mean, she'd booted Michael off the phone just to tell me about some dumb movie?

"Hello," Lilly said. "Movie. Of your life. You were portrayed as shy and awkward."

"I *am* shy and awkward," I reminded her.

"They made your grandmother all kindly and sympathetic to your plight," Lilly said. "It was the grossest mischaracterization I've seen since *Shakespeare in Love* tried to pass off the Bard as a hottie with a six-pack and a full set of teeth."

"That's horrible," I said. "Now can I please finish talking to Michael?"

"You didn't even ask how they portrayed *me*," Lilly said, accusingly, "your loyal best friend."

"How did they portray you, Lilly?" I asked, looking at the big fancy clock on top of the big fancy marble mantelpiece over my big fancy bedroom fireplace. "And make it quick, I've got a breakfast and then a ride with the Genovian Equestrian Society in exactly seven hours."

"They portrayed me as less than fully supportive of your royalness," Lilly practically screamed into the phone. "They made out like after you first got that stupid haircut, I mocked you for being shallow and a trend-follower!"

"Yeah," I said, waiting for her to get to the point of her

tirade. Because of course Lilly hadn't been very supportive of my haircut, or my royalness.

But it turned out Lilly had already gotten to the point of her tirade.

"I was never unsupportive of your royalness!" she shrieked into the phone, causing me to hold the receiver away from my head in order to keep my eardrums intact. "I was your number-one most supportive friend through the whole thing!"

This was so patently untrue, I thought Lilly was joking, and I started to laugh. But then I realized when she greeted my laughter with stone cold silence that she was totally serious. Apparently Lilly has one of those selective memories, where she can remember all the good things she did, but none of the bad things. Kind of like a politician.

Because of course if it were true that Lilly had been so supportive of me, I never would have become friends with Tina Hakim Baba, who I only started sitting with at lunch back in October because Lilly wasn't speaking to me on account of the whole princess thing.

"I sincerely hope," Lilly said, "that you are laughing in disbelief over the idea that I was ever anything less than a good friend to you, Mia. I know we've had our ups and downs, but any time I was ever hard on you, it was only because I thought you weren't being true to yourself."

"Um," I said. "Okay."

"I am going to write a letter," Lilly went on, "to the studio that produced that piece of libelous trash, demanding a written apology for their irresponsible screenwriting. And if they do not provide one—and publish it in a full-page ad in *Variety*—I will sue. I don't care if I have to take my case to the Supreme Court. Those Hollywood types think they can throw anything they want to in front of a camera and the viewing public will just lap it up. Well, that might be true for the rest of the proles, but *I* am going to fight for more honest portrayals of actual people and events. The man is not going to keep *me* down!"

I asked Lilly what man, thinking she meant the director or something, and she just went, "The man! The man!" like I was mentally challenged, or something.

Then Michael got back on the phone and explained that "the man" is a figurative allusion to authority, and that in the way that Freudian analysts blame everything on "the mother," blues musicians have historically blamed their woes on "the man." Traditionally, Michael informed me, "the man" is usually white, financially successful, middle-aged, and in a position of considerable power over others.

We discussed calling Michael's band The Man, but then dismissed it as having possibly misogynistic undertones.

Seven days until I can once again be in Michael's arms. Oh, that the hours would fly as fleetly as winged doves!

I just realized—Michael's description of "The Man" sounds a lot like my dad! Although I doubt all those blues musicians were talking about the Prince of Genovia. As far as I know, my dad has never even been to Memphis.

*8 p.m.–12 a.m.*
*Royal Genovian Symphony*

Just when it seems like maybe, just maybe, things might be starting to go my way, something always has to come along to ruin it.

And as usual, it was Grandmère.

I guess she could tell because I was so sleepy again today that I'd been up all night talking to Michael. So this morning between my ride with the Equestrian Society and my meeting with the Genovian Beachfront Development Society, Grandmère sat me down and gave me a lecture. This time it wasn't about the socially acceptable gifts to give a boy on his birthday. Instead, it was about Appropriate Choices.

"It is all very well and good, Amelia," Grandmère said, "for you to like *that boy*."

"I should think so!" I cried, with righteous indignation. "Considering you have never even met him! I mean, what do you even know about Michael, anyway? Nothing!"

Grandmère just gave me the evil eye. "Nevertheless," she went on. "I do not think it wise of you to allow your affection for this Michael fellow to blind you to other, more suitable consorts, such as—"

I interrupted to tell Grandmère that if she said the words *Prince William* I was going to jump off the Pont des Vierges.

Grandmère told me not to be more ridiculous than I already am, that I could never marry Prince William anyway, on account of his being Church of England. However, there are apparently other, infinitely more suitable romantic partners for a princess of the royal house of Renaldo than Michael. And Grandmère said she would hate for me to miss the opportunity to get to know these other young men just because I fancy myself in love with Michael. She assured me that, were the circumstances reversed, and Michael were the heir to a throne and a considerable fortune, she highly doubted he would be as scrupulously faithful as I was being.

I objected to this assessment of Michael's character very much. I informed Grandmère that, if she had ever bothered to get to know Michael, she'd have realized that in every aspect of his life, from his being editor in chief of the now defunct *Crackhead* to his role as treasurer in the Computer Club, he has shown nothing but the utmost loyalty and integrity. I also explained, as patiently as I could, that it hurt me to hear her saying anything negative about a man to whom I have pledged my heart.

"That is just it, Amelia," Grandmère said, rolling her scary eyes. "You are entirely too young to pledge your heart to anyone. I think it very unwise of you, at the age of fourteen, to decide who you are going to spend the rest of your life with. Unless, of course, it happened to be someone very, very special. Someone your father and I know. *Very, very* well. Someone who, while possibly *seeming* a bit immature, probably just needs the right woman to make him settle down. Girls mature much more quickly than young men, Amelia—"

I interrupted Grandmère to inform her that I will be fifteen in four months, and also that Juliet was fourteen when she married Romeo. To which Grandmère replied, "And that relationship turned out very nicely, didn't it!"

Grandmère clearly has never been in love. Furthermore, she has no appreciation whatsoever for romantic tragedy.

"And in any case," Grandmère added, "if you hope to

keep *that boy*, you are going about it all wrong."

I thought it was very unsupportive of Grandmère to be suggesting that I, after only having had a real boyfriend for twenty-five days, during which time I had spoken to him exactly three times on the phone, was already in danger of losing him to someone with multicolored eyes, and said so.

"Well, I'm sorry, Amelia," Grandmère said. "But I can't say you know what you're about if it's true you actually want to keep this young man."

I swear I do not know what came over me at that moment. But it was like all the pressure that had been building up—the parking-meter thing; missing Michael and my mom and Fat Louie; what I was going to say to Prince William; my zit—all became too much, and I heard myself spewing, "Of course I want to keep him! But how am I going to be able to do that, when I am an entirely un–self-actualized, talentless, breastless, un–Kate-Bosworth-like princess FREAK????"

Grandmère looked kind of surprised at my outburst. She didn't seem to know which issue to address first, my talentlessness or breastlessness. Finally she settled for saying, "Well, you could start by not staying on the phone with him until all hours of the night. You do not give him any reason to doubt your affections."

"Of course not," I said, horrified. "Why would I do that? I love him!"

"But you mustn't let him know that!" Grandmère looked ready to throw her mid-morning Sidecar at me. "Are you completely dense? *Never* let a man be sure of your affections for him! You did a very good job at first, with this business of forgetting his birthday. But now you are ruining everything with this calling all the time. If *that boy* realizes how you really feel, he will stop trying to please you."

"But Grandmère." I was way confused. "You married Grandpa. Surely he figured out you loved him if you went ahead and married him."

"Grandpère, Mia, please, not this vulgar *Grandpaw* you Americans insist upon." Grandmère sniffed and looked insulted. "Your grandfather most certainly did not 'figure out' my feelings for him. I made quite certain he thought I was only marrying him for his money and title. And I don't think I need to point out to you that we had forty blissful years together. And without separate bedrooms," she added, with some malice, "unlike *some* royal couples I could mention."

"Wait a minute." I stared at her. "For forty years, you slept in the same bed as Grandpère, but you never once told him that you loved him?"

Grandmère drained what was left of her Sidecar and laid an affectionate hand on top of Rommel's head. Since returning to Genovia and being diagnosed with OCD, most of Rommel's fur has started to grow back, thanks to the plastic cone around his head. White fuzz was starting to come out all over him, like down on a baby chicken. But it didn't make him look any less repulsive.

"That," Grandmère said, "is precisely what I am telling you. I kept your grandfather on his toes, and he loved every minute of it. If you want to keep this Michael fellow, I suggest you do the same thing. Stop this business of calling him every night. Stop this business of not looking at any other boys. And stop this obsessing over what you are going to get him for his birthday. *He* should be the one obsessing over what he is going to buy to keep *you* interested, not the other way around."

"*Me?* But my birthday isn't until May!" I didn't want to tell her that I had already figured out what I was getting for Michael. I didn't want to tell her because I had sort of snitched it out of the back of the Palais de Genovia museum.

Well, nobody else was using it, so I don't see why I can't. I'm the Princess of Genovia, after all. I own everything in that museum anyway. Or at least the royal family does.

"Who says a man should give a woman gifts only on her birthday?" Grandmère was looking at me like she pretty much despaired of me as a *Homo sapiens*. She held up her wrist. Dripping from it was a bracelet Grandmère wears a lot, one with diamonds big as Euro one-cent pieces hanging off it. "I got this from your grandfather on March fifth, forty years or so ago. Why? March fifth is not my birthday, nor is it any kind of holiday. Your grandfather gave it to me on that day merely because he thought that the bracelet, like me, was exquisite." She lowered her hand back down to Rommel's head. "That, Amelia, is how a man ought to treat the woman he loves."

All I could think was, *Poor Grandpère*. He couldn't have had any idea what he was getting himself into when it came to Grandmère, who'd been a total babe back when she was young, before she'd gotten her tattooed eyeliner and shaved off her eyebrows. I'm sure Gramps just took one look at her across that dance floor where they met back when he was just the dashing heir to the throne and she was a pert young debutante, and froze, like a graffiti artist caught in a cop car's headlights, never suspecting what lay ahead. . . .

Years of subtle mind games and Sidecar shaking.

"I don't think I can be like that, Grandmère," I said. "I mean, I don't want Michael to give me diamonds. I just want him to ask me to the Prom."

"Well, he won't do it," Grandmère said, "if he doesn't think there's a possibility you're entertaining offers from other boys."

"Grandmère!" I was shocked. "I would never go to the Prom with anybody but Michael!" Not like there was a big chance of anybody else asking me, either, but I felt that was beside the point.

"But you must never let him *know* that, Amelia," Grandmère said, severely. "You must keep him always in doubt of your feelings, always on his toes. Men enjoy the hunt, you see, and once they have taken their quarry, they tend to lose all interest. Here. This is for you to read. I believe it will adequately illustrate my point."

Grandmère had drawn out a book from her Gucci bag and handed it to me. I looked down at it incredulously.

"*Jane Eyre*?" I couldn't believe it. "Grandmère, I saw the movie. And no offense, but it was way boring."

"Movie," Grandmère said with a sniff. "Read that book, Amelia, and see if it doesn't teach you a thing or two about how men and women relate to one another."

"Grandmère," I said, not sure how to break it to her that she was way behind the times. "I think people who want to know how men and women relate to one another are reading *Men Are from Mars, Women Are from Venus* these days."

"READ IT!" Grandmère yelled, so loudly that she scared Rommel clear off her lap. He slunk off to cower behind a potted geranium.

I swear, I don't know what I did to deserve a grandmother like mine. Lilly's grandma totally worships Lilly's boyfriend, Boris Pelkowski. She is always sending him Tupperware tubs of kreplach and stuff. I don't know why I have to get a grandmother who is already trying to get me to break up with a guy I've only been going out with for twenty-five days.


Seven days, six hours, forty-two minutes until I see him again.

*8 a.m.–10 a.m.*
*Breakfast with members of Royal Genovian Shakespeare Society*
Jane Eyre v. boring—so far nothing but orphanages, bad haircuts, and a lot of coughing.

*10 a.m.–4 p.m.*
*Session of Genovian Parliament*
Jane Eyre looking up—she has gotten a job as governess in house of very rich guy, Mr. Rochester. Mr. Rochester v. bossy, much like Wolverine, or Michael.

*5 p.m.–7 p.m.*
*Tea with Grandmère and wife of prime minister of England*
Mr. Rochester=hottie. Going on my list of Totally Hot Guys, between Hugh Jackman and that Croatian dude from *ER*.

*8 p.m.–10 p.m.*
*Formal State dinner with prime minister of England and family*
Jane Eyre=total idiot! It was not Mr. Rochester's fault! Why is she being so mean to him?
And Grandmère shouldn't yell at me for reading at the table. She's the one who gave me this book in the first place.

Six days, eleven hours, twenty-nine minutes until I see him again.

Okay, I guess I understand what Grandmère was getting at with this book. But seriously, that whole part where Mrs. Fairfax warns Jane not to get too chummy with Mr. Rochester before the wedding was just because back in those days there was no birth control.

Still—and I may have to consult with Lilly on this—I am pretty sure it is unwise to pattern one's behavior after the advice of a fictional character, especially one from a book written in 1846.

However, I do get the general gist of Mrs. Fairfax's warning, which was this: Do not chase boys. Chasing boys is bad. Chasing boys can lead to horrible things like mansions going up in flames, hand amputations, and blindness. Have some self-respect and don't let things go too far before the wedding day.

I get this. I so get this.

*But what is Michael going to think if I just stop calling????* I mean, he might think I don't like him anymore!!!! And it isn't like I've got so much going for me in the first place. I mean, as a girlfriend, I pretty much suck. I'm not good at anything, I can't remember people's birthdays, and I'm a *princess*.

I guess that is Grandmère's point. I guess you are supposed to keep boys on their toes this way.

I don't know. But it seemed to work with Grandpère. And for Jane, in the end. I guess I could give it a try.

But it won't be easy. It is nine o'clock at night in Florida right now. Who knows what Michael is doing? He might have gone down to the beach for a stroll and met some beautiful homeless musician girl, who is living on the boardwalk and making a living off the tourists, for whom she plays wryly observant folk songs on her Stratocaster. I can't even play *tennis*, let alone an instrument.

I bet she is wearing fringy things and is all busty and snaggle-toothed, like Jewel. No boy could be expected just to walk on by when a girl like that is standing there.

No. Grandmère and Mrs. Fairfax are right. I've got to resist. I've got to resist the urge to call him. When you are less available, it drives men wild, just like in *Jane Eyre*.

Though I think changing my name and running away to live with distant relations like Jane did might be going a bit too far. As appealing as it seems.

Five days, seven hours, and twenty-five minutes until I see him again.

*Wednesday, January 14*
*Royal Daily Schedule*

*8 a.m.–10 a.m.*
*Breakfast with Genovian Society of Medicine*
So, so tired. This is the last time I stay up half the night reading nineteenth-century literature.

*10 a.m.–4 p.m.*
*Session of Genovian Parliament*
Filibuster by minister of finance! He says Genovia will have parking meters or perish!

*5 p.m.–7 p.m.*
*Session of Genovian Parliament*
Filibuster ongoing. Would like to slip out for an Orangina, but am afraid this would look unsupportive.

*8 p.m.–10 p.m.*
*Session of Genovian Parliament*
Can't take it anymore. Filibuster too boring. Plus René just poked his head in and smirked at me. Let him laugh. *He* won't have to rule a country someday.

Grandmère finally noticed my zit. I guess the idea of me meeting Prince William with a giant zit on my chin was too much for her, since she completely flipped out. I told her I had the situation under control, but Grandmère clearly does not put as much faith in toothpaste as a complexion aid as I do. She sent for the Royal Dermatologist. He injected my chin with something, then said not to put any more toothpaste on my face.

I can't even seem to handle a zit right. How am I ever going to rule a country?

### TO DO BEFORE LEAVING GENOVIA

1. Find a safe place to put Michael's present where it will NOT be found by grandmother or nosy ladies-in-waiting while packing my stuff (inside toe of combat boot?).

2. Say good-bye to kitchen staff, and thank them for all the vegetarian fare.

3. Make sure harbormaster has hung pair of scissors off every buoy in port for use of yachting tourists who didn't bring along their own set to snip six-pack holders.

4. Take funny nose and glasses off the statue of Grandmère in the Portrait Hall before she notices.

5. Practice my "Meeting Prince William" speech. Also "Good-bye Prince René" speech.

6. Break François's record of twenty feet, seven inches sock-sliding along Crystal Hallway.

7. Let all the doves in the palace dovecote go (if they want to come back, that is fine, but they should have the option to be free).

8. Let Tante Jean Marie know that this is the twenty-first century and that women no longer have to live with the stigma of dark facial hair, and leave her my Jolen.

9. Slip minister of finance details on parking-meter manufacturers that I got off the Internet.

10. Get scepter back from Prince René.

Tina spent all day yesterday reading *Jane Eyre* per my recommendation and agrees with me that there might be something to the whole letting-boys-chase-you-as-opposed-to-you-chasing-them thing. So she has decided not to e-mail or call Dave (unless he e-mails or calls first, of course).

Lilly, however, refuses to take part in this scheme, as she says game playing is for children and that her relationship with Boris is one that cannot be qualified by modern-day psychosexual mating practices. According to Tina (I can't call Lilly because Michael might pick up the phone and then he'll think I'm chasing him), Lilly says that *Jane Eyre* was one of the first feminist manifestos, and she heartily approves of us using it as a model for our romantic relationships. Although she sent a warning to me through Tina that I shouldn't expect Michael to ask me to marry him until after he's gotten at least one postgraduate degree, as well as a starting position with a company that pays at least two hundred thousand dollars a year, plus annual performance bonus.

Lilly also added that the one time she saw him ride a horse, Michael looked way unromantic, so I shouldn't get my hopes up that he's going to be jumping any stiles, like Mr. Rochester, any time soon.

But I find this hard to believe. I am sure Michael would look very handsome on a horse.

Tina mentioned that Lilly is still upset about the movie of my life they showed the other day. Tina saw it, though, and said it wasn't as bad as Lilly is making it out to be. She said the lady who played Principal Gupta was hilarious.

But Tina wasn't in the movie, on account of her dad having found out about it beforehand and threatening the filmmakers with a lawsuit if they mentioned his daughter's name anywhere. Mr. Hakim Baba worries a lot about Tina getting kidnapped by a rival oil sheik. Tina says she wouldn't mind being kidnapped though if the rival oil sheik was cute and willing to commit to a long-term relationship and remembered to buy her one of those diamond heart pendants from Kay Jewelers on Valentine's Day.

Tina says the girl who played Lana Weinberger in the movie did a fabulous job and should get an Emmy. Also that she didn't think Lana was going to be too happy about how she was portrayed, as a jealous princess wannabe.

Also the guy who played Josh was a babe. Tina is trying to find his e-mail address.

Tina and I vowed that if either of us ever felt like calling our boyfriends, instead we would call each other. Unfortunately I have no cell phone so it is not like Tina will be able to reach me if I am in the middle of knighting someone or anything. But I am fully going to hit my dad up for a Motorola tomorrow. Hey, I am heir to the sovereign of an entire country. At the very least I should have a beeper.

Note to self: look up word "stile."

Four days, twelve hours, and five minutes until I see Michael again.

Could there be a more boring sport than polo? I mean, besides golf? I think not.

Furthermore, I do not think it is very good for the horses, swinging mallets that close to their heads. It is like Silver, the Lone Ranger's horse. The Lone Ranger kept shooting off guns next to Silver's ear. It was no wonder the poor thing kept rearing.

Also, René isn't *too* competitive with Prince William, or anything. René keeps riding in front of the poor guy and stealing the ball from him every chance he gets . . . and they are supposed to be on the same team!

I swear, if René's team wins, and he pulls a Mia Hamm and swings his shirt around over his head, I will know he is just doing all of this for the benefit of the hordes of Prince William fans who are here. Which I guess is understandable. It probably is disconcerting to him that Wills is so much more popular than he is. And René does have pretty impressive pecs.

If only all those girls knew about the Enrique Iglesias lip-synching. . . .

Three days, seventeen hours, and six minutes until I see Michael again. Talk about impressive pecs . . .

*Saturday, January 17, 11 p.m.,
Royal Genovian bedchamber*

Grandmère so needs to get a life.

Tonight was the Farewell Ball—you know, to celebrate the end of my first official trip to Genovia in my capacity as heir to the throne.

Anyway, Grandmère's been going on about this ball for weeks, like this is going to be my big chance to redeem myself for the whole parking-meter thing. Not to mention the Prince William factor. In fact, between that and the whole not-thinking-Michael-is-suitable-consort-material, she's been laying it on so thick, I fully blame her for my zit— even though it's gone now, thanks to the miracle of modern dermatology. But still. Between the pressures Grandmère has been putting on me, plus the anxiety of knowing that my boyfriend might at this very moment be taking surfing lessons from some zit-free Kate Bosworth type, it is a wonder my complexion does not resemble that guy's they kept locked in the basement in that movie *The Goonies*.

Whatever. So Grandmère makes this big deal out of my hair (growing out and so becoming triangular-shaped again, but who cares, boys are supposed to like girls with long hair better than girls with short hair—I read that in French *Cosmo*) and she makes this big deal out of my fingernails (okay, so in spite of the whole New Year's resolution thing I still keep biting them. So sue me. The man is keeping me down.) and she makes this big deal out of what I am going to say to Prince William.

Then, after all this, we get to the stupid ball, and I walk up to Wills (who I will admit—though my heart still belongs to Michael—was looking quite studly in his tux) and I'm all set to go, "It's very nice to meet you," but it was like at the last second I forgot who I was talking to, because he turned those blue, blue eyes on me, like a pair of klieg lights, and I totally froze up, exactly the way I did that time Josh Richter smiled at me in Bigelow's drugstore. Seriously, like, I couldn't remember where I was or what I was doing there, I was just looking into those blue eyes and going, inside my head, *Oh, my God, they're the color of the sea outside the window of my Royal Genovian bedchamber*.

Then Prince William was going, "It's very nice to meet you," and shaking my hand, and I just kept on staring at him, even though I do not even like him in that way. I AM IN LOVE WITH MY BOYFRIEND.

But I guess that is the thing with the guy, he has that whole charisma thing going, kind of like Bill Clinton (only I never met him; I just read about it).

Anyway, that was it. That was the extent of my interaction with Prince William of England! He turned around after that to answer someone's question about Thoroughbred horse racing, and I was like, "Oh, look, baked mushroom caps," to cover my excruciating mortification and went chasing after the footman who was passing them around. That's all, the end.

Needless to say, I did not get his e-mail address. Tina is just going to have to learn to live with disappointment.

Oh, but my evening did not end there. Not at all. No, little did I know there was much, much more to come, in the form of Grandmère shoving me at *Prince René* all night, so that the two of us could dance in front of this *Newsweek* reporter who is in Genovia to do a story on our country's transition to the Euro. She SWORE that was the only reason: for the photo op.

But then while we were dancing—which, by the way, I am horrible at . . . dancing, I mean. I can box step if I look down the whole time and count inside my head, but that is about it, aside from slow dancing, but guess what? They so don't slow dance in Genovia . . . at least, not in the palace—I saw Grandmère totally going around, pointing us out to people, and it was so obvious what she was saying, you didn't even have to be a lip reader to know she was going, "Aren't they just the loveliest couple?"

EW!!!!!!!!!!!!!!!!!!!!!!!!!!!!!!!!!!!!!!!!!!!!!!!!!!!!!!!!!!!!

So then when the dance was over, just in case Grandmère was getting any ideas, I went up to her and I was all, "Grandmère, I am willing to cool it with the calling-Michael stuff, but that does not mean I am going to start going out with Prince René," who, by the way, asked me if I wanted to step outside onto the terrazzo and have a smoke.

I of course told him I do not smoke and that he shouldn't either as tobacco is responsible for half a million deaths a year in the United States alone, but he only laughed at me, all James Spader from *Pretty in Pink*–ishly.

So then I told him not to get any big ideas, that I already have a boyfriend and that maybe he didn't see the movie of my life, but I fully know how to handle guys who are only after me for my crown jewels.

So then René said I was adorable and I said, "Oh, for God's sake, cut the Enrique Iglesias act," and then my dad came up and asked me if I had seen the prime minister of Greece and I said, "Dad, I think Grandmère is trying to fix me up with René," and then my dad got all tight-lipped and took Grandmère aside and had "A Word" with her while Prince René slunk off to go make out with one of the Hilton sisters.

Afterward Grandmère came up and told me not to be so ridiculous, that she merely wanted Prince René and me to dance together because it was a nice photo op for *Newsweek* and that maybe if they ran a story on us, it would attract more tourists.

To which I replied that in light of our crumbling infrastructure, more tourists is exactly what this country doesn't need.

I suppose if my palace had been bought out from under me by some shoe designer, I would be pretty desperate, too, but I wouldn't hit on a girl who has the weight of an entire populace on her shoulders—and already *has* a boyfriend, besides.

On the bright side, if *Newsweek* does run the photo, maybe Michael will get all jealous of René the way Mr. Rochester did of that St. John guy, and he'll boss me around some more!!!

Two days, eight hours, and ten minutes until I see Michael again.

I CAN'T WAIT!!!!!!!!!!!!!!

I cannot believe that

A. my dad is staying in Genovia in order to resolve the parking crisis rather than coming back to New York with me.

B. he actually believed Grandmère when she said due to my poor performance in Genovia that my princess lessons need to continue.

C. she (not to mention Rommel) is coming back to New York with me.

IT IS NOT FAIR. I held up my part of the agreement. I went to every single princess lesson Grandmère gave last fall. I passed Algebra. I gave my stupid address to the Genovian people.

Grandmère says that in spite of what I might think, I still have a lot to learn about governance. Except that she is so wrong. I know she is only coming back to New York with me so she can go on torturing me. It is kind of like her hobby now. In fact, for all I know, it might even be her gift, her God-given talent.

At least she is lucky enough to have one. But it is still so not fair.

And yes, before I left, my dad slipped me a hundred Euros and told me if I didn't make a fuss about Grandmère, he'd make it up to me someday.

But there is nothing he can do to make this up to me. Nothing.

He says she is just a harmless old lady and that I should

try to enjoy her while I can because someday she won't be with us anymore. I just looked at him like he was crazy. Even he couldn't keep a straight face. He went, "Okay, I'll donate *two* hundred bucks a day to Greenpeace if you keep her out of my hair."

Which is funny, because of course my dad hasn't got any. Hair, I mean.

That is double the amount he was already donating in my name to my favorite organization. I sincerely hope Greenpeace appreciates the supreme sacrifice I am making for its sake.

So Grandmère is coming back to New York with me, and dragging a cowering Rommel along with her. Just when his fur had started to grow back, too. Poor thing.

I told my dad I'd put up with the whole princess-lesson thing again this semester, but that he'd better get one thing straight with Grandmère beforehand, and that is this: I have a serious boyfriend now. Grandmère had better not try to sabotage this, or think she can be trying to fix me up with any more Prince Renés. I don't care how many crown titles the guy has, my heart belongs to Mr. Michael Moscovitz, Esquire.

My dad said he'd see what he could do. But I don't know how much he was actually paying attention, since Miss Czech Republic was hanging around, twirling her sash kind of impatiently.

Anyway, a little while ago I told Grandmère myself that she better watch it where Michael is concerned.

"I don't want to hear anything more about how I'm too young to be in love," I said, over the lunch (poached salmon for Grandmère, three-bean salad for me) served by the royal Genovian flight attendants. "I am old enough to know my own heart, and that means I am old enough to give that heart away if I choose to."

Grandmère said something about how then I should get ready for some heartburn, but I ignored her. Just because her romantic life since Grandpa died has been less than satisfactory is no reason for her to be so cynical about mine. I mean, that is just what she gets for going out with media moguls and dictators and stuff.

Michael and I, on the other hand, are going to have a great love, just like Jane and Mr. Rochester. Or Jennifer Aniston and Brad Pitt.

Or at least we will, if we ever actually get to go out on a date.

One day, fourteen hours until I see him again.

I am so happy I feel like I could burst, just like that eggplant I once dropped out of Lilly's sixteenth-floor bedroom window.

I'm home!!!!!!! I'm finally home!!!!!!

I cannot tell you how good it felt to look out the window of the airplane and see the bright lights of Manhattan below me. It brought tears to my eyes, knowing I was once again in the air space over my beloved city. Below me, I knew, cab drivers were running down little old ladies (unfortunately not Grandmère), deli owners were shortchanging their customers, investment bankers were not cleaning up after their dogs, and people all over town were having their dreams of becoming singers, actors, musicians, novelists, or dancers completely crushed by soulless producers, directors, agents, editors, and choreographers.

Yes, I was back in my beautiful New York. I was back home at last.

I especially knew it when I stepped off the plane, and there was Lars waiting for me, ready to take over bodyguarding duty from François, the guy who had looked after me in Genovia and who had taught me all the French swear words. Lars looked especially menacing on account of being all darkly tanned from his month off. He had spent his winter break with Tina Hakim Baba's bodyguard, Wahim, snorkeling and hunting wild boar in Belize. He gave me a piece of ivory tusk as a memento of his trip, even though of course I don't approve of killing animals recreationally, even wild boars, who really can't help being so ugly and mean.

Then, after a delay of sixty-five minutes, thanks to a pileup on the Belt Parkway, I was home.

It was so good to see my mom!!!!! Her belly is starting to show now. I didn't want to say anything, because even though my mom says she does not believe in the Western standard of idealized beauty and that there is nothing wrong with a woman who is bigger than a size eight, I'm pretty sure though that if I had said anything like, "Mom, you're huge," even in a complimentary fashion, she would start to cry. After all, she still has quite a few months left to go.

So instead I just went, "That baby has to be a boy. Or if it's not, it's a girl who is going to be as tall as me."

"Oh, I hope so," my mom said, as she brushed tears of joy from her face—or maybe she was crying because Fat Louie was biting her ankles so hard in his effort to get near me. "I could use another you for when you aren't around. I missed you so much! There was no one to berate me for ordering roast pork and wonton soup from Number One Noodle Son."

"I tried," Mr. Gianini assured me.

Mr. G looks great, too. He is growing a goatee. I pretended I liked it.

Then I bent down and picked up Fat Louie, who was yowling to get my attention, and gave him a great big hug. I may be wrong, but I think he lost weight while I was away. I do not want to accuse anyone of purposefully starving him, but I noticed his dry food bowl was not completely full. In fact, it was perilously close to being only half full. I always keep Fat Louie's bowl filled to the brim, because you never know when there might be a sudden plague, killing everyone in Manhattan but cats. Fat Louie can't pour out his own food, having no thumbs, so he needs a little extra just in case we all die and there is no one around to open the bag for him.

But the loft looks so great!!!!!!!! Mr. Gianini did a lot to it while I was gone. He got rid of the Christmas tree—

the first time in the history of the Thermopolis household that the Christmas tree was out of the loft by Easter—and had the place wired for DSL. So now you can e-mail or go on the Internet anytime you want, without tying up the phone.

It is like a Christmas miracle.

And that's not all. Mr. G also fully redid the darkroom, leftover from when my mom was going through her Ansel Adams stage. He pulled the boards off the windows and got rid of all the noxious chemicals that have been sitting around since forever because my mom and I were too afraid to touch them. Now the darkroom is going to be the baby's room! It is so sunny and nice in there. Or at least it *was*, until my mom started painting the walls (in egg tempera, of course, so as not to jeopardize the welfare of her unborn child!) with scenes of important historical significance, such as the trial of Winona Ryder and the engagement of J.Lo and Ben Affleck, so that, she says, the baby will have an understanding of all the problems facing our nation (Mr. G assured me privately that he is going to have the whole thing painted over as soon as my mom gets admitted to the maternity ward. She will never know the difference once the endorphins kick in. All I can say is thank God Mom picked a man with so much common sense with whom to reproduce this time around).

But the best thing of all was what was waiting for me on the answering machine. My mom played it for me proudly almost the minute I walked through the door.

IT WAS A MESSAGE FROM MICHAEL!!!! MY FIRST RECORDED MESSAGE FROM MICHAEL SINCE I BECAME HIS GIRLFRIEND!!!!!!!!!!!!

Which of course means it worked. The my-not-calling-him thing, I mean.

The message goes like this:

*"Uh, hi, Mia? Yeah, it's Michael. I was just wondering if you could, uh, call me when you get this message. 'Cause I haven't heard from you in a while. And I just want to know if you're, uh, okay. And make sure you got home all right. And that there's nothing wrong. Okay. That's all. Well. Bye. This is Michael, by the way. Or maybe I said that. I can't remember. Hi, Mrs. Thermopolis. Hi, Mr. G. Okay. Well.*
*Call me, Mia. Bye."*

I took the tape out of the message machine and am keeping it in the drawer of my nightstand along with

A. some grains of rice from the bag Michael and I sat on at the Cultural Diversity Dance, in memory of the first time we ever slow danced together;

B. a dried-out piece of toast from the *Rocky Horror Picture Show*, which is where Michael and I went on our first date, though it wasn't really a date because Kenny came, too; and

C. a cut-out snowflake from the Nondenominational Winter Dance, in memory of the first time Michael and I kissed.

It was the best Christmas present I could ever have gotten, that message. Even better than DSL.

So then I came into my room and unpacked and played the message over about fifty times on my tape player, and my mom kept coming in to give me more hugs and asking me if I wanted to listen to her new Liz Phair CD and wanting to show me her stretch marks. Then about the thirtieth time she came in, I was playing Michael's message again, and she was all, "Haven't you called him back yet, honey?" and I went, "No," and she went, "Well, why not?" and I went, "Because I am trying to be like Jane Eyre."

And then my mom got all squinty-eyed like she does whenever they are debating funding for the arts on C-SPAN.

"Jane Eyre?" she echoed. "You mean the book?"

"Exactly," I said, tugging the little Napoleonic diamond napkin holders that the prime minister of France had given me for Christmas out from beneath Fat Louie, who had laid down inside my suitcase, I guess in the mistaken belief that I was packing, not unpacking, and he wanted to try to stop me from going away again. "See, Jane didn't chase Mr. Rochester, she let him chase her. And so Tina and I, we've both taken solemn vows that we are going to be just like Jane."

Unlike Grandmère, my mom didn't look happy to hear this.

"But Jane Eyre was so mean to poor Mr. Rochester!" she cried.

I didn't mention that this was what I had thought, too . . . at first.

"Mom," I said, very firmly. "What about the whole keeping Bertha locked up in the attic thing?"

"Because she was a lunatic," my mom pointed out. "It wasn't like they had psychotropic drugs back then. Keeping Bertha locked in the attic was kinder, really, than sending her to a mental hospital, considering what they were like during that era, with people chained to the walls. Really, Mia. I swear I don't know where you get half your ideas. Jane Eyre? Who told you about Jane Eyre?"

"Um," I said, stalling because I knew my mom wasn't going to like the answer. "Grandmère."

My mom's lips got so thin, they completely disappeared.

"I should have known," she said. "Well, Mia, I think it is commendable that you and your friends have decided not to chase boys. However, if a boy leaves a nice message on the answering machine like Michael did, it could hardly be construed as chasing for you to do the polite thing and return his call."

I thought about this. My mom was probably right. I mean, it isn't as if Michael has a crazy wife in the attic. The Fifth Avenue apartment where the Moscovitzes live doesn't even have an attic, so far as I know.

"Okay," I said, setting down the clothes I'd been putting away. "I guess I could return his call." My heart was swelling at the very idea. In a minute—less than a minute, if I could get my mom out of my room fast enough—I'd be talking to Michael! And there wouldn't be that weird swooshing sound there always is when you call from across the ocean. Because there would be no ocean separating us! Just Washington Square Park. And I wouldn't have to worry about him wishing I were Kate Bosworth instead of Mia Thermopolis, because there are no Kate Bosworth types in Manhattan . . . or at least if there are, they have to keep their clothes on, at least in winter.

"Returning calls probably doesn't count as chasing," I said. "That would probably be okay."

My mom, who was sitting on the end of my bed, just shook her head.

"Really, Mia," she said. "You know I don't like to contradict your grandmother"—this was the biggest lie I'd heard since René told me I waltzed divinely, but I let it slide, on account of Mom's condition—"but I really don't think you should be playing mind games with boys. Particularly a boy you care about. Particularly a boy like Michael."

"Mom, if I want to spend the rest of my life with him,

I have to play games with Michael," I explained to her, patiently. "I certainly can't tell him the truth. If he were ever to learn the depths of my passion for him, he'd run like a startled fawn."

My mom looked stunned. "A what?"

"A startled fawn," I explained. "See, Tina told her boyfriend Dave Farouq El-Abar how she really feels about him, and he pulled a total David Caruso on her."

My mom blinked. "A who?"

"David Caruso," I said. I felt sorry for my mom. Clearly she had only managed to snag Mr. Gianini by the skin of her teeth. I couldn't believe she didn't know this stuff. "You know, he disappeared for a really long time. Dave only resurfaced when Tina managed to scrounge Wrestlemania tickets for the Garden. And ever since, Tina says things have been really awkward." Done unpacking, I shooed Fat Louie out of the suitcase, closed it, and put it on the floor. Then I sat next to my mom on the bed. "Mom," I said. "I do *not* want that to happen to me and Michael. I love Michael more than anything else in the entire world, except for you and Fat Louie."

I just said the you part to be polite. I think I love Michael more than I love my mom. It sounds terrible to say, but I can't help it, it is just how I feel.

But I will never love anyone or anything as much as I love Fat Louie.

"So don't you see?" I said to her. "What Michael and I have, I don't want to mess it up. He's my Romeo in black jeans." Even though of course I have never seen Michael in black jeans. But I am sure he has some. It is just that we have a dress code at our school, so usually when I see him he is in gray flannel pants, as that is part of our uniform. "And the fact of the matter is, Michael could do way better than me, anyway. So I have to be especially careful."

My mom blinked at me sort of confusedly. "Better than you? What on earth are you talking about, Mia?"

"Well, you know," I said. "I mean, Mom, I am not exactly a catch. I'm not really pretty, or anything, and I think we both know how hard I had to work just to pass my first semester of freshman Algebra. And it isn't as if I am really good at anything."

"Mia!" My mom looked totally shocked. "What are you talking about? You're good at lots of things! Why, you know everything there is to know about the environment and Iceland and what's playing on the Lifetime Channel. . . ."

I tried to smile encouragingly at her, like I actually thought these things were talents. I didn't want to make my mom feel bad for not having passed any of her artistic gifts on to me. That is totally not her fault, just some faulty DNA strand somewhere.

"Yeah," I said. "But, see, Mom, those aren't actually talents. Michael is gorgeous and smart and he can play a bunch of instruments and write songs and is good at just about everything, and it's really only a matter of time until he gets snatched up by some totally pretty girl who can surf, or whatever—"

"I don't know why," my mom said, "you think that just because you had to work a little harder at Algebra than other people in your class that you are not good at anything, or that Michael is going to take up with a girl who can surf. But I do think that if you haven't seen a boy in a month, and he leaves a message for you, the decent thing to do is to call him back. If you don't, I think you can pretty much guarantee he is going to run. And not like a startled fawn, either."

I blinked at my mom. She had a point. I saw then that Grandmère's scheme—you know, of always keeping the man you love guessing as to whether or not you love him back—had some pitfalls. Such as, he could just decide you don't like him, and take off, and maybe fall in love with some other girl of whose affection he could be assured, such as Judith Gershner, president of the Computer Club and all-around prodigy, even though supposedly she is dating a boy from Trinity, but you never know, that could be a ruse to lull me into a false sense of security about Michael and let my guard down, thinking he is safe from Judith's fruit-fly–cloning clutches. . . .

"Mia," my mom said, looking at me all concerned. "Are you all right?"

I tried to smile, but I couldn't. How, I wondered, could Tina and I have overlooked this very serious flaw in our plan? Even now, Michael could be on the phone with Judith or some other equally intellectual girl, talking about quasars or photons or whatever it is smart people talk about. Worse, he could be on the phone with Kate Bosworth, talking about wave surface.

"Mom," I said, standing up. "You have to go. I have to call him."

I was glad the panic that was clutching my throat wasn't audible in my voice.

"Oh, Mia," my mom said, looking pleased. "I really think you should. Charlotte Brontë is, of course, a brilliant author, but you've got to remember, she wrote *Jane Eyre* back in the 1840s, and things were a little different then—"

"Mom," I said. Lilly and Michael's parents, the Drs. Moscovitz, have this totally hardfast rule about calling after eleven on schoolnights. It is verboten. And it was practically eleven. And my mom was still standing there, keeping me from having the privacy I would need if I were going to make this all-important call.

"Oh," she said, smiling. Even though she is pregnant, my mom still looks like a total babe, with all this long black hair that curls just right. Clearly I inherited my dad's hair, which I've actually never seen, since he's always been bald since I've known him.

DNA is so unfair.

Anyway, FINALLY she left—pregnant women move so slowly, I swear you would think evolution would have made them quicker so they could get away from predators or whatever, but I guess not—and I lunged for the phone, my heart pounding because at last, AT LAST, I was going to get to talk to Michael, and my mom had even said that it was all right, that my calling him wouldn't count as chasing since he'd called me first. . . .

And just as I was about to pick up the receiver, the phone rang. My heart actually did this flippy thing inside my chest, like it does every time I see Michael. It was Michael calling, I just knew it. I picked up after the second ring—even though I didn't want him dumping me for some more attentive girl, I didn't want him to think I was sitting by the phone waiting for him to call, either—and said, in my most sophisticated tone, "Hullo?"

Grandmère's cigarette-ravaged voice filled my ear. "Amelia?" she rasped. "Why do you sound like that? Are you coming down with something?"

"Grandmère." I couldn't believe it. It was ten fifty-nine! I had exactly one minute left to call Michael without running the risk of the wrath of his parents. "I can't talk now. I have to make another call."

"*Pfuit!*" Grandmère made her noise of disapproval. "And who would you be calling at this hour, as if I didn't know?"

"Grandmère." Ten fifty-nine and a half. "It's okay. He called me first. I am returning his call. It is the polite thing to do."

"It's too late for you to be calling that boy," Grandmère said.

Eleven o'clock. I had missed my opportunity. Thanks to Grandmère.

"You'll see him at school tomorrow, anyway," she went on. "Now, let me speak to your mother."

"My mother?" I was shocked by this. Grandmère never talks to my mom, if she can help it. They haven't gotten along since my mom refused to marry my dad after she got pregnant with me, on account of her not wanting her child to be subjected to the vicissitudes of a progenitive aristocracy.

"Yes, your mother," Grandmère said. "Surely you've heard of her."

So I went out and passed the phone to my mom who was sitting out in the living room with Mr. Gianini, watching *The Anna Nicole Show*. I didn't tell her who was on the phone, because if I had, my mom would have told me to tell Grandmère that she was in the shower, and then I would have had to talk to her some more.

"Hello?" my mom said, all brightly, thinking it was one of her friends calling to comment on the hijinks of Howard K. Stern and Bobby Trendy. I slunk out as fast as I could. There were several heavy objects lying around the couch that my mom could have hurled in my direction if I'd stayed within missile range.

Back in my room, I thought sadly about Michael. What was I going to say to him tomorrow, when Lars and I pulled up in the limo to pick him and Lilly up before school? That I'd gotten in too late to call? What if he noticed my nostrils flaring as I spoke? I don't know if he's figured out that they do that when I lie, but I think I'd sort of mentioned it to Lilly, since I have a complete inability to keep my mouth shut about stuff I really should just keep to myself, and supposing she told him?

Then, as I sat there dejectedly on my bed, pretty sleepy because in Genovia it was five in the morning and I was totally jet-lagged, I had a brilliant idea. I could see if Michael was logged on, and instant message him! I could do it even though my mom was on the phone with Grandmère, because we have DSL now!

So I scrambled over to my computer and did just that. And he was online!

*Michael*, I wrote. *Hi, it's me! I'm home! I wanted to call you, but it's after eleven, and I didn't want your mom and dad to get mad.*

Michael has changed his screen name since the demise of *Crackhead*. He's no longer CracKing. He's LinuxRulz, in protest of the stranglehold Microsoft has on the software industry.

LINUXRULZ: Welcome home! It's good to hear from you. I was worried you were dead or something.

So he had noticed I'd stopped calling! Which meant the plan that Tina and I had come up with was working perfectly. At least so far.

FTLOUIE: No, not dead. Just super busy. You know, fate of the aristocracy resting on my shoulders and all of that. So should Lars and I pick you and Lilly up for school tomorrow?

LINUXRULZ: That'd be good. What are you doing Friday?

What am I doing Friday? Was he asking me OUT? Were Michael and I actually going to have a date? At last????

I tried to type casually so he wouldn't know that I was so excited, I had already freaked Fat Louie out by jumping up and down in my computer chair and almost rolling over his tail.

FTLOUIE: Nothing, so far as I know. Why?

LINUXRULZ: Want to go to dinner at the Screening Room? They're showing the first *Star Wars*.

OH, MY GOD!!!!!!!! HE WAS ASKING ME OUT!!!!!!!!! Dinner and a movie. At the same time, because at the Screening Room you sit at a table and eat dinner while the movie is going. And *Star Wars* is only my favorite movie of all time, after *Dirty Dancing*. Could there BE a girl luckier than me? No, I don't think so. Bite me, Britney.

My fingers were trembling as I typed

FTLOUIE: I think that would be OK. I'll have to check with my mom. Can I let you know tomorrow?

LINUXRULZ: OK. So see you tomorrow? Around 8:15?

FTLOUIE: Tomorrow, 8:15.

I wanted to add something like I missed you or I love you, but I don't know, it just felt too weird, and I couldn't do it. I mean, it's embarrassing, telling the person you love that you love them. It shouldn't be, but it is. Also, it didn't seem like something Jane Eyre would do. Unless, you know, she had just discovered the man she loved had gone blind in a heroic attempt to rescue his crazy firebug wife from an inferno she'd set herself.

Asking me out to dinner and a movie didn't really seem the same, somehow.

Then Michael wrote

LINUXRULZ: Kid, I've been from one side of this galaxy to the other—

which is one of my favorite lines from the first *Star Wars*. So then I wrote

FTLOUIE: I happen to like nice men.

—jumping ahead to *The Empire Strikes Back*, to which Michael replied

LINUXRULZ: I'm nice.

Which is better than saying I love you, because right after Han Solo says that, he totally kisses Princess Leia. OH, MY GOD!!! It really is like Michael is Han Solo and I'm Princess Leia, because Michael is good at fixing stuff like hyper drives, and, well, I'm a princess, and I'm very socially conscious like Leia, and everything.

Plus Michael's dog, Pavlov, sort of looks like Chewbacca. If Chewbacca were a sheltie.

I could not imagine a more perfect date if I tried. Mom will let me go, too, because the Screening Room isn't that far away, and it's *Michael*, after all. Even Mr. Gianini likes Michael, and he doesn't like many of the boys who go to Albert Einstein—he says they are mostly all walking bundles of testosterone.

I wonder if Princess Leia ever read *Jane Eyre*. But maybe *Jane Eyre* doesn't exist in her galaxy.

I will never get to sleep now, I am too worked up. *I am going to see him in eight hours and fifteen minutes.*

And on Friday, I am going to be sitting next to him in a darkened room. All alone. With no one else around. Except all the waitresses and the other people at the movie.

The Force is *so* with me.

I barely made it out of bed this morning. In fact, the only reason I was able to drag myself out from beneath the covers—and Fat Louie, who laid on my chest purring like a weedwhacker all night long—was the prospect of seeing Michael for the first time in thirty-two days.

It is completely cruel to force a person of my tender years, when I should be getting at least nine hours of sleep a night, to travel back and forth between two such drastically different time zones, with not even a single day of rest in between. I am still completely jet-lagged, and I am sure it is going to stunt not only my physical growth (not in the height department because I am tall enough, thank you, but in the mammary-gland division, glands being very sensitive to things like disrupted sleep cycles), but my intellectual growth as well.

And now that I am entering the second semester of my freshman year, my grades are actually going to start to matter. Not that I intend to go to college or anything. At least not right away. I, like Prince William, intend to take a year off between high school and college. But I hope to spend it developing some kind of gift or talent, or, if I can't find one, volunteering for Greenpeace, hopefully in one of those boats that goes out between Japanese and Russian whaling ships and the whales. I don't think Greenpeace takes volunteers who don't have at least a 3.0 grade-point average.

Anyway, it was murder getting up this morning, especially when, after I'd dragged out my school uniform, I realized my Queen Amidala panties weren't in my underwear drawer. I have to wear my Queen Amidala underwear on the first day of every semester, or I'll have bad luck for the rest of the year. I *always* have good luck when I wear my Queen Amidala panties. For instance, I was wearing them the night of the Nondenominational Winter Dance, when Michael finally told me he loved me.

Not that he was IN LOVE with me, of course. But that he loved me. Hopefully not like a friend.

I have to wear my Queen Amidala panties on the first day of second semester, just like I'll have to send them to the laundry-by-the-pound place and get them washed before Friday so I can wear them on my date with Michael. Because I'm going to need extra good luck that night, if I'm going to have to compete with the Kate Bosworths of the world for his attentions . . . and also since I plan on giving Michael his birthday present that night. His birthday present that I'm hoping he'll like so much, he'll totally fall in love with me, if he hasn't already.

So I had to go into my mom's room, the one she shares with Mr. Gianini, and wake her up (thank God Mr. G was in the shower, I swear to God if I'd had to see them in bed together in the condition I was in at that time, I'd have gone completely Anne Heche) and be all, "Mom, where's my Queen Amidala underwear?"

My mom, who sleeps like a log even when she isn't pregnant, just went, "Shurnowog," which isn't even a word.

"Mom," I said. "I need my Queen Amidala underwear. Where are they?"

But all my mom said was, "Kapukin."

So then I got an idea. Not that I really thought there was any way my mom wasn't going to let me go out with Michael, after her uplifting speech about him the night before. But just to make sure she couldn't back out of it, I went, "Mom, can I go with Michael for dinner and a movie at the Screening Room this Friday night?"

And she went, rolling over, "Yeah, yeah, scuniper."

So I got that taken care of.

But I still had to go to school in my regular underwear, which creeped me out a little, because there's nothing special about it, it is just boring and white.

But then I kind of perked up when I got in the limo, because of the prospect of seeing Michael and all.

But then I was like, Oh, my God, what was going to happen when I saw Michael? Because when you haven't seen your boyfriend in thirty-two days, you can't just be all, "Oh, hi," when you see him. You have to, like, give him a hug or *something*.

But how was I going to give him a hug in the car? With everyone watching? I mean, at least I wasn't going to have to worry about my stepdad, since Mr. G fully refuses to take the limo to school with me and Lars and Lilly and Michael every morning, even though we are all going to the same place. But Mr. Gianini says he likes the subway. He says it is the only time he gets to listen to music he likes (Mom and I won't let him play Blood, Sweat and Tears in the loft, so he has to listen to it on his Discman).

But what about Lilly? I mean, Lilly was totally going to be there. How can I hug Michael in front of Lilly? And okay, it is partly because of Lilly that Michael and I got together in the first place. But that does not mean that I feel perfectly comfortable participating in, you know, public displays of affection with him *right in front of her*.

If this were Genovia it would be all right to kiss him on both cheeks, because that is the standard form of greeting there.

But this is America, where you barely even shake hands with people, unless you're, like, the mayor.

Plus there was the whole Jane-Eyre thing. I mean, Tina and I had resolved we were not going to chase our boyfriends, but we hadn't said anything about how to greet them again after not having seen them for thirty-two days.

I was almost going to ask Lars what he thought I ought to do when I had a brainstorm right as we were pulling up to the Moscovitzes' building. Hans, the driver, was going to hop out and open the door for Lilly and Michael, but I went, "I've got it," and then *I* hopped out, instead.

And there was Michael, standing there in the slush, looking all tall and handsome and manly, the wind tugging at his dark hair. Just the sight of him set my heart going about a thousand beats per minute. I felt like I was going to melt. . . .

Especially when he smiled once he saw me, a smile that went all the way up to his eyes, which were as deeply brown as I remembered, and filled with the same intelligence and good humor that had been there the last time I had gazed into them, thirty-two days earlier.

What I could not tell was whether or not they were filled with love. Tina had said I'd be able to tell, just by looking into his eyes, whether or not Michael loved me. But the truth was, all I could tell by looking into his eyes was that Michael didn't find me utterly repulsive. If he had, he'd have looked away, the way I do when I see that boy in the caf at school who always picks the corn out of his chili.

"Hi," I said, my voice suddenly super-squeaky.

"Hi," Michael said, his voice not squeaky at all, but really very thrillingly deep and Wolverine-like.

So then we stood there with our gazes locked on each other, and our breath coming out in little puffs of white steam, and people hurrying down Fifth Avenue on the sidewalk around us, people I barely saw. I hardly even noticed Lilly go, "Oh, for Pete's sake," and stomp past me to climb into the limo.

Then Michael went, "It's really good to see you."

And I went, "It's really good to see you, too."

From inside the limo, Lilly went, "Hello, it's like two below outside, will you two hurry it up and get in here already?"

So then I went, "I guess we better—"

And Michael went, "Yeah," and put his hand on the limo door to hold it open for me. But as I started to duck in there, he put his other hand on my arm, and when I turned around to see what he wanted (even though I kinda already knew) he went, "So can you go, on Friday night?"

And I went, "Uh-huh."

And then he kind of pulled on my arm in a very Mr. Rochester–like manner, causing me to take a step closer, and faster than I'd ever seen him move before, he bent down and kissed me, right on the mouth, in front of his doorman and all the rest of Fifth Avenue!

I have to admit, Michael's doorman and all of the people passing by, including everyone on the M1 bus that went barreling down the street at that very moment, didn't seem to take very much notice that the princess of Genovia was getting kissed right there in front of them.

But *I* noticed. *I* noticed, and it felt great. It made me feel like maybe all my worrying about whether Michael loved me as a potential life partner as opposed to just as a friend had maybe been stupid.

Because you don't kiss a friend like that.

I don't think.

So then I slid into the back of the limo with Lilly, a big silly smile on my face that I was totally afraid she might make fun of, but I couldn't help it, I was so happy, because in spite of not having on my Queen Amidala underwear, I was already having a good semester, and it wasn't even fifteen minutes old!

Then Michael got in beside me and closed the door, and

Hans started to drive and Lars said, "Good morning," to Lilly and Michael and they said good morning back and I didn't even notice that Lars was smirking behind his latte until Lilly told me when we got out of the limo at school.

"Like," she said, "we didn't all know what you were doing out there."

But she said it in a nice way.

I was so happy, I hardly even heard what Lilly was talking about on our way in to school, which was the whole movie thing. She had sent, she said, a certified letter to the producers of the movie of my life, and had no response, even though they had had it for more than a week.

"It is," Lilly said, "just another example of how those Hollywood types think they can get away with whatever they want. Well, I'm here to tell them they can't. If I don't hear back from them by tomorrow, I'm going to the news media."

That got my attention. I blinked at her. "You mean you're going to have a press conference?"

"Why not?" Lilly shrugged. "You did it, and up until recently, you could barely formulate a coherent sentence in front of a camera. So how hard can it be?"

Wow. Lilly is really mad about this movie thing. I guess I'm going to have to watch it myself to see how bad it is. The other kids at school don't seem to have thought much about it. But then they were all in St. Moritz or their winter homes in Ojai when it came on. They were too busy skiing or having fun in the sun to watch any stupid made-for-TV movie about the life of one of their classmates.

From the looks of the number of casts people are wearing—Tina was by far not the only one to sprain something on her vacation—everyone had a much better time on their break than I did. Even Michael says he spent most of the time at his grandparents' condo sitting on the balcony and writing songs for his new band.

I guess I am the only one who passed the whole of my break sitting in parliamentary sessions, trying to negotiate parking rates for casino garages in downtown Genovia.

Still, it's good to be back. It's good to be back because for the first time in my whole entire academic career, the guy I like actually likes—maybe even loves—me back. And I get to see him between classes and in Gifted and Talented fifth period—

Oh, my God! I totally forgot! It's a new semester! They are assigning us all new schedules! They are passing them out at the end of Homeroom, after the announcements. What if Michael and I aren't in the same Gifted and Talented class anymore? I am not even supposed to be in Gifted and Talented at all, seeing as how I am neither. They only put me in there when it became clear I was flunking Algebra, so I have an extra period for independent study. I was supposed to be in Tech Ed for that period. TECH ED! WHERE THEY MAKE YOU BUILD SPICE RACKS!

Second semester is Domestic Arts. IF I GET PUT IN DOMESTIC ARTS THIS SEMESTER INSTEAD OF GIFTED AND TALENTED I WILL DIE!!!!!!!

Because I ended up getting a B minus in Algebra last semester. They don't give you independent study periods if you are making B minuses. B minus is considered good. Except, you know, to people like Judith Gershner.

Oh, God, I knew it. I just KNEW something bad was going to happen if I didn't wear my Queen Amidala underwear.

So if I'm not in G and T, then the only time I will see Michael will be at lunch and between classes. Because he is a senior, and I am only a freshman, so it's not like I'll be in advanced calculus with him, or that he'll be in French II with me.

And I might not even be able to see him at lunch! We could conceivably not have the same lunch periods!

And even if we do, what is the likelihood that Michael and I are even going to sit together at lunch? Traditionally I always have sat with Lilly and Tina, and Michael always has sat with the Computer Club and upperclassmen. Is he going to come sit by me now? No way can I go sit at *his* table. All those guys over there ever do is talk about things I don't understand, like how Steve Jobs sucks and how easy it is to hack into India's missile defense system. . . .

Oh, God, they are passing out the new class schedules now. Please don't let me be in Domestic Arts. PLEASE PLEASE PLEASE PLEASE PLEASE PLEASE PLEASE PLEASE PLEASE PLEASE PLEASE PLEASE PLEASE PLEASE PLEASE PLEASE PLEASE PLEASE PLEASE PLEASE PLEASE PLEASE PLEASE PLEASE PLEASE PLEASE PLEASE PLEASE PLEASE PLEASE PLEASE PLEASE PLEASE PLEASE PLEASE PLEASE PLEASE PLEASE PLEASE PLEASE PLEASE PLEASE PLEASE PLEASE PLEASE PLEASE PLEASE PLEASE PLEASE PLEASE PLEASE PLEASE PLEASE PLEASE PLEASE PLEASE PLEASE PLEASE PLEASE PLEASE PLEASE PLEASE PLEASE PLEASE PLEASE PLEASE PLEASE PLEASE PLEASE PLEASE PLEASE PLEASE PLEASE PLEASE PLEASE PLEASE PLEASE PLEASE PLEASE PLEASE PLEASE PLEASE PLEASE PLEASE PLEASE PLEASE PLEASE PLEASE PLEASE PLEASE PLEASE PLEASE PLEASE PLEASE PLEASE PLEASE PLEASE PLEASE PLEASE PLEASE PLEASE PLEASE PLEASE PLEASE PLEASE PLEASE PLEASE PLEASE PLEASE PLEASE PLEASE PLEASE PLEASE PLEASE PLEASE PLEASE PLEASE PLEASE PLEASE PLEASE PLEASE PLEASE PLEASE PLEASE PLEASE PLEASE PLEASE PLEASE PLEASE PLEASE PLEASE PLEASE PLEASE PLEASE PLEASE

PLEASE PLEASE PLEASE PLEASE PLEASE PLEASE
PLEASE PLEASE PLEASE PLEASE PLEASE PLEASE
PLEASE PLEASE PLEASE PLEASE PLEASE PLEASE
PLEASE PLEASE PLEASE PLEASE

## Tuesday, January 20, Algebra

HA! My Queen Amidala underwear might be missing, but the power of The Force is with me nonetheless. My class schedule is EXACTLY the same as last semester's, except that by some miracle, I now have Bio third period instead of World Civ (Oh, God, please don't let Kenny, my former Bio partner and ex-boyfriend, have been switched to third-period Bio, too). World Civ is now seventh. And instead of PE fourth period, we all have Health and Safety.

And no Tech Ed or Domestic Arts, thank GOD!!!!! I don't know who told the administration that I am gifted and talented, but whoever it was, I am eternally grateful, and I will definitely try to live up to it.

And I happen to know that not only does Michael still have fifth-period G and T, but he has the same lunch hour as I do, too. I know that because after I got here to Algebra and sat down and got out my notebook and my Algebra I–II textbook, Michael came in!

Yes, he came right into Mr. G's second-semester freshman Algebra class, like he belonged there, or something, and everyone was staring at him, including Lana Weinberger, because you know seniors don't generally just go walking into freshman classes, unless they are working for the attendance office and bringing someone a hall pass or something.

But Michael doesn't work for the attendance office. He popped into Mr. G's class just to see *me*. I know, because he came right up to my desk with his class schedule in his hand and went, "What lunch have you got?" and I told him, "A," and he said, "Same as me. You have G and T after?" and I said, "Yes," and he said, "Cool, see you at lunch."

Then he turned around and walked out again, looking all tall and collegiate with his JanSport backpack and New Balances.

And the way he said, "Hey, Mr. G," all casually to Mr. Gianini—who was sitting at his desk with a cup of coffee in his hands and his eyebrows all raised—as he went walking out . . .

Well, you just can't get cooler than that.

And he had been in here to see me. ME. MIA THERMOPOLIS. Formerly the most unpopular person in the entire school, with the exception of that guy who doesn't like corn in his chili.

So now everyone who had not seen Michael and me kissing at the Nondenominational Winter Dance knows that we are going out, because you don't walk into someone else's classroom between periods to look at their schedule unless you are dating.

I could feel all the gazes of my fellow Algebra sufferers boring into me, even as the bell was ringing, including Lana Weinberger's. You could practically hear everybody going, "*He's* going out with *her*?"

I guess it *is* a little hard to believe. I mean, even *I* can hardly believe it's true. Because of course it's common knowledge that Michael's the third-best looking boy in the whole school, after Josh Richter and Justin Baxendale (though if you ask me, having seen Michael plenty of times without a shirt on, he makes those other guys look like that Quasimodo dude), so what is he doing with *me*, a talentless freak with feet the size of skis and no breasts to speak of and nostrils that flare when I lie?

Plus I am a lowly freshman, and Michael is a senior who has already been accepted early decision to an Ivy League school right here in Manhattan. Plus Michael is co-valedictorian of his class, being a straight-A student, whereas I barely scraped by Algebra I. Plus Michael is way involved with extracurriculars, including the Computer Club, Chess

Club, and Physics Club. He designed the school's website. He can play, like, ten instruments. And now he is starting his own band.

Me? I'm a princess. That's about it.

And that's only *recently*. Before I found out I was a princess, I was just this massive reject who was flunking Algebra and always had orange cat hair all over her school uniform.

So yeah, I guess you could say that a lot of people were kind of surprised to see Michael Moscovitz come striding up to my desk in Algebra to compare class schedules. I could feel them all staring at me after he left and the bell rang, and I could hear them buzzing about it among themselves. Mr. G tried to bring everybody to order, going, "Okay, okay, break's over. I know it's been a long time since you last saw one another, but we've got a lot to tackle in the next nine weeks," only of course nobody paid any attention to him but me.

In the desk in front of me, Lana Weinberger was already on her cell phone—the new one that I'd paid for, on account of my having stomped her old one to bits in a semi-psychotic fit last month—going, "Shel? You are not going to *believe* what just happened. You know that freaky girl in your Latin class, the one with the TV show and the flat face? Yeah, well, her brother was just in here comparing class schedules with Mia Thermopo—"

Unfortunately for Lana, Mr. Gianini has a thing about cell phone usage during class time. He fully pounced on her, snatched her phone away, put it up to his ear and said, "Ms. Weinberger can't speak to you right now as she is busy writing a thousand-word essay on how rude it is to make cell phone calls during class time," after which he threw her phone in his desk drawer and told her she'd get it back at the end of the day, once she'd handed in her essay.

I wish Mr. G would give Lana's cell phone to me, instead. I would fully use it in a more responsible manner than she does.

But I guess even if the teacher is your stepdad, he can't just confiscate things from other students and give them to you.

Which is a bummer because I could really use a cell phone right now. I just remembered I never asked my mom what Grandmère wanted when she called last night.

Oh, crud. Integers. Gotta go.


B = ($x$ : $x$ is an integer such that $x > 0$)

Defn: When integer is squared, the result is called a perfect square

# Tuesday, January 20, Health and Safety

This is so boring —MT

*You're telling me. How many times in our academic careers are they going to tell us having unprotected sex can result in unwanted pregnancy and AIDS? Do they think it didn't soak in the first five thousand times or something? —LM*

Apparently. Hey, did you see Mr. Wheeton open the door to the teachers' lounge, look at Mademoiselle Klein, then leave? He is so obviously in love with her.

*I know, you can totally tell, he is always bringing her lattes from Ho's. What is THAT about, if not luv? Wahim will be devastated if they start going out.*

Yeah, but why would she choose Mr. Wheeton over Wahim? Wahim has all those muscles. Not to mention a gun.

*Who can explain the vagaries of the human heart? Not I. Oh, my God, look, he's moving on to vehicular safety. Could this BE more boring? Let's make a list. You start it.*

OK.

# MIA THERMOPOLIS'S
## *NEW AND IMPROVED*
## LIST OF HOTTEST GUYS
### *with commentary by Lilly Moscovitz*

1. Michael Moscovitz *(Obviously I can't agree due to genetic link to said individual. Will concede he is not hideously deformed.)*

2. Ioan Griffud from the *Horatio Hornblower* series *(Agreed. He can shiver me timbers anytime he wants.)*

3. The guy from *Smallville (Duh—only they should have him join the school swim team because he needs to take his shirt off more per episode.)*

4. Hayden Christensen *(Again, duh. Ditto swim team. There must be one for Jedis. Even ones who have embraced the Dark Side.)*

5. Mr. Rochester *(Fictional character, but I agree he exudes certain rugged manliness.)*

6. Patrick Swayze *(Um, okay, maybe in* Dirty Dancing, *but have you seen him lately? The guy is older than your dad!)*

7. Captain von Trapp from *The Sound of Music (Christopher Plummer was a hottie extraordinaire. I would pit him against the Nazi horde anytime.)*

8. Justin Baxendale *(Agree. I heard an eleventh grader tried to kill herself because he looked at her. Seriously. Like, his eyes were so hypnotic, she went full-on Sylvia Plath. She is in counseling now.)*

9. Heath Ledger *(Oooh, in the rock-and-roll knight movie, totally. Not so much in* Four Feathers, *though. I found his performance in that film somewhat stilted. Plus he didn't take his shirt off enough.)*

10. Beast from *Beauty and the Beast (I think I know someone else who needs counseling.)*

I am so depressed.

I know I shouldn't be. I mean, everything in my life is going so great.

Great Thing Number One: The boy I have been madly in love with my entire life, practically, loves, or at least really likes, me back, and we are going out on our first real date on Friday.

Great Thing Number Two: I know it is only the first day of the new semester, but as of yet, I am not flunking anything, including Algebra.

Great Thing Number Three: I am no longer in Genovia, the most boring place on the entire planet, with the possible exception of Algebra class, and Grandmère's princess lessons.

Great Thing Number Four: I don't have Kenny for my Bio partner anymore. My new partner is Shameeka. What a relief. Which I know is cowardly (feeling relieved that I don't have to sit by Kenny anymore), but I am pretty sure Kenny thinks I am this horrible person to have led him on like that all those months, when really I liked someone else (though not the person he thought I liked). Anyway, the fact that I don't have to deal with any hostile looks from Kenny's direction (even though he fully has a new girlfriend, a girl from our Bio class, as a matter of fact—*he* didn't waste any time) is probably really going to boost my grade in that class. Plus Shameeka is really good at science. Actually Shameeka is really good at a lot of things, on account of her being a

Pisces. But like me, Shameeka has no *one particular talent*, which makes her my soul sister, if you think about it.

Great Thing Number Five: I have really cool friends who seem actually to want to hang around with me, and not just because I am a princess, either.

But that, see, is the problem. I have all these great things going for me, and I should be totally happy. I should be over the moon with joy.

And maybe it's only the jet lag talking—I am so tired I can barely keep my eyes open—or possibly PMS—I am sure my internal clock is way messed up from all this transcontinental flying—but I can't shake this feeling that I am . . .

Well, a total reject.

I started to realize it today at lunch. I was sitting there like always with Lilly and Boris and Tina and Shameeka and Ling Su, and then Michael came and sat down with us, which of course caused this total cafeteria sensation, since usually he sits with the Computer Club, and everyone in the entire school knows it.

And I was totally embarrassed but of course proud and pleased, too, because Michael *never* sat at our table back when he and I were just friends, so his sitting there must mean that he is at least slightly in love with me, because it is quite a sacrifice to give up the intellectual talk at the table where he normally sits for the kinds of talks we have at my table, which are generally, like, in-depth analyses of last night's episode of *Charmed* and how cute Rose McGowan's halter top was, or whatever.

But Michael was totally a good sport about it, even though he thinks *Charmed* is facile. And I really did try to steer the conversation around to things a guy would like, such as *Buffy the Vampire Slayer* or Milla Jovovich.

Only it turned out I didn't even need to, because Michael is like one of those lichen moths we read about in Bio. You know, the ones that turned black when the moss they fed on got all sooty during the industrial revolution? He can totally adapt to any situation, and feel at ease. This is an amazing talent that I wish I had. Maybe if I did, I wouldn't feel so out of place at meetings of the Genovian Olive Growers Association.

Anyway, today at the lunch table, someone brought up cloning, and everyone was talking about who would you clone if you could clone anyone, and people were saying, like, Albert Einstein so he could come back and tell us the meaning of life and stuff, or Jonas Salk so he could find a cure for cancer, and Mozart so he could finish his last requiem (whatever, that one was Boris's, of course), or Madame Pompadour so she could give us all tips on romance (Tina) or Jane Austen so she could write scathingly about the current political climate and we could all benefit from her cutting wit (Lilly).

And then Michael said he would clone Kurt Cobain, because he was a musical genius who died too young. And then he asked me who *I* would clone, and I couldn't think of anyone, because there really isn't anyone dead that I would want to bring back, except maybe Grandpère, but how creepy would that be? And Grandmère would probably freak. So I just said Fat Louie, because I love Fat Louie and wouldn't mind having two of him around.

Only nobody looked very impressed by this except for Michael who said, "That's nice," which he probably only said because he is my boyfriend.

But whatever, I could deal with that. I am totally used to being the only person I know who sits through *Empire*

*Records* every time it comes on TBS and who thinks it is one of the best movies ever made—after *Star Wars* and *Dirty Dancing* and *Say Anything* and *Pretty Woman*, of course. Oh, and *Tremors* and *Twister*.

I am content to keep the fact that I must watch the Miss America Pageant every single year without fail secret, even though I know it is degrading to women and *not* a scholarship fund, considering no one bigger than a size ten ever gets into it.

I mean, I know these things about myself. It is just the way I am, and though I have tried to improve myself by watching award-winning movies such as *Crouching Tiger, Hidden Dragon* and *Gladiator*, I don't know, I just don't like them. Everybody dies at the end and besides if there is not dancing or explosions, it is very hard for me to pay attention.

So okay, I am trying to accept these things about myself. They are just the way I am. Like, I am good at English class and not so good at Algebra. Whatever.

But it wasn't until we got to Gifted and Talented today, after lunch, and Lilly started working on the shot list for this week's episode of her cable access show, *Lilly Tells It Like It Is*, and Boris got out his violin and started playing a concerto (sadly, not in the supply closet because they still haven't put the door back on it), and Michael put on headphones and started working on a new song for his band, that it finally hit me:

There is not one thing that I am particularly good at. In fact, if it weren't for the fact that I am a princess, I would be the most ordinary person alive. It is not even that I can't surf, or weave a friendship bracelet. I can't do *anything*.

I mean, all my friends have these incredible things they can do: Lilly knows everything there is to know and isn't shy about saying it in front of a camera. Michael can not only play guitar and, like, fifty other instruments including the piano and drums, but he can also design whole computer programs. Boris has been playing his violin at sold-out Carnegie Hall concerts since he was, like, eleven years old, or something. Tina Hakim Baba can read, like, a book a day, and retain what she's read and quote it back practically verbatim, and Ling Su is an extremely talented artist. The only person at our lunch table besides me who has no discernible special gift is Shameeka, and that made me feel better for about a minute, before I remembered that Shameeka is totally smart and beautiful and gets straight As and people who work at modeling agencies are always coming up to her in, like, Bloomingdale's when she is shopping with her mom and asking her to let them represent her (even though Shameeka's dad says over his dead body will any daughter of his be a model).

But me? I do not know why Michael even likes me, I am so talentless and boring. I mean, I guess it's a good thing my destiny as the monarch of a nation is sealed, because if I had to go apply for a job somewhere, I so fully wouldn't get it, because I'm not good at anything.

So here I am, sitting in Gifted and Talented, and there really is no getting around this basic fact:

I, Mia Thermopolis, am neither gifted nor talented.

WHAT AM I DOING IN HERE????? I DO NOT BELONG HERE!!!! I BELONG IN TECH ED!!!! OR DOMESTIC ARTS!!!!! I SHOULD BE MAKING A BIRD-HOUSE OR A PIE!!!!

Just as I was writing this, Lilly leaned over and went, "Oh, my God, what is *wrong* with you? You look like you just ate a sock," which is what we say whenever someone looks super depressed, because that is how Fat Louie always looks whenever he accidentally eats one of my socks and has to go to the vet to have it surgically removed.

Fortunately Michael didn't hear her on account of having his headphones on. I would never have been able to confess in front of him what I confessed then to his sister, which is that I am a big talentless phony because then he would know I am nothing like Kate Bosworth and dump me.

"And they only put me in this class in the first place because I was flunking Algebra," I told her.

Then Lilly said the most surprising thing. Without batting an eye, she went, "You have a talent."

I stared at her, my own eyes wide and, I am afraid, filled with tears. "Oh, yeah, what?" I was really scared I was going to cry. It really must be PMS or something, because I was practically getting ready to start bawling.

But to my disappointment, all Lilly said was, "Well, if you can't figure it out, I'm not going to tell you." When I protested this, she went: "Part of the journey of achieving self-actualization is that you have to reach it on your own, without help or guidance from others. Otherwise, you won't feel as keen a sense of accomplishment. But it's staring you in the face."

I looked around, but I couldn't figure out what she was talking about. There was nothing staring me in the face that I could see. No one was looking at me at all. Boris was busy scraping away with his bow, and Michael was fingering his keyboard furiously (and silently), but that was about it. Everyone else was bent over their Kaplan review books or doodling or making sculptures out of Vaseline or whatever.

I still have no idea what Lilly is talking about. There is nothing I am talented at—except maybe telling a fish fork apart from a dinner one.

I can't believe that all I thought I needed in order to

achieve self-actualization was the love of the man to whom I have pledged my heart. Knowing Michael loves me—or at least really likes me—just makes it all worse. Because his incredible talentedness makes the fact that I am not good at anything even more obvious.

I wish I could go to the nurse's office and take a nap. But they won't let you do that unless you have a temperature, and I'm pretty sure all I have is jet lag.

I knew it was going to be a bad day. If I had had on my Queen Amidala underwear, I never would have come face-to-face with the truth about myself.

| Inventor | Invention | Benefits to Society | Costs to Society |
|---|---|---|---|
| Samuel F.B. Morse | Telegraph | Easier communication | Disrupted view (wires) |
| Thos. A. Edison | Electric light | Easier to turn on lights; less expensive than candles | Society didn't trust them; weren't successful at first |
| Ben Franklin | Lightning rod | Less chance of house being struck | Ugly |
| Eli Whitney | Cotton gin | Less work | Less employment |
| A. Graham Bell | Telephone | Easier communication | Disrupted view (wires) |
| Elias Howe | Sewing machine | Less work | Less employment |
| Chris. Sholes | Typewriter | Easier work | Less employment |
| Henry Ford | Automobile | Faster transportation | Pollution |

I will never invent anything, either of benefit or cost to any society, because I am a talentless reject. I couldn't even get the country I will one day rule to install PARKING METERS!!!!!!!!!!!!!!

HOMEWORK

Algebra: probs at beginning of Chapter 11 (no review session, Mr. G has mtgs—also, just started semester, so nothing to review yet. Also, not flunking anymore!!!!!!)
English: update journal (How I Spent My Winter Break—500 words)
Bio: read Chapter 13
Health and Safety: read Chapter 1, You and Your

Environment
G&T: figure out secret talent
French: Chapitre Dix
World Civ: Chapter 13: Brave New World

*Tuesday, January 20, in the limo on way to Grandmère's for princess lesson*

THINGS TO DO

1. Find Queen Amidala underwear.
2. Stop obsessing over whether or not Michael loves you vs. being in love with you. Be happy with what you have. Remember, lots of girls have no boyfriend at all. Or they have really gross ones with no front teeth like on Maury Povich.
3. Call Tina to compare notes on how not-chasing-boys thing is working.
4. Do all homework. Do not get behind first day!!!!!
5. Wrap Michael's present.
6. Find out what Grandmère talked to Mom about last night. Oh, God, please do not let it be something weird like wanting to take me skeet shooting. I don't want to shoot any skeets. Or anything else, for that matter.
7. Stop biting fingernails.
8. Buy cat litter.
9. Figure out secret talent. If Lilly knows, must be pretty obvious, as she hasn't even figured out about nostrils yet.
10. GET SOME SLEEP!!!!!!!!! Boys don't like girls who have huge, un–Kate-Bosworth-like purple bags under their eyes. Not even perfect boys like Michael.

*Tuesday, January 20, still in the limo on way to Grandmère's for princess lesson*

Draft for English Journal:

## HOW I SPENT MY WINTER BREAK

I spent my winter break in Genovia, population 50,000. Genovia is a principality located on the Côte d'Azur between Italy and France. Genovia's main export is olive oil. Its main import is tourists. Recently, however, Genovia has begun suffering from considerable damage to its infrastructure due to foot traffic from the many cruise ships that dock in its harbor and

-

-

-

-

Oh, my God. I must have been even more tired than I thought yesterday. Apparently I fell asleep in the limo on the way to Grandmère's, and Lars couldn't even wake me up for my princess lesson! He says that when he tried, I swatted him away and called him a bad word in French (that is François's fault, not mine).

So he had Hans turn around and drive me back to the loft, then Lars carried me up three flights of stairs to my room (no mean feat, I weigh as much as about five Fat Louies), and my mom put me to bed.

I didn't wake up for dinner or anything. I slept until seven this morning! That is fifteen hours straight.

Wow. I must have been fried from all the excitement of being back home and seeing Michael, or something.

Or maybe I really did have jet lag, and that whole I-am-a-talentless-bum thing from yesterday wasn't rooted in my low self-esteem, but was due to a chemical imbalance from lack of REM. You know they say that people who are sleep deprived start suffering from hallucinations after a while. There was a DJ who stayed up for eleven days straight, the longest recorded period of time anyone has ever gone without sleep, and he started playing nothing but Phil Collins, and that's how they knew it was time to call the ambulance.

Except that even after fifteen hours of sleep, I still feel like a bit of a talentless bum. But at least today I don't feel like it's such a tragedy. I think sleeping for fifteen hours straight has given me some perspective. I mean, not everyone can be super geniuses like Lilly and Michael. Just like not everyone can be a violin virtuoso like Boris. I have to be good at *something*. I just need to figure out what that something is. I asked Mr. G today at breakfast what he thinks I am good at, and he said he thinks I make some interesting fashion statements sometimes.

But that cannot have been what Lilly was referring to, as I was wearing my school uniform at the time she mentioned my mystery talent, which hardly leaves room for creative expression.

Mr. G's remark reminded me that I still haven't found my Queen Amidala underwear. But I wasn't about to ask my stepfather if he'd seen them. EW! I try not to look at Mr. Gianini's underwear when it comes back all folded from the laundry-by-the-pound place, and thankfully he extends the same courtesy to me.

And I couldn't ask my mom because once again she was dead to the world this morning. I guess pregnant women need as much sleep as teenagers and DJs.

But I had seriously better find them before Friday, or my first date with Michael will be a full-on disaster, I just know it. Like, he'll probably open his present and be all, "Uh . . . I guess it's the thought that counts."

I probably should have just followed Mrs. Hakim Baba's rules and gotten him a sweater.

But Michael is so not the sweater type! I realized it as we pulled up in front of his building today. He was standing there, looking all tall and manly and Heath Ledger–like . . . except for having dark hair, not blond.

And his scarf was kind of blowing in the wind, and I could see that part of his throat, you know, right beneath his Adam's apple and right above where his shirt collar opens, the part that Lars once told me if you hit someone hard enough, it would paralyze them. Michael's throat was so nice-looking, so smooth and concave, that all I could think about was Mr. Rochester, out on Mesrour, his horse, brooding about his great love for Jane. . . .

And I knew, I just knew, I was right not to have gotten

Michael a sweater. I mean, Kate Bosworth would never have given her quarterback boyfriend a *sweater*. Ew.

Anyway, then Michael saw me and smiled and he didn't look like Mr. Rochester anymore, because Mr. Rochester never smiled.

He just looked like Michael. And my heart turned over in my chest like it always does when I see him.

"Are you okay?" he wanted to know, as soon as he got into the limo. His eyes, so brown they are almost black—like the peat bogs Mr. Rochester was always striding past out there on the moor, because if you step into a peat bog, you can sink in up to your head and never be heard from again . . . which in a way is like what happens every time I look into Michael's eyes: I fall and fall and am pretty sure I will never be able to get out of them again, but that's okay, because I love being there—looked deeply into mine. My eyes are merely gray, the color of a New York City sidewalk. Or parking meter.

"I called you last night," Michael said, as his sister pushed him to move over on the seat so that she could get into the limo, too. "But your mom said you'd passed out—"

"I was really, really tired," I said, delighted by the fact that he appeared to have been worried about me. "I slept for fifteen hours straight."

"Whatever," Lilly said. She was clearly not interested in the details of my sleep cycle. "I heard from the producers of your movie."

I was surprised. "Really? What did they say?"

"They asked me to take a breakfast meeting with them," Lilly said, sounding like she was trying not to brag. Only she wasn't succeeding terribly well. You could totally hear the gloating in her voice. "Friday morning. So I won't be needing a ride."

"Wow," I said, impressed. "A breakfast meeting?

Really? Will they serve bagels?"

"Probably," Lilly said.

I was impressed. I have never been invited to a breakfast meeting with producers before. Just the Genovian ambassador to Spain.

I asked Lilly if she had come up with a list of demands for the producers, and she said she had, but she wouldn't tell me what they were.

I think I am going to have to watch this movie, and see what's making her so mad. My mom has it on tape. She said it was one of the funniest things she has ever seen.

But then, my mom laughs all through *Dirty Dancing*, even the parts that aren't supposed to be funny, so I don't know if she is the best judge.

Uh-oh. One of the cheerleaders (sadly, not Lana) tore her Achilles tendon doing pilates over the break, so they just announced they are holding tryouts for a replacement, as the team's alternate got transferred to a girls' school in Massachusetts due to having too wild of a party while her parents were in Martinique.

I sincerely hope Lilly is too busy protesting the movie of my life to protest the new cheerleading tryouts. Last semester she made me walk around with a big sign that said CHEERLEADING IS SEXIST AND NOT A SPORT, which I am not even sure is technically true, since they have cheerleading championships on ESPN. But it is a fact that there are no cheerleaders for the female sports in our school. Like Lana and her gang never turn out for the girls' basketball team or the girls' volleyball team, but they never miss a boys' game. So maybe the sexist part is true.

Oh, God, a geek just came in with a hall pass. A hall pass for me! I am being summoned to the office! And I didn't even do anything! Well, not this time, anyway.

*Wednesday, January 21,*
*Principal Gupta's office*

I can't believe it is only the second day of second semester, and already I am sitting here in the principal's office. I might not have finished my homework, but I fully have a note from my stepdad. I turned it in to the administrative office first thing. It says:

> *Please excuse Mia for not completing her home-*
> *work for Tuesday, January 20. She was crippled*
> *with jet lag, and unable to attend to her academic*
> *responsibilities last evening. She will of course make*
> *up the work tonight.*
>
> — *Frank Gianini*

It kind of sucks when your stepdad is also your teacher.

But why would Principal Gupta object to this? I mean, I realize it is only the second day of second semester, and already I've fallen behind. But I'm not *that* far behind.

And I haven't even seen Lana today, so it's not like I could have done anything to her or her personal belongings.

OH, MY GOD. It just occurred to me. What if they realize they made a mistake, putting me back in Gifted and Talented? I mean, because I have no gifts or talents? What if I was only put in there in the first place because of some computer glitch, and now they've corrected it, and they're going to put me in Tech Ed or Domestic Arts, where I belong? I will have to make a spice rack!!! Or worse, a western omelet!!!

And I will never see Michael anymore! Okay, I will see him on the way to school and during lunch and after school and on weekends and holidays, but that's it. By taking me out of Gifted and Talented class, they will be depriving me of five whole hours of Michael a week! And true, during class we don't talk all that much, because Michael really is gifted and talented, unlike me, and needs to use that class period to hone his musical abilities instead of tutoring me, which is what he generally ends up doing thanks to my uselessness at Algebra.

But still, at least we are *together*.

Oh, God, this is awful! If I really do turn out to have a talent—which I doubt—WHY didn't Lilly just tell me what it is? Then I could throw it in Principal Gupta's face when she tries to deport me back to Tech Ed.

Wait . . . who does that voice belong to? The one coming from Principal Gupta's office? It sounds kind of familiar. It sounds kind of like . . .

I cannot believe Grandmère just did this. I mean, what kind of person DOES this? Just yanks a teenager out of school like this?

She is supposed to be the adult. She is supposed to be setting a good example for me.

And what does she do instead?

Well, first she tells a big fat LIE, and *then* she removes me from school property under false pretenses.

I am telling you, if my mom or dad finds out about this, Clarisse Renaldo will be a dead woman.

And not like she didn't practically give me a heart attack, you know. Good thing my cholesterol and everything is so low thanks to my vegetarian diet, otherwise I might have suffered a serious cardial infarction, she scared me so bad, coming out of Principal Gupta's office like that and being all, "Well, yes, we are of course praying for his quick recovery, but you know how these things can be—"

I felt all the blood run out of my face at the sight of her. Not just because, you know, it was Grandmère, talking to Principal Gupta, of all people, but because of what she was saying.

I stood up fast, my heart pounding so hard, I thought it might go flying right out of my chest.

"What is it?" I asked, all panicky. "Is it my dad? Is the cancer back? Is that it? You can tell me, I can take it."

I was sure, from the way Grandmère was talking to Principal Gupta, that my dad's testicular cancer was back, and that he was going to have to go through treatment for it all over again—

"I will tell you in the car," Grandmère said to me, stiffly. "Come along."

"No, really," I said, trailing after her, with Lars trailing after me. "You can tell me now. I can take it, I swear I can. Is Dad all right?"

"Don't worry about your homework, Mia," Principal Gupta called to us as we left her office. "You just concentrate on being there for your father."

So it was true! Dad *was* sick!

"Is it the cancer again?" I asked Grandmère as we left the school and headed down to her limo, which was parked out front by the stone lion that guards the steps up to Albert Einstein High. "Do the doctors think it's treatable? Does he need a bone marrow transplant? Because you know, we're probably a match, on account of my having his hair. At least, what his hair must have looked like, back when he had some."

It wasn't until we were safely inside the limo that Grandmère gave me a very disgusted look and said, "Really, Amelia. There is nothing wrong with your father. There is, however, something wrong with that school of yours. Imagine, not allowing their pupils any sort of absences except in the case of illness. Ridiculous! Sometimes, you know, people need a day. A personal day, I think they call it. Well, today, Amelia, is your personal day."

I blinked at her from my side of the limo. I couldn't quite believe what I was hearing.

"Wait a minute," I said. "You mean . . . Dad isn't sick?"

"*Pfuit!*" Grandmère said, her drawn-on eyebrows raised way up. "He certainly seemed healthy enough when I spoke to him this morning."

"Then what—" I stared at her. "Why did you tell Principal Gupta—"

"Because otherwise she would not have allowed you out of class," Grandmère said, glancing at her gold-and-diamond watch. "And we are late, as it is. Really, there is nothing worse than an overzealous educator. They think they are helping, when in reality, you know, there are many different varieties of learning. Not all of it takes place in a classroom."

Comprehension was beginning to dawn. Grandmère had not pulled me out of school in the middle of the day because anyone in my family was sick. No, Grandmère had pulled me out of school because she wanted to teach me something.

"Grandmère," I cried, hardly able to believe what I was hearing. "You can't just drive over and yank me out of school whenever you want to. And you certainly can't tell Principal Gupta that my dad is sick when he isn't! How could you even *say* something like that? Don't you know anything about self-fulfilling prophecies? I mean, if you go around lying about stuff like that all the time, it could actually come true—"

"Don't be ridiculous, Amelia," Grandmère said. "Your father is not going to have to go back to the hospital just because I told a little white lie to an academic administrator."

"I don't know how you can be so sure of that," I said angrily. "And anyway, where do you think you're taking me? I can't afford to just be leaving school in the middle of the day, you know, Grandmère. I mean, I am not as smart as most of the other kids in my class, and I've got a lot of catching up to do, thanks to the fact that I went to bed so early last night—"

"Oh, I *am* sorry," Grandmère said, very sarcastically. "I know how much you enjoy your Algebra class. I am sure it is a very great deprivation to you, missing it today. . . ."

I couldn't deny that she was right. At least partially. While I wasn't all that thrilled about the method by which she'd done it, the fact that Grandmère had extracted me from Algebra wasn't exactly something I was about to cry over. I mean, come on. Integers are not my best thing.

"Well, wherever we're going," I said severely, "we better be back in time for lunch. Because Michael will wonder where I am—"

"Not *that boy* again," Grandmère said, lifting her gaze to the limo's sunroof with a sigh.

"Yes, *that boy*," I said. "That boy I happen to love with all of my heart and soul. And Grandmère, if you could just meet him, you'd know—"

"Oh, we're here," Grandmère said, with some relief, as her driver pulled over. "At last. Get out, Amelia."

I got out of the limo, then looked around to see where Grandmère had brought me. But all I saw was the big Chanel store on Fifty-seventh Street. But that couldn't be where we were headed. Could it?

But when Grandmère untangled Rommel from his Louis Vuitton leash, put him on the ground, and began striding purposefully toward those big glass doors, I saw that Chanel was exactly where we were headed.

"Grandmère," I cried, rushing after her. "Chanel? You pulled me out of class to take me *shopping*?"

"You need a gown," Grandmère said with a sniff, "for the black-and-white ball at the Contessa Trevanni's this Friday. This was the soonest I could get an appointment."

"Black-and-white ball?" I echoed as Lars escorted us into the hushed white interior of Chanel, the world's most exclusive fashion boutique—the kind of store that, before I found out I was a princess, I would have been too terrified even to set foot in . . . although I can't say the same for my friends, as Lilly once filmed an entire episode of her cable access show from inside a dressing room at Chanel. She'd barricaded herself in and was trying on Karl Lagerfeld's latest creations and wouldn't come out until security broke the door down and escorted her to the sidewalk. It had been a show on how haute couture designers are completely sizeist, seeing as how it is impossible to find leather pants in anything larger than a misses' size ten. "What black-and-white ball?"

"Surely your mother told you," Grandmère said, as a tall, reed-thin woman approached us with cries of, "Your Royal Highnesses! How delightful to see you."

"My mother didn't tell me anything about a ball," I said. "When did you say it was?"

"Friday night," Grandmère said to me. To the sales-lady she said, "Yes, I believe you've put aside some gowns for my granddaughter. I specifically requested white ones." Grandmère blinked owlishly at me. "You are too young for black. I don't want to hear any arguing about it."

Argue about it? How could I argue about something I hadn't even begun to understand?

"Of course," the saleslady was saying with a big smile. "Come with me, won't you, Your Highness?"

"Friday night?" I cried, that part, at least, of what was going on beginning to sink in. "Friday night? Grandmère, I can't go to any ball on Friday night. I already made plans with—"

But Grandmère just put her hand in the center of my back and pushed.

And then I was tripping after the saleslady, who didn't even blink an eye, as if princesses in combat boots go trip-ping after her all the time.

And now I am sitting in Grandmère's limo on my way back to school, and all I can think about are the number of people I would like to thank for my current predicament, foremost among which is my mother, for forgetting to tell me that she had already given Grandmère permission to drag me to this thing; the Contessa Trevanni, for having a black-and-white ball in the first place; the salespeople at

Chanel, who, although they are very nice, are really all just a bunch of enablers, as they have enabled my grandma to garb me in a white diamanté ball gown and drag me to something I have no desire to attend in the first place; my father, for setting his mother loose upon the helpless city of Manhattan without anyone to supervise her; and of course Grandmère herself, for completely ruining my life.

Because when I told her, while the Chanel people were throwing yards of fabric over me, that I cannot possibly attend Contessa Trevanni's black-and-white ball this Friday night, as that is the night Michael and I are supposed to have our first date, she responded by giving me a big lecture about how a princess's first duty is to her people. Her heart, Grandmère says, must always come second.

I tried to explain how this date could not be postponed or rescheduled, as *Star Wars* would only be showing at the Screening Room that night, and that after that they would go back to showing *Moulin Rouge*, which I won't see because I heard someone dies at the end.

But Grandmère refused to see that my date with Michael was anywhere near as important as Contessa Trevanni's black-and-white ball. Apparently Contessa Trevanni is a very socially prominent member of the Monaco royal family, besides being some kind of distant cousin (who isn't?) of ours. My not attending her black-and-white ball here in the city with all the other debutantes would be a slight from which the royal house of Grimaldi might never recover.

I pointed out that my not attending *Star Wars* with Michael will be a slight from which my relationship with my boyfriend might never recover. But Grandmère said only that if Michael really loves me, he'll understand when I have to cancel on him.

"And if he doesn't," Grandmère said, exhaling a plume of gray smoke from the Gitanes she was sucking down, "then he was never appropriate consort material to begin with."

Which is very easy for Grandmère to say. *She* hasn't been in love with Michael since the first grade. *She* doesn't spend hours and hours attempting to write poems befitting his greatness. She doesn't know what it is to love, since the only person Grandmère has ever been in love with in her entire life is herself.

Well, it's true.

And now we are pulling up to the school. It is lunchtime. In a minute I will have to go inside and explain to Michael how I cannot make it to our first date, or it will cause an international incident from which the country over which I will one day rule may never recover.

Why couldn't Grandmère just have sent me to boarding school in Massachusetts instead?

I couldn't tell him.

I mean, how could I? Especially when he was being so nice to me during lunch. Everybody in the whole school, it seemed, knew that Grandmère had come and taken me away during homeroom. In her chinchilla cape, with those eyebrows, and Rommel at her side, how could anyone have missed her? She is as conspicuous as Cher.

Everyone was all concerned, you know, about the supposed illness in my family. Michael especially. He was all, "Is there anything I can do? Your Algebra homework, or something? I know it isn't much, but it's the least I could do. . . ."

How could I tell him the truth—that my father wasn't sick; that my grandmother had dragged me off in the middle of school to take me *shopping*? Shopping for a dress to wear at a ball to which he was not invited, and which was to take place during the exact time we were supposed to be enjoying dinner and a space fantasy set in a galaxy far, far away?

I couldn't. I couldn't tell him. I couldn't tell anyone. I just sat there at lunch being all quiet. People mistook my lack of talkativeness for extreme mental distress. Which it was, actually, only not for the reasons they thought. Basically all I was thinking as I sat there was I HATE MY GRANDMOTHER. I HATE MY GRANDMOTHER. I HATE MY GRANDMOTHER. I HATE MY GRAND-MOTHER.

I really, really do.

As soon as lunch was over, I snuck off to one of the pay phones outside the auditorium doors and called home. I knew my mom would be there instead of at her studio because she is still working on the nursery walls. She'd gotten to the third wall, on which she was depicting a highly realistic painting of the fall of Saigon.

"Oh, Mia," she said, when I asked her if there wasn't something she'd possibly forgotten to mention to me. "I am so sorry. Your grandmother called during *Anna Nicole*. You know how I get during *Anna Nicole*."

"Mom," I said through gritted teeth. "Why did you tell her it was okay for me to go to this stupid thing? You told me I could go out with Michael that night!"

"I did?" My mom sounded bewildered. And why shouldn't she have? She clearly did not remember the conversation she'd had with me about my date with Michael . . . primarily of course because she'd been dead to the world during it. Still, she didn't need to know that. What was important was that she was made to feel as guilty as possible for the heinous crime she had committed. "Oh, honey. I am so sorry. Well, you're just going to have to cancel with Michael. He'll understand."

"Mom," I cried. "He will not! This was supposed to be our first real date! You've got to do something!"

"Well," my mom said, sounding kind of wry. "I'm a little surprised to hear you're so unhappy about it, sweetheart. You know, considering your whole thing about not wanting to chase Michael. Canceling your first date with him would definitely fall into that category."

"Very funny, Mom," I said. "But Jane wouldn't cancel her first date with Mr. Rochester. She just wouldn't call him all the time beforehand, or let him get to second base during it."

"Oh," my mom said.

"Look," I said. "This is serious. You've got to get me out of this stupid ball!"

But all my mom said was that she'd talk to my dad about it. I knew what that meant, of course. No way was

I getting out of this ball. My dad has never in his life forsaken duty for love. He is full-on Princess Margaret that way.

So now I've been sitting here (trying to do my Algebra homework, as usual, because I am neither gifted nor talented), knowing that at some point or another I am going to have to tell Michael our date is canceled. Only how? How am I going to do it? And what if he's so mad, he never asks me out again?

Worse, what if he asks some other girl to see *Star Wars* with him? I mean, some girl who knows all the lines you're supposed to shout at the screen during the movie. Like when Ben Kenobi goes, "Obi-Wan. Now that's a name I haven't heard in a long time," you're supposed to shout, "How long?" and then Ben goes, "A very long time."

There must be a million girls besides me who know about this. Michael could ask any one of them instead of me and have a perfectly wonderful time. Without me.

Lilly is bugging me to find out what's wrong. She keeps passing me notes, because they are fumigating the teachers' lounge, so Mrs. Hill is in here today, pretending to grade papers from her fourth-period computer class. But really she is ordering things from a Garnet Hill catalog. I saw it beneath her gradebook.

*Is your dad super sick?* Lilly's latest note reads. *Are you going to have to fly back to Genovia?*

*No*, I write back.

*Is it the cancer?* Lilly wants to know. *Did he have a recurrence?*

*No*, I write back.

*Well, what is it, then?* Lilly's handwriting is getting spiky, a sure sign she is becoming impatient with me. *Why won't you tell me?*

*Because*, I want to scrawl back, in big capital letters.

*The truth will lead to the imminent demise of my romantic relationship with your brother, and I couldn't bear that! Don't you see I can't live without him?*

But I can't write that, because I'm not ready to give up yet. I mean, am I not a princess of the royal house of Renaldo? Do princesses of the royal house of Renaldo just give up, just like that, when something they hold as dearly as I hold Michael is at stake?

No, they do not. Look at my ancestresses, Agnes and Rosagunde. Agnes jumped off a bridge in order to get what she wanted (not be a nun). And Rosagunde strangled a guy with her own hair (in order to not have to sleep with him). Was I, Mia Thermopolis, going to let a little thing like the Contessa Trevanni's black-and-white ball get in the way of my having my first date with the man I love?

No, I was not.

Perhaps this, then, is my talent. The indomitability that I inherited from the Renaldo princesses before me.

Struck by this realization, I wrote a hasty note to Lilly:

*Is my talent that I, like my ancestresses before me, am indomitable?*

I waited breathlessly for her response. Although it was not clear to me what I was going to do if she replied in the positive. Because what kind of talent is being indomitable? I mean, you can't get paid for it, the way you can if your talent is playing the violin or songwriting or producing cable access television programs.

Still, it would be good to know I'd figured out my talent on my own. You know, as far as climbing the Jungian tree to self-actualization went.

But Lilly's response was way disappointing:

*No, your talent is not that you're indomitable, dinkus. God, U R so dense sometimes. WHAT IS WRONG WITH YOUR DAD?????*

Sighing, I realized I had no choice but to write back, *Nothing. Grandmère just wanted to take me to Chanel, so she made up the thing about my dad being sick.*

*God*, Lilly wrote back. *No wonder you're looking like you ate a sock again. Your grandmother sucks.*

I could not agree more. If only Lilly knew the full extent of how much.

Emergency meeting of the followers of the Jane Eyre technique of boyfriend-handling. We are of course in peril of discovery at any moment, as we are skipping French in order to gather here in the stairwell leading to the roof (the door to which is locked, of course: Lilly says in the movie of my life, the kids got to go on the roof of their school all the time. Just another example of how art most certainly does not imitate life), so that we can lend succor to one of our sisters in suffering.

That's right. It turns out that I am not the only one for whom the semester is off to an inauspicious beginning. Not only did Tina sprain her ankle on the ski slopes of Aspen—no, she also got a text message from Dave Farouq El-Abar during fifth period over her new cell phone. It said, U NEVER CALLED BACK. AM TAKING JASMINE TO RANGER GAME. HAVE A NICE LIFE.

I have never in my life seen anything so insensitive as that message. I swear, my blood went cold as I read it.

"Sexist pig," Lilly said when she saw it. "Don't even worry about it, Tina. You'll find somebody better."

"I d-don't want someone b-better," Tina sobbed. "I only want D-Dave!"

It breaks my heart to see her in such pain—not just emotional pain, either: it was no joke trying to get up to the third-floor stairwell on her crutches. I have promised faithfully to sit with her while she works through her anguish (Lilly is taking her through Elisabeth Kübler-Ross's five stages of break-up grief: Denial—I can't believe he would do this to me; Anger—Jasmine is probably a cow who Frenches on the first date; Bargaining—maybe if I tell him I'll call him faithfully every night, he'll take me back;

349

Depression—I'll never love another man again; Acceptance—well, I guess he *was* kind of selfish). Of course being here with Tina, instead of in French class, means I am risking possible suspension, which is the penalty for skipping class here at Albert Einstein.

But what is more important, my disciplinary record, or my friend?

Besides, Lars is keeping a lookout at the bottom of the stairs. If Mr. Kreblutz, the head custodian, comes along, Lars is going to whistle the Genovian anthem, and we'll flatten ourselves against the wall by the old gym mats (which are quite smelly, by the way, and undoubtedly a fire hazard).

Although I am deeply saddened for her, I can't help feeling that Tina's situation has taught me a valuable lesson: that the Jane Eyre technique of boyfriend-handling is not necessarily the most reliable method by which to hang on to your boyfriend.

Except that, according to Grandmère, who did manage to hang on to a husband for forty years, the quickest way to turn a guy off is to chase after him.

And certainly Lilly, who has the longest-running relationship of any of us, does not chase after Boris. Really, if anything, *he* is the one doing the chasing. But that is probably because Lilly is too busy with her various lawsuits and projects to pay much more than perfunctory attention to him.

Somewhere between the two of them—Grandmère and Lilly—must lie the truth to maintaining a successful relationship with a man. Somehow I have got to get the hang of this, because I will tell you one thing: if I ever get a message from Michael like the one Tina just got from Dave, I will fully be taking a swan dive off the Tappan Zee. And I highly doubt any cute coast guard captain is going to come along and fish me out—at least, not in one piece. The Tappan Zee Bridge is *way* higher than the Pont des Vierges.

And of course you know what this means—this whole thing with Tina and Dave, I mean. It means that I can't cancel my date with Michael. No way, no how. I don't care if Monaco starts lobbing SCUD missiles at the Genovian House of Parliament: I am not going to that black-and-white ball. Grandmère and the Contessa Trevanni are just going to have to learn how to live with disappointment.

Because when it comes to our men, we Renaldo women don't mess around. We play for keeps.

## HOMEWORK

Algebra: probs at beginning of Ch. 11,
PLUS . . . ??? Don't know, thanks to Grandmère
English: update journal (How I Spent My Winter
Break—500 words), PLUS . . . ??? Don't know, thanks
to Grandmère
Bio: read Chapter 13, PLUS . . . ??? Don't know,
thanks to Grandmère
Health and Safety: Chapter 1, You and Your
Environment, PLUS . . . ??? Don't know, thanks to
Grandmère
G&T: figure out secret talent
French: *Chapitre* Dix, PLUS . . . Don't know, due to
skipping!!!!
World Civ: Chapter 13: Brave New World; bring in
current event illustrating how technology can cost
society

While I might never actually figure out what my own talent is—if I even have one—Grandmère's is only too painfully obvious. Clarisse Renaldo has a total gift for completely destroying my life. It is abundantly clear to me now that this has been her goal all along. The simple fact of the matter is, Grandmère can't stand Michael. Not, of course, because he's ever done anything to her. Never done anything to her except make her granddaughter superbly, sublimely happy. She's never even met him.

No, Grandmère doesn't like Michael because Michael is not royal.

How do I know this? Well, it became pretty obvious when I walked into her suite for my princess lesson today, and who should just be coming in from his racquetball game at the New York Athletic Club, swinging his racquet and looking all Andre Agassi-ish? Oh, only Prince René.

"What are YOU doing here?" I demanded in a manner that Grandmère later reproved me for (she said my question was unladylike in its accusatory tone, as if I suspected René of something underhanded, which, of course, I did. I practically had to beat him over the head back in Genovia to get my scepter back).

"Enjoying your beautiful city," was how René replied. And then he excused himself to go shower, because, as he put it, he was a bit ripe from the court.

"Really, Amelia," Grandmère said, disapprovingly. "Is that any way to greet your cousin?"

"Why isn't he back in school?" I wanted to know.

"For your information," Grandmère said, "he happens to be on a break."

"Still?" This sounds pretty suspicious to me. I mean,

what kind of business college—even a French one—has a Christmas break that goes practically into February?

"Schools like René's," was Grandmère's explanation for this, "traditionally have a longer winter holiday than American ones, so that their pupils can make full use of the ski season."

"I didn't see any skis on him," I pointed out craftily.

"*Pfuit!*" was all Grandmère had to say about it, however. "René has had enough of the slopes this year. Besides, he adores Manhattan."

Well, I guess I could see that. I mean, New York *is* the greatest city in the world, after all. Why, just the other day, a construction worker down on Forty-second Street found a twenty-pound rat! That's a rat that's only five pounds lighter than my cat! You won't be finding any twenty-pound rats in Paris or Hong Kong, that's for sure.

So, anyway, we were going along, doing the princess-lesson thing—you know, Grandmère was instructing me about all the personages I was going to meet at this black-and-white ball, including this year's crop of debutantes, the daughters of socialites and other so-called American royalty, who were "coming out" to Society with a capital S, and looking for husbands (even though what they should be looking for, if you ask me, is a good undergraduate program, and maybe a part-time job teaching illiterate homeless people to read. But that's just me.) when all of a sudden, it occurred to me, the solution to my problem:

Why couldn't Michael be my escort to the Contessa Trevanni's black-and-white ball?

Okay, granted, it was no *Star Wars*. And yeah, he'd have to get his hands on a tux and all. But at least we would be together. At least I could still give him his birthday present in a forum that was outside of the cinderblock walls of Albert Einstein High. At least I wouldn't have to cancel on him altogether. At least the state of diplomatic affairs between Genovia and Monaco would remain at DefCon Five.

But how, I wondered, was I ever going to get Grandmère to go along with it? I mean, she hadn't said anything about the Contessa letting me bring a date.

Still, what about all those debutantes? Weren't they bringing dates? Wasn't that what West Point Military Academy was *for*? Providing dates to debutante balls? And if those girls could bring dates, and they weren't even princesses, why couldn't I?

How I was going to get Grandmère to let me bring Michael to the black-and-white ball, after all of our long discussions about how you mustn't let the object of your affection even know that you like him, was going to be a major obstacle. I decided I would have to exercise some of the diplomatic tact Grandmère had taken so much trouble to teach me.

"And please, whatever else you do, Amelia," Grandmère was saying, as she sat there running a hairpick through Rommel's sparse fur, as the royal Genovian vet had instructed, "do not stare too long at the Contessa's face-lift. I know it will be difficult—it looks as if the surgeon botched it horribly. But actually, it's exactly the way Elena wanted it to look. Apparently she has always fancied resembling a walleyed bass—"

"Listen, about this dance, Grandmère," I started in, all subtly. "Do you think the Contessa would mind if I, you know . . . brought someone?"

Grandmère looked at me confusedly over Rommel's pink, trembling body. "What do you mean? Amelia, I highly doubt your mother would have a very nice time at the Contessa Trevanni's black-and-white ball. For one thing, there won't be any other hippy radicals there—"

"Not my mom," I said, realizing that perhaps I had been a little *too* subtle. "I was thinking more, you know. Of an escort."

"But you already have an escort." Grandmère adjusted Rommel's diamond-flake-encrusted collar.

"I do?" I did not recall asking anyone to scrounge up a West Pointer for me.

"Of course you do," Grandmère said, still not, I noticed, meeting my gaze. "Prince René has very generously offered to serve as your escort to the ball. Now, where were we? Oh, yes. About the Contessa's taste in clothes. I think you've learned enough by now to know that you aren't to comment—at least to her face—on what any of your hostesses happen to be wearing. But I think it necessary to warn you that the Contessa has a tendency to wear clothes that are somewhat young on her, and that reveal—"

"*René* is going to be my escort?" I stood up, nearly knocking Grandmère's Sidecar over as I did so. "*René* is taking me to the black-and-white ball?"

"Well, yes," Grandmère said, looking blandly innocent—a little too blandly innocent, if you asked me. "He is, after all, a guest in this city—in this country, as a matter of fact. I would think that you, Amelia, would be only too happy to make him feel welcome and wanted—"

I narrowed my eyes at her. "What is going on here?" I demanded. "Grandmère, are you trying to fix up René and me?"

"Certainly not," Grandmère said, looking genuinely appalled by the suggestion. But then, I'd been fooled by Grandmère's expressions before. Especially the one she puts on when she wants you to think that she is just a helpless old lady. "Your imagination most definitely comes from your mother's side of the family. Your father was never as fanciful as you are, Amelia, for which I can only thank God. He'd have driven me to an early grave, I'm convinced of it, if he'd been half as capricious as you tend to be, young lady."

"Well, what else am I supposed to think?" I asked, feeling a little sheepish over my outburst. After all, the idea that Grandmère might, even though I was only fourteen, be trying to fix me up with some prince that she wanted me to marry *was* a little outlandish. I mean, even for Grandmère. "You made us dance together—"

"For a magazine pictorial." Grandmère sniffed.

"—and then your not liking Michael—"

"I never said I didn't like him. From what I know of him, I think he is a perfectly charming boy. I just want you to be realistic about the fact that you, Amelia, are not like other girls. You are a princess, and have the good of your country to think of."

"—and then René showing up like this, and you're announcing he's taking me to the black-and-white ball—"

"Is it wrong of me to want to see the poor boy have a nice time while he is here? He has suffered so many hardships, losing his ancestral home, not to mention his own kingdom—"

"Grandmère," I said. "René wasn't even alive when they kicked his family out—"

"All the more reason," Grandmère said, "you should be sensitive to his plight."

Great. What am I supposed to do now? About Michael, I mean? I can't bring both him *and* Prince René to the ball. I mean, I look weird enough, with my half-grown-out hair and my androgyny (although judging by Grandmère's description of her, the Contessa might look even weirder than I do) without hauling two dates and a bodyguard around with me.

I wish I were Princess Leia instead of me, Princess Mia. I'd *so* rather take on the Death Star than a black-and-white ball.

*Wednesday, January 21, the loft*

Well, my mom getting hold of my dad about the Contessa's ball was a washout. Apparently the whole parking-meter debate has gotten way out of control. The minister of tourism is conducting a filibuster of his own, in response to the one from the minister of finance, and there can't be a vote until he stops talking and sits down. So far he's been talking for twelve hours, forty-eight minutes. I don't know why my dad doesn't just have him arrested and put in the dungeon.

I am really starting to be afraid that I am not going to be able to get out of this ball thingie.

"You better let Michael know," my mom just poked her head in to say, helpfully. "That you won't be able to make it Friday. Hey, are you writing in your journal again? Aren't you supposed to be doing your homework?"

Trying to change the subject from my homework (hello, I am totally doing it, I am just taking a break right now), I went, "Mom, I am not saying anything to Michael until we've heard from Dad. Because there's no point in my running the risk of Michael breaking up with me if Dad's just going to turn around and say I don't have to go to the stupid ball."

"Mia," my mom said. "Michael is not going to break up with you just because you have a familial commitment you cannot get out of."

"I wouldn't be so sure," I said darkly. "Dave Farouq El-Abar broke up with Tina today because she didn't return his call."

"That's different," my mom said. "It's just plain rude not to return someone's calls."

"But Mom," I said. I was getting tired of having to explain this stuff to my mom all the time. It is a wonder to

358

me she ever got a single guy in the first place, let alone two of them, when she clearly knows so little about the art of dating. "If you are too available, the guy might think all the thrill has gone out of the chase."

My mother looked suspicious. "Don't tell me. Let me guess. Your grandmother told you that?"

"Um," I said. "Yes."

"Well, let me give you a little tip my mother once gave me," my mom said. I was surprised. My mom doesn't get along so well with her parents, so it is rare that she mentions either of them ever giving her a piece of advice worthy of passing down to her own daughter.

"If you think there's a chance you might have to cancel on Michael for Friday night," she said, "you'd better cat-on-the-roof him now."

I was understandably perplexed by this. "Cat on the whatta?"

"Cat on the roof," my mother said. "You need to begin mentally preparing him for the disappointment. For instance, if something had happened to Fat Louie while you were in Genovia—" My mouth must have fallen open, since my mom went, "Don't worry, nothing did. But I'm just saying, if something had, I would not just have blurted it right out to you, over the phone. I'd have prepared you gently for the eventual letdown. Like I might have said, 'Mia, Fat Louie escaped through your window, and now he's up on the roof, and we can't get him down.'"

"Of course you could get him down," I protested. "You could go up by the fire escape and take a pillowcase and when you get near him, you could throw the pillowcase over him and scoop him up and carry him back down again."

"Yes," my mom said. "But supposing I told you I'd try that. And the next day I called you and said it hadn't worked, Fat Louie had escaped to the neighbor's roof—"

"I'd tell you to go to the building next door and make someone let you in, then go up to their roof." I really did not see where this was going. "Mom, how could you be so irresponsible as to let Fat Louie out in the first place? I've told you again and again, you've got to keep my bedroom window closed, you know how he likes to watch the pigeons. Louie doesn't have any outdoor survival skills—"

"So naturally," my mom said, "you wouldn't expect him to survive two nights out of doors."

"No," I practically wailed. "I wouldn't."

"Right. See. So you'd be mentally prepared when I called you on the third day to say despite everything we'd done, Louie was dead."

"OH, MY GOD!" I snatched up Fat Louie from where he was lying beside me on the bed. "And you think I should do that to poor Michael? He has a dog, not a cat! Pavlov's never going to get up on the roof!"

"No," my mother said, looking tired. Well, and why not? Her life's essence was being slowly devoured by the insatiable fetus growing inside her. "I'm saying you should begin mentally preparing Michael for the disappointment he is going to feel if indeed you need to cancel on him Friday night. Call him and tell him you might not be able to make it. That's all. Cat-on-the-roof him."

I let Fat Louie go. Not just because I finally realized what my mom was getting at, but because he was trying to bite me in order to get me to loosen the stranglehold I had on him.

"Oh," I said. "You think if I do that—start mentally preparing him for my not being able to go out with him on Friday—he won't dump me when I get around to breaking the actual news?"

"Mia," my mom said. "No boy is going to dump you

because you have to cancel a date. If any boy does, then he wasn't worth going out with anyway. Much like Tina's Dave, I'd venture to say. She's probably better off without him. Now, do your homework."

Only how could anyone expect me to do my homework after receiving a piece of information like that?

Instead I went online. I meant to instant message Michael, but instead, I found that Tina was instant messaging me.

ILUVROMANCE: Hi, Mia. What R U doing?

She sounded so sad! She was even using a blue font!

FTLOUIE: I'm just doing my Bio. How are you?

ILUVROMANCE: OK, I guess. I just miss him so much!!!!!!!!!!!!!!!!!!!!! I wish I had never even heard of stupid Jane Eyre.

Remembering what my mom had said, I wrote

FTLOUIE: Tina, if Dave was willing to break up with you just because you didn't return his calls, then he was not worthy of you. You will find a new boy, one who appreciates you.

ILUVROMANCE: Do U really think so?

FTLOUIE: Absolutely.

ILUVROMANCE: But where am I going to find a boy who appreC8s me at AEHS? All the boys who go there are morons. Except MM of course.

FTLOUIE: Don't worry, we'll find someone for you. I have to go IM my dad now—

I didn't want to tell her that the person I really had to IM was Michael. I didn't want to rub it in that I had a boyfriend and she didn't. Also, I hoped she didn't remember that in Genovia, where my dad was, it was four o'clock in the morning. Also that the Palais de Genovia isn't exactly state-of-the-art, technologically speaking.

FtLouie: —so TTYL.

ILuvRomance: OK, bye. If U feel like chatting later, I'll be here. I have nowhere else to go.

Poor, sweet Tina! She is clearly prostrate with grief. Really, if you think about it, she is well rid of Dave. If he wanted to leave her for this Jasmine girl so badly, he could have let her down gently by cat-on-the-roofing her. If he was any kind of gentleman, he would have. But it was all too clear now that Dave was no gentleman at all.

I'm glad *my* boyfriend is different. Or at least, I hope he is. No, wait—of course he is. He's MICHAEL.

FtLouie: Hey!

LinuxRulz: Hey back atcha! Where have you been?

FtLouie: Princess lessons.

LinuxRulz: Don't you know everything there is to know about being a princess yet?

FtLouie: Apparently not. Grandmère's got me in for some fine tuning. Speaking of which, is there, like, a later showing of *Star Wars* than the seven o'clock?

LinuxRulz: Yeah, there's an eleven. Why?

FtLouie: Oh, nothing.

LinuxRulz: WHY?

But see here was the part where I couldn't do it. Maybe because of the capital letters, or maybe because my conversation with Tina was still too fresh in my mind. The unparalleled sadness in her blue Us was just too much for me. I know I should have just come right out and told him about the ball thingie right then and there, only I couldn't go through with it. All I could think about was how incredibly smart and gifted Michael is, and what a pathetic talentless freak I am, and how easy it would be for him to go out and find someone worthier of his attentions.

So instead, I wrote

FtLouie: I've been trying to think of some names for your band.

LinuxRulz: What does that have to do with whether or not there's a later showing of *Star Wars* Friday night?

FtLouie: Well, nothing, I guess. Except what do you think of Michael and the Wookiees?

LinuxRulz: I think maybe you've been playing with Fat Louie's catnip mouse again.

FtLouie: Ha ha. OK, how about the Ewoks?

LinuxRulz: The EWOKS? Where did your grandma take you today when she hauled you out of homeroom? Electric shock therapy?

FtLouie: I'm only trying to help.

LinuxRulz: I know, sorry. Only I don't think the guys would really enjoy being equated with furry little muppets from the planet Endor. I mean, I know one of them is Boris, but even he would draw the line at Ewoks, I hope—

FtLouie: BORIS PELKOWSKI IS IN YOUR BAND????

LinuxRulz: Yeah. Why?

FtLouie: Nothing.

All I can say is, if I had a band, I would not let Boris in it. I mean, I know he is a talented musician and all, but he is also a mouth breather. I think it's great that he and Lilly get along so great, and for short periods of time, I can totally put up with him and even have a nice time with him and all. But I would not let him be in my band. Not unless he stopped tucking his sweaters into his pants.

LinuxRulz: Boris isn't so bad, once you get to know him.

FtLouie: I know. He just doesn't seem like the band type. All that Bartok.

LinuxRulz: He plays a mean bluegrass, you know. Not that we'll be playing any bluegrass in the band.

This was comforting to know.

LinuxRulz: So will your grandmother let you off on time?

I genuinely had no idea what he was talking about.

364

LinuxRulz: On Friday. You've got princess lessons, right? That's why you were asking about later showings of the movie, wasn't it? You're worried your grandmother isn't going to let you out on time?

This is where I screwed up. You see, he had offered me the perfect out—I could have said, "Yes, I am," and chances were, he'd have been like, "Okay, well, let's make it another time, then."

BUT WHAT IF THERE WERE NO OTHER TIME????

What if Michael, like Dave, just blew me off and found some other girl to take to the show????

So instead, I went

FtLouie: No, it will be okay. I think I can get off early.

WHY AM I SO STUPID???? WHY DID I WRITE THAT???? Because of COURSE I won't be able to get off early, I will be at the stupid black-and-white ball ALL NIGHT!!!!!

I swear, I am such an idiot, I don't even deserve to have a boyfriend.

*Thursday, January 22, Homeroom*

This morning at breakfast, Mr. G was all, "Has anyone seen my brown corduroy pants?" and my mom, who had set her alarm so that she could wake up early enough to possibly catch my dad on a break between Parliament sessions (no such luck) went, "No, but has anyone seen my Free Winona T-shirt?"

And then I went, "Well, I still haven't found my Queen Amidala underwear."

And that's when we all realized it: Someone had stolen our laundry.

It is really the only explanation for it. I mean, we send our laundry out to the Thompson Street laundry-by-the-pound place, and then they do it for us and deliver it all folded and stuff. Since we don't have a doorman, generally the bag just sits in the vestibule until one of us picks it up and drags it up the three flights of stairs to the loft.

Only apparently no one has seen the bag of laundry we dropped off the day before I left for Genovia! (I guess I am the only one in my family who pays attention to things like laundry—clearly because I am the talentless one, and have nothing deeper to think about than clean underwear.)

Which can only mean that one of those freaky news reporters (who regularly go through our garbage, much to the chagrin of Mr. Molina, our building's superintendent) found our bag of laundry, and any minute we can expect a groundbreaking news story on the front cover of the *Post:* OUT OF THE CLOSET: WHAT PRINCESS MIA WEARS, AND WHAT IT MEANS, ACCORDING TO OUR EXPERTS.

AND THEN THE WHOLE WORLD WILL FIND OUT THAT I WEAR QUEEN AMIDALA PANTIES!

I mean, it is not like I go around *advertising* that I have *Star Wars* underwear, or even that I have any kind of lucky panties at all. And by rights, I should have taken my Queen Amidala underwear with me to Genovia, for luck on my Christmas Eve address to my people. If I had, maybe I wouldn't have gone off on that parking-meter tangent.

But whatever, I had been too caught up in the whole Michael thing, and had completely forgotten.

And now it looks like someone has gotten hold of my special lucky underwear, and the next thing you know, it will be showing up on eBay! Seriously! Who is to say a pair of my panties wouldn't sell like hotcakes? Especially the fact that they are Queen Amidala panties.

I am so, so dead.

Mom has already called the Sixth Precinct to report the theft, but those guys are too busy tracking down real criminals to go after a laundry swiper. They practically laughed her off the phone.

It is all very well for her and Mr. G; all they lost were regular clothes. I am the only one who lost underwear. Worse, my lucky underwear. I fully understand that the men and women who fight crime in this city have more important things to do than look for my underwear.

But the way things have been going, I really, really need all the good luck I can get.

*Thursday, January 22, Algebra*

## THINGS TO DO

1.  Have Genovian ambassador to the UN call the CIA. See if they can dispatch some agents to track down my underwear (if it falls into the wrong hands, there could be an international incident!).

2.  Get cat food!!!!!

3.  Check on Mom's folic acid intake.

4.  Tell Michael I will not be able to make first date with him.

5.  Prepare to be dumped.

<u>Defn</u>: Square root of perfect sq is either of the identical factors.
<u>Defn</u>: Positive sq root is called the principle sq root. Negative numbers have no sq root.

*Thursday, January 22, Health and Safety*

*Did you see that? They are meeting at Cosi for lunch!*

Yes. He so loves her.

*It's so cute when teachers are in love.*

So are you nervous about your breakfast meeting tomorrow?

*Hardly. THEY are the ones who should be nervous.*

Are you going all by yourself? Your mom and dad aren't going with you, are they?

*Please. I can handle a bunch of movie executives on my own, thanks. How can they keep stuffing this infantile swill down our throats, year after year? Don't they think we know by now that tobacco kills? Hey, did you get all your homework done, or were you up all night IMing my brother instead?*

Both.

*You two are so cute, it makes me want to puke. Almost as cute as Mr. Wheeton and Mademoiselle Klein.*

Shut up.

*God, this is boring. Want to make another list?*

Okay, you start.

## LILLY MOSCOVITZ'S GUIDE TO
## WHAT'S HOT AND WHAT'S NOT ON TV
*(with commentary by Mia Thermopolis)*

### 7th Heaven

*Lilly: A complex look at one family's struggles to maintain Christian mores in an ever-evolving, modern-day society. Fairly well acted and occasionally moving, this show can turn "preachy," but does depict the problems facing normal families with surprising realism, and only occasionally sinks to the banal.*

Mia: Even though the dad is a minister and everyone has to learn a lesson at the end of every episode, this show is pretty good. High point: When the Olsen twins guest starred. Low point: When the show's cosmetologist gave the youngest girl straight hair.

### Popstars

*Lilly: A ridiculous attempt to pander to the lowest common denominator, this show puts its young stars through a humiliatingly public "audition," then zeroes in as the losers cry and winners gloat.*

Mia: They take a bunch of attractive people who can sing and dance and make them audition for a place in a pop group, and some of them get it and some of them don't, and the ones who do are instant celebrities who then crack up, all while wearing interesting and generally navel-baring outfits. How could this show be bad?

### Sabrina the Teenage Witch

*Lilly: Though based on comic-book characters, this show is surprisingly affable, and even occasionally amusing.*

*Although, sadly, actual Wiccan practices are not described. The show could benefit from some research into the ages-old religion that has, through the centuries, empowered millions, primarily females. The talking cat is a bit suspect: I have not read any believable documentation that would support the possibility of transfiguration.*

Mia: Totally awesome during the high school/Harvey years. Good-bye Harvey = good-bye show.

## Baywatch

*Lilly: Puerile garbage.*

Mia: Most excellent show of all time. Everyone is good-looking; you can fully follow every plotline even while instant messaging; and there are lots of pictures of the beach, which is great when you are in dark, gloomy Manhattan in February. Best episode: When Pamela Anderson got kidnapped by that half man/half beast, who after plastic surgery became a professor at UCLA. Worst episode: Anytime Mitch adopts a son.

## Powerpuff Girls

*Lilly: Best show on television.*

Mia: Ditto. 'Nough said.

## Roswell

*Lilly: Now, sadly, canceled, this show offered an intriguing look at the possibility that aliens live among us. The fact that they might be teenagers, and extraordinarily attractive ones, at that, stretches the show's credibility somewhat.*

Mia: Hot guys with alien powers. What more can you

ask? High point: Future Max; any time anybody made out in the eraser room. Low point: When that skanky Tess showed up. Oh, and when it got canceled.

## Buffy the Vampire Slayer

*Lilly: Feminist empowerment at its peak, entertainment at its best. The heroine is a lean, mean, vampire-killing machine, who worries as much about her immortal soul as she does about messing up her hair. A strong role model for young women—nay, people of both genders and all ages will benefit from the viewing of this show. All of television should be this good. The fact that this show has, for so long, been ignored by the Emmys is a travesty.*

Mia: If only the Buffster could just find a boyfriend who doesn't need to drink platelets to survive. High point: Any time there's kissing. Low point: None.

## Gilmore Girls

*Lilly: Thoughtful portrayal of single mother struggling to raise teenage daughter in a small northeastern town.*

Mia: Many, many, many, many, many, many cute boys. Plus it is nice to see single moms who sleep with their kid's teacher getting props instead of lectures from the Moral Majority.

## Charmed

*Lilly: While this show at least accurately portrays SOME typical Wiccan practices, the spells these girls routinely do are completely unrealistic. You cannot, for instance, travel through time or between dimensions without creating rifts in the space-time continuum. Were these girls really to transport themselves to seventeenth-century Puritan*

*America, they would arrive there with their esophagi ripped inside out, not neatly stuffed into a corset, as no one can travel through a wormhole and maintain their mass integrity. It is a simple matter of physics. Albert Einstein must be spinning in his grave.*

Mia: Hello, witches in hot clothes. Like Sabrina, only better, because the boys are cuter, and sometimes they are in danger and the girls have to save them.

Tina is so mad at Charlotte Brontë. She says *Jane Eyre* ruined her life.

She announced this at lunch. Right in front of Michael, who isn't supposed to know about the whole Jane Eyre technique of not-chasing-boys thing, but whatever. He admitted to never having read the book, so I think it is a safe bet he didn't know what Tina was talking about.

Still, it was way sad. Tina said she is giving up her romance novels. Giving them up because they led to the ruination of her relationship with Dave!

We were all very upset to hear about this. Tina *loves* reading romances. She reads about one a day.

But now she says that if it weren't for romance novels, she, and not Jasmine, would be going to the Rangers game with Dave Farouq El-Abar this Saturday.

And my pointing out that she doesn't even like hockey didn't seem to help.

Lilly and I both realized that this was a pivotal moment in Tina's adolescent growth. It needed to be pointed out to her that Dave, not Jane Eyre, was the one who'd pulled the plug on their relationship . . . and that, when looked at objectively, the whole thing was probably for the best. It was ludicrous for Tina to blame romance novels for her plight.

So Lilly and I very quickly drew up the following list, and presented it to Tina, in hopes that she would see the error of her ways:

## MIA AND LILLY'S LIST OF
## ROMANTIC HEROINES AND THE
## VALUABLE LESSONS EACH TAUGHT US

1. Jane Eyre from *Jane Eyre*:
   Stick to your convictions and you will prevail.

2. Lorna Doone from *Lorna Doone*:
   Probably you are secretly royalty and an heiress,
   only no one has told you yet
   (this applies to Mia Thermopolis, as well).

3. Elizabeth Bennet from *Pride and Prejudice*:
   Boys like it when you are smart-alecky.

4. Scarlett O'Hara from *Gone With the Wind*:
   Ditto.

5. Maid Marian from *Robin Hood*:
   It is a good idea to learn how to use a bow and
   arrow.

6. Jo March from *Little Women*:
   Always keep a second copy of your manuscript
   handy in case your vindictive little sister throws
   your first draft on the fire.

7. Anne Shirley from *Anne of Green Gables*:
   One word: Clairol.

8. Marguerite St. Just from *The Scarlet Pimpernel*:
   Check out your husband's rings before you marry
   him.

9.  Catherine, from *Wuthering Heights*:
    Don't get too big for your britches or you, too,
    will have to wander the moors in lonely heart-
    break after you die.
10. Tess from *Tess of the d'Urbervilles*:
    Ditto.

Tina, after reading the list, admitted tearfully that we
were right, that romantic heroines from literature really
were her friends, and that she could not, in good con-
science, forsake them. We were all just breathing a sigh of
relief (except for Michael and Boris—they were playing on
Michael's GameBoy) when Shameeka made a sudden
announcement, even more startling than Tina's:

"I'm trying out for cheerleading."

We were, of course, stunned. Not because Shameeka
would make a bad cheerleader—she is the most athletic of
all of us, also the most attractive, and knows almost as
much as Tina does about fashion and makeup.

It was just that, as Lilly so bluntly put it, "Why would
you want to go and do something like *that*?"

"Because," Shameeka explained. "I am tired of letting
Lana and her friends push me around. I am just as good as
any of them. Why shouldn't I try out for the squad, even if
I'm not in their little clique? I have just as good a chance
of getting on the team as anybody else."

Lilly said, "While this is unarguably true, I feel I must
warn you: Shameeka, if you try out for cheerleading, you
might actually get on the squad. Are you prepared to subject yourself to the humiliation of cheering for Josh Richter
as he chases after a ball?"

"Cheerleading has, for many years, suffered under the
stigma of being inherently sexist," Shameeka said. "But I
think the cheerleading community in general is making

strides at asserting itself as a fast-growing sport for both men and women. It is a good way to keep fit and active, it combines two things I love dearly: dance and gymnastics, and will look excellent on my college applications. That is, of course, the only reason my father is allowing me to try out. That and the fact that George W. Bush was a cheerleader. And that I won't be allowed to attend any post-game parties."

I didn't doubt this last part. Mr. Taylor, Shameeka's dad, was way strict.

But as for the rest of it, well, I wasn't sure. Plus, her speech sounded a little planned and, well, defensive.

"Does that mean that if you get on the squad," I wanted to know, "you'll stop eating lunch with us, and go sit over there?"

I pointed at the long table across the caf from ours, at which Lana and Josh and all of their school-spirit-minded, incredibly well-coifed cronies sat. The thought of losing Shameeka, who was always so elegant and yet at the same time sensible, to the Dark Side made my heart ache.

"Of course not," Shameeka said disparagingly. "Getting on the Albert Einstein High School cheerleading squad is not going to change my friendships with all of you one iota. I will still be the camera person for your television show—" She nodded to Lilly "—and your Bio partner—" to me "—and your lipstick consultant—" to Tina "—and your portrait model—" to Ling Su. "I just may not be around as much, if I get on the squad."

We all sat there, reflecting upon this great change that might befall us. If Shameeka made the squad, it would, of course, strike a blow for geeky girls everywhere. But it would also necessarily rob us of Shameeka, who would be forced to spend all of her free time practicing doing the splits and taking the bus to Westchester for away games with Rye Country Day.

But there was even more to it than that. If Shameeka made the cheerleading squad, it would mean she is good at something—REALLY REALLY good at something, not just a little good at everything, which we already knew about her. If Shameeka turned out to be REALLY REAL-LY good at something, then I would be the ONLY one at our lunch table without a recognizable talent.

And I swear it wasn't for this reason alone that I was hoping so fervently that Shameeka wouldn't make the team. I mean, I seriously wanted her to make it, if that was really what she wanted.

Only . . . only I REALLY don't want to be the only one who doesn't have a talent!!!! I REALLY REALLY don't!!!!!!!

The silence at the table was palpable . . . well, except for the *bing-bing-bing* of Michael's electronic game. Boys—apparently even perfect boys, like Michael—are immune to things like mood.

But I can tell you, the mood of this year so far has been pretty bad. In fact, if things don't start looking up soon, I may have to write this entire year off as a do-over.

Still no clue as to what my secret talent might be. One thing I'm pretty sure it's *not* is psychology. It was hard work talking Tina out of giving up her books! And we didn't manage to convince Shameeka not to try out for cheer-leading. I guess I can see why she'd want to do it—I mean, it might be a *little* fun.

Though why anyone would willingly want to spend that much time with Lana Weinberger is beyond me.

Mademoiselle Klein is *not* happy with Tina and me for skipping yesterday.

Of course I told her we didn't skip, that we had a medical emergency that necessitated a trip to Ho's for Tampax, but I am not sure Mademoiselle Klein believed me. You would think she would show some feminine solidarity with the whole surfing the crimson wave thing, but apparently not. At least she didn't write us up. She let us off with a warning and assigned us a five-hundred-word essay each (in French, of course) about the Maginot Line.

But that isn't even what I want to write about. What I want to write about is this:

MY DAD RULES!!!!!

And not just a country, either. He totally got me out of the Contessa's black-and-white ball!!!!

What happened was—at least according to Mr. G, who just caught me outside in the hall and filled me in—the filibuster over the parking meters was finally broken (after thirty-six hours) and my mom was finally able to get through to my dad (those in favor of charging for parking meters won. It is a victory for the environment as well as for me. But I cannot feel fully vindicated for the post-introduction-speech-to-my-people mocking I endured at Grandmère's hands, due to the fact that the true winner in all of this is the Genovian infrastructure).

Anyway, my dad fully said that I did not have to go to the Contessa's party. Not only that, but he said he had never heard anything so ridiculous in his life, that the only feud going on between our family and the royal family of Monaco is Grandmère's. Apparently she and the Contessa have been in competition since finishing school, and Grandmère had just wanted to show off her granddaughter, about whom books have been written and movies have been made. Apparently the Contessa's only granddaughter will also be at the ball, but she's never had a movie based on her life, and in fact is kind of like a sad-sack who got kicked out of finishing school for never learning how to ski right, or something.

So I am free! Free to spend tomorrow night with my only love! I cat-on-the-roofed Michael for nothing! Everything is going to be all right, despite my lack of lucky underwear. I can feel it in my bones.

I am so happy, I feel like writing a poem. I will shield it from Tina, however, because it is unseemly to gloat over one's own fortunes when the fortunes of another are so exceedingly wretched (Tina found out who Jasmine is: a girl who goes to Trinity, with Dave. Her father is an oil sheik, too. Jasmine has aquamarine braces and her screen name is IluvJustin2345).

## HOMEWORK

Algebra: probs at end of Chapt. 11
English: in journal, describe feelings pertaining to reading John Donne's *The Bait*
Bio: don't know, Shameeka is doing it for me
Health and Safety: Chapter 2, Environmental Hazards and You
G&T: figure out secret talent
French: *Chapitre Onze, écrivez une narratif*, 300 words, double spaced, plus 500 wds on snails
World Civ: 500 words, describe origins of Armenian conflict

## Poem for Michael

Oh, Michael,
soon we'll be parkin'
in front of Grand Moff Tarkin
Enjoying veggie moo shu
to the beeps of R2-D2
And maybe even holding hands
while gazing upon the Tatooine sands
And knowing that our love by far
has more fire power than the Death Star
And though they may blow up our planet
and kill every creature living on it
Like Leia and Han, in the stars above,
they can never destroy our love—
Like the Millennium Falcon in hyperdrive
our love will continue to thrive and thrive.

It takes a big person to admit she's wrong—Grandmère is the one who taught me that.

And if it's true, then I must be even bigger than my five feet nine inches. Because I've been wrong. I've been wrong about Grandmère. All this time, when I thought she was inhuman and perhaps even sent down from an alien mothership to observe life on this planet and then report back to her superiors? Yeah, turns out Grandmère really is human, just like me.

How did I find this out? How did I discover that the dowager princess of Genovia did not, after all, sell her soul to the Prince of Darkness as I have often surmised?

I learned it today when I walked into Grandmère's suite at the Plaza, fully prepared to do battle with her over the whole Contessa Trevanni thing. I was going to be all, "Grandmère, Dad says I don't have to go, and guess what, I'm not going to."

That's what I was going to say, anyway.

Except that when I walked in and saw her, the words practically died on my lips. Because Grandmère looked as if someone had run over her with a truck! Seriously. She was sitting there in the dark—she had had these purple scarves thrown over the lampshades because she said the light was hurting her eyes—and she wasn't even dressed properly. She had on a velvet lounging robe and some slippers and had a cashmere throw blanket covering her lap and that was it, and her hair was all in curlers and if her eyeliner hadn't been tattooed on, I swear it would have been all smeared. She wasn't even enjoying a Sidecar, her favorite refreshment, or anything. She was just sitting there, with Rommel trembling on her lap, looking like death warmed over. Grandmère, not the dog.

"Grandmère," I couldn't help crying out, when I saw her. "Are you all right? Are you sick or something?"

But all Grandmère said was, in a voice so unlike her own normally quite strident one that I could barely believe it belonged to the same woman, "No, I'm fine. At least I will be. Once I get over the humiliation."

"Humiliation? What humiliation?" I went over to kneel by her chair. "Grandmère, are you sure you aren't sick? You aren't even smoking!"

"I'll be all right," she said, weakly. "It will be weeks before I'll be able to show my face in public. But I'm a Renaldo. I'm strong. I will recover."

Actually Grandmère is technically only a Renaldo by marriage, but at that point I wasn't going to argue with her, because I thought there was something genuinely wrong, like her uterus had fallen out in the shower or something (this happened to one of the women in the condo community down in Boca where Lilly and Michael's grandmother lives. Also it happens a lot to the cows in *All Creatures Great and Small*).

"Grandmère," I said, kind of looking around, in case her uterus was lying on the floor somewhere or whatever. "Do you want me to call a doctor?"

"No doctor can cure what is wrong with me," Grandmère assured me. "I am only suffering from the mortification of having a granddaughter who doesn't love me."

I had no idea what she was talking about. Sure, I don't like Grandmère so much sometimes. Sometimes I even think I hate her. But I don't not love her. I guess. At least I've never said so, to her face.

"Grandmère, what are you talking about? Of course I love you—"

"Then why won't you come with me to the Contessa

Trevanni's black-and-white ball?" Grandmère wailed.

Blinking rapidly, I could only stammer, "Wh-what?"

"Your father says you will not go to the ball," Grandmère said. "He says you have no wish to go!"

"Grandmère," I said. "You know I don't want to go. You know that Michael and I—"

"*That boy!*" Grandmère cried. "*That boy* again!"

"Grandmère, stop calling him that," I said. "You know his name perfectly well."

"And I suppose this Michael—" Grandmère sniffed "—is more important to you than *I* am. I suppose you consider *his* feelings over mine in this case."

The answer to that, of course, was a resounding *yes*. But I didn't want to be rude. I said, "Grandmère, tomorrow night is our first date. Mine and Michael's, I mean. It's really important to me."

"And I suppose the fact that it was really important to *me* that you attend this ball—that is of no consequence?" Grandmère actually looked, for a moment, as she sat gazing down at me so miserably, like she had tears in her eyes. But maybe it was only a trick of the not very clear light. "The fact that Elena Trevanni has been, since I was a little girl, always lording it over me, because she was born into a more respected and aristocratic family than I was? That until I married your grandfather, she always had nicer clothes and shoes and handbags than my parents could afford for me? That she still thinks she is so much better than me, because she married a *compt* who had no responsibilities or property, just unlimited wealth, whereas I have been forced to work my fingers to the bone in order to make Genovia the vacation paradise it is today? And that I was hoping that just this once, by revealing what a lovely and accomplished granddaughter I have, I could show her up?"

I was stunned. I'd had no idea why this stupid ball was so important to her. I thought it had just been because she'd wanted to try to split Michael and me up, or get me to start liking Prince René instead, so that the two of us could unite our families in holy matrimony someday and create a race of super-royals. It had never occurred to me that there might be some underlying, mitigating circumstance. . . .

Such as that the Contessa Trevanni, was, in essence, Grandmère's Lana Weinberger.

Because that's what it sounded like. Like Elena Trevanni had tortured and teased Grandmère as mercilessly as I had been tortured and teased by Lana through the years.

I wondered if Elena, like Lana, had ever suggested to Grandmère that she wear Band-Aids on her boobs instead of a bra. If she had said this to Clarisse Renaldo, she was a far, far braver soul than I.

"And now," Grandmère said, very sadly, "I have to tell her that my granddaughter doesn't love me enough to put aside her new boyfriend for one single night."

I realized, with a sinking heart, what I had to do. I mean, I knew how Grandmère felt. If there had been some way—any way at all—that I could have shown up Lana— you know, besides going out with her boyfriend, which I had already done, but that had ended up humiliating *me* way more than it had Lana—I'd have done it. Anything.

Because when someone is as mean and cruel and just downright nasty as Lana is—not just to me, either, but to all the girls at Albert Einstein High who weren't blessed with good looks and school spirit—she fully deserves to have her nose rubbed in it.

It was so weird to think about someone like Grandmère, who seemed so incredibly sure of herself, having a Lana Weinberger in her life. I mean, I had always pictured Grandmère being the type of person who, if Lana flipped her long blonde hair onto her desk, would go all Crouching Tiger on her and deliver a Ferragamo to the face.

But maybe there was someone even Grandmère was a little bit afraid of. And maybe that person was Contessa Trevanni.

And while it is not true that I love Grandmère more than I love Michael—I do not love anyone more than I love Michael, except of course for Fat Louie—I did feel sorrier for Grandmère at that moment than I did for myself. You know, if Michael ended up dumping me because I canceled our date. It sounds incredible, but it's true.

So I went, even as I said them not quite believing the words were coming out of my mouth, "All right, Grandmère, I'll put in an appearance at your ball."

A miraculous change overcame Grandmère. She seemed to brighten right up.

"Really, Amelia?" she asked, reaching out to grasp one of my hands. "Will you really do this for me?"

I was, I knew, going to lose Michael forever. But like my mother had said, if he didn't understand, then he probably hadn't been right for me in the first place.

I am such a pushover. But she just looked so happy. She flung off the cashmere throw—and Rommel—and rang for her maid to bring her a Sidecar and her cigarettes, and then we moved on to the day's lesson—how to ask for the number of the nearest taxi company in five different languages.

All I want to know is: What.

Not about why I would ever need to call a taxi in Hindustani.

I mean what—WHAT????—am I going to tell Michael? I mean, seriously. If he doesn't dump me now then there's something wrong with him. And since I know there is nothing wrong with him, I know that I am about to be dumped.

For which all I can say is THERE IS NO JUSTICE IN THE WORLD. NONE.

Since Lilly has her breakfast meeting with the producers of the made-for-TV movie of my life tomorrow morning, I guess I will break the news to Michael then. That way he can dump me in time for Homeroom. Maybe then I will have stopped crying before Lana sees me in Algebra first period. I don't think I'll be able to take her mockery, after already having my heart ripped from my body and flung across the floor.

I hate myself.

I saw the movie of my life. My mom taped it for me while I was in Genovia. She thought Mr. G recorded a Jets game over it, but it turned out he hadn't.

The guy who played Michael was a total babe. In the movie, he and I end up together in the end.

Too bad that in real life, he is going to dump me tomorrow . . . even though Tina doesn't think so.

This is very nice of her and everything, but the fact is, he is totally going to. I mean, it really is a matter of pride. If a girl with whom you have been going out for a full thirty-four days cancels your very first date, you really have no choice but to break up with her. I mean, I totally understand. *I* would break up with me. It is clear now that royal teens can't be like normal ones. I mean, for people like me and Prince William, duty will always have to come first. Who is going to be able to understand that, let alone put up with it?

Tina says Michael can, and will. Tina says Michael won't break up with me because he loves me. I said yes he will, because he only loves me as a friend.

"Clearly Michael loves you as more than just a friend," Tina keeps saying into the phone. "I mean, you guys kissed!"

"Yes," I say. "But Kenny and I kissed, and I did not like him as more than just a friend."

"This is a completely different situation," Tina says.

"How?"

"Because you and Michael are meant to be together!" Tina sounds exasperated. "Your star chart says so! You and Kenny were never meant for one another, he is a Cancer."

Tina's astrological predictions notwithstanding, there

is no evidence that Michael feels more strongly for me than he does for, say, Judith Gershner. Yes, he wrote me that poem that mentioned the L word. But that was an entire month ago, during which period I was in another country. He has not renewed any such protestations since my return. I think it highly likely that tomorrow will be the straw that broke the hot guy's back. I mean, why would Michael waste his time on a girl like me, who can't even stand up to her own grandmother? I'm sure if Michael's grandmother had been all, "Michael, you've got to go to Bingo with me Friday night, because Olga Krakowski, my childhood rival, will be there, and I want to show you off," he'd have been all, "Sorry, Gram, no can do."

No, I'm the spineless one.

And I'm the one who now must suffer for it.

I wonder if it is too late in the school year to transfer. Because I really don't think I can take going to the same school as Michael after we are broken up. Seeing him in the hallway between classes, at lunch, and in G and T, knowing he was once mine, but that I'd lost him, might just kill me.

But is there another school in Manhattan that might take a talentless, spineless reject like me? Doubtful.

For Michael

*Oh, Michael, my one true love*
*We had all new pleasures yet to prove*
*But I lost you due to my lack of spine*
*And now through the years, for you I will pine.*

Well. That's it. I told him.

He hasn't dumped me. Yet. In fact, he was way nice about the whole thing.

"No, really, Mia," was what he said. "I understand. You're a princess. Duty comes first."

Maybe he just didn't want to dump me at school, in front of everyone?

I told him that I would try to get out of the ball early if I could. He said that if I did, I should stop by. The Moscovitzes' apartment, I mean.

I know what this means, of course:

That he is going to dump me there.

OH, MY GOD, WHAT IS WRONG WITH ME?????
I have known Michael for years and years. He is NOT the type of boy who would dump a girl just because she has a family obligation that must take precedence over a date with him. HE IS NOT LIKE THAT. THAT IS WHY I LOVE HIM.

But why can't I stop thinking that the only reason he didn't dump me right then and there is because he couldn't do it in my own limo, in front of my bodyguard and driver? I mean, for all Michael knew, Lars might be trained to beat up boys who try to dump me in front of him.

I HAVE GOT TO STOP THIS. MICHAEL IS NOT DAVE FAROUQ EL-ABAR. He is NOT going to dump me because of this.

Except why do I feel like I know now how Jane Eyre must have felt when she learned the truth about Bertha on her wedding day? No, Michael doesn't have a wife, that I know of. But it's entirely possible that my relationship with him, like Jane's with Mr. Rochester, is coming to an end. And I can think of no earthly way it can ever be repaired.

I mean, it's possible that tonight, when I go by the Moscovitzes' place, it will be in flames, and I will be able to prove myself worthy of Michael's love by selflessly saving his mother, or perhaps his dog, Pavlov, from the fire.

But other than that, I don't see us getting back together. I will of course give him his birthday present, because I went to all the trouble of stealing it.

But I know it won't do any good.

What is WRONG with me???? This better be PMS. Because if this is what love is like all the time, I don't want to be in love anymore!!!!!!!!!!!!!!!!!!!!!!!!!!!!!

They just announced the name of the newest member of the Albert Einstein High junior varsity cheerleading squad. It is Shameeka Taylor.

Great. Just great. So that's it. I am now officially the only person I know who has absolutely no discernible talent.

I am a reject in *every* way.

Michael did not stop by here between classes. It is the first day all week that he hasn't slipped in to say hi on his way to AP English, three classrooms away from this one.

I am totally trying not to take it personally, but there is this little voice inside of me going, *That's it! It's over! He's dumping you!*

I'm sure Kate Bosworth doesn't have a voice like this that lives inside her. WHY couldn't I have been born Kate Bosworth instead of me, Mia Thermopolis?

To make matters worse—as if I can even care about something so trivial—Lana just turned around to hiss, "Don't think just because your little friend made the squad that anything is going to change between us, Mia. She's as much of a pathetic geekette as you are. They only let her on the squad to fill our freak quota."

Then she whipped her head around again—but not as fast as she should have. Because a lot of her hair was still draped across my desk.

And when I slammed my Algebra I–II text closed as hard as I could—which is what I did next—a lot of her silky, awapuhi-scented locks got trapped between pages 210 and 211.

Lana shrieked in pain. Mr. G, up at the chalkboard, turned around, saw where the screaming was coming from, and sighed.

"Mia," he said, tiredly. "Lana. What now?"

Lana stabbed an index finger in my direction. "She slammed her book on my hair!"

I shrugged innocently. "I didn't know her hair was in my book. Why can't she keep her hair to herself, anyway?"

Mr. Gianini looked bored. "Lana," he said. "If you can't keep your hair under control, I recommend braids.

Mia, don't slam your book. It should be open to page two eleven, where I want you to read from Section Two. Out loud."

I read out loud from Section Two, but not without a certain primness. For once, vengeance on Lana had been mine, and I had NOT been sent to the principal's office. Oh, it was sweet. Sweet, sweet vindication.

Although I don't even know why I have to learn this stuff, it isn't as if the Palais de Genovia isn't full of dweeby staffers who are just dying to multiply fractions for me.

Polynomials
term: variable(s) multiplied by a coefficient

monomial: Polynomial w/ one term
binomial: Polynomial w/ two terms
trinomial: Polynomial w/ three terms

Degree of polynomial = the degree of the term with the highest degree

In my delight over the pain I had brought upon my enemy, I almost forgot about the fact that my heart is broken. Must keep in mind that Michael is dumping me after the black-and-white ball tonight. Why can't I FOCUS???? Must be love. I am sick with it.

*Why do you look like you just ate a sock?*

I don't. How was your breakfast meeting?

*You do, too. The meeting went GREAT.*

Really? Did they agree to print a full-page letter of apology in *Variety*?

*No, better. Did something happen between you and my brother? Because I saw him looking all furtive in the hallway just now.*

FURTIVE? Furtive like how? Like he was looking for Judith Gershner to ask her out tonight????

*No, more like he was looking for a pay phone.*
*Why would he ask out Judith Gershner?*
*How many times do I have to tell you, he likes you, not J.G.*

He used to like me, you mean. Before I was forced to cancel our date tonight due to Grandmère forcing me to go to a ball.

*A ball? Really. Ugh. But excuse me. Michael isn't going to ask some other girl to go out with him tonight just because you can't make it. I mean, he was really looking forward to going with you. Not just for concupiscent reasons, either.*

REALLY????

*Yes, you loser. What did you think? I mean, you guys are going out.*

But that's just it. We haven't. Gone out yet, I mean.

*So? You'll go out sometime when you don't have a ball to go to instead.*

You don't think he's going to dump me?

*Uh, not unless something heavy fell on his head between now and the last time I saw him. Guys with cranial damage can't generally be held responsible for their actions.*

Why would something heavy fall on his head?

*I'm being facetious. Do you want to hear about my meeting, or not?*

Yes. What happened?

*They told me they want to option my show.*

What does that mean?

*It means that they will take* Lilly Tells It Like It Is *around to the networks to see if anybody wants to buy it. To be a real show. On a real channel. Not like public access. Like ABC or Lifetime or VH1 or something.*

Lilly!!!! THAT IS SO GREAT!!!!

*Yes, I know. Oops, gotta go. Wheeton's looking this way.*

Note to self: Look up words *concupiscent* and *facetious*.

Lunch was just one big celebration today. Everyone had something to be happy about:

- Shameeka, for making the cheerleading squad and striking a blow for tall geeky girls everywhere (even though of course Shameeka looks like a supermodel and can wrap both her ankles around her head, but whatever).
- Lilly, for getting her TV show optioned.
- Tina, for finally deciding to give up on Dave but not on romance in general and get on with her life.
- Ling Su for getting her drawing of Joe, the stone lion, into the school art fair.
- And Boris for just, well, being Boris. Boris is always happy.

You will notice that I did not mention Michael. That is because I do not know what Michael's mental state at lunch was, whether or not he was happy or sad or concupiscent or whatever. That is because Michael didn't show up to lunch. He said, when he breezed by my locker just before fourth period, "Hey, I've got some things to do, I'll see you in G and T, okay?"

*Some things to do.*

I should, of course, just ask him. I should just be like, "Look, are you going to break up with me over this, or what?" Because I would really like to know, one way or the other.

Except that I can't just go up and ask Michael what the deal is between us, because right now he is busy with Boris, going over band stuff. Michael's band is comprised of (so far) Michael (precision bass), Boris (electric violin), that tall guy Paul from the Computer Club (keyboards), this guy from the AEHS marching band called Trevor (guitar), and Felix, this scary-looking twelfth grader with a goatee that's bushier than Mr. Gianini's (drums). They still don't have a name for the band, or a place to practice. But they seem to think that Mr. Kreblutz, the head custodian, will let them into the band practice rooms on weekends if they can get him tickets to the Westminster Kennel Show next month. Mr. Kreblutz is a huge bichon-frise fan.

The fact that Michael can concentrate on all this band stuff while our relationship is falling apart is just further proof that he is a true musician, completely dedicated to his art. I, being the talentless freak that I am, can of course think of nothing *but* my heartbreak. Michael's ability to remain focused in spite of any personal pain he might be suffering is evidence of his genius.

Either that or he never cared that much about me in the first place.

I prefer to believe the former.

Oh, that I had some kind of outlet, such as music, into which to pour the suffering I am currently feeling! But alas, I'm no artist. I just have to sit here in silent pain, while around me, more gifted souls express their innermost angst through song, dance, and filmography.

Well, okay, just through filmography since there are no singers or dancers in fifth-period G and T. Instead we just have Lilly, putting together what she is calling her quintessential episode of *Lilly Tells It Like It Is*, a show that will explore the seamy underbelly of that American institution known as Starbucks. It is Lilly's contention that Starbucks, through the introduction of the Starbucks card (with which caffeine addicts can pay for their fix electronically) is actually a secret branch of the Central Intelligence Agency that is tracing the movements of America's intelligentsia—writers, editors, and other known liberal agitators—through their coffee consumption.

Whatever. I don't even like coffee.

Aw, crud. The bell.

HOMEWORK

Algebra: Who cares?
English: Everything sucks.
Bio: I hate life.
Health and Safety: Mr. Wheeton is in love, too. I
should warn him to get out now, while he still can.
G&T: I shouldn't even be in this class.
French: Why does this language even exist? Everyone
there speaks English anyway.
World Civ: What does it matter? We're all just going
to die.

Grandmère made me come here straight after school so that Paolo could start getting us ready for the ball. I didn't know Paolo makes house calls, but apparently he does. Only for royalty, he assured me, and, of course, Madonna.

I explained to him about how I am growing out my hair on account of boys liking long hair better than short hair, and Paolo made some tut-tutting noises, but he slapped some curlers into it to try to get rid of the triangular shape, and I guess it worked, because my hair looks pretty good. All of me looks pretty good. On the outside, anyway.

Too bad that inside, I'm completely busted.

I am trying not to show it, though. You know, because I want Grandmère to think I am having a good time. I mean, I am only doing this for her. Because she is an old lady and my grandmother and she campaigned against the Nazis and all of that, for which someone has to give her some props.

I just hope someday she appreciates it. My supreme sacrifice, I mean. But I doubt she ever will. Seventy-something-year-old ladies—particularly dowager princesses—never seem to remember what it was like to be fourteen and in love.

Well, I guess it is time to go. Grandmère has on this slinky black number with glitter all over it. She looks like Diana Ross. Only with no eyebrows. And old. And white.

She says I look like a snowdrop. Hmmm, just what I always wanted, to look like a snowdrop.

Maybe that's my secret talent. I have the amazing ability to resemble a snowdrop.

My parents must be so proud.

Yep. In the bathroom. In the bathroom once again, where I always seem to end up at dances. Why is that?

The Contessa's bathroom is a little bit overdone. It is nice and everything, but I don't know if I'd have chosen flaming wall sconces as part of my bathroom decor. I mean, even at the palace, we don't have any flaming wall sconces. Although it looks very romantic and *Ivanhoe*-y and all, it is actually a pretty serious fire hazard, besides being probably a health risk, considering the carcinogens they must be giving off.

But whatever. That isn't even the real question—why anyone would have flaming wall sconces in the bathroom. The real question, of course, is this: if I am supposedly descended from all these strong women—you know, Rosagunde, who strangled that warlord with her braid, and Agnes, who jumped off that bridge, not to mention Grandmère, who allegedly kept the Nazis from trashing Genovia by having Hitler and Mussolini over for tea—why is it that I am such a pushover?

I mean, seriously. I totally fell for Grandmère's whole riff about wanting to show up Elena Trevanni with her pretty and accomplished—yeah, and looking like a snow-drop—granddaughter. I actually felt sorry for her. I had empathy for Grandmère, not realizing then—as I do now—that Grandmère is completely devoid of human emotion, and that the whole thing was just a charade to trick me into coming so she could parade me around as PRINCE RENÉ'S NEW GIRLFRIEND!!!!!!!!!!!!!!!

To his credit, René seems to have known nothing about it. He looked as surprised as I was when Grandmère presented me to her supposed archrival, who, thanks to the skill of her plastic surgeon, looks about thirty years younger than Grandmère, though they are supposedly the same age.

But I think the Contessa maybe went a little far with the surgery thing—it is so hard to know when to say when. I mean, look at poor Michael Jackson—because she really does, just like Grandmère said, resemble a walleyed bass a little bit. Like her eyes are sort of far apart on account of the skin around them being stretched so tight.

When Grandmère introduced me—"Contessa, may I present to you my granddaughter, Princess Amelia Mignonette Grimaldi Renaldo" (she always leaves out the Thermopolis)—I thought everything was going to be all right. Well, not everything, of course, since directly after the ball, I knew I was going to go over to my best friend's house and maybe-possibly-probably get dumped by her brother. But you know, everything at the ball.

But then Grandmère added, "And of course you know Amelia's beau, Prince Pierre René Grimaldi Alberto."

Beau? BEAU??? René and I exchanged quick glances. It was only then that I noticed that, standing right next to the Contessa, was a girl who had to have been her own granddaughter, the one who'd been kicked out of finishing school. She was kind of plain and sad-looking, though her slinky black dress was exactly the kind I'd have wanted to wear to the Prom—were I ever asked. Still, she wasn't exactly wearing it with confidence.

So while I was standing there getting totally red in the face, and probably not resembling a snowdrop as much as a candy cane, the Contessa cocked her head so she could look at me and went, "So that rascal René has finally been snatched up, and by *your* granddaughter, Clarisse. How satisfying that must be for you."

Then the Contessa shot her own granddaughter—

whom she introduced to me as Bella—a look of pure malevolence that caused Bella to cringe.

And I realized all at once what, exactly, was going on.

Then Grandmère said, "Isn't it, though, Elena?" And then to René and me she went, "Come along, children," and we followed her, René looking amused, but me? I was *seething*!

"I can't believe you did that," I cried, as soon as we were out of the Contessa's earshot.

"Did what, Amelia?" Grandmère asked, nodding to some guy in traditional African garb.

"Told that woman that René and I are going out," I said, "when we most certainly are not. I know you only did it to make me look better than poor Bella."

"René," Grandmère said, sweetly. She can be very sweet when she wants to be. "Be an angel and see if you can find us some champagne, would you?"

René, still looking cynically amused—the way Enrique always looks in Doritos commercials—moved off in search of libation.

"Really, Amelia," Grandmère said, when he was gone. "Must you be so rude to poor René? I am only trying to make your cousin feel welcome and at home."

"There is a difference," I said, "between making my cousin feel welcome and wanted, and trying to pass him off as my boyfriend!"

"Well, what's so wrong with René, anyway?" Grandmère wanted to know. All around us, elegant people in tuxedos and evening gowns were heading to the dance floor, where a full orchestra was playing that song Audrey Hepburn sang in that movie about Tiffany's. Everyone was dressed in either black or white or both. The Contessa's ballroom bore a significant resemblance to the penguin enclosure at the Central Park Zoo, where I had once sobbed my eyes out after discovering the truth about my heritage.

"He's extremely charming," Grandmère went on, "and quite cosmopolitan. Not to mention devilishly handsome. How can you possibly prefer a high school boy to a *prince*?"

"Because, Grandmère," I said. "I love him."

"Love," Grandmère said, looking toward the big glass ceiling overhead. "*Pfuit!*"

"Yes, Grandmère," I said. "I do. The way you loved Grandpère—and don't try to deny it, because I know you did. Now you've got to stop harboring a secret desire to make Prince René your grandson-in-law, because it is not going to happen."

Grandmère looked blandly innocent. "I don't know what you can mean," she said, with a sniff.

"Cut it out, Grandmère. You want me to go out with Prince René, for no other reason than that he is a royal, and it will make the Contessa feel bad. Well, it isn't going to happen. Even if Michael and I were to break up"— which might possibly happen sooner than she thought—"I wouldn't get together with *René*!"

Grandmère finally began to look as if she might believe me. "Fine," she said, without much grace. "I will stop calling René your beau. But you must dance with him. At least once."

"Grandmère." The last thing in the world I felt like was dancing. "Please. Not tonight. You don't know—"

"Amelia," Grandmère said, in a different tone of voice than she'd used thus far. "One dance. That is all I am asking for. I believe you owe it to me."

"*I* owe it to *you*?" I couldn't help bursting out laughing at that one. "How so?"

"Oh, only because of a little something," Grandmère

said, all innocently, "that was recently found to be missing from the palace museum."

All of my Renaldo fighting spirit went right out the Contessa's French doors to her backyard patio when I heard this. I felt as if someone had punched me in my snowdrop stomach. Had Grandmère really said what I *thought* she'd said???

Swallowing hard, I went, "Wh-what?"

"Yes." Grandmère looked at me meaningfully. "A priceless object—only one out of a group of several, almost identical items—that were given to me by my very dear friend, Mr. Richard Nixon, the deceased former American president, has been found to be missing. I realize the person who took it thought it would never be missed, because it wasn't the only such item, and they all did look much alike. Still, it held great sentimental value for me. Dick was such a dear, sweet friend to Genovia while he was in office, for all his later troubles. *But you wouldn't happen to know anything about any of this, would you, Amelia?*"

She had me! She had me, and she knew it. I don't know how she knew—undoubtedly through the black arts, in which I suspect Grandmère of being well versed—but clearly, she knew. I was dead. I was so, so dead. I don't know if, being a member of the royal family and all, I was above the law back in Genovia, but I for one did not want to find out.

I should, I realize now, merely have dissembled. I should have been all, "Priceless object? What priceless object?"

But I knew it was no good to lie. My nostrils would give me away. Instead, I went, in this squeaky, high-pitched voice I barely recognized as my own, "You know what, Grandmère? I'll be happy to dance with René. No problem!"

Grandmère looked extremely satisfied. She said, "Yes,

I thought you would feel that way." Then her drawn-on eyebrows went up. "Oh, look, here comes Prince René with our drinks. Sweet of him, don't you think?"

Anyway, that's how it happened that I was forced to dance with Prince René—who is a good dancer, but whatever, he's no Michael. I mean, he's never even seen *Buffy the Vampire Slayer* and he thinks Windows is pretty swell.

While we were dancing, though, this incredible thing happened. René went, "Could you believe that Bella Trevanni? Look at her, over there. She looks like a plant someone forgot to water."

I glanced around to see what he was talking about, and sure enough, there was poor sad Bella, dancing with some old guy who must have been a friend of her grandmother's. She looked extremely pained, like the old guy was talking to her about his investment portfolio or something. Then again, with someone like the Contessa for a grandmother, maybe pained was an expression Bella wore all the time. And my heart swelled with sympathy for her, because I so know what it is like to be somewhere you don't want to be, dancing with someone you don't like. . . .

I looked up at René and said, "When this dance is over, ask her for the next one."

It was René's turn to look pained. "Must I?"

"Come on, René," I said, severely. "Ask her to dance. It will be the thrill of her life to be asked to dance by a handsome prince."

"But not so much for you, eh?" René said, still wearing his cynical smile.

"René," I said. "No offense. But I already met my prince, long before I ever met you. The only problem is, if I don't get out of here soon, I don't know how much longer he's going to be my prince, because I already missed the movie we were supposed to see together, and pretty soon it's going to be too late even for me to stop by—"

"Never fear, Your Highness," René said, twirling me around. "If fleeing the ball is your desire, I will see to it that your wish is fulfilled."

I looked at him kind of dubiously. I mean, why was René being so nice to me all of a sudden? Maybe for the same reason I wanted him to dance with Bella? Because he felt sorry for me?

"Um," I said. "Okay."

And that's how I ended up in this bathroom. René told me to hide, and that he'd get Lars to flag down a cab, and once he'd gotten one, and the coast was clear, René would knock three times, signaling that Grandmère was too otherwise occupied to notice my defection. Then, René promised, he'd tell her I must have eaten a bad truffle, since I'd looked queasy, and Lars had taken me home.

It doesn't matter, of course. Any of this, I mean. Because I am just going to end up at Michael's in time for him to dump me. Maybe he'll feel bad about it, you know, after I give him his birthday present. Then again, maybe he'll just be glad to be rid of me. Who knows? I've given up trying to figure out men. They are a breed apart.

Oops, there's René's knock. Gotta go.

To meet my fate.

Now I know how Jane Eyre must have felt when she returned to Thornfield Hall to find it all burned to the ground and everyone telling her everybody inside of it was killed in the fire.

Only then she finds out Mr. Rochester didn't die, and Jane's, like, super happy, because, you know, in spite of what he tried to do to her, she loves him.

That's how I feel right now. Super happy. Because I fully don't think Michael is going to break up with me after all!!!!

Not that I ever thought he was going to . . . well, not REALLY. Because he is NOT that kind of guy. But I was really, really scared he might when I was standing outside the Moscovitzes' apartment, you know, with my finger on the buzzer. I was standing there going, *Why am I even doing this? I am fully just walking into heartbreak. I should turn around and have Lars flag down another cab and just go back to the loft*. I hadn't even bothered changing out of my stupid ball gown, because what was the point? I was just going to be on my way home in a few minutes anyway, and I could change there.

So I'm standing there in the hallway, and Lars is behind me going on about his stupid boar hunt in Belize, because that is all he talks about anymore, and I hear Pavlov, Michael's dog, barking because someone is at the door, and I'm going, inside my head, *Okay, when he breaks up with me, I am NOT going to cry. I am going to remember Rosagunde and Agnes, and I am going to be strong like they were strong. . . .*

And then Michael opened the door. He looked kind of taken aback by my apparel, I could tell. I thought maybe it was because he hadn't counted on having to break up with a snowdrop. But there was nothing I could do about that, though I did remember at the last minute that I was still wearing my tiara, which I suppose might intimidate, you know, some boys.

So I took it off and went, "Well, I'm here," which is a toolish thing to say, because, well, duh, I was standing there, wasn't I?

But Michael kind of seemed to recover himself. He went, "Oh, hey, come in, you look . . . you look really beautiful," which of course is exactly the kind of thing a guy who is about to break up with you would say, you know to kind of bolster your ego before he grinds it beneath his heel.

But whatever, I went in, and so did Lars, and Michael went, "Lars, my mom and dad are in the living room watching *Dateline*, if you want to join them," which Lars totally did, because you could tell he didn't want to hang around and listen to the Big Breakup.

So then Michael and I were alone in the foyer. I was twirling my tiara around in my hands, trying to think of what to say. I'd been trying to think what to say the whole way down in the cab, but I hadn't been very successful.

Then Michael went, "Well, did you eat yet? Because I've got some veggie burgers. . . ."

I looked up from the parquet floor tiles, which I had been examining very closely, since it was easier than looking into Michael's peat-bog eyes, which always suck me in until I feel like I can't move anymore. They used to punish criminals in ancient Celtic societies by making them walk into a peat bog. If they sank, you know, they were guilty, and if not, they were innocent. Only you always sink when you walk into a peat bog. They uncovered a bunch of bodies from one in Ireland not too long ago, and they, like, still had all their teeth and hair and stuff. They were totally preserved. It was way gross.

That's how I feel when I look into Michael's eyes. Not preserved and gross, but like I'm trapped in a peat bog. Only I don't mind, because it's warm and nice and cozy in there. . . .

And now he was asking me if I wanted a veggie burger. Do guys generally ask their girlfriends if they want a veggie burger right before they break up with them? I wasn't very well versed in these matters, so the truth was, I didn't know.

But I didn't think so.

"Um," I said, intelligently. "I don't know." I thought maybe it was a trick question. "If you're having one, I guess."

So then Michael went, "Okay," and gestured for me to follow him, and we went into the kitchen, where Lilly was sitting, using the granite countertop to lay out her storyboards for the episode of *Lilly Tells It Like It Is* she was filming the next day.

"Jeez," she said, when she saw me. "What happened to you? You look like you swapped outfits with the Sugar Plum Fairy."

"I was at a ball," I reminded her.

"Oh, yeah," Lilly said. "Well, if you ask me, the Sugar Plum Fairy got the better deal. But I'm not supposed to be here. So don't mind me."

"We won't," Michael assured her.

And then he did the strangest thing. He started to cook.

Seriously. He was *cooking*.

Well, okay, not really cooking, more like reheating. Still, he fully got out these two veggie burgers he'd gotten from Balducci's, and put them on some buns, and then put the buns on these two plates. And then he took some fries that had been in the oven on a tray and put them onto the two plates, as well. And then he got ketchup and mayo and mustard out of the fridge, along with two cans of Coke, and he put all that stuff on a tray, and then he walked out of the kitchen, and before I could ask Lilly what in the name of all that was holy was going on, he came back, picked up the two plates, and went, to me, "Come on."

What could I do, but follow him?

I trailed after him into the TV room, where Lilly and I had viewed so many cinematic gems for the first time, such as *Valley Girl* and *Bring It On* and *Attack of the 50 Foot Woman* and *Crossing Delancey*.

And there, in front of the Moscovitzes' black leather couch, which sat in front of their thirty-two-inch Sony TV, sat two little folding tables. Michael lowered the plates of food he'd prepared onto them. They sat there, in the glow of the *Star Wars* title image, which was frozen on the TV screen, obviously paused there.

"Michael," I said, genuinely baffled. "What *is* this?"

"Well, you couldn't make it to the Screening Room," he said, looking as if he couldn't quite believe I hadn't figured it out on my own yet. "So I brought the Screening Room to you. Come on, let's eat. I'm starved."

He might have been starved, but I was stunned. I stood there looking down at the veggie burgers—which smelled divine—going, "Wait a minute. Wait a minute. You aren't breaking up with me?"

Michael had already sat down on the couch and stuffed a few fries in his mouth. When I said that, about breaking up, he turned around to look at me like I was demented. "Break up with you? Why would I do that?"

"Well," I said, starting to wonder if maybe he was right, and I really *was* demented. "When I told you I couldn't make it tonight you . . . well, you seemed kind of distant—"

"I wasn't distant," Michael said. "I was trying to figure out what we could do instead of, you know, going to the movie."

"But then you didn't show up for lunch. . . ."

"Right," Michael said. "I had to call and order the veggie burgers and beg Maya to go to the store and get the rest of the stuff. And my dad had loaned our *Star Wars* DVD to a friend of his, so I had to call him and make him get it back."

I listened in astonishment. Everyone, it seemed—Maya, the Moscovitzes' housekeeper; Lilly; even Michael's parents—had been in on Michael's scheme to re-create the Screening Room right in his own apartment.

Only I had been in ignorance of his plan. Just as he had been in ignorance of my belief that he was about to break up with me.

"Oh," I said, beginning to feel like the world's number-one dork. "So . . . you don't want to break up?"

"No, I don't want to break up," Michael said, starting to look mad now—probably the way Mr. Rochester looked when he heard Jane had been hanging out with that St. John guy. "Mia, I love you, remember? Why would I want to break up with you? Now come sit down and eat before it gets cold."

Then I wasn't *beginning* to feel like the world's number-one dork: I *totally* felt like it.

But at the same time, I felt incredibly, blissfully happy. Because Michael had said the L word! Said it right to my face! And in a very bossy way, just like Captain von Trapp or the Beast or Patrick Swayze!

Then Michael hit the play button on the remote, and the first chords of John Williams's brilliant *Star Wars* theme filled the room. And Michael went, "Mia, come on. Unless you want to change out of that dress first. Did you bring any normal clothes?"

Still, something wasn't right. Not completely.

"Do you just love me like a friend?" I asked him, trying to sound cynically amused, you know, the way René would, in order to keep the truth from him—that my heart was pounding a mile a minute. "Or are you *in* love with me?"

Michael was staring over the back of the couch at me. He looked like he couldn't quite believe his ears. I couldn't believe my own. Had I really just asked him that? Just come out and asked him, flying in the face of all Tina and I had discussed?

Apparently—judging from his incredulous expression, anyway—I had. I could feel myself starting to turn redder, and redder, and redder, and redder. . . .

Jane Eyre would so never have asked that question.

But then again, maybe she ought to have. Because the way Michael responded made the whole embarrassment of having had to ask completely and totally worth it. And the way he responded was, he reached out, took the tiara from me, laid it down on the couch beside him, took both my hands in his, pulled me toward him, and gave me a really long kiss.

On the lips.

Of the French variety.

We missed the entire scrolling prologue to the movie, due to kissing. Then finally when the sound of Princess Leia's starship being fired upon roused us from our passionate embrace, Michael said, "Of course I'm in love with you. Now come sit down and eat."

It truly was the most romantic moment of my entire life. If I live to be as old as Grandmère, I will never be as happy as I was at that moment. I just stood there, thrilled to pieces, for about a minute. I mean, I could barely get over it. He loved me. Not only that, he was *in* love with me! Michael Moscovitz is in love with me, Mia Thermopolis!

"Your burger is getting cold," he said.

See? See how perfect we are for each other? He is so practical, while I have my head in the clouds. Has there ever been as perfect a couple? Has there ever been as perfect a date?

We sat there, eating our veggie burgers and watching *Star Wars*, he in his jeans and vintage Boomtown Rats T-shirt, and me in my Chanel ball gown. And when Ben Kenobi said, "Obi-Wan? That's a name I haven't heard in a long time," we both went, right on cue, "How long?" And Ben said, as he always does, "A very long time."

And when, just before Luke flies off to attack the Death Star, Michael put it on pause so he could go get dessert, I helped him clear the plates.

And then, while he was making the ice-cream sundaes, I snuck back into the TV room, and put his present on his TV table, and waited for him to come back and find it, which he did, a few minutes later.

"What's this?" he wanted to know, as he handed me my sundae, vanilla ice cream drowning in a sea of hot fudge, whipped cream, and pistachios.

"It's your birthday present," I said, barely able to contain myself, I was so excited to see what he'd think of it. It was way better than candy or a sweater. It was, I thought, the perfect gift for Michael.

I feel like I had a right to be excited, because I'd paid a pretty hefty price for Michael's gift . . . weeks of worrying about being found out, and then, after having been found out, being forced to waltz with Prince René, who was a good dancer, and all, but who kind of smelled like an ashtray, to tell the truth.

So I was pretty stoked as Michael, with a puzzled expression on his face, sat down and picked up the box.

"I told you that you didn't have to get me anything," he said.

"I know." I was bouncing up and down, I was so excited. "But I wanted to. And I saw this, and I thought it was *perfect*."

"Well," Michael said. "Thanks." He untied the ribbon that held the minuscule box closed, then lifted the lid. . . .

And there, sitting on a wad of white cotton, it was. A dirty little rock, no bigger than an ant. Smaller than an ant, even. The size of the head of a pushpin.

"Huh," Michael said, looking down at the tiny speck. "It's . . . it's really nice."

I laughed delightedly. "You don't even know what it is!"

"Well," he said. "No, I don't."

"Can't you guess?"

"Well," he said, again. "It looks like . . . I mean, it closely resembles . . . a rock."

"It *is* a rock," I said. "Guess where it's from."

Michael eyed the rock. "I don't know. Genovia?"

"No, silly," I crowed. "The moon! It's a moon rock! From when Neil Armstrong was up there. He collected a bunch of them, and then brought them back and gave them to the White House, and Richard Nixon gave my grandmother a bunch of them when he was in office. Well, he gave them to Genovia, technically. And I saw them and thought . . . well, that you should have one. Because I know you like space stuff. I mean how you've got the glow-in-the-dark constellations on the ceiling over your bed and all . . ."

Michael looked up from the moon rock—which he'd been staring down at like he couldn't quite believe what he was seeing—and went, "When were you in my room?"

"Oh," I said, feeling myself beginning to blush again. "A long time ago—" Well, it *had* been a long time ago. It had been way back before I'd known he liked me, when I'd been sending him those anonymous love poems "—once when Maya was cleaning in there."

Michael said, "Oh," and looked back down at the moon rock.

"Mia," he said, a few seconds later. "I can't accept this."

"Yes, you can," I said. "There's plenty left back at the palace museum, don't worry. Richard Nixon must have really had a thing for Grandmère, because I'm pretty sure we got more moon rocks than Monaco or anybody else. "

"Mia," Michael said. "It's a rock. From the *moon*."

"Right," I said, not certain what he was getting at. Did he not like it? It *was* kind of weird, I guess, to give your boyfriend a rock for his birthday. But it wasn't just any rock. And Michael wasn't just any boyfriend. I'd really thought he'd like it.

"It's a rock," he said again, "that came from two hundred thirty thousand miles away. From Earth. Two hundred thirty thousand miles away from Earth."

"Yes," I said, wondering what I had done wrong. I had only just gotten Michael back, after having spent a whole week convinced he was going to dump me over one thing, only to discover that he was going to dump me over something else entirely? There is seriously no justice in the world. "Michael, if you don't like it, I can give it back. I just thought—"

"No way," he said, moving the box out of my grasp. "You're not getting this back. I just don't know what I'm

418

going to get you for your birthday. This is going to be a hard act to follow."

Was that all? I felt my blush receding.

"Oh, that," I said. "You can just write me another song."

Which was kind of vixenish of me to say, because he had never admitted that the song, the first one he'd ever played me, "Tall Drink of Water," was about me. But I could tell by the way he was smiling now that I'd guessed correctly. It was. It *totally* was.

So then we ate our sundaes and watched the rest of the movie, and when it was over and the credits were rolling, I remembered something else I'd meant to give him, something I'd thought of in the cab on the way down from the Contessa's, when I'd been trying to think up what I was going to say to him if he broke up with me.

"Oh," I said. "I thought of a name for your band."

"Not," he said with a groan, "the X-Wing Fighters. I beg of you."

"No," I said. "Skinner Box." Which is this thing this one psychologist used on all these rats and pigeons to prove there's such a thing as a conditioned response. Pavlov, the guy Michael had named his dog after, had done the same thing, but with dogs and bells.

"Skinner Box," Michael said carefully.

"Yeah," I said. "I mean, I just figured, since you named your dog Pavlov—"

"I kind of like it," Michael said. "I'll see what the guys say."

I beamed. The evening was turning out so much better than I had originally thought it would, I couldn't really do anything *but* beam. In fact, that's why I locked myself in the bathroom. To try to calm down a little. I am so happy, I can barely write. I—

*Saturday, January 24, the loft*

Oops. I had to break off there last night, because Lilly started banging on the bathroom door, wanting to know whether I'd suddenly become bulimic or something. When I opened it (the door, I mean) and she saw me in there with my journal and my pen, and she went, all crabby (Lilly is more of a morning person than a night person), "Do you mean to say you've been in here for the past half hour *writing in your journal*?"

Which I'll admit is a little weird, but I couldn't help it. I was so happy, I HAD to write it down, so I would never forget how it felt.

"And you *still* haven't figured out what you're good at?" she asked.

When I shook my head, she just stomped away, all mad.

But I couldn't be annoyed with her, because . . . well, because I'm so in love with her brother.

The same way I can't really be mad at Grandmère, even though she did, in essence, try to foist me off on this homeless prince last night. But I can't blame her for trying. She was only trying to make herself look better in front of her friend.

Besides, she called here a little while ago, wanting to know if I was feeling all right after the bad truffle I'd ingested. My mom, playing along, assured her that I was fine. So then Grandmère wanted to know if I could come over and have tea with her and the Contessa . . . who was just dying to get to know me better. I said I was busy with homework. Which ought to impress the Contessa. You know, with my diligent work ethic.

And I can't be mad at René, either, after the way he fully came to my aid last night. I wonder how he and Bella

420

got along. It would be pretty funny if they hit it off . . . well, funny to everyone but Grandmère.

And I can't even be mad at Thompson Street Cleaners for losing my Queen Amidala underwear, because this morning there was a knock on the door to the loft, and when I opened it, our neighbor Ronnie was there with a big bag of our laundry, including Mr. G's brown cords and my mom's Free Winona T-shirt. Ronnie says she must have accidentally picked up the wrong bag from the vestibule, and then she'd gone to Barbados with her boss for the holidays, and only just now noticed that she had a bag of clothing that was not her own.

Although I am not as happy about getting my Queen Amidala underwear back as you might think. Because clearly, I can get along without them. I was thinking about asking for more of them for my birthday, but now I don't have to, because Michael, even though he doesn't know it, has already given me the greatest gift I've ever gotten.

And no, it's not his love—although that is probably the second greatest thing he could have given me. No, it's something that he said after Lilly went stomping away from the bathroom.

"What was that all about?" he wanted to know.

"Oh," I said, putting away my journal, "she's just mad because I haven't figured out what my secret talent is."

"Your what?" Michael said.

"My secret talent." And then, because he'd been so honest with me, with the whole being in love thing, I decided to be honest with him, too. So I explained, "It's just that you and Lilly, you're both so talented. You guys are good at so many things, and I'm not good at anything, and sometimes I feel like . . . well, like I don't belong. At least not in Gifted and Talented class, anyway."

"Mia," Michael said. "You're totally gifted."

"Yeah," I said, fingering my dress. "At looking like a snowdrop."

"No," Michael said. "Although now that you mention it, you're pretty good at that, too. But I meant writing."

I have to admit, I kind of stared at him, and went, in a pretty unprincesslike manner, "Huh?"

"Well, it's pretty obvious," he said, "that you like to write. I mean, your head is always buried in that journal. And you always get A's on your papers in English. I think it's pretty obvious, Mia, that you're a writer."

And even though I had never really thought about it before, I realized Michael was right. I mean, I *am* always writing in this journal. And I do compose a lot of poetry, and write a lot of notes and e-mails and stuff. I mean, I feel like I am *always* writing. I do it so much, I never even thought about it as being a *talent*. It's just something I do all the time, like breathing.

But now that I know what my talent is, you can bet I am going to start working on honing it. And the first thing I'm going to write is a bill to submit before the Genovian Parliament to get some traffic lights downtown. The intersections there are *murder*. . . .

Right after I get home from going bowling with Michael and Lilly and Boris. Because even a princess has to have fun sometimes.

To: Mel Fuller <melissa.fuller@thenyjournal.com>
From: Human Resources
<human.resources@thenyjournal.com>
Subject: Tardiness

Dear <u>Melissa Fuller</u>,
This is an automated message from the Human Resources Division of the *New York Journal,* New York City's leading photo-newspaper. Please be aware that according to your supervisor, <u>managing editor George Sanchez</u>, your workday here at the *Journal* begins promptly at <u>9 AM</u>, making you <u>68</u> minutes tardy today. This is your <u>37th</u> tardy exceeding twenty minutes so far this year, <u>Melissa Fuller</u>.

We in the Human Resources Division are not "out to get" tardy employees, as was mentioned in last week's unfairly worded employee newsletter. Tardiness is a serious and expensive issue facing employers all over America. Employees often make light of tardiness, but routine lateness can often be a symptom of a more serious issue, such as
- alcoholism
- drug addiction
- gambling addiction
- abusive domestic partner
- sleep disorders
- clinical depression
- and any number of other conditions. If you are suffering from any of the above, please do not hesitate to contact your Human Resources Representative, <u>Amy Jenkins</u>. Your Human Resources Representative will be only too happy to enroll you in the *New York Journal*'s Staff Assistance Program, where you will be paired with a mental health professional who will work to help you achieve your full potential.

<u>Melissa Fuller</u>, we here at the *New York Journal* are a team. We win as a team, and we lose as one, as well. <u>Melissa Fuller</u>, don't you want to be on a winning team? So please do your part to see that you arrive at work on time from now on!

Sincerely,
Human Resources Division
New York Journal

**Please note that any future tardies may result in suspension or dismissal.**

To: George Sanchez <george.sanchez@thenyjournal.com>
From: Mel Fuller <melissa.fuller@thenyjournal.com>
Subject: Where the hell I was

Since it is apparently so important to you and Amy Jenkins that your employees account fully for every moment they spend away from the office, I will provide you with a detailed summary of my whereabouts while I was unavoidably detained.

Mel's Morning:
7:15—Alarm rings. Hit snooze button.
7:20—Alarm rings. Hit snooze button.
7:25—Alarm rings. Hit snooze button.
7:26—Wake to sound of neighbor's dog barking. Turn off alarm.
7:27—Stagger to bathroom. Perform morning ablutions.
7:55—Stagger to kitchen. Ingest nourishment in form of Nutrigrain bar and Tuesday night's take-out kung pao.
7:56—Neighbor's dog still barking.
7:57—Blow dry hair.
8:10—Check Channel One for weather.
8:11—Neighbor's dog still barking.
8:12—Attempt to find something to wear from assorted clothes crammed into studio apartment's single, refrigerator-sized closet.
8:30—Give up. Pull on black rayon skirt, black rayon shirt, black sling-back flats.
8:35—Grab black bag. Look for keys.
8:40—Find keys in bag. Leave apartment.
8:41—Notice that Mrs. Friedlander's copy of the *New York Chronicle* (yes, George, my next-door neighbor subscribes to our biggest rival) is still lying on the floor in front of her apartment door. She is normally up at six to walk her dog, and takes the paper in then.
8:42—Notice that Mrs. Friedlander's dog is still barking. Knock on door to make sure everything is all right. (Some of us New Yorkers actually care about our neighbors, George. You wouldn't know that, of course, since stories about people who actually care for others in their community don't make for very good copy.)
8:45—After repeated knocks, Mrs. Friedlander still does not come to

door. Paco, her Great Dane, however, barks with renewed vigor.

8:46—Try handle to Mrs. Friedlander's apartment door. It is, oddly enough, unlocked. Let myself inside.

8:47—Am greeted by Great Dane and two Siamese cats. No sign of Mrs. Friedlander.

8:48—Find Mrs. Friedlander facedown on living room carpet.

Okay, George? Get it, George? The woman was facedown on her living room carpet! What was I supposed to do, George? Huh? Call Amy Jenkins down in Human Resources?

No, George. That lifesaving class you made us all take paid off, see? I called 911 and waited with her until the ambulance came. With the ambulance, George, came some cops. And guess what the cops said, George? They said it looked to them as if Mrs. Friedlander had been struck. From behind. Some creep whacked that old lady on the back of the head!

I don't know what this city is coming to, George, when little old ladies aren't even safe in their apartments. But I'm telling you, there's a story here—and I think I should be the one to write it.

Whadduya say, George?